AN UNHOLY COMMUNION

By the same author

A Very Private Grave
A Darkly Hidden Truth

THE MONASTERY MURDERS

AN UNHOLY COMMUNION

BOOK 3

DONNA FLETCHER CROW

LION FICTION

Text copyright © 2013 Donna Fletcher Crow
This edition copyright © 2013 Lion Hudson

Published by Lion Fiction
an imprint of
Lion Hudson plc
Wilkinson House, Jordan Hill Road,
Oxford OX2 8DR, England
www.lionhudson.com/lionfiction

ISBN 978 1 78264 004 2
e-ISBN 978 1 78264 005 9

First edition 2013

A catalogue record for this book is available from the British Library

Printed and bound in the USA, February 2013

With deep gratitude to my sisters in crime
Sally Wright
and
Dolores Gordon-Smith
Without whom it wouldn't have happened

Acknowledgments

Thank you so much to Father Stephen Gallagher, his wonderful team and my fellow pilgrims that took me to their hearts as a considerably over-age pilgrim on the amazing experience of walking from London to Walsingham (126 miles) to celebrate the 950th anniversary of the founding of the shrine. Father Antony wouldn't have had any idea how to go about leading his little band of pilgrims across Wales without their great example.

And to Dolores Gordon-Smith, who did lead me through Wales in sun and driving rain. And to Sisters Alma and Nora for their gracious hospitality at St Non's retreat house and for giving me the room with the stunning view which later became Felicity's.

You can see pictures of all our adventures at www.DonnaFletcherCrow.com

TIME LINE

304	Julius and Aaron martyred at Caerleon
500 (c.)	Non gives birth to St David
546	St David preaches at the Synod of Brefi, is named Bishop of Caerleon
1150 (c.)	Cistercians establish Llantarnam Abbey
1188	Gerald tours Wales
1203	Llantarnam establishes manor at Penrhys
1328–47	Henry de Gower is Bishop of St David's
1538	Shrine of Our Lady of Penrhys destroyed
1904	Welsh Revival
1953	Statue of Our Lady of Penrhys erected

The Bishop's Palace

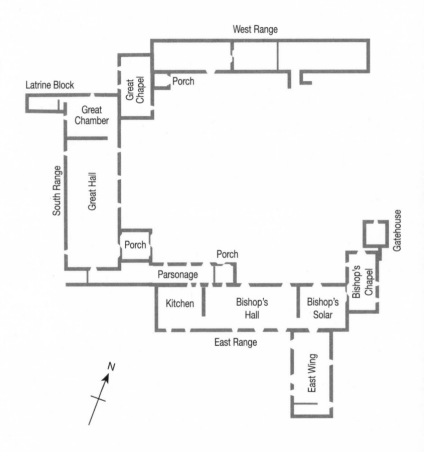

Glossary

Arcade: A succession of arches

Argentiferous: Rock containing silver

Ascension: Feast commemorating the bodily Ascension of Jesus into heaven, fortieth day after Easter

Aspergillum: Liturgical implement used to sprinkle holy water

Aurochs: Ancient type of wild cattle

Barbour: Exclusive waterproof jackets for country wear

Camlan: King Arthur's final battle

Cairn: Manmade pile of stones, usually for ceremonial purposes

Caractacus: A first century British chieftain of the Catuvellauni tribe

Castra: Roman word for fort

Clerestory: Windows in an upper level to bring in light and air

Compline: Final Office of the day in the canonical hours

Coney: Rabbit

Corpus Christi: A joyous feast celebrating the presence of Christ in the Eucharist

Crockford's: Clerical directory of biographies of Anglican clergy in UK

Croeso: Welsh for welcome

Cwm: Welsh for valley

Cymru: Welsh name for Wales

Dolomitic: Sedimentary rock containing calcium magnesium carbonate

Epipen: Instrument for injecting allergy medication into outer thigh

Frigidarium: Cold pool in Roman baths

Frontal: Altar cloth covering the entire front of the altar

Garth: Celtic word for field

HobNob: British biscuit (cookie) made from oats

Hollow way: A road which has over time fallen significantly lower than the land on either side

Ipecac: Syrup used to cause vomiting

Kyrie eleison: Lord have Mercy (Greek)

Lemsip: Brand of lemon-flavoured hot drink for colds containing paracetamol

Llan: Welsh for church

Malefice: An evil deed

Menevia: Ancient name for St. David's

Metaled road: Road built on a bed of crushed rock

Miter: Liturgical headdress worn by bishops and abbots

Mithraism: Religion popular in Roman army worshipping the sun-god Mithra

Mizzle: Drizzle; light, depressing rain

Motte: Mound topped with structure known as a keep in castle construction

Nightwish: Symphonic metal band from Finland

Ordinand: One studying for ordination

Pelagius: Fifth-century preacher who denied original sin as well as Christian grace

Paracetamol: Analgesic similar to aspirin

Paraments: Liturgical hangings around the altar, altar cloth

Parapet: A wall-like barrier at the edge of a roof

Pediment: Low-pitched gable surmounting the façade of a classical building

Pilum: Javelin used in Roman army

Pinny: Wrap-around apron, cover-all

Piscina: Place near the altar used for washing communion vessels

Portico: Porch leading to the entrance of a building

Potholer: Spelunker, a person who explores caves

Pulpitum: Massive screen, usually stone, dividing choir from nave in a cathedral

Refectory: Dining room, especially in a monastery

Renesmee: Child of hero and heroine in Twilight vampire series

Reredos: Screen or decoration behind the altar

Rood Screen: An ornate partition between the chancel and nave of a church

Satnav: GPS

Satsumas: Small, loose-skinned orange, seedless Mandarin Orange

Scrynne: Used to contain precious writings or sacred relics, forerunner of a shrine

Sidesman: Usher

Silures: Celtic tribe occupying much of present Wales

Snogging: Vernacular for kissing

Spatha: Longer sword used by the Roman cavalry

St. John Ambulance: First Aid charity in UK

Stations of the Cross: Fourteen prayers and meditations on scenes in the passion of Christ

Summer Solstice: June 21, beginning of summer in the northern hemisphere

Swot: Vernacular for study

Tepidarium: The warm room in Roman baths

Thelemic: Occult mystical system to achieve understanding

Thurible: Metal censer suspended from chains in which incense is burned for worship

Titania, **Oberon**: Faeries in Shakespeare's A Midsummer Night's Dream

Triangulation: Process of determining the location of a point by measuring angles to it from known points

Tump: Hillock

Tussock: A small mound of coarse grass

Tyburn: Historically the principal place for execution in London, near present Marble Arch

Vallum: Earthwork rampart around a Roman camp

Versicle: A short sentence spoken by a priest and followed by a response from the congregation

Viaticum: Latin, "food for the journey" reference to Communion

Volturi: Coven of vampires in Twilight series

The Dawn of Promise

Non is old now. Old and frail, her skin white and thin as gossamer. The stones are warm behind her head. She can feel the heat through her veil. It warms the fine silver hair that was once a cascade of gold, longer than her veil is now. She smiles. Thin, pale lips that were once the lush red of cherries curve in soft remembrance. Her blue eyes are still clear, yet it is not the scene before her that brings a smile to her lips and softness to her face, but the scene in her mind.

Non is old now. Old and frail, her skin white and thin as gossamer. But when her skin was smooth and golden as thick cream, she was loved by a king and a great thing came of that love.

It was her favorite walk atop the cliffs above Whitesands Bay in her faraway, beloved Wales. The waves crashed on the shore below her, spewing white foam on the black rocks. The bay beyond was blue, bluer even than the sky swept free of clouds by the wind that tossed her hair in the sunlight and billowed the skirt of her grass-green gown. She had been listening so intently to the call of the seabirds wheeling and diving over the bay that she had not heard the approach of the horseman.

It was a lifetime ago. It was yesterday. Sandde leapt from his horse and would have taken her that moment in his urgency had it not been for her maidenly insistence on her virtue. She was horrified. Sandde was not old; he was barely half again her age. Sandde was not without position; of the family of Cunedda Wledig, descended from Bran the Blessed, he ruled the neighboring canton. Sandde had not come with the intention of taking her in dishonor; he had just come from forming a liaison with her family. Yet she would not. Could not. She had made her choice.

It was a lifetime ago. It was yesterday. Non was to be vowed to the religious life. It had been in her heart and her prayers, always. The nearby convent at Ty Gwyn was the home of her choice, not the castle of Ceredigion. But Sandde would have her. So in the end, it was a matter of force. And the rejected suitor rode back to his people and left Non to go on alone. Yet not alone, for she carried the marvelous child within her.

Three months she had carried her child that day when she went to church as usual. And as usual the priest Gildas, a lemon-sucking man with deeply furrowed brow, declaimed his scowling sermon. "Know ye not, oh ye wretched, that it is God's will that ye be slaughtered and enslaved by the Saxons? The puerile progeny of our leaders are sadly degenerated from the excellence of our ancestors. And now the hangdog enemy—" He was struck dumb mid sentence.

Non smiled as she felt again the child leap in her womb. Did ever infant announce himself with such violent quickening since John the Baptist leapt in his mother's womb at the sight of the Mother of our Lord? Gildas fell to his knees before her, silent like the stricken Zechariah, making known by gestures and hasty scribblings that Non's child was to excel all religious teachers.

It was then that the holy Nonnita knew that she must go to the house of Sisters above Whitesands Bay, for in her deepest heart of hearts, she had never left her desire for the vowed life. She would make her profession now. Six months later it was there that she was brought to bed.

Nothing could have been a greater contrast to the day of David's conception than the day of his birth. No place could the sun shine brighter and the breezes blow more sweetly than on the green peninsula thrust so far into the sea at the westernmost edge of the land, and no place could the black clouds hang lower or the winds beat more violently. And so the storm raged. Hour after hour, as black as night in the middle of the day, the sound of the howling wind and crashing sea pounded in Non's ears with increasing ferocity as the intensity of her pains grew. The noise of the storm, the shaking of the conical thatched roof over her head and the relentlessness of her gripping pains were so all-consuming that she was not aware of the ministrations of the nursing Sisters, but hung all the more tightly to the large, smooth stone beside her pallet, giving her something to push against in her labor.

The peak of the storm and the peak of her labour climaxed together. "A son." "It is a son." "A fine, strong, prince of a son." "Praise God for a miracle."

"And another miracle, holy Mother. Look." Little Sister Bryn pointed at the stone to which Non had clung. In sympathy for her pain it lay crumbled, the fragments bearing Non's fingerprints.

And yet the wonders were not ceased. Sister Elspeth, blind these many years, rushed into the room like a romping child. "A well, a holy well." She pointed across the field just beyond the wall encircling the clutch of convent huts. "New sprung. I heard it bubbling forth and felt along the turf until my hands came away wet. I wiped them on my eyes, and I can see!"

At that moment the infant in Non's arms wrinkled his face and gave a great howl. Miracles or no, David would not be ignored.

Non took her son to Aberaeron in Ceredigion that he might be baptized by his cousin Eilfyw and educated by the most learned, most holy men in the kingdom: Colman, Illtud and Paulinus. And so Non returned to her convent and gave over the nurturing and educating of her son into other hands. But she did not give over the praying.

Non is old now. Old and frail, her skin white and thin as gossamer. She has lived these many years in Brittany, a nun professed. And every day for all the years of her son's life hers has been the deepest joy of all. The joy of praying for the holy child that was born to her in the midst of that great storm on that rocky cliff edge so far away. She sits now in a sunny corner in the cloister and thinks long thoughts. And smiles.

Chapter 1

The thickened light engulfed her. Fighting the heaviness, she opened her mouth. But no sound came out. The black figure plunged over the edge of the tower and hurtled toward the earth. Then, as the skirt of his cassock flared like a parachute, the scene changed to even more horrifying slow motion. Falling, falling, falling.

Would he never reach the bottom? Felicity screamed. But still the figure fell. She screamed again.

And woke up. "Oh, no!" She grasped her alarm clock and groaned. How could she have overslept this morning of all mornings? She had looked forward to this day so much. In Oxford it had been May Morning when she had stood below Magdalen's Great Tower to listen to the college choir singing up the sun. And Ascension morning at the College of the Transfiguration was going to be just like that only better, because she would be up on the tower with her fellow ordinands singing "God is Gone Up on High" and all the wonderful Ascension hymns she only got to sing once a year.

But now it was all wrong. And the phantom of her nightmare hanging over her like an incubus was the least of it. She had so carefully set her alarm last night. Then failed to switch it on. If her scream hadn't wakened her... Sunrise at 4:49, *BBC Weather* had said. That gave her twenty minutes.

She thrust her tangled duvet off, splashed water on her face and pulled on her jeans. Still clumsy with sleep, her fingers tangled as she struggled to do up all the thirty-nine self-covered buttons of her long, black cassock— a task which it never paid to rush. How could she have made such a stupid mistake? What was the point of all this scramble if she was late? Her frenzy increased when she had to waste time searching under her bed for her second shoe.

The moment she flung open her door, however, she found herself engulfed by the fresh, golden air of an early June daybreak. The spirit of the day that had seemed to have fled now captivated her. The first shafts of sunlight pierced the trees and an exultant dawn chorus rang in her ears as she raced up the hill toward the tallest building in the grounds.

She would surely have made it on time if the slick-damp stones under her feet hadn't brought her to disaster in a border of lady's mantle, coral bells and creeping geranium. She picked herself up, brushed impatiently at the stains on her cassock and raced on.

As she started up the steep green mound that led to the tower, a triumphant shout and enthusiastic clanging of handbells told her she was too late. Her fellow ordinands had already ascended the tower of Pusey Hall to sing in Ascension, celebrating the fortieth day after Easter by hymning Christ upward as He ascended to heaven. Felicity would be relegated to observing from the ground rather than singing from the top of the tower herself.

Putting her frustration aside and determining to make the best of the experience, even though she was by nature a doer rather than a watcher, Felicity sought a reasonably secure footing on the slope of the precipitous embankment. At least her presence on the ground provided an earthly audience for her fellows as well as their heavenly one. With one more burst of tintinnabulation they began the hymn "Hail Thee, Festival Day."

Felicity stood alone in the peaceful garden, gazing upward just as that band of disciples must have done on the hill outside Jerusalem on the first Ascension morning. Trying to picture what that first day would have been like, Felicity's mind scrolled through the artists' interpretations she had seen all the way from full-length paintings of a ghostly, white-draped Christ floating in the air, to a silver gilt plastic cloud with just the nail-pierced soles of Jesus' feet poking through. Her favorite depiction of all, though, was one she had seen in some cathedral with Christ looking back down through the clouds, His hand raised in blessing, appearing for all the world as if He were waving to her.

Felicity wasn't sure whether she was gesturing to the ascended Christ or to her fellow ordinands as she flung her arm upward. "Blessed day to be hallowed forever;/Day when our risen Lord/Rose in the heavens to reign." At the end of the song the jubilant singers leant over the parapet shouting and ringing their bells until Felicity wanted to shout at them to be careful—a warning that she herself needed to heed, as her vigorous waving almost caused her to lose her footing on the steep hillside covered with wet grass.

> *See, the Conqueror mounts in triumph; see the King in*
> *   royal state,*
> *Riding on the clouds, His chariot, to His heavenly*
> *   palace gate.*
> *Hark! the choirs of angel voices joyful alleluias sing,*
> *And the portals high are lifted to receive their heavenly*
> *   King.*

The next hymn was as much shouted as sung, but the words were almost drowned out by the crashing of bells in a determined attempt to rouse any of their fellow students who might have been so foolish as to think they could sleep in that morning. The sunrise exuberance continued with a shouted versicle from the tower: "The Lord is gone up on high, Alleluia."

And Felicity cupped her hands around her mouth to shout the response: "And has led captivity captive, Alleluia."

The tower-top choir began, "Hail the day that sees Him rise … Christ, awhile to mortals given, Alleluia!/Reascends His native heaven, Alle—"

The final Alleluia never registered in Felicity's ears. It was extinguished by a much nearer shriek. Her own.

The piercing scream tore a second time from her throat as she watched in horrifying slow motion a cassock-clad figure from the back of the choir catapult across the parapet and arc over the side of the tower.

The singing must have continued, as no one on the tower appeared to have seen the terrifying spectacle. But Felicity heard no music, only the shuddering thud as the body hit the earth. Then, appallingly, rolled down the steep hill to come to rest at her feet.

Too shocked to run, Felicity stood frozen, staring with unbelieving eyes. This wasn't real. It was her morning's dream replaying in her subconscious. She squeezed her eyes shut so hard they hurt. The ghastly specter would be gone when she opened them.

But it wasn't. This was no dream. Somehow the earlier chimera had translated itself into flesh and blood—a slow trickle of blood oozing from blue lips and trickling into a matted black beard.

Felicity pulled her mesmerized gaze away from the staring black eyes and followed the line of the out-flung arm to the hand that was almost touching her foot. She jerked her foot away and moaned when she realized she had kicked the white hand. It opened to release a folded scrap of paper.

Felicity bent to pick it up with fingers so stiff they could hardly grasp the paper. Shaking, she unfolded it and glanced at the strange emblem drawn there. Then shrieked again and flung it from her as the paper burst into flame.

Chapter 2

"**A**re you talking about literal fire? Just *pouf,* like a stage magician?" Detective Inspector Nosterfield made no attempt to keep the skeptical tone out of his voice. "Sure you didn't flick it with a lighter?"

"I don't even own a lighter. I wish I did. I wish I had some explanation." Felicity looked around as if one might appear.

"You use a lot of candles up 'ere," Nosterfield suggested.

"There were no candles!" Felicity sounded desperate.

Antony knew she had had enough of Nosterfield's badgering. "Inspector, I don't know anything about stage magic, but even I have heard of flash paper."

"You can be assured we'll test the ashes. I expect we'll find nitric acid. But that still doesn't explain—"

Antony stepped forward, determined to shift Nosterfield's focus from Felicity. "I thought you wanted to know more about the victim."

The stocky inspector in his crumpled suit turned to the priest still clad in the white alb and stole he had donned in preparation for the mass that was to have followed the singing from the tower. "Knew him, did you, Father?"

"Shall we, er—" Antony indicated the chairs in the classroom Father Clement, principal of the college, had offered to the police to use as an incident room.

"Oh, yes. Yes, sit down." Nosterfield sounded as if he were struggling to keep the irritation out of his voice. Antony thought he probably didn't want to sit in case he needed to charge out of the room and back up the hill to the spot his uniformed officers were marking off with yellow crime scene tape. "Sergeant Silsden," he summoned a young officer from the other side of the room. The sergeant pulled a notebook from his pocket and they all sat rather uncomfortably in student desks, except Nosterfield who leaned against the heavy lectern. The pale lavender walls in the north-facing room increased the chill of the atmosphere.

"Hwyl. He's Hwyl Pendry." Antony gave Felicity a concerned glance. She looked so pale—her face was almost as white as her T-shirt and her blonde hair fell in tangled tendrils down her back. It gave her a heart-wrenchingly childlike look. Far younger than her twenty-six years. He didn't want to upset her further.

Felicity's shrieks had brought Antony running from the church at such a speed he had reached her side before any of the students made it down from the tower. He had taken her trembling body in his arms and held her tightly, murmuring calming phrases to her until at last she was quiet. By then the hillside around them was covered with the black-robed figures of ordinands, priests and monks from the college and Community of the Transfiguration. He longed to hold her again, but Nosterfield cleared his throat meaningfully.

"He was an ordinand here several years ago," said Antony.

"Knew him well, did you?"

Antony shook his head. "I only had him in one class."

"And that was?"

Antony hesitated. He knew the response his answer would elicit. "Er—Spiritual Warfare."

Nosterfield's head jerked up. "Oh, yes? Still teaching witch hunts, are you?"

Antony didn't reply. This was hardly the time or place for a discourse on the power of evil. One would expect a detective to be all too well acquainted with that reality. But perhaps that was what had made Nosterfield cynical.

"So you hadn't seen 'im for a few years? Are you certain it was 'im? People change."

Antony closed his eyes and shook his head to ward off the shattering images. He was back again on that hillside, holding Felicity as they both gazed at the broken body that had seemingly plummeted from the sky to land at her feet in a horrible reversal of the Ascension story. He saw again the black hair, the thick beard and the single silver stud in the earlobe. Yes, he was changed. Terribly changed by style, by time and by death, and yet Antony was certain.

He gave himself a little shake and answered Nosterfield's question. "He came back once for Deacon's Weekend. Most of our students do. But I hadn't seen him since. We didn't keep in touch, but I'd heard that he had married."

"You don't know where he lived?"

"I think he went back to Wales, but I don't know where. It'll be in *Crockford's*. There's a copy in the library." Antony pointed out the window to the next building.

"*Crockford's?*"

"Clerical directory. It's very complete. It will tell you how to get in touch with him. Er, I mean his wife or bishop or whoever."

"In the library, you say?" Nosterfield gestured for Silsden to dispatch himself and acquire the volume. He pushed away from the lectern and took a step toward Felicity. "Well, well, Miss 'oward. You're making a habit of this, aren't you?" He stood in front of her, legs apart and arms akimbo.

"I… I don't know—I was just there to sing in Ascension Morn—"

"Inspector, is this necessary? Miss Howard has received

a severe shock—" Antony attempted to quell the aggressive inspector.

"Oh, really? I'd think she'd be getting used to it by now."

"Inspector, this is hardly a matter for levity."

"You're quite right, Father. But still, I'm not sure I'd want to be one of Miss 'oward's friends."

Antony started to reply, but Felicity put a hand on his arm and sat up straighter. "It's all right, Antony. I can answer his questions."

Nosterfield returned to leaning against the lectern. "Tell me about this paper you pulled out of the dead man's 'and." As Felicity opened her mouth to answer, the detective held up his hand. "And I suggest you think carefully. You realize I could 'ave you up for destroying evidence."

"I didn't destroy it—" she began, then looked at her hand as unbelieving as if the paper were still burning there. "And I didn't pull it out of his hand. He dropped it and I picked it up. It was a reflex."

Nosterfield waited for her to continue. "It was folded. I unfolded it. The paper was light. Like tissue paper, only stiffer. I only had a moment to look at it, but it had a strange marking on it. Heavy black lines. A triangle with horns. Or maybe snakes, I don't know…" She started to trace the pattern in the air with her finger, but Nosterfield held out a notepad and pen to her.

Her fingers were so stiff she dropped the pen. Antony picked it up and held her hand in both of his before giving it back to her. "Felicity, this can wait. Let me get you some tea."

She gave him a wavering smile then lifted her chin. Ah, this was his courageous Felicity. Her hand was still shaking, but she drew the pattern.

"Right." Nosterfield retrieved his notebook. "And what does this mean?"

"I haven't any idea." She shook her head.

"Father?" He looked at Antony with his eyebrows raised.

Antony cleared his throat. "The triangle is a symbol of the Holy Trinity: Father, Son and Holy Spirit. But I have no idea what this rendering could mean." Nosterfield continued to hold the drawing out for consideration, so Antony tried again. "The center appears to be a foreshortened triangle. As if it were coming forward. The dark object sitting on it could be a stringless lyre or bulls' horns with knobs on them, or a two-headed snake?" He shook his head. "Sorry, just wild guesses, I'm afraid."

Silsden returned with a thick mulberry-colored hardback book and handed it to his superior. Nosterfield found the listing for Hwyl Pendry and held it out to Antony. "Perhaps you'd care to interpret for us, Father?"

Antony took the volume. "Yes, name, date of deaconing, date of priesting, address, phone number. I think that's all quite straightforward." He started to return the book.

Nosterfield thumped his finger on the listing. "So 'e was priest in charge of St David's in Whitchurch. Straightforward enough, I suppose. But what does this mean?"

Antony looked where the inspector's finger was pointing. "Ah, deliverance minister. Well, that means he is the priest in the dioceses that is called on for situations dealing with the, er—unusual. That is, extrasensory." How to make Nosterfield understand without sensationalizing it? "Paranormal," he finished.

Nosterfield blinked. "I thought that was all you people ever dealt with."

"Shall we say instances from the other side of the coin, Detective Inspector?"

"Right. So this 'wyl friend of yours," with Nosterfield's heavy northern accent the name came out as Owl, "is a ghostbuster, and 'e dies in inexplicable circumstances clutching a piece of paper with a strange mark on it which just 'appens to burst into flame when Miss 'oward 'ere picks it up." He was silent long enough for his sarcasm to sink in. "Sergeant Silsden, I think someone is 'aving us on."

"I realize how it looks, Inspector," Antony protested, "but that is what happened. I'm sure you'll agree with me, though, that most instances of the seeming occult have perfectly rational explanations."

"I'm relieved to hear you say that, Father. I wasn't intending to organize a séance."

"I would hardly be recommending that. I should point out, though, that there are instances—"

"Yes, I'm sure there are, Father. But we'll leave that to your lot." The detective inspector gave Antony a long, level look before snapping his notebook shut. "You'll remain available for the investigation." His gaze shifted to include both Felicity and Antony.

Felicity started to nod, but Antony cut her off. "I'll be happy to leave my contact information with you, of course. But I'm afraid I have plans. That is—something has come up." He spoke more directly to Felicity than to Nosterfield.

"What?" Felicity looked at Antony in wide-eyed surprise.

"And what plans are these?" Nosterfield's question was leveled at Antony, but Antony turned directly to Felicity to answer.

"I hadn't had a chance to tell you yet, Felicity. Father Stephen rang last night. The Youth Walk pilgrimage in Wales our ecumenical council is sponsoring…"

"Yes, you were advising on the church history."

"That's right. But Stephen broke his leg—ironically,

hillwalking to get in shape for the walk. He asked if I could lead it."

She sat blinking at him as Nosterfield cut in, "Another pilgrimage?" His brow furrowed. "Do a lot of that, don't you?"

"It is an important aspect of our tradition, yes. And the young people are very keen. This is an interfaith walk. If we can break down the barriers among the youth, it gives great hope for the church of the future."

Nosterfield shook his head. "You'd think people in a monastery would stay put. So you'll be where?"

"Caerleon," Nosterfield scribbled in his notebook as Antony recited, "then from Llantarnam to Penrhys."

"And what's that when it's at 'ome?"

"Er, from near Newport to the Rhondda. And then on to St David's by bus. It's part of a reconstruction of a pilgrim route called the Cistercian Way that circles Wales. It was extremely popular in the Middle Ag—"

Nosterfield cut him off with an impatient gesture. "I'm sure it was. And this 'ere 'wyl just 'appens to be from Wales. You aren't thinking of meddling again are you?"

"No!" The exclamation came from Antony and Felicity with equal vehemence.

Antony could tell by the look on Felicity's face that she, just as he, was recalling their harrowing experiences retracing their beloved Father Dominic's pilgrimage route searching for clues to his brutal murder, and then, more recently, Felicity's journey of discernment which was interrupted by their discovery of their friend's body in a shallow grave. But this was nothing like that. In a sense, lightning had struck three times in the same place, but this sudden death of a slight acquaintance could have nothing to do with them.

Nosterfield shook his head. "You'll get a soaking, but go on then. Leave your details with Sergeant Silsden."

Nosterfield gave Antony his card. "Ring if you think of anything you've forgotten to mention." Antony gave his mobile number to the sergeant and promised to get a copy of their itinerary for him. Then he and Felicity departed, leaving the police to interview the others who had been so jubilantly singing in the morn just a short time ago.

As if by mutual consent, Felicity and Antony turned their steps toward the church. They walked in silence, so close their arms brushed. The heavy wooden door grated on the stone floor, then shut behind them leaving only the remembered echo of a clang. The comfort of lingering incense, soft light filtering through leaded glass, and the sweetness of air filled seven times a day with whispered prayers cocooned them. They took sheltered seats in the choir and sat long, clinging to one another's hands.

At last Felicity broke the silence with a long intake of breath. "So. You're going to Wales?"

"I'm sorry, Felicity. That was a terrible way to break it to you."

"I thought we were going to have some peaceful time together. Plan our wedding…" She took her hands from his and her voice took on an edge of anger. "But of course, if this youth walk thing is more important to you—"

"Felicity, nothing is more important to me than you are. I intended to ask you right after mass."

"*Ask* me? You were going to ask? How thoughtful."

Antony looked at her. The words sounded sarcastic, but her voice was level. He waited for her next words.

"So go ahead, then. Nosterfield is right, though, you will get soaked." She rose to her feet as if the matter was decided.

Antony grabbed her hand and tugged her back to her seat. "No, Felicity. You don't understand." He ran his fingers backward through his hair, then stopped, remembering that he was trying to break that habit. "I was hoping it would be 'we.'"

She frowned as if she were translating his words. "You what? You want me to spend my break slogging across Wales with a gang of noisy, spotty teenagers?"

"It could be fun, Felicity. If we did it together. Relaxing, even. We'll be walking through some beautiful country—"

"On trails like the one Father Stephen broke his leg on?"

Antony ignored that and pressed on. "We'll stay in lovely old churches, visit ancient holy sites, and the second part will be entirely relaxing—ten whole days on retreat at St Non's. St David's is one of the most charming cathedral cities in Britain, and—"

"Wait!"

Felicity looked down and shivered. Antony could tell she was reliving the horror of having a dead body drop at her feet. "Peace and quiet. You promise?"

"Absolutely. Nothing could be more peaceful."

Her smile was brave, if wobbly. "I'm just not sure an isolated hillside in Wales will be far enough away from here."

Chapter 3

Felicity stepped off the train at Newport with her head buzzing. Antony handed her backpack and borrowed bedroll down, and jumped off behind her. The schedule had allowed only a day and a half for her to get her gear together and, more importantly, to get her mind adjusted to this whole new adventure she was setting out on. How could the world have changed so suddenly? Every one of the forty days she and Antony had been engaged had been like living inside a golden bubble as the Yorkshire countryside filled with greening trees, May flowers and tottering lambs. A bubble filled with Easter songs and friends' congratulations, and shining visions of the future in a world of peace and love. Then a body had fallen from the sky and the bubble burst.

And here she was, after a four-hour journey from Yorkshire, standing in one of the busiest train stations in Wales, wondering what was next.

"Where do we meet this Michael?" She asked as she snapped the clip on her rucksack over her chest. "Do you know what he looks like?"

"I'm afraid Stephen was a bit vague—I think he was on rather strong pain medication. Tall with dark hair, he said. Mostly he assured me what a reliable driver Michael is—"

"Driver? I thought we were walking," Felicity interrupted.

"We will, but we need a minibus to transport luggage and bedrolls—offer respite to anyone who gets tired, that sort of thing. Anyway, as I was saying, Stephen said Michael would have all the maps and contact information with him..." he paused and sighed. "Which will all be fine once we make contact, of course."

Felicity squeezed his arm as they moved out of the line of bustling passengers into the station. "So you feel a bit like you've been dropped in the soup, too, do you?"

He grinned. "I'd feel a lot worse if you weren't here. I want this to be a really good time for you, Felicity. Thank you so much for agreeing to come."

She looked at Antony and barely stopped herself caressing the crease of concern in his wide brow. Concern for the youth he had promised to lead; concern for her. And the love shining from his eyes. How could she not have accepted his plea? Two weeks walking with Antony, working with Antony, just being with Antony. There was no place on earth she would rather be. She shrugged and gave him a little smile. "Whither thou goest..."

They stood in the middle of the station looking hopefully at each tall male with dark hair, hoping it would be their contact. Felicity felt the tension rise. What if this Michael person didn't show up? She bit her lip.

"Father Antony?" A harried young man rushed toward them, looking as relieved to see them as they were to see him. "I was afraid you might not be wearing your collar. Didn't know how I'd spot you." They shook hands all around, and Michael picked up Felicity's bedroll and started toward the door. "I've got the others in the minibus. Nancy had an early train from Bristol, but Lydia and Adam's bus was late, then I thought we were to connect with Colin—his mum is bringing him down from Monmouth—but she rang and said she'd just go straight to Caerleon..." His monologue continued as he led the way to the parking lot at a speed that even long-legged Felicity had trouble keeping up with. She didn't get any of the names of either people or places, but she assumed it would right itself in time.

Once their bags were stowed in the back of the large silver vehicle, Michael made the introductions to the three passengers already inside: Lydia, a ruddy-cheeked, auburn-haired young woman with narrow shoulders and more than ample hips; her pale, thin little brother, Adam, and a young woman in the back—Nancy, with nut-brown hair, wide blue eyes and a shy smile.

Felicity went over their names in her mind: Michael, Lydia, Adam and Nancy. Antony had mentioned that he especially wanted her to look out for Adam who, at thirteen, would not have been allowed on the walk except for the fact that his sister was accompanying them as nurse to look after emergencies and the inevitable blisters.

As soon as Felicity opened her mouth to return their greetings they wanted to know how an American wound up in the south of Wales preparing for such an adventure, so, omitting more recent events, Felicity spent the drive northward from Newport explaining about her exchange program studying Classics at Keble College, Oxford, that led to her spending a year living with a vicar and her husband in London, teaching Latin at a church school; a year in which the teacher definitely learned more than the students. What she primarily learned was that she didn't want to be a teacher.

"And so on Rebecca's recommendation— she was the vicar I was living with— I went off to the College of the Transfiguration." The subsequent events of that whirlwind year that had led to her becoming engaged to marry her church history lecturer—she interrupted her thoughts to steal a sideways glance at Antony's handsome profile— she would leave for another day.

Nancy leaned forward from her corner in the back. "Just like that? What did your DDO say? How did you get through Selection Conference so fast?"

Felicity shook her head, feeling her long blonde braid tickle the back of her neck. "It was definitely a case of fools rushing in where angels fear to tread. I just went up and interviewed and signed up. I thought it was like going to grad school in America. I'm afraid I didn't have enough background to know about such things as Diocesan Directors of Ordinands or selection conferences." Her own words amazed her to think how rash and innocent she had been in that fairly recent past when she thought she knew everything. "I guess you could say this year has been my 'discernment process.'" A year ago she had never heard the term.

They crossed the River Usk on an old stone bridge, followed a curving road into a small village, and pulled up in front of a classical building with four enormous Doric columns supporting a pedimented portico. "You might as well get out here," Michael said. "Car park's up the street." He turned to Antony. "Hope this is all right with you, Father. Father Stephen said you'd want to fill us in on the importance of the Romans here for your history bit, so I thought this would be a good meeting place. When I mentioned it, Colin's mum said he's wild about Roman artifacts."

"That's perfect," Antony replied. "Getting a feel for Roman Britain is important to understanding the first part of our pilgrimage."

Before Antony had even paid their admission to the museum, a woman in faded jeans with tired-looking hair hurried to him from the large display room beyond. "Oh, Father Stephen, I'm so glad you're here. I really must be getting back home. I have younger children, you know. Now, Colin has all his kit and I know he won't be any trouble, but you will see that he takes his allergy meds, won't you? He's so keen on all this, I don't know if you'll be able to drag him out. This is really the most wonderful opportunity for him. He's doing his GCSE in archeology and you know AQA axed its course, so he has to do it all online—"

At last she paused for breath and Antony managed to get a word in. "Ah, Mrs., er—" He pulled the list of pilgrims' names from his pocket. "Mrs Warder. I'm Father Antony. Father Stephen has had an accident and I'll be leading the walk. But I can assure you we'll take excellent care of your son. You might want to discuss Colin's medications with our nurse in training." He turned to Lydia. "This is Lydia Bowen."

"Oh, you have trained medical help. How very wise."

"Well, almost." Lydia stepped forward. "I've completed the theory work for my nursing diploma. I start my practical placement in a clinic this September. I did bring a well-stocked first aid kit, so I'll be glad to keep his tablets there if you like."

"Oh, no. I don't want to embarrass him. But you will keep an eye on him, won't you?" She hurried off to bid her son goodbye. Observing from across the room, Felicity was afraid Mrs Warder might try to kiss him farewell, but the plump, sandy-haired youth was sufficiently enthralled with a glass case displaying iron weapons from the third century that he barely responded. "Look, a real pilum head." He glanced up. "Oh, yeah. Bye, Mum."

As a classicist this was right up Felicity's alley, too. "Wonderful display, isn't it?" She peered at the assortment of spearheads in the same case.

Colin needed little encouragement. "The Second Augustan legion came here in the year 74 and stayed for more than three hundred years. There were around six thousand men stationed here. The fortress was called Isca from the River Usk, but the Welsh called it Caerleon." He said all that without taking his eyes off the displays as he moved on to survey bits of chain mail and scale armor.

"Yes, I know," Felicity said. "Caerleon, a corruption of *Castra Legionis*, the Fort of the Legion."

Colin looked up from the array of armor buckles and tie-loops to regard Felicity open-mouthed. "You know?"

"Uh-huh." She gave a little shrug. "I studied this stuff."

"That's champion." He responded with a grin that even lit up his freckles, and moved on to the display of letters and writing materials.

Felicity was as enchanted as Colin. She had long felt that nothing could make one feel so in touch with another age as holding—or in this case, seeing—letters written to family, friends or business associates from people living long ago. It was perhaps as close as one could come to actually hearing a voice from the past. How amazing that these had survived almost two thousand years.

The case contained a pottery inkwell, an iron stylus, a seal-box and a lead property-marker inscribed "Century of Vibius Proculus" arranged beside a wax tablet like the one on which Vibius Proculus might have written his military reports or letters to his family in Rome. Or they to him, as letters were carried in every direction across all parts of the Empire.

"Look," Colin pointed to a crumbling leather pouch. "This once held letters probably sent to a legionnaire stationed here— this is totally cool."

Next was a wooden tablet with its ink inscription still readable. Felicity couldn't make out the words, but the card beside it offered a translation of the account of guards sent to collect the legionaries' pay and of parties collecting building timber. Nearby displays showed more leather pouches, wooden boxes and clay jars which could have contained similar missives on papyrus or parchment. Felicity tingled to get her hands on such treasures to translate them for herself. She well understood Colin's enthusiasm.

"Oh, stop moaning." Felicity's thoughts of antiquities were interrupted by Lydia's sharp rebuke to her brother on the other side of the freestanding display case.

"But I'm hungry," Adam persisted.

"And I'm sure you're not alone in that," Antony turned to their youngest pilgrim, who didn't even look his thirteen years. "I've heard a rumor that the chip shop up the road should be open now."

The consent was unanimous. They were just leaving the display room when an object in a case in the corner caught Felicity's eye. She grabbed Antony's arm. "Look!"

They bent closer to the protective glass. Antony read the label: "'Copper alloy hook in the form of a horned serpent.'"

A chill ran through Felicity. "What does it mean? Why would a hook used to secure the shoulder piece of Roman armor be on a symbol in Hwyl's hand?"

"You're sure it's the same design? You only saw it for a minute."

Felicity closed her eyes, remembering. "It's the same, only double. See, the hole on the bottom of this one where it attached to the armor—if you had two hooks and placed one hole on top of the other, it would be just the same. It's burned into my mind. No pun intended. It's like my mind took a flash photo of it."

Antony steered her from the museum. "I'll ring Nosterfield and let him know, in case it's of any importance." But first he gave Felicity a reassuring hug. "Try to put this behind you. You're here to forget about these things."

She tossed her head and lifted her chin as if to defy the fates. "Absolutely. This is another world. Nothing is going to interrupt our idyll."

Chapter 4

Saturday, continued

A ntony's advice was easy enough to follow a few minutes later when Felicity, who was equally as hungry as the ravenous Adam, bit through the crispy batter into succulent white flakes of fillet of cod. "Mmmm, my favorite food. It was worth immigrating for."

Antony paused with a long, crispy chip halfway to his mouth. "Just this?"

Without even bothering to see if anyone was watching, she leaned over and gave his cheek a quick peck. "All this and heaven, too."

"Glad I talked you into coming on the pilgrimage?"

Her smile was her answer.

"Right, then, on to the barracks block?" Colin tossed his fish and chips wrapper in the bin. "That *is* next, isn't it?"

Felicity continued to nibble on her chips as they walked up the street past walls covered with flowering clematis and honeysuckle and gardens filled with hydrangea, lupin and geranium. And just behind Felicity, Colin continued his narrative. "The Romans were brilliant organizers. Across the empire, every fort was built on the same plan so when troops were posted to a new location they wouldn't have to waste time getting oriented. Of course, Britannia was the most troublesome province in all the empire. And the Welsh were the hardest of all to subdue." Felicity smiled at the ring of pride in his voice. "Caractacus held the Romans off for almost thirty years before they captured him. Then the Romans built a string of fortresses like this one along the border." Felicity smiled and nodded. That was all that was required of her to qualify as a good audience for the lecture.

They crossed a street and entered a wide green field ringed with trees. On the far side was a rectangular pattern of stone footings, no more than two feet high. Colin went straight to the information board and read out for any who cared to listen, "These are the only visible remains of a Roman legionary barracks in Europe. At first built around 74 AD, they would have been of timber, but were replaced in stone in the second century." He studied the rest of the board, then walked through the footings, explaining it all.

No one else was paying any attention to Colin, so Felicity, fearing his feelings would be hurt, stayed with him as he paced through the ruins. "This would have been the verandah along the front of each building." They stepped over a low footing. "These smaller outer rooms were for each soldier to store his kit and equipment." He gestured to what would once have been a wall. "Their shields were enormous, covered the whole body; they must have lined them up along here." He moved to a larger room at the back. "Eight men would have slept in here. Each building housed a single century—80 to 100 men. Six centuries made a cohort. There were ten cohorts in the legion." His explanation had taken them to a much more spacious officer's room at the end of the building, where Antony stood with the others.

"You've really got this down, Colin. You're going to make an excellent archeologist," Felicity assured her guide. He beamed.

"Right now," Antony addressed the group. "Why don't you make yourselves as comfortable as you can here?" He indicated they should find seats on the barracks' foundations. "It's probably time for me to start earning my keep. I think you all know that I was just supposed to supply the church history background for Father Stephen to use as he led you through the trails of this green and pleasant land."

"At least we know it's green. We hope it'll be pleasant," Michael commented to Lydia, sitting beside him.

Antony smiled and looked around him. "I'm sure you all know of St Alban, England's first martyr, but you might not be as well acquainted with the next two, Julius and Aaron, although their martyrdoms are recounted together from the chronicler Gildas the Wise by the Venerable Bede."

Antony picked up where Colin's discourse had left off: "It's quite easy to picture daily life in the Roman army when Aaron and Julius served here in the year 303." He pointed to the rooms marked by the stone footings. "We don't know how the legionaries slept in these rooms—bunks seem the most sensible, but beds or mattresses are possible. Latrines were along that wall where the ditches kept the water flowing; soldiers did their own cooking. Their cookpots would probably have hung over fires along that wall, bubbling with porridge or stew. The parade ground and practice field," he indicated a wide expanse of green, "are these modern playing fields. And the fortress baths were back the way we came, just up the street from the museum. That would have been across the main street from the headquarters— where the church is now." Again he pointed and heads turned. Felicity took in the green sweep of lawn and the church tower through the trees.

"Little beyond the fact of their martyrdom is recorded about these comrades who probably came from different parts of the empire—Julius perhaps from Gaul, Aaron probably from Palestine—but their daily life would undoubtedly have been the same as any legionary in the Second Augustan." Felicity smiled as Antony's voice took on the familiar ring that told his listeners they were going to hear the story in the you-are-there style that had made him the most popular lecturer in the college.

At a barked order from the primus Pilus, the cohort was dismissed from drilling on the parade ground to go to the amphitheater for spatha practice. After what seemed like hours spent thrusting and hacking his broad-bladed sword at a wooden practice post while wielding a forty-pound shield, Aaron's arms ached and his vision blurred. Then finally the "Cohort dismissed" command freed them.

"Time to make for the baths, I think." Aaron fell into step with Julius on the way back to their barracks.

"I'll meet you in the tepidarium. I want to go by headquarters. I heard that a mail packet arrived. I haven't heard from my family in months."

Aaron cuffed his companion on the arm. "Family, my donkey's ear. You're thinking of that dark-eyed Achiella you're forever boring us all about."

Julius just grinned as they stored their kit in the outer room of their barracks.

Aaron made his way along the Via Pretoria and through the high masonry wall surrounding the tile-roofed bathing complex. He crossed the open courtyard with the long, narrow swimming pool where, even in the chill of the evening, many legionnaires were swimming laps.

Aaron, however, preferred to go straight to the frigidarium, with its controlled climate under a high-vaulted ceiling. After a refreshing plunge that left his skin tingling, he anointed his body with oils from the green and blue glass bath flasks supplied by slaves, then donned a pair of wooden sandals to protect his feet from the hot tiled floors of the heated rooms, and purchased a dish of olives before settling down to relax in the tepidarium. He savored the oily brininess of a small black olive and spit the seed into the pool. The Roman drain system could handle anything.

When Julius entered the pool beside him a few minutes

later, he turned to offer him an olive but stopped at the look of horror on his friend's face.

"Julius! What is it? You look like you've just seen into Tartarus."

"I have. It's started."

Aaron spat another olive seed into the pool. "What? Another of those cursed Silurian uprisings?"

"No. The persecution of Christians. We knew it would happen. You remember that rumor that Galerius had finished his campaigns and moved into the palace at Nicomedia with Diocletian? They say he even wanted to persuade the Augusta to move ahead with stamping out the 'atheistic' Christian cult."

Aaron looked around to be certain no other bathers were within earshot. "But Galerius is only a caesar—not half the power Diocletian Augusta holds. Diocletian has been moderate."

Julius shook his head. "But Galerius is married to Diocletian's daughter, and Diocletian will do anything to strengthen the empire. Anyway, he's not being moderate now."

"What's happened? Did you receive a letter?"

Julius's white face showed the strain of his control. "From my sister, Carola. She's married to a centurion in the Theban Legion serving in Gaul—*was* married." He turned his face away and swallowed.

"Has he divorced her?"

"He's dead. Quintillian, along with the entire legion."

"An uprising?"

Julius turned back to him and now his formerly pallid face was flushed with anger. "Put to the sword. Maximian ordered a general sacrifice. The whole army was ordered to burn incense to Caesar before they set about wiping out Christianity in Gaul."

Aaron grabbed his friend's shoulder. "Your family. They're all Christians."

Julius gave a jerk of a nod. "They've survived so far. But the legion." He paused again, fighting for control. "Aaron, the entire legion was Christian—every man of them. Not a single one would perform the sacrifice or swear the oath. So Maximian ordered the legion decimated."

"Literally, you mean?"

"A literal decimation. Divided the legion into groups of ten. Each group drew straws. The short straw was put to the sword. Maximian had to call in a special auxiliary to do it. Then Maximian ordered the sacrifice again."

"And?"

"Not a one." Julius shook his head. "Not a single man gave in. So Maximian ordered a second decimation. The remaining soldiers stood firm. They drew up a petition to Diocletian, swore their allegiance to empire and emperor, but asserted their privilege as Roman citizens to worship their God."

Aaron caught his breath. He suspected the answer. "Diocletian refused?"

"He put them to the sword. The whole legion. More than six thousand loyal, well-trained fighting men. He had them slaughtered."

Wordlessly the two men got out of the warm water and went to the frigidarium for a final cold rinse. Neither spoke until they were well beyond the bath house. Aaron broke the silence. "The edict is universal."

"Yes. It will come here."

"There will be no need of a decimation of the Augustan."

"No, Mithra worship is strong here. We may well be the only Christians in the legion."

Aaron regarded the man he had joked with and fought

beside and prayed with for so long. "When it comes, I hope I can stand firm."

Julius's countenance cleared for the first time since he began his account. "We will, my brother. We know our Lord stood firm at his trial."

Aaron nodded. "Yes, we will stand also." Then he thought. There was something he must do. His family's *hereditaria* must not fall into the wrong hands. The enforcement of the edict could come at any moment.

Back in the barracks he took the amphora from the bottom of his chest, seized a shovel and went out into the night.

Antony's gaze swept the faces of his listeners. "In his *De Excidio et Conquestu Britanniae*, Gildas records that, 'God, in the time of persecution, lest Britain should be completely enveloped in the thick darkness of black night, kindled for us bright lamps of holy martyrs.' He names Alban and 'Aaron and Julius, citizens of Caerleon, who stood firm with lofty nobleness of mind in Christ's battle.'"

Nancy sighed. "That was beautiful, Father. Thank you."

The others were going on to the amphitheater, but Felicity felt as though she couldn't move. She always loved it when Antony spun his web of storytelling. Well, she hadn't always. It used to irritate her no end. But she had come to appreciate the depth—of both the stories and the storyteller. "That was wonderful."

His lopsided half-smile told her how much her compliment meant to him. "Would you like to see their memorial in the church?"

"Yes, if we don't have to keep up with the others."

"Michael will look after them and we can catch them up soon."

They walked over the field then down High Street toward the square Norman tower of the stone church. Antony paused at the corner of High and Museum streets. "This would have been where the Via Pretoria made a T-junction with the Via Principalis, the main streets of the fortress. And this," he led into a green churchyard, dotted with gravestones and altar-like monuments, "would have been the courtyard of the headquarters building. The first church may have been built of wood, but this, like most of the older buildings in Caerleon, is built of reused Roman stone."

Felicity placed her hand on the rough stone of St Cadoc's Church. What history that block of stone stood witness to. They entered the cool, dim nave, afternoon light coming through the colorful stained-glass windows all around them.

"These windows were given to the church in the middle of the eighteenth century by a local lad who killed his cousin in a duel, fled to Turkey where he made his fortune and, on a pardon from Queen Anne, returned to London." Antony pointed to the Gothic east window above the dark carved wood of the reredos. "Our Savior in Glory in the red robes in the centre, St Julius on Christ's right, St Aaron on his left. In the smaller light beneath, Julius is being put to the sword by a Roman soldier as Aaron is led to his execution."

They walked on around the church, admiring the scenes from the life of Christ told in glowing stained glass. Felicity paused at a table at the back of the church to purchase a book about the history of St Cadoc's and its windows. As she was putting her 20p in the box she noticed a red and gold folder with a striking figure of St David on it. "Support The Bishop's Palace Appeal," it implored. Intrigued, she put it in her bag with the book, intending to read it later.

They were walking back along the former Via Principalis toward the amphitheater when Felicity asked, "What did you mean about Aaron burying his family papers before his martyrdom?"

Antony furrowed his brow. "Did I say that? I'm afraid I get rather wrapped up in my accounts sometimes. Seems they have a way of taking on a life of their own. But it does make sense. If he did have letters or documents, he wouldn't have wanted them to fall into the hands of inquisitors."

Felicity nodded. "Yes, we know some were saved somehow— by accident or on purpose—or they wouldn't be in the museum now."

They had gone only a bit further when she asked, "Julius and Aaron—would they have worn horned snake hooks on their armor?"

Antony stopped and turned to her, his hand warm on her shoulder. "They would have worn armor, certainly. And chain mail was standard issue. But Felicity," his grip tightened, "you're to forget about that."

She gave a rueful grin. "Yeah, I know. I forgot. I must remember to forget."

Afternoon shadows were beginning to lengthen as they walked across another stretch of verdant grass to the amphitheater. Felicity, as always, was reveling in the greenness of the world around her—so different from her native Idaho.

As they approached the amphitheater, Felicity heard shouts, laughter and applause. They walked up the nearest sloping bank of the arena and looked into the great green oval where Colin and Adam were locked in deadly gladiatorial combat while Lydia and Michael, standing on the rim to the left where the dignitaries' box seats would have been, cheered. Nancy sat a bit apart, looking on, but not engaging with the action.

Felicity held her breath as Colin, the lion, launched a fresh attack. It was only horseplay, but she didn't want anyone to get hurt. Adam was slightly built, but spunky. Colin was the older and broader, but softer. Weaponless, they grappled hand to hand. Then Adam broke off and sprinted around the arena, Colin in hot pursuit. A good tactic on Adam's part to tire his opponent.

Antony swept the site with his arm. "It's the only fully excavated Roman amphitheater in Britain." The mounds of carpeted green looked as soft as cushions, as if made of cotton batting and velvet rather than of stone buttressed by banked earth.

"The seating would have been a massive timber structure." Antony pointed high above their heads. "It seated around six thousand to accommodate the full legion."

Below them Colin caught up with his prey, giving a mighty roar. "Come on, Julius! Bite him back," Lydia shouted.

Antony led the way to the dignitaries' box their companions occupied. "This box would have been above a waiting room for the combatants." He pointed to a brick structure built into the wall. "That was a shrine. Most likely dedicated to Nemesis."

Felicity shivered. The goddess of fate and vengeance. How many brave men, and perhaps women, met their nemesis here?

In the arena, Colin overpowered his opponent as Michael, in best Roman style, cheered for the lion. It was all in jest.

But Felicity wondered. The window in the church had shown Julius dying by the sword, but the means of the martyrs' death wasn't recorded. Did Julius and Aaron actually die in the center of this soft green oval?

The roar of 6,000 bloodthirsty legionnaires rang in Felicity's ears, and in her mind's eye the grass ran red with blood. As the grass at her feet had been stained with Hwyl's blood on Ascension morning.

Chapter 5

Saturday, continued

A ntony looked at his watch as the re-enactors joined them. "Time to get back into town. Ryan should be arriving soon. Where did you say we'd meet up?" He turned to Michael.

"The Olde Bull. I told him we would meet him there for dinner. He was cadging a ride with a mate, so I hope his timing works out." Michael led the way back toward the High Street.

Antony was glad the youth walk members would be assembling in intervals over the weekend. It would give him a chance to get to know them as individuals, and to get a grip on this adventure he had been thrust into so suddenly. Knowing the history and having detailed maps of the terrain were small steps, indeed, to the actual job of leading almost a dozen people across the rugged Welsh countryside. The youth walk had seemed such a good idea months ago when the energetic Stephen, along with Antony's support, had proposed it to the Ecumenical Council: Get young people involved in endeavoring together, learning about some little known heroes of the faith... They had written to all the congregations in Wales and across southern and western England that supported the council, asking them to encourage their youth to join the walk. Stephen had been disappointed that there hadn't been more takers—he had envisioned twenty or thirty pilgrims. Antony felt overwhelmed with eight, plus Michael and Felicity.

Antony and Felicity were the last to enter the black and white timbered pub in the center of town. The group was just finding seats around tables near the fireplace when a large young man in a plaid shirt entered. His face lit up when he saw Antony's collar. "Ah, Father Stephen."

"His locum, I'm afraid. You must be Ryan." Antony explained about the substitution and introduced the newcomer to the group.

Under the ensuing bustle of shifting seats, sorting out drinks orders, and discussing menus, Felicity invited, "Tell us about yourself, Ryan."

His voice was soft, but Antony caught the essentials that their newest pilgrim was from Swindon, doing his gap year working in a garden center, and had a place at uni to study geography this fall. "That's why I'm looking forward to this walk so much; we'll be going right through some of the most famous glaciated valleys and moraines in the world."

His listeners were spared attempting an intelligent reply by the approach of the amiable host. "Welcome to the Olde Bull. I hope you're finding all to your liking." He eyed Antony's collar with apparent interest.

"Yes, thank you. We're a pilgrimage group. Walking to Penhrys," Antony attempted an explanation.

"Oh, interested in history, are you?" He would almost certainly have been expansive even without the encouragement of nodding heads. "Well, now, you'll want to know you're sitting in the oldest inn in Caerleon. I'm sure you know our car park was the courtyard of the Roman baths. And across the street, now," he waved his arm in the general direction, "you would have noticed the Priory. It's a hotel these days, but it started out as a monastery—some say even the very site of St David's himself. Founded in the twelfth century, it was, by Hywel ap Iorwerth, the Lord of Caerleon.

"Later on, Caerleon grew and got too noisy for the monks, so they moved on and founded Llantarnam Abbey. Kept this as their town house, though.

"Now here's the good bit, if you'll pardon me, Father." He leaned closer to the table, looking around to be sure he had everyone's attention. "There's an underground passage from the Priory to the Olde Bull. The inn used to be the monks' kitchen, you see. And this passage is what the monks and nuns used when they were getting up to no good." He finished by tapping the side of his nose with his forefinger and giving an exaggerated wink.

Antony was about to reply that he wasn't aware that there had been nuns here as well—there certainly hadn't been in St David's day, but Michael intervened to get everyone's drinks order. A few minutes later, Antony noticed his driver chatting up the barmaid as she filled their orders.

When Michael returned, though, his attention was all on Lydia, who seemed to be attempting to persuade him to her viewpoint on something as ardently as Colin was working to fill in gaps in Nancy's archeological education. Antony smiled. The energetic conversation around the tables indicated that the pilgrims were getting well acquainted. Later, though, he was enjoying his steak and mushroom pie when he noted Michael disappearing around the corner of the bar. Antony hoped he wasn't going to have a problem with his driver. He relied on Michael for all the practical arrangements. If he were to be slipping off for drinks or women…

Just then Felicity returned from the loo with a stricken look that drove all other concerns from his mind. "What is it?" He jumped from his seat and strode to her. "Are you ill?"

"Come see." Her voice was tight.

Back along the passageway to the car park, she pointed to the wall outside the loo. A community noticeboard was plastered with various announcements of rewards for missing dogs, bring-and-buy sales and housecleaning services. "Here, look."

Antony saw immediately: A notice bearing the emblem of a triangle spouting horned snakes. Felicity looked even paler than a moment ago. Antony put his arm around her for support. "The Thelemic Society of The Orbis Astri," he read.

"I know the last bit means Circle of the Star," Felicity said, "but what's a thelemic society?"

"Essentially an order that tells people to do whatever feels good. It's an abbey in the novel by Rabelais where the only rule was 'do what you will.'" Antony looked at the notice again. "Yes, just like this: 'Become the master of your own life, the architect of your own destiny,'" he read aloud. This society was sponsoring a lecture on how each person could become a Master of Existence and reach an inner state of perfection and power.

"'Inside each person exists all the good of the universe. You, too, can become an adept, a Master of Existence,'" Felicity read the last line in a weak voice.

Antony turned to reassure her, but one look told him she had made one of those quick recoveries he was becoming accustomed to. She looked far readier to march into battle than to faint. "What nonsense! Do you think Hwyl was killed over some new age mumbo-jumbo?"

"I'm sure it was more than that, but I'll certainly report this to Nosterfield."

Felicity turned back to the notice. "It was a shock to see the emblem again, but this is just moonshine."

Antony shook his head. "I don't know. It might be, but, as little as we like to face it, evil is a very powerful force." He didn't want to frighten her, but he knew all too well how rash she could be, so maybe just a small caution would be in order.

When they returned to the table, Michael was calling the group to attention. "All right, boys and girls, time. We need to be getting on to our lavish accommodations for the evening. You'll appreciate that no expense has been spared for your comfort."

He led the way up Church Street to the hall beside the square white Methodist church with their silver minibus parked outside. Michael opened the back doors and began handing out bags, bedrolls and assorted equipment. In a few minutes the hall was a buzz of pilgrims inflating air mattresses and arranging belongings as each established their space. Felicity, Nancy and Lydia settled in the far end of the hall. Antony dropped his bag beside Michael, Ryan, Colin and Adam nearer the door.

This would be as good a time as any to ring the number Sergeant Silsden had given him. It was likely the detective inspector would want the local constabulary to check out this Thelemic Society of The Orbis Astri. Antony stepped out into the dark and walked a way into the churchyard before clicking on the number he had entered into his phone. Silsden answered on the third ring and seemed genuinely appreciative of Antony's information, if puzzled. "Sounds a load of codswallop, doesn't it? But still, you never know. I'm sure the inspector will want to check it out. Thanks for ringing."

Antony stood for a moment, pondering whether he would have felt better if the policeman had assured him there was nothing to the horned snake emblem, or if he was glad to think they might have found a clue. He had promised Felicity a peaceful getaway. He hoped he could make good on that. For the first time he questioned his wisdom in encouraging Felicity to join this pilgrimage. What had he gotten her into?

He had taken one step back toward the hall when the door opened quietly and a dark figure slipped out and headed down the street. There was nothing wrong with any member of the party taking a walk. So why the furtive air?

Inside the hall it took only a quick glance to see that Michael was missing. Rendezvous with the barmaid, perhaps?

The others seemed ready to settle, so he called them into the sanctuary before they were all cocooned in their sleeping bags. "It's a little late for evening prayers, so I think we'll say Compline." He chose to stand on the floor before the pews rather than behind the pulpit which, in good Methodist fashion, occupied center place at the front of the church.

"The Lord Almighty grant us a quiet night and a perfect end," he began.

"Amen," the little band replied.

Felicity was glad he had chosen this, the quietest and most contemplative of all offices. It invited reflection on the events of the day past. And what a day it had been. It seemed like a week ago she had stood, disoriented, on the train station at Newport. Then following that she had spent most of her day in Roman times. Little wonder if she felt jetlagged.

And then there had been those two vivid reminders of the event that had catapulted her into this journey. She shivered and forced the image from her mind. *Concentrate on the prayers*, she told herself. "Visit, O Lord, this dwelling, and drive away all snares of the enemy; may the angels preserve us in peace, and your blessing be ever upon us…"

Her "Amen" was hearty.

"In peace, we will lie down and sleep…" Antony declared.

"For you alone, Lord, make us dwell in safety," came the response.

"The almighty and merciful God, the Father, the Son, and the Holy Spirit, bless us and preserve us."

With the final "Amen" they were dismissed to their beds.

Felicity barely mumbled a "goodnight" to Nancy and Lydia on either side of her before she was asleep.

Hours later she jerked awake so violently she bolted upright with her sleeping bag around her. She stared into the thick blackness of the hall, listening to the rhythmic breathing of the mounds around her. Why was it so dark? She held a hand out tentatively as if she could touch the darkness, mold it in her hand like play dough.

Ridiculous. She must have been sounder asleep than she thought. She shook her head to clear it. Surely everyone was as deeply asleep as she had been moments ago. And yet she had been so sure. The voice had been clear. Antony calling her. "Felicity." Then a pause. "Felicity." And a third time, more insistent. "Felicity." She didn't think she had been dreaming.

Carefully, so as not to disturb anyone, she unzipped her sleeping bag and padded barefoot across the tiled floor, slowly, with her hands in front of her to ward off the dark. Her foot touched Antony's bag and she knelt, feeling his shape. The bag rose and fell rhythmically with his slow, steady breathing. She put her hand on his shoulder, but didn't shake him. Dead to the world was the expression. But she didn't like that.

It was possible he could have called out in his sleep, but if so, he slumbered soundly now.

She crossed the floor on her hands and knees. She told herself it was easier. Of course it wasn't that she didn't want anything to see her in the dark. She crawled into her bag and zipped herself in. But this time it didn't feel cozy. It felt confining. The bag was part of the dark pressing down on her.

She would need her sleep if she were to function at her best as assistant leader tomorrow, but her eyes wouldn't close. The black burned itself into her eyeballs. *This is silly*, she told herself sternly. She forced her eyes closed and concentrated on stilling her breathing. But she did not sleep. Instead double-headed horned serpents writhed on the back of her eyelids.

Throwing off her restricting bag and pulling jeans and sweater from her pack, she slipped silently into her clothes to go for a predawn walk. Some caretaker must have been attentive to oiling the hinges because the door opened silently. Felicity stepped into the adumbral world. She took a deep breath to steady herself, and filled her lungs with the fresh air. *You're breathing the darkness in*. She silenced the taunting voice.

A single note from a bird in the branches above her head signaled that dawn was not far off. *Hold to the coming of the light*, she told herself. Still, for the moment she must watch carefully where she stepped so as not to trip over a half-buried stone or crash into a bush.

She could make out the shape of the nearby St Cadoc's Church just across an expanse of lawn, so turned that direction, but had taken only a few steps when she stopped. She had thought herself alone in the world awaiting daybreak. Just herself and one solitary bird. But now she distinctly heard voices only a few feet away, on the other side of that mound of bushes. Not exactly arguing, but one at least was very insistent.

Was it some of their group? She had assumed all the sleeping bags were occupied when she left the hall, but she hadn't actually checked. She took two steps across the dew-soaked grass.

"You must know something. You're so keen on the subject. I saw you looking at the letters." Michael's voice, she was certain.

The muttered reply was softer. A lighter, younger voice. Male. Colin? "I don't know anything about a missing letter. Ask Father Antony. He's the one…"

The figures emerged from behind the bush. Felicity stepped back into the shelter of the nearest tree.

"I'm sorry I couldn't be more help, Michael. It was a brilliant adventure anyway, huh?"

She could tell now Michael was smiling. "Yeah, it was all right. But it's our secret, right?"

"Right."

Felicity turned and followed a distance behind, thinking they would go into the church hall, but instead they made for the van. At Michael's instruction, Colin flicked on the torch he carried so the driver could see to unlock the rear door. Felicity just made out that he stored a small spade before relocking the vehicle.

What had these two been up to with spade and torch in the dark of night?

Chapter 6

Sunday After Ascension
Caerleon to Llantarnam

Felicity was still rolling up her sleeping bag and wishing she had slept better when three grey-haired Methodist ladies bustled in with boxes of cereal and bags of fruit. Antony and several pilgrims who had been more efficient than she at their morning ablutions in the rather primitive washroom began folding out the tables stacked against the wall and setting out chairs. Sounds of boiling kettles and popping toasters came from the kitchen.

"Sorry to hurry you along, luv." One of the ladies, her rotund figure swathed in a flowered pinny over her Sunday dress, gave Felicity a warm, motherly smile. "It's just that we have a Sunday school class meeting in here in an hour."

"Oh, no. That's absolutely fine." Felicity did up the zipper on the duffle that held the sleeping bag, air mattress, and battery-powered pump she had borrowed from a friend in Kirkthorpe. "Thank you so much for bringing in our breakfast. It's absolutely lovely of you."

"Oh, it's no trouble a'tall. We're happy to help out. It's an extraordinary thing you're doing, isn't it? Walking all these young people across the ancient ways. Not enough youngsters interested in such things these days. Seems like all most of them want to do is play those video games. I know that's what my grandchildren do."

Felicity smiled. "Yes, and I think we have three more joining. It should be a good group."

"Ah, that's lovely. Come have your tea, now."

Felicity couldn't have been happier to obey. As she sliced a banana onto her cornflakes she surreptitiously watched Colin and Michael. Had that mud been on Colin's boots yesterday? Whatever they had been up to, neither Colin nor Michael looked any worse for their escapade. Neither had dark circles under their eyes like she did.

The activity in the room whirled around her as Antony, his plate stacked high with toast, took a seat next to Adam. "Sleep all right, did you?"

Adam answered readily enough, but Lydia, sitting on the other side, chided her brother for putting too much sugar in his tea. Felicity flinched. There was sure to be antagonism if Lydia insisted on mothering her younger brother.

Then she looked around. Where was Nancy? That solemn young woman was so quiet one tended to overlook her. And yet Felicity was certain there was a depth there that would be well worth getting to know. A moment later her question was answered when Nancy emerged from the door to the church and tucked her prayer book and Bible in her neatly packed bag before getting a mug of black tea.

"Is that all you're having?" Felicity asked. "I think it's something like seven miles on to Llantarnam."

Nancy gave her a brilliant smile that made her chestnut eyes sparkle. "Oh, I'll be fine. It's no matter."

Felicity suspected she was being scrupulous about a pre-Eucharistic fast. It would be a long time though before they joined the nuns for their morning service.

As it turned out it was to be even longer than she thought, because Antony announced that as soon as the van was loaded they would go back to the field beyond the amphitheater for one more bit of history before leaving Caerleon. Nancy beamed, but Felicity was almost certain she heard Lydia groan. Felicity smiled at her, thinking how well she knew the feeling. It had been such a short time ago that she herself had thought she would go cross-eyed if she had to listen to one more history lecture—until she learned the relevance such ancient accounts could have. In their recent experience, the understanding of historical events had become a matter of life and death. Felicity gave a soft sigh of relief that this time no such desperate import attached to Antony's lectures. She could simply enjoy them for the sake of the story.

Felicity stepped into the kitchen to thank their hostesses one more time, then picked up her luggage and took it to the van where Michael was loading. It required a bit of moving her bags around, but she managed to position herself so that her glance could fall seemingly naturally on the shovel tucked along the side of the back seat. "What's that for?"

Michael looked where she was pointing and shrugged. "Standard equipment. Mud can get pretty deep on some of the back roads if we have a good rainstorm."

She nodded and handed him her bag, not mentioning the fresh-looking clay on the blade.

At least they didn't appear to be in danger of a rainstorm today. The morning sun shone brightly as they gathered around Antony who stood with the green mounds of the amphitheater behind him. "All right, you'll be hearing a lot about St David, especially in the second week of our time together when we'll be in his city and staying at the retreat center that bears his mother's name, but I wanted you to have the Caerleon part of his story before we move on westward, following pretty much the path David and his monks would have taken when he moved his see.

"I don't suppose there's anyone here who doesn't know that David is the patron saint of Wales." If there was, no one raised their hand. "You all wear daffodils on St David's Day, do you?"

"I wear a leek," Colin declared. "St David ordered his soldiers to wear leeks on their helmets—they were fighting the Saxons in a field of them."

Antony smiled. "Or, more realistically perhaps, because of its importance to the national diet in days of old, especially in Lent." Colin frowned at such a mundane idea.

Felicity wondered about wearing such a pungent vegetable on one's shoulder, but she could imagine Colin doing just that.

"Getting back to David," Antony continued. "He was of noble lineage, his father, Sandde, was descended from Bran the Blessed, his mother, Non, of the family of Vortigern. We'll be seeing his birthplace in a convent on the cliff overlooking the Irish Sea.

"David was dedicated to the church at an early age. He lived and studied at Henfynyw monastery in Menevia, the city that now bears his name. While still young he is said to have healed his teacher Paulinus of blindness. David grew to be six feet tall and exceptionally strong. He believed in self-denial—living on bread and vegetables and drinking only water. As a result he was known as the Waterman, an appropriate title, as he also stood up to his neck in cold water as a penance." Antony smiled as several of his listeners shivered.

"David put all his physical strength and moral vigor into his passion for proclaiming the Word of God and establishing monasteries. With his own energy and his gift for leading others, he built a string of twelve monasteries around Wales from which the nation was Christianized. This circuit of monasteries forms a path around Wales, part of which we'll be walking as we follow in St David's footsteps.

"But David's greatest gift was in fighting heresy. The event he is best remembered for occurred west of here at Llanddewi Brefi. His eloquence so put the heretics to confusion and made such an impact that the synod at once elected him archbishop of Caerleon and primate of the Cambrian church:

Light gathered in the clouds over his head as David, standing near the bank of the River Brefi, its waters running blue and swift, surveyed the vast crowd covering the field before him. The popularity of the message being preached by the British monk Pelagius in Rome was much talked of even here in their rugged land beyond the shielding mountains. Many church officials in Rome and throughout what little was left of the empire had been persuaded of Pelagius's enticing doctrine that there was no such thing as original sin. Humankind was basically good and could overcome evil and make itself fit for heaven by its own efforts. There was no need for the atoning sacrifice of Christ, only for strength of will and energy of activity.

David shook his head. His mane of gold-shot brown hair tossed in the breeze behind the half moon tonsure that left the front of his head clean-shaven. The white dove that had followed him since his childhood hovered near his shoulder. That so many had assembled for the debate proved the correctness of Archbishop Dubricius's decision to call this synod. And David feared it would be a debate, not an automatic acclamation of acceptance for the historic faith delivered by the apostles. Even priests and monks from some of the houses he himself had founded had fallen under the spell of this heretical teaching. David closed his eyes and raised a fervent prayer that Archbishop Dubricius would be able to persuade them to stand strong for the orthodox faith.

David opened his eyes and started when he saw Dubricius himself standing before him. "My lord Archbishop, I pray for your strength and wisdom. This heresy must be uprooted before it spreads like a virulent weed throughout our land. Already its poisonous tentacles are gripping much of the church."

Dubricius nodded his head in a kind of bow. "And I pray for your wisdom. And success in persuading your hearers."

It was a moment before the significance of Dubricius's words struck him. "My lord, you would have me address the synod?"

"I know of no one else so well qualified in the skills of debate and proclamation. Ever you have stood strong for the historic ways. May your strength not fail you today."

David looked at the throng of churchmen gathered across the field. An image of our Lord teaching and then feeding the 5,000 came to him. He could not refuse to do the archbishop's bidding. But he felt so inadequate. So unprepared. And the stakes were so high. The very gospel itself was at risk. The truth must be preserved for future generations.

"My lord Archbishop," he bowed his head. "I humbly accept. Permit me a few moments' preparation."

Dubricius raised his arms to call the congregation to order and began a chant that was half prayer, half hymn: "All the paths of the Lord are mercy and truth unto such as keep His covenant and His testimonies."

And across the field the antiphonal response came: "Let Thy loving kindness and Thy truth continually preserve me."

The plea for the triumph of truth ringing in his ears, David entered his cell. He lifted the carved chest and drew out the cherished document. No time now for study, but it would serve as a focus to guide his prayers.

Minutes later his fears were calmed; he knew what he would say.

The chant was concluding, the echoes ringing from side to side of the field, as David walked to the head of the assemblage: "Truth shall spring out of the earth; and righteousness shall look down from heaven."

David joined in the doxology: "Great is our God which keepeth truth for ever."

David raised his arms, aware of the dove fluttering just at his right shoulder. "My brothers, it is the keeping of the truth, the historic faith of the prophets, the apostles and the fathers I declare to you. The precious faith of the death and resurrection of our Lord Jesus Christ. This we must not sacrifice for any easy doctrine, no matter how honeyed the words."

David was aware that those standing near him—even those he knew disagreed with his position—were listening intently. But he could sense a restlessness at the back of the throng. And little wonder; they could neither hear nor see him. How could they be persuaded of so sensitive an issue?

He looked around. The riverbank offered a slight elevation. He took a few steps backward to gain perhaps a foot or two of height, but not enough for even his powerful voice to reach to the back.

All he could do was carry on. And pray. He raised his voice, "Always the new ways glitter. The easy ways entice. How pleasant to believe that we carry no stain..." His words continued, the arguments flowing easily, but David was less aware of his own words than of the look of amazement on the faces of his hearers. He could feel the air vibrate with the intensity of their attention.

And then he realized he could see their faces. Even those as far back as the monastery wall—he could see them. And they him.

He looked down and saw that where all had been a level field, he was now standing on a raised hill the height of a man's head. And the dove no longer fluttered, but sat on his shoulder.

David's heart rejoiced. His plea had been heard. His voice increased in vigor as his appeal reached to the farthest corners: If no sin, there was no need of God's grace. If man could save himself by his own righteous acts, what use then Christ's saving act through His great loving sacrifice?

It was the hard way they must take. As our Lord had taken. The hard but true way. The way delivered unto the saints. The way opened for all by our Lord's sacrifice.

He didn't know how long he spoke. Afterward he could not recount the arguments he had made. But when he was finished he descended the hill, not knowing that his face was shining.

Nor, thought Felicity, did Antony know his face was shining when he finished his story. But then, perhaps she was prejudiced. It could just have been the morning sun.

Chapter 7

Sunday, continued

Befote they set out on the walk to Llantarnam Abbey, Felicity, Antony and Michael got their heads together over their maps. Ordnance Survey Explorer maps with a scale of two and a half inches to the mile; a well-marked set each for the driver and for the leader of the walk. Both cut into the size of a sheet of A4 paper and neatly put in order in a clear plastic folder, with a shoulder strap for the walk leader. Every detail had been seen to.

Michael traced the dark blue highlighted line with his finger, starting at Isca Roman Fortress, clearly indicated with a drawing of the amphitheater below it. "Walking route's about the same as I'll be driving. Back through town, then along Malthouse Road, then north at Craig Wood to the abbey. I'll head on up and get the minibus unloaded. Ring me on your mobile if you need me to come back for anything—anyone sprains an ankle or anything."

Felicity gave a little shiver. He said it as a joke and she wasn't really superstitious or anything; still, she had an impulse to knock on wood. Michael handed her the set of walking maps, but she held up her hand. "Er—" She turned to Antony. "Do you mind awfully? I know the idea was for me to lead so you could stay back with any stragglers, but I'm afraid I'll be the straggler myself this morning. I really hate to admit it, but I didn't sleep very well last night."

Both men were instantly solicitous. "Of course, ride with me. I'd be delighted for the company," Michael said.

"Felicity, you should have said." Antony looked worried.

Felicity forced a laugh and felt guilty. Well, she *was* feeling less than refreshed, but her real reason for wanting to ride was to see if she could learn anything about what Michael had been up to last night. She certainly didn't want to cause Antony concern. "Oh, no worries. Sorry. But it would feel good to sit down. I do feel a slacker, though, I heard Colin declaring this morning that he intended to walk every step of the trail and here's me sitting out before we start."

Antony placed a warm hand on her shoulder. "That's the time to do it—before we start. Official starting point for medieval pilgrims was St Michael's Church. We start out from there tomorrow. So, by all means, take a break now. We'll meet you at the abbey." Without even looking to see whether or not anyone was looking, he leaned forward and kissed her.

She was still smiling as she settled into the seat that in America would have been on the driver's side. It still required a conscious effort on her part to get it right. Or to smile at the teasing that always ensued when she got it wrong. "Thinking of driving, were you?"

Waving to the pilgrims on the ground, Felicity sat back as the van rolled through the town toward the open countryside. She pretended to be captivated by the scenery as she struggled to form a question that would help her learn what Michael had been up to without giving away that she had been spying on him. "Tell me about yourself. What do you do?" Seemed as safe a place as any to start.

"I'm from Llandaff—well, that's Cardiff, really. I work in the diocesan office with Father Stephen."

"Ah, so that's how you got roped into this job?"

"In a way. My job is to promote the church's Tourism

Network, so I guess helping with a pilgrimage is pretty much a natural. That's what Father Stephen thought, anyway."

"Church Tourism Network? You mean there is such a thing?"

Michael grinned. "'Putting tourism into church and church into tourism' is the motto. Not a bad idea, really. Make people aware of our spiritual heritage. Get some tourist money to help restore some of the old sites."

"Evangelism and practicality."

"Exactly. And we work with the Ecumenical Council because we promote nonconformist chapels just as much as the medieval sites."

"Do you drive for these tourist groups?"

"No. No, nothing like that. Just sit in the office mostly and look up things on the computer to answer queries, recommend religious venues for tours, suggest accommodations near chapels or abbeys that groups are interested in seeing. Lot more enthusiasm for a site if they know there's a good pub or leisure park nearby."

"You must have been invaluable for Father Stephen in planning this."

"We worked on it all for months, yeah. Walked a lot of it together—so I don't mind driving now; I've already done most of it. There are so many alternative routes to choose from. Had to be sorted out ahead the best we could. Such a shame he has to miss it."

"Did you know any of the pilgrims before?"

"Not really. I took the registrations as they came in, answered their questions about what they'd need to bring, where to meet up, that sort of thing. When Lydia registered to come along with her little brother and mentioned her nurse's training, Stephen asked me to contact her about being prepared to do first aid, so we've corresponded a bit."

Felicity smiled. Ah, perhaps that was it. Maybe a letter from Lydia? They were both in their early twenties, a good age for a romance. She thought for a moment. Yes, they would make a cute couple. That could make the pilgrimage interesting. Or difficult. She would keep her eyes open. And mention it to Antony. But that hardly explained the dirt on the shovel. And would Michael really discuss a budding romance with Colin? What had Michael and Colin been doing last night?

Recently trimmed hedgerows lined both sides of the narrow road, giving the sense of driving in a deep, narrow canyon. The road wound up the side of a hill. Just as they reached the crest, the sun came out from behind a cloud like a spotlight across the green, sheep-dotted fields, intersected by hedgerows. All the while Felicity was thinking about the predawn excursion she had witnessed.

"Did you sleep all right last night?" she asked. "That floor was awfully hard, wasn't it? I suppose we'll have to get used to it, though."

"I slept fine." Just then they met a car, requiring Michael to reverse to a spot barely wide enough to allow the other vehicle to pass. "That is, I would have if that wet Colin had let me."

"Colin?"

"Said he'd had a bad dream. Wanted to go for a walk. Seemed easier to comply than argue. After all, I was awake by then."

Check, thought Felicity. That still didn't explain the spade, but she simply couldn't think of any way to approach that.

Felicity argued with herself for the rest of the brief journey. She knew she had an overactive imagination. And how many times in the past had it led her astray? She had had trouble sleeping, so why shouldn't some of the others? She had wakened from a dream, thinking Antony was calling her. What was unnatural or to be feared about that? She had gone for a walk and heard Colin and Michael arguing. No, they weren't even arguing, just talking intently. And she had no business to be eavesdropping—much less following them. And what was so alarming about Michael carrying a spade? Colin probably wanted to collect some soil samples from a historic Roman site. Or maybe examine the footings of the Roman fortress more closely. Probably with the idea of some original research for an essay. Or maybe...

In the dark? A small niggling voice said at the back of her head. But, well, Colin was pretty obsessive. She was still spooked from that awful experience back at Kirkthorpe—which she had come all this way to forget, she reminded herself sternly. She really must concentrate on the bucolic scenery, and relax.

Now the road was lined on the left by a stone wall with little purple flowers growing between its stones, and grassy banks of green with yellow flowers at its feet. Ponies grazed in the field beyond. They swung around a corner and there before them was the ornate Gothic, stone gatehouse of Llantarnam Abbey at the end of a long, wooded drive, with ivy covering the trunks of all the trees. Signs pointed them to *Ty Croeso*, the House of Welcome.

They parked between ancient cedar trees taller than the abbey, and crunched across the gravel to the courtyard. The bell was marked "Please Ring" so they rang. A tall, thin woman wearing a brown cardigan over a beige skirt and blouse answered the door. She introduced herself as Sister Alicia.

When Michael explained who they were, Sister Alicia offered a tour. "That way you can show the others around when they arrive." She started down the hall, pointing out the comfortable visitors' lounge, each comfy chair carefully provided with an antimacassar to protect its upholstery from soil. "We are forty Sisters, but I'm afraid many are elderly and keep to the infirmary. And many Sisters go out from here to work in schools, parishes and hospitals. Above all, we are a place of prayer and we are most happy to provide hospitality for those who would join us for quiet days."

Felicity thought of the clutch of energetic pilgrims walking their way, and hoped that, indeed, it would be a quiet day.

Along another hall, Sister Alicia opened the door onto a warm room with golden oak wainscoting and a carved oak ceiling. "Our refectory. It was the men's billiard room when owned by the Morgan family."

"Oh, was this a private home?" Felicity had been sure it was an ancient monastery. Hadn't the monks at Caerleon moved here for more quiet?

"Yes, it was in private hands for many years." Alicia led the way across the room and opened a door onto a sunny, glassed walk lined with pots of orange lilies. "We record our history from the middle of the twelfth century when the Cistercians established a monastery here. Although they say St David may have had a community here earlier. Of course, it was all confiscated by Henry VIII. William Morgan obtained the land. He was directly descended from Hywel ap Iorweth, the founder of the abbey."

"Was Hywel an abbot?" Felicity asked.

"No, no. Most definitely not. He was a man of war. In his own words he said he gave the lands to the White Monks 'for the salvation of my soul and that of my parents and predecessors.' It was frequently the case that a wealthy member of the nobility would endow a monastery in return for the prayers of the monks."

"How amazing that it then came back to his family."

"It is, yes. The land stayed with the Morgan descendants until the twentieth century. The building was used as an American Air Force storage depot during the Second World War and the Sisters of St Joseph— that's us—came here in 1946 to make it a house of prayer again."

She turned to the front of the house. "Here now, the entrance hall was part of the original pre-Reformation abbey. It was the entrance hall for the family. And let me just show you something amazing." With a mischievous smile she opened a door marked "Gents" and invited her visitors to look in.

"Oh!" Felicity couldn't repress a small giggle at the sight of an ornate pink marble loo with a decorated plaster ceiling, and the Morgan coat of arms in stained glass in the window.

"We think that's rather fun." Another sister, this one shorter and plumper than Sister Alicia, wearing a beige skirt and white blouse and her soft face framed in a flowing veil, joined them. "The Morgans and their guests lived quite well, it seems."

Their guide introduced Sister Florence, and Felicity and Michael explained about their pilgrimage before she wished them a blessed stay in their house before departing by the side door. "Sister Florence is our sacristan; she'll be seeing everything is ready for Father Giles. He comes over from Newport to give us mass after he finishes in his parish," she explained as she led the way down a hall.

Sister Alicia stepped into the library, giving her visitors a glimpse of parquet floor and stacks of books. Seconds later she emerged with a small booklet which she handed to Felicity. "Here you are. The whole history of us."

Felicity thanked her and started to comment on the sweeping gardens beyond the glassed walk. It seemed one couldn't look out a window without seeing something beautiful. But Sister Alicia had turned to lead up a magnificent oak stairway to point out the guest rooms. Felicity sighed in anticipation. Tonight she would sleep in a bed. And there were bathrooms with tubs and showers. She knew that once they started on the pilgrims' trail there would be no more such luxuries.

After showing them their rooms, Sister Alicia left them to settle in. Michael and Felicity had just finished unloading the van, although they had not carried the gear up that grand staircase, when the merry walkers crunched up the gravel path. Ryan, their enthusiastic geographer, who had apparently taken on the map-reading task, led the file with the map case hanging around his neck. Nancy, her red jumper tied around her waist and her brown pony tail bobbing, walked beside him. Antony and Colin came last, Colin swinging his walking stick and talking nonstop. Felicity's heart gave that little skip it always did when Antony came into view, and went out to meet them.

"Have Kaylyn and Evie arrived yet?" Antony took a long pull on his water bottle.

"Oh, are those the walkers meeting us here? I haven't seen anyone."

The words were no more than out of Felicity's mouth than a large black car swept up the drive. Gravel crunched as the driver braked hard. Two teenage girls emerged from the back seat. Felicity had to check that her mouth wasn't gaping. Not stereotypical pilgrims.

"Hi, I'm Evie." The plump girl with spiked maroon hair and multiple piercings and tattoos gave a giggle. "This is Kaylyn."

Kaylyn was almost a head taller than Evie and thin, emaciated, with long, shaggy, kohl-black hair. She swept the group with a bored glance and said nothing.

Antony stepped forward. "Welcome. Did you have a good journey from Brighton?" He had apparently checked his notes.

Again, Evie was the spokesperson. "It was fast. Kaylyn's brother drove us." She giggled again and looked toward the window shielding the driver. "Gareth, he is." Her smile said that the youth hiding behind the tinted glass was, to her way of thinking, pretty special.

"Fine, let us help you with your gear." Apparently the delightful Gareth wasn't planning to lift a hand because he merely pulled the lever to unlatch the boot without getting out of the car. Antony had barely slammed the boot shut when Gareth spun out of the driveway, spewing gravel behind him. "He's in a hurry," Evie explained unnecessarily, accompanied by her apparently perpetual giggle.

Antony held his hands up and called for attention. "All right, everyone. Well done on your first bit of walking. A good warm-up, yes? We have almost an hour to settle in. Then you can take another walk around the grounds if you like." He smiled at the chorus of groans. "Or have a rest. Eucharist will be at one o'clock. Dinner in the refectory after that."

The next half hour or so was a flurry of activity as pilgrims were assigned rooms, and toted their bags up the grand staircase of the abbey-cum-manor house-cum-abbey. Finally Felicity had a chance to corner Antony. "We need to talk. That is, I want to talk to you. Er, I mean, I missed you."

A huge smile, several times the kilowatt power of Antony's usual little lopsided grin, split his face. "That's great. Even if it was just over two hours."

Felicity noticed he didn't say, "I missed you, too." But that was all right. She knew he did. "There's a gazebo at the foot of the garden—garth, they call it. Let's go there."

Felicity had spotted the gazebo on her earlier tour, standing in the far corner against the high, grey stone garden wall. Square, formed of natural golden brown wooden slats. "Sister Alicia said it was donated to them by a lady. It was vandalized in the lady's garden, so she gave it to the Sisters."

Antony surveyed the fortress-like wall. "Should be safe enough from vandals here."

"Yes, Sister Alicia gave me a booklet about the history of the order. It's titled *Behind the Walls*. She said they chose that title because so many first-time visitors say, 'Oh, I always wondered what was behind the walls.'"

They sat on the lattice-backed wooden bench and Felicity breathed deeply. "Ah, mock orange. I love that scent. At home we call it syringa. It's the Idaho state flower because it grows wild in our mountains." By mutual consent they reached for each other and clasped hands. "I've been thinking I would like to wear a halo of syringa over my veil. This absolutely confirms it."

Antony squeezed her hand. "Good. See, you did get a bit of wedding planning done."

Felicity sighed even though she was still smiling. "Yes, sitting around reading *Today's Bride* would have seemed too—I don't know—too flippant, I guess... After what happened. Anyway, I'm not sure if they have such things in England."

"I rather think it's simply called *Brides*."

Felicity's mouth dropped open. "Fancy you knowing that!"

"Gwena kept them under her bed as a teenager. Ironic, really, given how many er—relationships she's had, and no weddings."

Felicity blinked. Gwena? Oh, yes, Antony spoke so seldom of Gwendolyn, his sister, but she suspected he missed her. "Oh, yes. I do hope she'll be able to come to our wedding. And your aunt and uncle." They were all that was left of Antony's family after his parents had drowned in a sailing accident when he and his sister were young.

"And your brothers," he added, then shook his head. "It hardly seems real, does it? Our families getting together from such a distance. And your mother. And father. Have you heard anything?"

Felicity shook her head. "Mother decided not to take the transfer to Los Angeles and is definitely staying with the law firm in Boise. I guess that's hopeful. But I haven't heard much from her. I keep hoping they'll get back together."

They sat in silence for several moments. Bees buzzed around the mock orange bush outside the lattice and a thrush sang from a tree further away. At last Felicity got her thoughts together. As much as they would come together sitting in such an idyllic spot with the man she loved. "But Antony, I didn't ask you to come here to talk about wedding plans. Actually, I need to tell you something."

In her breathless, headlong way she recounted the eerie feeling of being wakened by a voice—his voice—in the dark hall. "At first it was comforting—hearing your voice. No, more enticing, maybe. I can't really describe it... Anyway, there was no question, I just untangled from my sleeping bag and groped my way across the floor. It was pitch black. And cold. And there you were, sleeping like—well, I don't know what like. Just really soundly. I thought of waking you and asking if you wanted anything, but that would have been silly, wouldn't it?

"And then I looked around. Well, listened mostly because I couldn't really see anything. And everyone was totally flat out. Sounded like a room full of steam engines, or something. I don't really know what a room of steam engines would sound like.

"And then I felt sort of, I don't know—claustrophobic, I guess. Anyway, I really needed some fresh air. And then I found out not quite everyone else was asleep." She repeated the snatches of overheard conversation the best she could recall. The whole affair was more and more taking on the indefiniteness of a dream. At least her glimpses of the mud-caked spade were more definite. Then she told him about her conversation with Michael that morning, and her attempts to explain it all in a reasonable light. She held her breath for his reaction.

To her relief, Antony didn't rebuke her for her mild bit of probing. Nor did he dismiss the whole thing as overactive imagination. Surprisingly, the thing he seemed most concerned about was her dream. "You're certain it was my voice?"

"Absolutely. I'm not likely to fail to recognize those plummy vowels in your beautiful tenor voice."

As her flowery compliments always did, this caused him to duck his head and swallow a chuckle. "Er—right. And you were soundly asleep? Dreaming?"

"I'm not aware that I was dreaming. I think I heard you call my name three times. Twice to waken me. Then again after I was awake."

Antony became very still and turned more directly toward her. "You're certain? You were awake?"

She thought carefully. "As certain as one can be when they've been wakened from a sound sleep in a strange place." She closed her eyes to relive the experience. "It was spooky. So silent. The darkness was, well—thick.

"It was like being alone on the edge of a cliff. And then the voice. Calling me over."

"Over the cliff? And moments later you were aware of all the snoring and deep breathing in the room?"

"That's right. It wasn't silent at all. And I didn't have any sense of crawling over a cliff. I was going to you. How strange."

Antony was silent for several moments, squeezing the hand he still held in both of his. "Felicity, be careful."

"Why—"

The bells began ringing from the Abbey Chapel at the side of the grounds. Antony looked at his watch. "Five minutes. Better go see that the troops are organized." He gave her a peck of a kiss, then stopped to make a proper job of it.

"I'll meet you there." Felicity watched him go, but she didn't want to leave this tiny, golden shelter. Telling Antony about last night's experience had sharpened it in her mind, and yet made it all the harder to understand. The sense of being outside time, outside reality. Easy enough to explain for a dream. But the sharper consciousness was from when she was awake. She touched the wooden slats of the bench she sat on. Cool in the shade. But nothing like the chill of the floor she had touched last night. Yes, she had definitely been awake.

The bell began again with more insistence this time, forcing her to race across the garth, through the small side gate in the wall, and across the gravel path to the church beside the convent. The cool sanctuary slowed her rush. It was beautiful with its ceiling and sunburst corona soaring above the stone altar in the apse. The stained-glass window behind her, representing the hills and valleys of Wales beneath sun and sky, sent glowing swirls of rainbow that warmed the space with color.

Felicity chose a pew behind the rows of beige-clad Sisters, next to Nancy, who was kneeling in prayer. The sacristan Sister Florence lit the candles on the altar, her veil falling softly over her face as she made a solemn bow, and returned to her seat. Felicity was aware of the other pilgrims straggling in, the newly arrived Evie and Kaylyn the last, with Antony behind them. One of the Sisters began a hymn on the organ in the loft at the back. Father Giles took the pot of holy water from the credence table and walked up and down the aisle, flinging drops of water over the worshipers to remind them of their baptism as all stood to sing on this, the Sunday after Ascension, "Let the earth rejoice and sing, alleluia!/At the triumph of our King, alleluia!/He ascends from mortal sight…"

Felicity should have been comforted as the melody soared upward with the angelic voices of the nuns and light from the stained-glass window pooling around her. She should have been rejoicing, as Nancy beside her obviously was. But instead her mind filled with the horrifying image of a black-cassocked figure arching over the edge of a high stone tower, seeming to soar for a moment like a great, black bird, and then plummeting to earth.

She looked at the pool of green light at her feet and almost screamed as a shadow seemed to roll over it. "…Thou didst shatter Satan's might,/Rising glorious from the fight…" She gripped the back of the pew in front of her and concentrated on the words of the hymn. *Focus on the candles, their flames reaching upward, spreading the light.*

Father Giles stepped forward and held out his arms, making his white chasuble unfurl like angels' wings, "Let us pray. God our Father, make us joyful in the ascension of your Son, may we follow him into the new creation…"

Felicity's breathing steadied. She relaxed, and the service swirled around her with its familiar, comforting rhythms. Everything was fine. She was overwrought. She needed to relax. Have faith.

Felicity's complacence grew as the mass continued in its stately order through readings, homily, prayers. The only jarring note came when Felicity's gaze, seeking a comforting look at Antony's serene profile, fell instead on Kaylyn. She might not have noticed if the girl hadn't been so stiffly expressionless before, but the glittering intensity of her face made Felicity catch her breath. There should be nothing discordant about a worshiper looking triumphant at Eucharist, especially on a feast day, but somehow Kaylyn's look chilled Felicity.

Concentrate on the liturgy, she told herself. Everyone rose as the organ began a hymn and Sister Florence stepped forward to present the gifts of bread and wine to Father Giles. The priest, on his side of the altar, took the elements from her hands and gave a nod as if to say, "Thank you."

Sister Florence returned the bow, her veil shifting forward.

Felicity cried out as the nun's veil ignited.

Sister Florence became a giant paschal candle.

Father Giles grabbed the pot of holy water he had used for the asperges and dumped it on the blaze.

It was all over in seconds. The entire congregation gave a sigh of relief. The Reverend Mother took the trembling Sister Florence aside to tend to her singed hair and veil.

"I hope it'll not be taken amiss if I comment that Pentecost is next Sunday." Father Giles' comment quelled the alarm. Even Sister Florence managed a weak smile. The service continued.

All was well. It had been a simple accident.

Felicity could have convinced herself of that if she hadn't seen the candle flame leap sideways as if blown by unseen lips to grab the nun.

And if she hadn't caught the gleam of satisfaction on Kaylyn's face.

Chapter 8

Monday
Llantarnam to Llandderfel

*F*eeling refreshed and energized after a good night of sleep in a real bed, a shower, a solid abbey breakfast and brief morning prayers with the Sisters, they set out early the next morning. Antony strode along the path through the abbey grounds toward the little town of Llantarnam. Sheep baaed softly in the pasture and birds called from fir trees on the far side of the field. The sun played hide-and-seek with the fluffy clouds overhead and the fresh morning air grew alternately warm and cool accordingly.

He watched Felicity walking at the head of the crocodile of marching pilgrims and gave thanks that she seemed in good spirits in spite of her fright over yesterday's mishap with the candle. Ryan, the official map-bearer, followed closely behind her, his tread measured by rhythmic swings of his hiking pole, and the others straggled along the narrow brown line through the green.

It would be easy to get overconfident on such a pleasant morning. But that would be the worst thing one could do. He didn't know what they were dealing with here; whether the disturbing events of the past days had been simple human action caused by the malice and greed one encountered on an almost daily basis—especially in his business—or whether they were threatened with something—well, something less normal.

Nosterfield had been very right to be skeptical of any such suggestion. But Antony's training and experience had taught him that it wasn't outside the realm of possibility. Constant vigilance. And prayer. That was Antony's job.

As they crossed the A road and walked along a village street, the square, sharply crenelated tower of St Michael's Church came into view. Built by the Llantarnam monks for the use of the local community, this had been the official starting point for pilgrimages like theirs for ten centuries. The massive, arched wooden door stood open. Felicity led the little band up the wide walkway through the churchyard dotted with lichen-covered tombstones leaning at various angles.

The minibus which had been obliged to take a longer route around the fields crunched into the gravel parking space. And Michael got out, alone. "Where's Jared?" Antony asked, pleasure in the freshness of the morning receding. "His email said he would be at the abbey no later than ten o'clock."

Antony had been concerned about this final addition to their group. As if what Felicity had told him about Kaylyn's strange attitude wasn't enough to worry about, Stephen's notes informed him that Jared's lengthy, consistent record of troublemaking had caused him to be excluded from school. He was now in a special program where he did very abbreviated school days. At the request of his single mother and his grandmother's priest, Jared had been entrusted to Father Stephen—and now passed over to Antony—to participate in this experience for "therapeutic" reasons. Antony could only hope it would be therapeutic for the group as well as for Jared; if he deigned to show up. Surely Antony or the Ecumenical Council wouldn't be held responsible if the boy had done a bunk.

Michael held up his mobile. "He rang. Said he'd been delayed. He'll meet us here."

This was not an auspicious start to Jared's "therapy." And

Antony did not want to be delayed. His perusal of the route had already told him that they had many miles to walk today. Over some exceedingly rough terrain. He didn't want to be looking for their accommodation after dark tonight.

"All right, everyone inside," Antony called to those who were wandering over the churchyard. He gave them a few minutes to look around the historic church. The stone walls were cool and the small windows limited the light, and yet the golden oak pews and gleaming golden altar cross seemed to give off a light of their own. The massive tomb bearing the arms of the Morgan family bore silent testimony to the patrimony of the area.

"Let's gather at the back." The little band filed obediently into the rear pews. This was his time to set the tone for the coming days, to lay out some ground rules, to let them know what he expected of them. Nine pairs of eyes met his. Lydia and Michael to his right. Was it only happenstance they sat together, or was Felicity correct to suspect a budding romance? If so, Antony hoped it wouldn't distract either of them. Michael as driver and Lydia as nurse were both key to the success—survival, even—of the pilgrimage.

Colin, the budding archeologist, was talking nonstop to Ryan, the geography student. Their interests should keep them focused on the terrain and hopefully not too bored by his lectures.

Kaylyn and Evie sat in the farthest corner. Evie's magenta hair looking brighter than ever next to the scarlet shirt she wore today, while Kaylyn was swathed in her ritual black with silver studs. Odd that this pair would have chosen—or at least consented—to join a pilgrimage. Perhaps they were looking for answers to questions they didn't want to admit, or didn't realize, they were asking. If so, God give him wisdom.

Nancy, her hands folded in her lap, her brown hair in a neat braid coiled atop her head, bent sideways to the diminutive Adam who sat beside her. The pale youth was such a scrap of humanity

Antony wondered about his ability to accomplish their vigorous itinerary. But then, his sister was a nurse and he could always ride in the minibus.

Ah, and in the corner nearest the door where the light shining through fell on her pale hair—his Felicity. They exchanged brief smiles as their eyes met, then he swallowed hard at the incredible thought that this amazing young woman was soon to be his. He cleared his throat. "Right then, just a few ground rules so we'll all know what's expected of us. First, order of march. The person carrying the map, which will usually be Felicity," he looked at the large youth in front of him with the map case around his neck, "or Ryan, will stay toward the front. I'll pretty much stay at the back with anyone who hits a slower pace. This isn't to be a forced march, but we must stay together. There's some rough terrain out there and we can't have anyone going off and getting lost.

"Michael will touch points with us every few miles. There's no stigma attached to taking a break. Much better to ride a few miles now and then, than to overdo and not be able to finish.

"Be sure you keep your water bottles filled. You can refill them from the minibus when we stop for breaks."

Lydia held up her hand. "And I've got sunblock for anyone who needs it."

"Thank you, Lydia. And we're well supplied with plasters and anything else you might need in that line, so don't be afraid to speak up."

Evie raised her hand. "Um, what about—er, facilities?" She swallowed the word in a giggle.

Antony smiled. "A fair question. Rest stops are indicated on the route map. Other than that, I'm afraid you'll have to find a bush." Evie gasped and giggled again. It was probably an honest question, but if she'd asked it to embarrass him, it was clear that it had backfired.

"I can't stress enough that this is a community exercise. We're in this together. It isn't a race or an endurance contest. I'm sure you'll all be good about helping each other. And as you walk, don't just walk with your friend. Be sure you walk with different people, get to know each other. And no iPods or any such thing in your ears. That cuts against community.

"Now, we'll be saying the Stations of the Cross every day. It'll be a good way to help mark the miles and to remember what we're all about. Also, we have a cross to carry, which Father Stephen made for us. We'll pass it around. Again, it will remind us what we're about and let others know as well.

"We'll start with the first Station out in the churchyard." As the pilgrims filed back out into the midmorning, Antony looked at his watch. Jared was more than an hour late. He hated to walk on and leave the minibus to wait. It wasn't good to get too far apart. Would they be stuck here all day? No wonder the boy had run afoul of authority if he was this irresponsible.

The deep grass gave off its distinctive scent as they walked to the far side of the yard to stand in a ragged circle under a spreading beech tree. Michael brought the cross from the van, perhaps five feet tall, fashioned from rough tree limbs lashed together with heavy cord. A powerful symbol, indeed. Antony unfolded the paper he took from his pocket. "I've chosen a Stations service that follows the way of the cross through the thoughts of a Roman centurion. I thought it would be appropriate since we'll be encountering some Roman sites on our walk, and those of you who were with us in Caerleon heard the story of two of Britain's first martyrs who were Roman soldiers.

"'The first Station, Jesus is condemned…' The brief scripture passage recalling Pilate asking the mob clamoring for Jesus' crucifixion, 'Why? What harm has he done?' was followed by the centurion's musing on Jesus' demeanor: 'He didn't shout and rave like most of them; just took it all calmly…'"

They knelt in the soft, unmown grass for the final prayer. "We praise you and bless—"

The ending was ragged as they were interrupted by a cheery shout. "Halloo, sorry about being late. I mean, I coulda walked faster than that coach from Swansea." A tall, lanky, redheaded youth strode across the churchyard, stepping over the lower tombstones rather than going around them. He wore a camouflage rucksack and carried a large, well-stuffed duffel bag as if it were weightless.

Antony stood, and stepped toward the newcomer. "You must be Jared." Recriminations over his late arrival dispersed at the young man's wide, open smile that lit up his blue eyes.

"Got it in one." He stooped and unzipped a side pocket from his bag. "Hope I'm not too late, I mean, this being St Michael's Church and all, I wanted to give you these before we left." He started handing around small cards bearing the image of an avenging St Michael the Archangel subduing the Evil One even as flames from the pit of hell reached out to devour him. "My church—well, my gran's, really—is St Michael's, so they sent these to everyone."

Antony turned his card over. *May the prayers of St Michael and All Angels sustain you on your pilgrimage. You will be remembered each day of your journey by our congregation.* The cards had been printed especially for them. The thoughtfulness and devotion that had provided these cards warmed him.

"The priest, er, like, blessed them, too. He said to say. He's an old geezer, but he's cool." Jared was obviously embarrassed by all the holy stuff he had been commissioned to relay. He let out a long breath when his duty had been performed.

But the sense of comfort Antony had first felt ended in a shiver. "Your priest. What's his name?"

"Father Finan."

"Gray hair, long? Beard?" Antony held his hands out from his face to indicate a substantial bush.

"Tha's it. You know him?" Jared seemed pleased.

"Not personally." But Antony knew his reputation. Father Finan had written an important book on his experiences as a deliverance minister. How appropriate that he was now vicar at a church dedicated to St Michael the Archangel, of whom demons were particularly afraid.

Did this prescient, experienced exorcist have a premonition that they were going to be in special need of his prayers?

Chapter 9

Monday, continued

Felicity volunteered to be first to carry the cross, although when she picked it up she was surprised at its weight. Carrying this up and down mountains could amount to more than a symbolic burden. Still, with all that had been going on, she wanted personal contact with this concrete reminder to pray. The weight of the cross felt good.

If only it were the only weight she felt. Even in the late morning sunshine, she had a sense of brooding darkness as if clouds surrounded the sun, rather than only scattered bits of stratus. She tightened her grip on the uneven bark and raised the cross aloft. What was she thinking to let depression get her down? This wasn't like her at all. Good vigorous exercise was what she needed to shake off this mood. She would outwalk the darkness.

She gave her head a hearty shake, making her hair cascade across her back, raised her chin and looked at Ryan for directions.

"Cross the road in front of the church," he pointed. "Then take the track to your left. On up a bit when the track becomes a driveway to houses, you'll turn left and follow the way-marked footpath round the back of the industrial buildings." He held the map out for her to see.

"Industrial buildings." Felicity groaned and looked at the dispiriting buildings and tarmac before them. This was supposed to be a bucolic ramble through green hillsides dotted with safely grazing sheep. She looked closer at the map: Industrial park, industrial estate, tight clusters of buildings drawn on the map.

How was she going to outstrip her depression in such dismal surroundings?

Ryan consulted the notes accompanying his map. "The traditional route out of Llantarnam followed an ancient trackway which was used in 1179 as the boundary of the land given by Hywel ab Iorwerth to the monks. Unfortunately, it's now a suburban main road." He shrugged and smiled as if to say, "Can't fight progress."

Right. Best thing was just to get through it. Felicity led out. Once everyone was safely across the road she half turned to Ryan. "So you're doing your gap year?" That part of the educational schedule for so many British young people was an intriguing idea to Felicity. That it should be an accepted thing for a student to take a year off their formal studies to work, travel, do volunteer work, or explore new interests before going on to university was not part of the American system. Of course, many young people had to take some time to work to get money to go to college or university, but taking a gap year would more likely be viewed as slacking.

"Yeah, it's been good. I've had time to think. I worked in a garden center and volunteered at a youth club. This pilgrimage sort of brings it all together."

"Being out in nature—getting close to the geography, you mean?"

"Well, yeah, there's that. We'll be walking through some amazing land formations, but I meant more the spiritual side. I wouldn't have wanted to come on this a year ago, but working with the kids at the club—a lot of them were pretty troubled— made me appreciate my family."

They continued to chat intermittently, but the whizzing Monday midday traffic in the heavily built-up area made sustained conversation difficult. Still, Felicity held in her mind the idea that she would soon be above all this, on the cool green mountainside she occasionally glimpsed in the distance. Then she could begin the "getting away from it all" that Antony had promised her when she had signed on to this adventure. Whenever her steps started to flag with the weight she carried at the back of her mind, she gave herself another shake and pushed forward with a lengthened stride.

Walking along the canal offered a bit of a respite, and the stone buildings lining the high street of Old Cwmbran held traces of its quieter, perhaps more picturesque, past. But Felicity was finding the upward slope of the street to be deceptively steep.

"Shall I carry the cross for you?"

Felicity smiled at Ryan and handed it over gratefully. "I'll take the map, then." But after she looked at it and saw that they had next a retail park and then an industrial park to go through, she wished she hadn't looked ahead. Walking through urban industrial areas was not her idea of what a pilgrimage should be. Still, there, just on a bit was the Greenmeadow Community Farm where they would meet the minibus for lunch, and the second Station.

The path up to the farm grew increasingly steeper, the traffic along the road below the footpath noisier, until the now-wooded trail moved off to skirt around the back of a housing estate on their left. Felicity was happy to be walking on a dirt path after all the pavement, but in spite of the leafy branches overhead, the path was anything but idyllic. The way was marred by litter caught in the bushes, rusty wire coiling along the side, and shards of broken glass in the walkway. Ryan lowered the cross to lead them through a damp, shadowy underpass where a couple stood wrapped in each other's arms continuing their intense kissing unperturbed by the train of pilgrims passing only a couple of feet beside them.

Out of the tunnel, the air cleared as the path emerged on the edge of a green, wooded hillside. The sun had ducked behind a cloud; it was almost misty. Felicity took in a great gulp of air and looked around in wonder. "It's so peaceful after all of that."

Jared gave the wide, loose-lipped smile that covered half of his face. "Have to take the good with the bad, don't you?"

Remembering Antony's admonition that the walkers should get to know each other, Felicity asked, "Jared, what are you interested in?"

He looked puzzled at first, as if he couldn't think of anything. And then his face lit up. "Llamas."

"You're interested in llamas?"

"Yeah, I guess I sort of am. But I mean—look."

The hillside to their right was dotted with the woolly, long-necked creatures with their floppy ears and gentle eyes. "Supposed to be the largest herd of breeding llamas in Wales," Ryan turned back to say. "All kinds of animals here."

Jared looked back over his shoulder for as long as the animals were in sight, until the path veered to the left. Felicity wondered if he had found an interest; perhaps boredom was the root of his history as a troublemaker.

Felicity's stomach growled and she began looking around for the familiar silver van. She felt as if they had been walking for ages. It couldn't have been more than two or three hours, yet it seemed like days since they had thanked Sister Alicia and the fully recovered Sister Florence for their gracious hospitality, and set out walking in a scraggly queue across the abbey grounds.

Around another curve in the steep path, a familiar figure strode toward them. Michael raised a hand in greeting. "Anyone hungry?" A chorus of assenting groans greeted his implied invitation. "I found a nice green spot just up here a bit."

A green spot sounded wonderful, but Felicity was so hungry she would have accepted a cup of tea and a sandwich even if it had meant standing in a musty underpass with a fondling couple beside her. When they arrived at the rolling green hillside dotted with scrub brush and deciduous trees, however, she was happy, indeed, to be beyond such unsavory surroundings. Now, a nice cup of tea, some nourishment, a bit of a rest and the real pilgrimage could begin. No more gloomy doldrums, she vowed. Her earlier megrims were merely low spirits. Nothing more sinister than that.

"Michael, you're a genius." She surveyed the feast he had spread for them, even unfolding a small camp table to hold all the sandwich-makings he had purchased in Cwmbran for everyone to assemble their lunch from. Felicity started to fall ravenously on the food, then realized she was supposed to be the hostess. "Come on, Adam." She steered the boy who was looking even smaller and paler than usual to the buffet. "How did you do with all that walking?"

"Oh, it was brill," he said, grabbing a slice of bread and slathering it with mayonnaise before stacking on cold cuts and pickle. He grinned. "Did you see those two snogging? And—"

"That's enough, Squib," Lydia cut her brother off with a sharp rebuke. Pink tinged his cheeks, and his shoulders slumped as he returned silently to his sandwich-making.

Felicity moved on to see if she could help Michael serve the tea from the large flasks he had prepared before they left the abbey, but again Lydia preempted her as the auburn-haired woman began filling bright plastic beakers with steaming liquid.

After everyone had eaten their fill, and Lydia had efficiently repacked the leftover food while Felicity was enjoying her second cup of tea, Antony strolled over to join her. He sat on the grass, his back against a small, scrubby tree. "Not bad for our first official morning, do you think? How did you get on?"

"Brilliant. Great!" Then she realized her brightness sounded too forced. "Well, OK after the yucky bits. But it'll be fine now." Her smile felt only slightly stiff.

Michael joined them, holding out his map. "Right. St Derfel's Chapel next stop. Only a few miles, but this bit," he indicated the contouring on the map, "will be plenty steep." He grinned at Antony. "Might want to say a Station before you start down that, Father."

"And then we start up again." Ryan, who joined them around the map, spoke up. "Steep grade there. I assume that cross is where we're going." He pointed to the tiny black mark on the map.

Antony nodded. "St Derfel's Chapel. Well, what little is left of it, anyway. Still, a traditional stop for pilgrims. We'll have Eucharist there, and tea."

"I'll do my best," Michael said. "It's a bit off the road, so the satnav can't find it."

"What, no postcode for a ruined sixth-century chapel?" Colin chimed in.

Felicity's mind boggled at the idea of keying an ancient chapel named after an obscure saint into a GPS. "Maybe they should come out with a new version that can pick up on vibes—halo nav."

Antony called the rest of the group, scattered across the green hillside, together. Jared arrived with Evie and Kaylyn, Evie walking with a jaunty step and giggling as she tipped her head back to look up at their tall escort, Kaylyn still in her remote shell. Lydia shooed Adam forward sharply. "Wake up, Squib. Must you always be daydreaming?" Then added to no one in particular, "That child is a constant plague."

Nancy picked up the cross Ryan had leaned against a bush, and carried it forward for the reading of Jesus taking up His cross. Then, refreshed by the stop, they moved forward. Felicity soon noticed their path was significantly lower than the land on either side. "A hollow way," Ryan explained before she could ask "Over time they are created incrementally by erosion, by water, and traffic."

The way was steep, but with such a definite trail there was no risk of losing their way here. They passed a few houses which Ryan told her were nineteenth century. That sounded old to Felicity, but she realized it was brand-spanking new from the perspective of St Derfel.

The going was hard as the way climbed steadily. They crossed a road near some cottages to ascend a steep hill, and eventually joined a rough road near a farm called *Gelli Grafog.* "Do you know what that means?" she asked Ryan.

"Roughly, small wood or copse."

"Do you speak Welsh?"

He shrugged. "Not really speak. But I can get the sense of most things. With something like that—it helps one understand the geography."

Now the way led as sharply downhill as it had earlier been up. Felicity was aware of less general conversation among the walkers, although she could hear a steady hum that told her Colin was talking nonstop to Antony, and an occasional giggle from Evie who dogged Jared's heels on the single track path. Felicity hoped they wouldn't have trouble finding this chapel. She knew Antony was concerned that they were behind their expected pace, and the sun was already arching toward the west. Even with her determination, she was feeling her energy lag.

And then from just ahead of her a light soprano voice led out, "Walk, walk in the light…" Ryan, nearest to Nancy, picked it up. A breeze blew the words back and others joined in. "Walk in the light of God…" Felicity tuned her ear to catch Antony's rich tenor, but was surprised to hear Jared's deep bass, and then a pure soprano that she at first thought must be Evie and then realized was Adam—a chorister any cathedral would boast of. What an interesting group this was. She wondered what other surprises these diverse personalities held.

By the time they reached the bottom of the draw her legs

were aching, but her spirits were the best they had been all day. Nancy had been inspired to start singing. This quiet young woman was certainly going to be an asset to the group, thought Felicity. Less than a mile on and a small signpost read "Llandderfel Farm." Ah, that was what they were looking for.

"What does llan mean? That prefix seems to be everywhere," Felicity asked Ryan, whom she was quickly coming to consider a source of all knowledge. It was no wonder he had won a place at Oxford for the fall term.

"Llan originally referred to an enclosure; later it came to mean 'church.'"

"Oh, so this was Derfel's church!"

"Right. We'll have you speaking Cymru before you go home."

Felicity laughed. "Oh, I doubt that. But I would love to pick up a few words."

They gathered on the track below the stone farmhouse nestled on the green hillside and said a Station. Felicity was glad enough to take a breather as she took a long draw on her water bottle, but was becoming more concerned for their time.

At the end of the brief meditation, Adam stepped forward and held out a hand to Nancy. "I'll carry it now, if I may."

The cross was taller than he was, and Felicity could see Nancy's hesitation to hand it over.

"What nonsense are you about, Squib?" A sharp voice demanded.

"Of course you may!" Nancy thrust the cross into Adam's hands even before his face could fall at his sister's sharp rebuke.

"Wait here," Antony directed. "I'll just check with the farmer. It's supposed to be cleared for us to go into his field."

Felicity looked around. There was no sign of a silver van. Perhaps Michael's "halo nav" had let him down. They hadn't seen an actual road for some time, but the land was crisscrossed with farm tracks. How would Michael ever find them? The sun now seemed to be lodged permanently behind a gray cloud bank, and a chill breeze was rising. She shivered. She had heard how quickly mists could come up, shrouding whole hillsides.

Antony, however, returned smiling, and led the way up a dirt lane. Behind a low, iron-roofed stone barn the farmer stood in his Wellington boots, holding a gate open for them. "Ye may get a mite muddy up there, but ye're right welcome. Lot of interest in that old pile of stones, it seems."

They all greeted him and said "thank you" as they entered. "Right, you are. It's noo trouble. Just make certain you lock the gate when ye're done." Antony assured him they would, and led the way on up the hill to, as the farmer had said, to a pile of scattered stones, indicating the broken walls of an ancient building.

Colin was the first to ask, "So who was this St Derfel?"

Felicity was glad it was a Welsh pilgrim who asked; it made her feel less ignorant. She was hoping she wasn't the only one completely in the dark.

Antony gave his "I'm glad you asked that" smile. "Actually, Derfel is little known outside his home territory. I'll admit to having swotted him up in preparation for the lecture Father Stephen was supposed to be giving you here today." His smile didn't speak of dissatisfaction with the new arrangement, however.

"Local legend holds that Derfel was a warrior of King Arthur. Derfel Gadarn—*Gadarn* meaning mighty, valiant or strong—was reputedly born around 566. He is said to be one of seven warriors of Arthur left standing after the Battle of Camlan. Derfel the Mighty is said to have survived by his strength alone. After Camlan, Welsh tradition is unanimous that Derfel entered the religious life."

"And had a monastery or hermitage or something here?" Colin asked, looking around for more evidence of such activity.

"Tradition suggests he was a hermit for a while. That wouldn't have been unusual, especially for one who had been a warrior. After that he is said to have entered a monastery and to have founded 'Derfyl's Church' on this spot. It's all a bit speculative, of course, but at a minimum, it's likely he preached here, although the structure these stones represent would have been of later construction, dedicated to him."

Colin looked satisfied. "All right, then. I was just going to point out that little building in stone was done in any part of Britain before the Norman Conquest." Colin turned to Jared, who was standing nearest him, and continued his monologue about the inaccuracies of Arthurian tales that place sixth-century warriors in stone castles.

Antony selected the smoothest mound of stones, standing almost waist-high, and opened his rucksack. He donned a white stole and spread a small white linen cloth over the stones, turning them instantly into an altar. He set his prayer book to one side, placed a chalice and paten on the fair linen and proceeded to arrange the elements. Felicity was amazed. She knew Antony had planned to celebrate Eucharist at the chapel, but she had no idea he had all that in his backpack. It was a good thing he hadn't left them on the van because there was no sight of it yet.

Antony was efficient in his preparations, but even in that short time it seemed the sky had grown darker and the wind keener. Felicity shivered.

Antony faced his little congregation with outstretched hands, and gave the Easter season greeting: "Alleluia. Christ is risen."

They responded, "The Lord is risen indeed. Alleluia." Felicity, aware that some of their pilgrims had sketchy worship backgrounds, to say the least, spoke out clearly to provide a lead.

Antony led an abbreviated liturgy with only readings from the book of Acts and the Gospel of John, then stepped forward to give his brief homily. "Fellow pilgrims," he surveyed the small circle, looking each one in the eye and offering a smile. "Here we are on a green Welsh hillside, come from our various locations and various occupations. Each one with our own hopes and our own problems. But we've come together as a community. A band of seekers. As brothers and sisters. It's my hope that as we walk on through these coming days, that we will cease to be isolated individuals, but a true community. To do that, walls will need to come down, perhaps some old ideas jettisoned, some new attitudes taken on board. I pray that that will happen.

"What happens will be different for each one of us; how much happens will be controled by how much each of you allow. But I can offer you one means that can lead to allowing the power of God's Holy Spirit in your life. It is the means He ordained for us on the night before He was crucified. That is coming together around His table to receive His Body and Blood."

Antony stopped. He looked for a moment as if he would say more, then changed his mind. He returned to stand behind the altar. "The Lord be with you." He held out his hands.

"And also with you," Felicity led the response.

The wind picked up sharply as Antony began the prayer of consecration over the elements: "...You sent Jesus Christ, Your only and eternal Son, to share our human nature, to live and die as one of us, to reconcile us to You, the God and Father of all."

The fury of the gale beat on the tiny band of worshipers, driving spatters of icy rain into them like tiny nails. Felicity feared the vessels would be swept from the altar, but Antony continued as if he were in a monastery church: "He stretched out His arms upon the cross and offered Himself. In obedience to Your will, a perfect sacrifice for the sins of the whole world. Recalling now His death, resurrection, and ascension, we offer You these gifts. Sanctify them to be for us the Body and Blood of Your Son, the holy food and drink of new and unending life in Him."

Instinctively the group huddled together as the only source of shelter on the open hillside. "Sanctify us also, that we may faithfully receive this holy Sacrament, and serve You in unity, constancy and peace…" Antony's last words were whipped away in a roar of wind.

As if an angry spirit were tearing them away, Felicity thought with a gasp of horror.

The darkness seemed so thick Felicity wasn't sure she could grope her way to the altar only a few feet in front of her. The wind lashed as if it would fling her from the hillside. She didn't want to stumble against a fallen stone.

And then something reached out to grab her. A tentacle trying to encircle her wrist. Pale and ghostly. She opened her mouth to scream, then realized it was the end of Antony's stole, whipping in the wind. Now Antony was before her, sheltering her from the fury of the wind. Her mouth remained open, but not in fright. "The Body of our Lord Jesus Christ, which was given you, preserve your body and soul unto everlasting life." He placed the wafer on her tongue.

She crossed herself.

Miraculously, all the pilgrims made it through the gale to the altar, and Antony concluded, "Let us go forth in the name of Christ."

And then, as quickly as it had risen, the wind dropped. A weak sun came out from behind the cloud bank, looking as uncertain as Felicity felt, and cast late afternoon shadows over the scene.

All the way through the arduous afternoon trek, Felicity had been looking forward to that afternoon tea break. I must be becoming English, she thought. But to be honest, it wasn't just the tea. She had glimpsed the store of cakes Michael had laid in. But now, no Michael, no van, no tea and cakes.

Antony, having repacked his communion vessels, approached her holding out his mobile and shaking his head. "No reception up here. Nothing to do, really, but to carry on. We have accommodation at a farm tonight."

"Not a church?" Felicity asked.

"Nothing in convenient distance." Ryan held out the map. "Not too far to go now." He looked around at the sun sinking behind the mountain. "We'll be all right if the weather holds. This track here past the chapel is a green lane, hollowed by centuries of use, so easy enough to follow. Fairly steep going, though. And it will be really important for everyone to stay on the path." He raised his voice. "We're going past the remains of an old colliery. All this area," he pointed to the map, "was disturbed by mining. There will be tips, broken masonry around old upcast shafts, steep drops into quarries." Felicity shivered as Ryan continued detailing the possible dangers, but he seemed entranced by the thought. "We'll want to make good time. It would be a shame to go through such an interesting site in the dark."

Felicity shook her head at his focus. She was far more worried about getting off the mountain safely in the dark than missing a geological site. "Are you all right to lead, Ryan? I'd like to walk to the back for a bit if that's OK."

"Certainly. No problem."

"And keep an eye out for Adam; he doesn't have to walk to the front to carry the cross, but I think he means to." Adam stood on the trail, the cross held aloft in both hands like the crucifer in a liturgical procession, rather than resting it over his shoulder as most had chosen to do.

Ryan smiled. "He's a good kid. No worries." And Felicity believed him. This tall, broad Welshman in a Barbour coat and cloth cap with his soft voice and passion for the land inspired confidence.

She wished she felt as confident about some of the other members of their group. Holding back, she watched them as they moved forward behind the leaders. Jared had been such a surprise: who would have thought their troubled youth—she refused to think juvenile delinquent—would be so charmingly relaxed, with such a winning smile?

Or their nurse so pushy? She thought as Lydia hefted her rucksack and fell into step behind Evie and Kaylyn, another pair of enigmas. Her thoughts went back to Lydia with her ruddy cheeks and auburn hair, her narrow shoulders and wide hips. Hard to imagine a more unlikely brother and sister pair than Lydia and the frail Adam. But Lydia would need her strength in the demanding profession of nursing, Felicity concluded, before moving on to consider Nancy, her head bent to listen to Colin, her serenity undisturbed by his never-ending flow of words.

Felicity and Antony fell in close behind. As Ryan had warned, it wouldn't do to get separated in the gathering dusk, but Felicity wanted to be far enough back that they could talk, hopefully undisturbed.

She reached for his hand and they simply stood, looking at each other for a heart-stopping moment, then moved forward. The path was too narrow to allow comfortable hand-in-hand walking. Under the cover of Colin's words she said as quietly as she could, "Antony, that storm… I mean— it was awfully violent. And the timing…"

He was quiet for several paces until she began to wonder if he had heard her. Then, "It wouldn't do to make too much out of it. Weather can change very quickly this time of year on the mountains. As we've experienced." Again he was quiet for a moment.

Felicity smiled. Always thoughtful, always careful, thinking everything through. That was her Antony. She, on the other hand… Well, she *was* learning to be less rash, less headstrong. At least she hoped she was. Although she wasn't sure what she had gotten herself into just now.

"On the other hand," Antony picked up the conversation thread. "It could be a dangerous mistake to dismiss all the, er—unusual things that have happened lately as merely nothing."

"You mean you think something *is* going on? Something—" now it was her turn to stumble over her word, "as Nosterfield said, something paranormal?"

Antony nodded. "I think that was my word, but Nosterfield accepted it. I dislike using it because it's overused and over-hyped by the media. But still, it can be useful because we need to realize that things do happen—inexplicable things—that are outside our 'normal' experience."

Felicity shivered and zipped up the waterproof jacket she had donned against the evening chill. "You mean demon possession?" She couldn't help her eyes seeking out Kaylyn. It would be easy enough to imagine that sullen young woman participating in something occult.

"Whoa. That's the problem with such terms. People tend to jump to the most sensational examples. Of course, as a priest, I know it exists. There are enough examples in the Bible. But oppression is often a far more useful word and not so emotion-charged."

"Yes! That's it exactly. That's what I felt all day. And then that storm at Eucharist. It was like an *assault*." She breathed deeply. "Oppression. Amazing how it can help just to put the right word on something. Thank you."

The sense of comfort lasted for several yards. "So, you *do* think something is going on?"

"Like I said, you could find natural explanations for everything that's happened, but I believe we would dismiss them at our peril."

Felicity looked at her hand and saw again the paper bursting into flame. Felt the instantaneous heat. Smelt the sulfur.

A large black bird flew overhead. A scream rose in her throat as she thought of Hwyl plummeting from the tower. She stifled it immediately. *Focus on your surroundings*, she commanded herself. She looked up at the mountain looming over them to the right. In the growing dark she sensed more than saw the abandoned tip from the old colliery. Nature was reclaiming its own as scrubby bushes and coarse grasses pushed their way over the rocks. She hoped they held. The top must have been 100 feet above them, the hillside terraced like wide stair steps with a few trees clinging to the shallow earth.

Ryan stopped before a crumbling stone structure built into the hillside; a tall tower, the curve of its Roman-arched doorway repeated in two more arches on the top. Beside it, a lower structure of the same sturdy stone, its wide, arched opening gaping like a hungry mouth. The hillside above loomed threateningly; dead branches among the trees seeming to reach forward. "The entrance and fan house to the old mine," Ryan announced. "Careful of all the broken bits in the grass," he warned the walkers who gathered around him.

"Foul air was sucked from the mine workings by a large steam-driven fan. Fresh air then entered the mine by airshafts dotted around the mountainside. There was a terrible accident here when a tram jolted off the rails and slammed into a boiler pipe, spewing out the entire contents of the boiler."

Felicity didn't want to know that, but Ryan was unfazed. "Want to say a Station here, Father?"

Antony shook his head. "Too dark. Let's press on. We're already late for dinner. I hope they've held it for us." They could meditate on the cross after dinner.

Ryan pulled a torch from his pocket and shone it on the map. *Pant-yr-yrfa* Farm just here."

"That's 'career valley.'" Colin interpreted. "Odd name."

"It's only about a mile or so on, I'd say," Ryan continued. "Looks like the nearest road comes up here, then there's a track, so Michael should be all right."

"Great. Press on." Antony raised his voice to reach the little clump of walkers. "Everybody all right, then? Just a bit further on. Then it'll probably be shepherd's pie and bed."

Felicity could only fantasize about how good her bedroll would feel. And a full stomach. "Oh!" She cried out and clutched Antony for support as she stumbled over a stone on the path. How good it all would feel if she could just manage to get there.

Then up ahead a familiar melody rang out, "Guide me, O thou great Jehovah…" What could possibly be more appropriate than to be singing "Cum Rhondda" as they trekked toward the Rhondda Valley? Blessing Nancy, Felicity joined in with far more energy than she knew she possessed: "… pilgrim through this barren land…"

A light from a single window shone through the gloom, leading them forward. The isolated farmhouse took shape against the hill as the pilgrims increased their pace. Soon, they were inside.

"Ah, warmth!"

"Oh, that smells so good!"

"Oooh, I want to take my boots off and not move for hours and hours!"

Felicity, leaning against the wall of the welcoming, rustic kitchen, smiled. Through rough terrain, delays and sudden storm they had triumphed. The first day of any new adventure was always the hardest. The going would be easier now. She grinned at Antony across the room as she savored the blessed relief of pulling her boots off.

Chapter 10

Tuesday
Llandderfel to Pontyminster

*I*n spite of his fatigue from the unaccustomed hillwalking yesterday, Antony woke early. He stepped into his trousers, black as always, but these of a waterproof fabric, and pulled a sweater over his head—what Felicity would call a sweatshirt. He would get back into his regular walking attire later: black shorts with his clerical shirt, sleeves rolled up, walking boots well padded with two pairs of gray walking socks. He picked up his office book and, moving as silently as possible through the roomful of sleeping bodies, he let himself out the front door.

The sky was tinged an early morning pink and gold, the coarse grass dew-damp and fresh-smelling. The occasional birdsong could hardly be called a dawn chorus, but it lightened his troubled thoughts as he made his way to a rustic bench overlooking the valley at the side of the house.

His cautious words to Felicity had been perfectly sincere, but he still felt uneasy over yesterday's events. He paused and rephrased his thought to make it a question: What *had* happened yesterday? Had the sudden violence been a perfectly natural phenomenon of the weather patterns in this part of the country? Or something far more sinister?

And if the latter—why? And what should he do about it?

Why should any evil power bother attacking their little group of pilgrims? Certainly their goal was to be a presence for good everywhere they trod, and to foster spiritual growth and unity among their members but, praise-worthy as that might be, it hardly seemed worth calling down the wrath of the Evil One in such a spectacular effort.

He thought again of the fury of the wind that felt as if it would snatch the Body of Christ from his hands. It had felt so— well, so personal.

Certainly every mass was an affront to Satan, a declaration of the triumph of the risen Christ over his enemy: *Christ has died, Christ is risen, Christ will come again.* He repeated the familiar words in his mind. But why pick on this small, remote band?

And if yesterday's storm, the flame attacking Sister Florence, the voice calling Felicity… If all the recent anomalies they had encountered added up to some sort of attack—he shuddered at the thought—what should he do about it?

Aborting the pilgrimage, sending everyone home, seemed unthinkable, just the logistics unimaginable. And would accomplish little. Giving in to a bully never worked. The dark had to be confronted. Besides, he was a priest. This was what he was trained to deal with, wasn't it?

He took a deep breath of the fresh, damp air and opened his book to the Morning Office. Even with the sun breaking in the east, however, the sense of lightlessness persisted in his mind. So he chose to begin with an evening collect: "Look down, O Lord, from your heavenly throne; illuminate the darkness of this night with your celestial brightness; and from the children of light banish the deeds of darkness…"

Three hours later, their stomachs warmed with baked beans, homemade bread, and bacon and sausage produced right there at *Pant-yr-yrfa*, the energy among the pilgrims was tangible. Antony called them all together to begin the day's journey with a Station of the Cross. "Well, you know what they say about the best laid plans of mice and men," he began.

"Yeah, and the way to you-know-where being paved with good intentions," Jared quipped.

Antony grinned at him. "As I was saying—the plan was to say all the Stations each day, but since we only managed four yesterday, I think we'll just cycle through them as we go. Today we'll pick up at the fifth Station, Simon of Cyrene takes the cross: 'He was looking tired,' the fictional centurion narrated. 'He had to be kept going, so I called a man out of the crowd.'" As if on cue, Jared stepped forward and grasped the cross.

When the brief prayers were over, he continued walking by Antony, waving as the minibus pulled out ahead of them and they followed the narrow track back to the path along the side of the treeless green hill.

"So what do you like to do, Jared?" Antony was happy to have this chance to get to know the lad better.

Jared's smile was self-deprecating. "Nothing special. Just hang out, like."

"How did you happen to come on this youth walk?"

"My gran, really. It was her idea. She convinced my unit officer—you know, the teacher who, like, sees to it I study and stay out of trouble."

"You don't seem like a troublemaker to me, Jared."

The youth shrugged. "Nah. Well, yeah. I don't know really. Incorrigible was what they said. I don't even know what it means."

"You live with your gran?"

"Yeah."

"Is that an all right arrangement?"

Another shrug, making the cross swing dangerously close to Antony's head. "She's a'right. Me mam's...well—away a lot."

Antony nodded. He had read the report. Single mother, on drugs, in and out of jail. Little wonder Jared lacked direction.

Antony suspected wayward friends. Jared seemed like an accommodating personality who could easily be led astray—or led to the good. A challenging goal for the priest suddenly put in charge of him.

They walked on with strides lengthened by the invigorating morning air and cheering sunshine. At this pace they would easily cover the day's miles. Antony would welcome a restful evening at St Mary's in Risca. He was enjoying thoughts of the possibility of a quiet time with Felicity until he heard a whoop from Colin, walking at the front with Ryan. "Bronze Age burial cairns!"

Antony smiled. At least Colin was predictable. No problem with that one lacking direction for his energies.

"Where?" But there was a surprise. Antony could have sworn that excited query came from the hitherto nearly silent Kaylyn. He had heard her voice so little, though, it was hard to be certain.

"Colin, wait!" No mistaking that voice as Felicity strove to halt Colin's downhill plunge toward the mounds of stone with Evie and Kaylyn right behind him.

Whether it was Felicity's warning or the unevenness of the ground that made them decelerate, Colin and the girls slowed enough for the others to catch up with them.

"Don't rush," Antony cautioned Colin. "Those stones have been there for thousands of years. They aren't going anywhere now."

Colin grinned. "Actually, about four thousand years."

"Oooh, older than the Volturi." If Antony hadn't been so near he wouldn't have heard Evie's whisper to Kaylyn; as it was, the reference was meaningless.

Michael, who had arrived at the farmhouse in the middle of the night blaming his late arrival on a flat tire, parked the minibus along the road and joined them. Lydia walked over to stand by him. "So what's all this?" he asked.

"Burial cairns." Colin indicated three piles of stones spread across the field with small yellow and white wildflowers growing in the long grass around them. A larger standing stone stood somewhat apart from the others with sheep grazing near it. Even to the untrained eye, the long mounds surrounding sunken hollows could indicate burial grounds.

Michael seemed instantly interested. "Any archeology done here?"

"Oh, yes. I read about the digs here when I knew we'd be coming this way. They recovered a bunch of prehistoric flint tools."

Michael walked around the nearest cairn, examining it carefully. "I thought your interest was the Romans, Colin."

"Yeah, they're my favorite. But the Romans were the first to work a lot of these mines. No reason there couldn't be Roman artifacts here, too." He knelt down beside the largest of the cairns as if he would begin digging with his hands.

Nancy walked over to the standing stone and leaned against it, gazing out over the valley with Cwmbran spread out below them. Her long brown hair sparkled with red highlights in the midmorning sun. "Oh, don't move!" Evie approached her with a camera. "That's so cool, you look just like Bella."

Nancy's blank look showed her puzzlement at the reference, but she posed for several pictures. "This is so perfect! Can't you just imagine Bella and Edward here?" Evie gushed.

Kaylyn, apparently the only one who knew what she was talking about, agreed and entered into directions for the photoshoot. "Get a picture of Adam by those stones—looking uphill with that big ridge in the background."

"Oh, yes. If Renesmee had a brother, he would look just like Adam, wouldn't he?" She clicked a photo. "Except Adam's skin doesn't glisten." She giggled.

Antony was as puzzled by the two girls' sudden animation as

by their references. He was glad to see them taking an interest in something, but he was troubled by the brittle ebullience of their excitement, and their apparent sense of superiority in sharing esoteric knowledge. It was as if they felt a power in an awareness that they were the only ones in on a secret.

Felicity had also been observing the girls. Now she walked around the nearest trench and stood by him. "Do you have any idea what they're talking about?" he asked.

"I'm guessing vampires."

Antony boggled. "What? Are you serious?"

"I think they are. If you hadn't spent most of this century in a monastery on a remote hillside you'd know that vampires are more popular than Harry Potter. Evie and Kaylyn are exactly the target market for those books."

Antony grinned and shook his head. "You're making that leafy hillside in Yorkshire sound better by the minute. Why did I ever leave it?"

Michael finished his examination of the cairns and approached them. "Want me to get out the tea while we're stopped here, Father?"

"We'll stop for drinks when we get back up to the road, but I want to say a Station here, first." Antony couldn't define his discomfort, but this was a place that needed prayer, not one where he wanted to picnic.

Back at the minibus, Antony gratefully accepted a mug of sweet, well-milked tea from Lydia. "Ah, thank you. Wouldn't make it without tea." She gave him a bright smile and moved on to serve others in her efficient way.

Ryan and Michael approached, already deep in comparing routes on their maps. "Medieval travelers would have followed this line around the shoulder of the mountain and along the forest road." Ryan traced the line on the map that indicated going through the thick stand of conifers in the distance.

"I'm sure you're right. It would have been easier walking in that day," Michael responded. "Unfortunately, Father Stephen walked over this and found that although the Forestry Commission left the right of way unplanted, trees have fallen across it and seeded themselves into it. It's almost impossible to follow these days. A simpler route goes this way." He pointed to the dotted green line indicating a public footpath, then smiled at Ryan. "Besides, any geographer worth his salt will certainly want to go on up Twmbarlwm." Now he didn't point to the map, but to the long green ridge of the hill commanding the highest point in the area.

Colin turned with predictable excitement to endorse the idea. "The Romans had a signal station there, you know." To him that obviously settled the matter.

But it was Jared who had the most surprising tale. "Yeah, the Tump, thas what my gran calls it. There's a giant buried there with his treasure. Guarded by swarms of bees." He grinned. "Well, thas what Gran says."

"Legend I heard says the druids regarded it as a sacred site and a place of judgment," Michael said. "Undoubtedly because there was a giant buried there," he added in deference to Jared's gran.

Normally Antony would be completely complacent about visiting sites of ancient pagan worship, but the recent disturbances gave him a bit of hesitation. Still, interest in climbing the Tump seemed to be unanimous. The decision settled, they emptied their teacups and set out.

A little over an hour's walking brought them to the spot where the track left the narrow road and climbed the mountainside. Michael, and Lydia who had gone on ahead in the van with him, had emptied the coolers and bags and had the lunch-makings set out in readiness, including a new selection of flavored crisps, tasty humus spreads and a bag of satsumas. "This is amazing," Felicity cried. "Where did all this come from?"

"Oh, Michael and I zipped into Risca and did a spot of shopping while you lot dawdled up the hillside." Lydia took the lid off a carton of macaroni salad to place on the table.

Throughout lunch Antony kept one eye on the giant tumulus above them, almost as if he expected it to pounce on them, or the giant's swarm of bees to show themselves. By the time they had eaten, however, he could think of no rational reason not to proceed. The sky had remained clear all morning. Only one tiny dark cloud showed itself in the horizon. "Anyone feeling tired? Blisters? This would be a good chance to catch your breath if anyone wants to wait in the minibus." Michael had indicated he would lock it up securely and walk up with them. There were no takers.

"Right then, up we go."

The smooth green ground rose steeply under their feet, causing the walkers to use muscles Antony suspected many of them were unaccustomed to exercising. A thick stand of conifers grew to their left, to the right the open landscape swept away toward the Severn Estuary.

Perhaps a thousand meters on, they crossed the deep ditch that could have been the first defensive structure when the Tump was an Iron Age hill fort—or perhaps late Bronze Age. Built by the Silures, if Ryan or Colin or whoever of his remarkably well-informed charges had it right—and it seemed they usually did. In spite of the effort of the climb, Antony smiled to himself. He had to admit this was something of a new experience for him. He had been roped into this exercise for his knowledge on church history, but he seldom found himself in circumstances so far outside his field of expertise. It was fortunate that his charges included such enthusiastic students.

"*Vallum,* the Romans would have called it," he heard Colin explaining to Nancy, "although it's unlikely the Romans would have bothered to fortify a signal station. Of course, the Normans would certainly have made the most of it. The motte may be no older than thirteenth century."

The trail dipped deeply down into the dry ditch and then sharply up the side of the motte. It would undoubtedly have been deeper in its day and have offered a formidable defense. Four hundred meters on across the rounded hillside, at the far end, they came to the mound that was probably the hill fort itself, or the bailey in a later age. Whatever it might have been, it was clear why the locals called the earthwork crowning the Tump—"the Pimple."

A grassy stairway cut into the side led to the summit, offering a blessedly easy ascent. Antony stood on the top, for a moment fancy overtaking him as he imagined a Silurian warrior, a Roman soldier or a Norman noble standing on that spot, glimpsing the sun shining on the Bristol Channel in the distance, just as he was. Until a sudden stiff wind made him shiver. Looking behind him, Antony realized he had been too sanguine about the weather. The tiny black cloud he had dismissed earlier had grown to alarming proportions, threatening to descend as a mist. "All right, everyone," Antony had to project his voice against the rising wind to get the attention of all his group, spread like wandering sheep over the summit of the Tump. "Let's go down now. I don't want to get caught up here in a mist."

Predictably, Colin, who seemed to be intent on circling Twmbarlwm walking in the *vallum*, and Evie and Kaylyn who had wandered the furthest away, were slowest to respond, but Antony greatly appreciated Felicity's efficiency in gathering Ryan with his map, and Jared, still carrying the cross and heading them down the path. The others straggled behind.

The cloud bank rolled toward them and the first fingers of mist touched Antony's cheek before he had crossed the motte. By the time they had descended the Tump and were on the path back to the minibus, the fog was so thick he could barely glimpse the cross at the head of the line of march. Fortunately, Felicity had pulled on her red sweater against the sudden chill. The vibrant color offered a beacon.

The mist thinned at the lower elevation and the silver van shone through. Antony gave thanks. The afternoon walk into Risca was all downhill. They should be all right if the mist stayed thinner at lower elevations.

His hopeful thought lasted about thirty seconds. "Oh, this is so typical!" Lydia's voice held more than a tinge of asperity. She raised her volume to a clear shout: "Squib! Get over here now. Don't you dare go off into that mist. If you get lost, it'll be your own fault. Serve you right if we left you." She paused. "I will. I mean it, so help me." She upped the threat.

"What is it?" Antony strode to her side. "Has Adam wandered off? He isn't lost, is he?"

Lydia's disgust was clear. "Oh, he's always doing something like this. He does it to attract attention, you know. Always has, since Ma died and Da took that job in Dubai."

"When did you last see him?"

She shrugged her narrow shoulders. "I don't remember exactly. He was on that Pimple thing, I think." She turned away and started back up the path. "Squib! Come here now. I mean it."

Antony held his breath, hoping to see a small, blue-clad figure materialize from the mist.

None did. "Lydia, come back. Gather round, everybody. We need to get organized." Wisps of mist floated before his eyes, momentarily blurring his sight of the faces before him, then clearing. "Was anyone walking with Adam?"

"He was beside me most of the way up the Tump," Nancy said. "Then he went on up the Pimple. I don't remember after that."

No one could recall anything more concrete. Evie thought maybe she had seen him on the back side of the Tump, "Sort of running. Well, almost dancing. But I didn't really pay much attention."

That seemed to be a unanimous problem. Antony wondered if that was the story of Adam's life: No one paid attention.

"Trust me, he either followed a bird over a hill or he's sitting on a rock somewhere making up a story in his head. Probably about that sleeping giant. Dozy. He's just so dozy. Drives me spare."

Lydia was undoubtedly correct in her assessment of her brother's personality, but more sisterly concern would have seemed appropriate at that moment. Antony was getting seriously worried. The wandering off might have been innocent enough, but what hazard might the child have run afoul of after that? Antony realized he must be a more careful shepherd in future.

Picturing a lost lamb caught in a thick bramble or fallen into a crevice, he made his decision. "Michael, Ryan, you come with me. We'll search the hill. The rest of you have a cup of tea in the minibus—out of this damp. And pray."

"No, we'll all come with you." Felicity was the first to speak up, but the others agreed.

Antony appreciated their support, but he stood firm. "No, not in this mist. It's too dangerous. The last thing we need is more of you lost in the fog."

"I'm coming." Antony was more surprised by Lydia's contrite tone than by her words. "I was too harsh. Sorry. It's just so irritating because he's always doing this. But, but..."

Michael, standing closest to her, put an arm around her shoulders. "Of course you can come." He looked at Antony for confirmation. Antony nodded. "We'll find him. Don't worry."

Antony had barely put a foot on the path when he heard Felicity behind him urging the remaining pilgrims into the van. "Kaylyn, can you reach the mugs from that box in the back? Nancy, this would be a good time for a song, I think."

The mist thickened as they traced their way back up the incline. Antony, fighting a rising sense of claustrophobia, kept to the path by feeling for the rocky surface rather than the surrounding grass with every step. Every few feet they stopped and shouted. "Adam!" "Adam, can you hear us?" "Adam!"

The cotton wool silence that met each repeated plea stifled Antony's spirits even more than the shrouding mist muffled all sounds.

A few more feet fumbling upward, then they repeated the process. "Adam!" Still the enveloping silence.

It seemed impossible that the mist could keep getting thicker. Antony felt it like a weight pressing on him. He wanted to lash out and push it away with his hands. He had to fight an urge to bite and spit to clear a channel to breathe. His cough was a mere reflex. Still, he fought for breath. "Adam!" His voice sounded weak to his own ears. Michael and Lydia, walking so close he could touch them, sounded distant. Ryan at the back was a mere echo.

They could pass within a few feet of Adam and miss him. And yet the answering silence rang in his ears.

His mind knew that the mist was weightless, still it pressed on him, an oppressive burden. They hadn't climbed enough for the height to make him dizzy, and yet he had to fight the impulse to sit down by the side of the path. He was so weary. His limbs so heavy. His head spun. His knees buckled.

Strong hands gripped him on either side. "Watch it. Ground's rough here." Michael pulled him upright, supported by Lydia.

"I judge we're almost to the ditch." Ryan offered encouragement.

Antony shook his head to clear his thoughts, even if he couldn't clear the mist. "Good. Thanks. I think we should circle around to the right when we get there since there seemed to be an impression he went down the back of the Tump." That was the thing—focus on a plan. And keep going. Keep calling. "Adam!"

Was that a reply? "Adam!" He tried again. Holding his breath, Antony willed the sound to come again. Then it did, and he wished it hadn't. Thunder. This clap louder. Nearer over their head. A rumble followed like a roar from their sleeping giant.

"Probably get hail now," Michael said. Antony was amazed how ordinary the local man made it sound. Perhaps it was.

Michael had no more than spoken than a third roar of thunder shook the ground under their feet and the hailstorm started. Marble-sized hailstones assailed the walkers from every side at once as the wind whirled the ice pellets around them. It was no use trying to go forward. By common consent they huddled together, pulling their jackets over their heads.

The assault probably didn't last more than ten minutes, but as they stood there with hail peppering their anoraks like bullets, it seemed like hours. With a final clap and rumble the storm moved on, leaving the tumulus dotted with mounds of white pellets that must have been what manna looked like in the Sinai.

Then Antony realized he was actually *seeing* the piles of hailstones. The mist had lifted. "Adam!" He gave a push on his trekking pole and leapt forward with long strides that carried him to the back of the hill. Then he stopped. The lower slope was reforested with a dense, dark stand of conifers. If Adam was in there that would have provided useful cover from the hailstorm. But if he was injured and unable to answer their call, they would never find him. All along, Antony had assumed they would find the boy on the wide, open slope of Twmbarlwm, probably with a sprained ankle from tripping over a stone, or dazed from having fallen downhill and hit his head. Now any such easy sighting seemed unlikely.

"Shall I go back and get the others to help search, now that the mist has lifted?" Ryan asked.

"Yes. Good idea." Still Antony was reluctant to split up. "Let's all go, though. We can get dry clothes and a cuppa before we start again."

Antony spent most of the walk back organizing the search in his mind—how he would divide the walkers into teams; responsible ones with… well, with others; how he would divide the areas to be searched. This time they would do a proper job with each team carrying food and drink and bandages. He pulled his mobile out of his pocket, hoping there might be reception so teams could communicate. A forlorn hope, however.

They were still some distance from the van when Antony saw a red-clad figure with a flying blonde braid hurtling up the path toward him. "Oh, Antony! I was so worried." Felicity flung herself into his arms. She continued to cling to him for several moments. "Oh, I'm so thankful!"

"Did Adam show up?"

She pulled away. "No. Isn't he with you? I thought…" She look round, then hurled herself back into his arms. "Oh, but I was worried for you, too. The storm was awful. And after yesterday, I thought… Well, I don't know what I thought. And then when Jared didn't come back, either…"

"Jared? Where did he go? I told you to keep everyone in the minibus." He hadn't meant it to come out as such an accusation.

"I know. But after we had tea, he had to—well, he needed to find a bush."

Antony nodded. "He wouldn't have needed to go far in that fog."

"I know. I thought he'd be right back. But then there was all that thunder. And the hail! You should have heard it beating the roof of the van. I was afraid it would break the windshield."

"Yes, I know."

"Oh, I expect you do, don't you? Up close and personal." She gave him another hug and, her arm still around him, pulled him toward the van. "So, of course, I thought Jared was just sheltering under his bush. But then the storm passed and the mist lifted and—" She swept the area with her arm. "No one. No Jared. No Adam. No *you*." Her voice caught on the last word.

Antony turned his head to give her a peck on the cheek. "I'm fine. We all are. But now—" he turned back. "Michael, I think we'd better drive into Risca and get proper help. They must have a mountain rescue team. Or maybe we'll be able to ring them when we get down off the mountain." He looked at his watch, trying to calculate how long they had before dark.

They had barely reached the vehicle when a jaunty "Cooee!" caught Antony's ear. He turned to see Jared's tall, loose-limbed figure striding toward them from around the west wide of Twmbarlum, with a small Adam bouncing beside him like a puppy.

In moments they were engulfed in a rejoicing cluster. Lydia, who had actually outstripped everyone and reached her brother first, held Adam aloft like a trophy. It was several moments before the babble of excited voices and questions died down enough for Adam to explain, in a voice that showed his bewilderment at the hubbub, "I was fine. The lady asked me to help her pick those funny spotted flowers. Fly catcher, she called them. Did you know they actually eat flies?" Adam rambled on.

One look at Jared, however, told Antony that he had seen nothing of any such lady.

Chapter 11

Wednesday
Pontyminster to Bedwas

The next morning, crossing the Old Bridge into Pontyminster, where the medieval monks kept a grange, Felicity reflected on how much they had to be thankful for in spite of the desultory drizzle falling on them from a leaden sky. She smiled and supposed the first thing to give thanks for was that it was merely a light sprinkle and not the tearing sheets of rain she had been warned of in this area. Nor was it a hailstorm like they had experienced yesterday. And there was almost no wind like the day before that. She pulled her hood up and concluded that, considering the alternatives, it was positively balmy.

They walked down Mill Road, named, Ryan informed her, for the mill the monks built on the river in the early 1200s, then crossed the Afon Ebwy by the Old Bridge into Pontyminster— "Pont meaning bridge, and minster for the grange the Llantarnam monks had here," her informant told her.

She smiled and nodded but, in spite of her "could be worse" determination, she was missing the comforts of the accommodations provided by St Mary's Church last night. In spite of their delayed arrival, the weary pilgrims had been met by two gray-haired ladies and a bald, jolly priest bearing shepherd's pie, salad and treacle tart for their supper in the church hall. After supper they had gone into the church where Nancy led the group in evening prayers. Felicity wasn't surprised that Nancy would do a graceful job of leading the service, but she was surprised Antony had asked a pilgrim to lead rather than doing it himself. When Antony explained, however, that Nancy was in the discernment process to sort out her calling, Felicity understood.

Felicity paused to massage the aching calf of her left leg. Looking back on yesterday, it was impossible to believe they had walked only about six miles. But then, most of those miles had been straight up and down.

And sure enough, she no sooner had the thought than the path started up again. Felicity was thankful for the clear plastic covering over the map which she was carrying this morning. She wiped a few drops of water away as she paused to consider the alternative routes offered. Ryan looked over her shoulder. "Far more interesting to go over the top of Mynydd Machen. Bronze Age, Roman and medieval sites up there."

"Amazing, the amount of ancient activity in what seems like such a remote area."

Ryan looked up at the gray mizzle. "Don't know what Father A would think about it in this weather, but it would be a shame to miss those sites."

Felicity looked through the mist at yet another green mountain before them, and felt again the panic rising in her throat at the remembered fear of thinking they had lost Adam on the Tump. She had noticed that he was staying closer to his sister today—or she to him—and that was good. But the disquiet remained: Who had Adam met? And where had she gone?

At that moment, Antony joined them. "Take the path to the right. Just past *Heol Las* Farm. We'll stop at the old chapel for Eucharist." He pointed to the spot on the map, then smiled at Ryan. "We can go on up the mountain after that if the weather clears."

Felicity would settle for it just not getting worse, but Antony's optimism was comforting.

The old chapel, as Felicity had expected, was little more than a foundation marked by broken walls and scattered stones; still, it had once been a place of worship. And today, it was again as Antony prepared in his careful way, using a section of broken wall for his altar. The pilgrims stepped over the rough footings and turned to the east, facing Antony.

He cleared his throat and smiled at them. "The Lord be with you." He held out his hands to encompass them all.

"And also with you," Felicity's reply surprised even herself with its enthusiasm. The events of the recent days made her more thankful than ever for this sacramental moment.

And Antony was obviously thinking in a similar vein as he began his homily. "*Viaticum*—food for the journey. That's what our Lord offers us in His Body and Blood. These past days have been challenging. No doubt more challenges await us. So it has always been for those on pilgrimage. And that is as it should be, because a pilgrimage is meant to be a symbol of life. Always in life, as on pilgrimage, hazards lurk. But always we have what we need if we will avail ourselves of it. Strength for the journey. *Viaticum*."

He proceeded to the consecration, then held the elements out to all of them, "The gifts of God for the people of God."

The last of the pilgrims was partaking when lances of intermittent sunshine broke through the final wisps of grey cloud, making the damp stones of the old chapel glisten. The warming rays awoke the scent in a froth of white wildflowers growing around the foundations, giving the impression of spicy incense. Evie apparently noticed it too, because she bent to pluck a blossom, sniffed it, then picked several more of the clusters before handing the nosegay to Kaylyn, who nodded almost formally as if accepting her due.

What enigmas those girls are, Felicity thought, then recalled Antony's admonition that they should walk with different pilgrims and get to know each other. Right, off-putting as Kaylyn's silence was, she would try.

Felicity pulled the strap of the map case over her head and offered it to Ryan. "You don't mind, do you? Especially now that the weather has cleared so we can explore the interesting sites."

Ryan took the map and his place at the head of the line with alacrity, Colin beside him. Felicity held back, waiting for Evie and Kaylyn. Kaylyn, still holding her posy, moved forward. In spite of her impassivity, or perhaps because of it, the girl had an admirable dignity. The path was wide enough here to allow walking three abreast, so Felicity joined them. "Lovely lacy flowers, aren't they?" She nodded toward the bouquet. "Such an unusual scent. Almost like licorice. I wonder what they're called."

Predictably, Evie giggled, but Kaylyn's terse answer was startling. "Mother-die."

"What?" Felicity couldn't have heard right.

Kaylyn shrugged, apparently gratified to have shocked Felicity. "More commonly called cow parsley, but mother-die is a common name. It's from the hemlock family."

Felicity shivered. "Oh, how interesting." She would need to think of another topic of conversation. "Are you doing biology in school?" Kaylyn certainly didn't strike her as someone who would be interested in gardening.

The kohl-lined eyes peered from beneath the shaggy black bangs to give Felicity a *Don't be ridiculous* look. "Creeping Hemlock is a publisher."

"They do some of our favorite books," Evie explained.

Felicity understood. Zombies again. "Oh." She paused. "Well, what are you studying? Do you go to the same school?"

"You could say that. We're both home-schooled," Evie explained. "Kaylyn's mother's really—er—involved, busy, like, so my mum oversees both of us. That's why she sent us here."

Felicity looked blank.

"It's an RE thing. Have to get our hours in, visiting churches, learning church history—stuff like that. Seemed a good way to get it done."

Felicity was still lost. "RE?"

"Religious Education. It's required." Kaylyn looked at her as if she wondered what planet this American woman was from, but Evie smiled. "It's cool, really. We learn all kinds of religious stuff. Did you know Michael is thinking of becoming an RE teacher? I told him he should. It's brilliant." She paused. "I think I might do it, too."

It was fortunate that the walking demanded her attention as the trail started uphill again to slope around the side of the mountain, because Felicity really couldn't think of anything to reply to such information. Evie teaching religion?

On up a bit they came to a wide, fairly level spot, and Antony called for them to stop for a Station. To Felicity's astonishment, Kaylyn handed the cow parsley to her before turning to Jared and offering to carry the cross. The fact that she was doing this for school credit was the only explanation Felicity could imagine.

"Jesus meets the women of Jerusalem," Antony read the meditation for the eighth Station, bringing to mind Jesus' love for his mother and the mourning women. Felicity looked at the flowers in her hand. Was it just because she knew the nickname that they now smelled acrid?

As they moved on, Ryan pointed out some old mine workings. "The path we're on was probably a tramway to the quarry over there." He pointed to their right. "The stone here is dolomitic limestone, which was used in the iron industry. It has veins of argentiferous lead in it, and quarrying has exposed old lead workings—"

Evie burst into giggles and Jared punched him on the arm. "Speak English, man."

But Colin jumped in, "Most likely Roman. There was a Roman mining station down in the valley. They found its bath house a few years ago."

Jared shook his head. "Get your head out of the encyclopedia." He and Evie moved ahead to catch up with Kaylyn.

But Colin was undaunted. "The abundance of mineral resources in Britannia was likely one of the reasons for the Roman conquest. They were able to use advanced technology to find and extract valuable minerals on a scale unequaled again until the late Middle Ages. That's very important because lead was essential to the smooth running of the Roman Empire, you see. It was used for pipes for aqueducts and plumbing, pewter, gutters for villas, even for coffins. Just six years after the conquest of Britain, the Romans had Welsh lead mines up and running at full shift."

Felicity wasn't sure which was more amazing, that Colin could remember all that or that he could spurt it out without catching his breath while ascending a mountain. No telling what more she might have learned if their beaten earth trail hadn't abruptly turned steep enough to subdue even the loquacious Colin. As was most of the terrain they had walked through, the ground was hummocky, covered with coarse grass with piles of scattered stones peeking through, and occasional scrubby bushes. The summit of Mynydd Machen above them was apparent for miles around, as it was topped with a television transmission mast; excellent as a landmark, but of little interest to the antiquarians among them.

Felicity walked toward a square, whitewashed cement pillar standing more than waist-high, assuming it must be a monument of some sort. Perhaps to another Celtic saint?

"That's a trig point," Ryan explained before she could ask.

"A what?"

"Triangulation point. A fixed station, used for surveying. They're usually set up on hilltops by the government for plotting road construction and the like. But over there," his voice took on a ring of greater interest as he pointed to a large rounded pile of stones near the crest of the hill looking out over the wide green valley, "that's a Bronze Age burial mound. It's one of a line stretching for several miles along the hilltop." He pointed westward. "That means the route along the ridge is probably prehistoric. There are more cairns and a burial mound with an enclosure where burial ceremonies for the dead were probably performed."

"A line of burial mounds!" Felicity had never heard Kaylyn speak with such excitement.

"You mean this was a *ritual path*?" Evie's voice matched Kaylyn's fervor.

"Sick!"

From Kaylyn's tone, Felicity took the last word to mean "good." The two Goths turned and walked to the cairn with a measured step that suggested they were in a procession themselves.

"And over here," Ryan turned to the northwest, "under that heather are the foundations of a number of medieval platform houses, built by peasant farmers in the twelfth and thirteenth centuries when the weather was better than it is now, and crops could be grown on these mountains."

He had addressed the whole group of walkers who stood clustered around the trig point, and as he turned toward the medieval site the group followed. "Apparently rabbit husbandry was an important part of their economy because we have pillow mounds all over this area. See those bumps? There are interconnected stone-lined tunnels under them—a housing estate for the coneys medieval farmers raised for their skin and meat."

The group moved on for closer examination of the site, but Felicity looked over her shoulder and saw that Kaylyn and

Evie were still at the cairn, standing as one might at a family graveside. Kaylyn, who had handed the cross to Jared when the trail became steep, laid the rather wilted cow parsley bouquet she had reclaimed from Felicity at the base of the pile of stones.

"You go on. I'll stay with Kaylyn and Evie," Felicity told Antony.

The girls were so deep in their focus on the cairn that Evie seemed startled when Felicity stood beside her. "Want to go see the medieval site?" Felicity suggested.

The numerous silver rings and studs in Kaylyn's piercings glinted in the midday sun as she glared at Felicity before dismissing her suggestion with disdain. "We're meditating." Kaylyn took a seat on a flat stone as if it were a pew in church.

The surprise would have been enough to make Felicity sit down, even if it hadn't seemed the best course. She didn't want to leave the girls alone, and they obviously wouldn't choose to come with her peaceably. She backed off a little way and sat on a clump of grass under a bush covered with small unripe berries. A closer examination revealed the flat, ridged bottoms on the tiny berries and Felicity realized they were huckleberries, so ubiquitous in her Idaho mountains. The hours she had spent filling her sand pail with the little purple beads when her father took her and her brothers to a mountain lake in those long-ago summers.

She had heard little from her mother since Cynthia had returned home after Easter, hoping to rebuild her shattered marriage. Felicity assumed that her mother was still working on it.

"They're sobbing!" Evie's cry burst into Felicity's reverie.

"Ohhh, horrible!" Kaylyn covered her ears with her black-tipped, be-ringed hands.

"Somebody help them!" Evie began sobbing herself.

Felicity's surprise turned to irritation. What were those girls playing at? She stood up.

"Voices of the dead!" wailed Evie.

"That's enough. Time to go." Felicity had only spent one year teaching, but she could still summon a school teacher voice when she needed to.

Her words bounced back at her as if they hit an impenetrable shield. Felicity was chilled. They weren't acting. Whatever it was, Evie and Kaylyn believed they were hearing something. Something that to them was far more real than her presence only a few feet away.

"Not dead, mourning for the dead," murmured Kaylyn.

"Both—both living and dead, mingling their voices. Terrible—a chant of doom," cried Evie.

Felicity stood frozen as the girls' terror reached out to engulf her. For a heart-stopping moment she saw it: not a granite boulder in front of her but a gray, haunted face with hollow eyes, its features twisted in agony. Matted hair swirled around the head like snakes, vipers that would entangle and sting.

"No!" she cried, looking away and clutching the small cross she wore around her neck.

The image morphed back into the weather-beaten rock.

"All right." Pretending a courage she was far from feeling, Felicity strode forward.

Still shaking herself, she grabbed Evie's shoulders and shook her. "Evie, come on. Wake up. This is a nightmare." It was inadequate, but the simplest explanation she could think of. They hadn't used drugs, had they? Something she had inhaled a whiff of herself?

Evie looked up at her with wild, staring eyes. "Don't you hear them? It's so loud! There must be hundreds." She shook off Felicity's gripping fingers.

Felicity closed her ears, refusing the sounds she sensed assaulting her. "Kaylyn!" she all but shouted.

The girl didn't seem to hear her. She appeared to be in

a trance, staring fixedly at the largest of the roughhewn stones about halfway up the side of the cairn. She cried out, then her gaze froze on another, held for several long moments, then moved to another. "See!" she cried. "Faces! Horrible. Misshapen! Don't you see them?"

Felicity refused to look, focusing on the girls instead.

Kaylyn held her hands out as if to ward off the specters. "Their flesh! It's shriveling and falling off. Oh, I can't look."

But neither could she look away. "Skulls! Gaping eyes— staring at me!" Her voice came out in jerky sobs. Now she addressed the stones. "Stop it! Be quiet." She clasped her hands to her ears. "Stop screaming at me. I can't help you. I can't! I can't. Can't…" The last was a whimper. If Felicity hadn't caught her, Kaylyn would have fallen off her stone seat.

"Kaylyn, wake up. You're all right. There's nothing to be afraid of." She had to say that, even though her own terror was barely in check. Only a few nights ago, she had heard a voice. Far less terrible, yet someone or something calling her.

Still, she must calm Kaylyn. "Don't be silly. You were dreaming. They're rocks. Nothing more. Come. Feel them." She grasped the girl's hand to guide it forward.

"No! I don't want to touch it. I won't!" Kaylyn jerked away from Felicity, her hysteria rising.

Felicity turned to run for Antony, but he was at her side. "I heard the screams. What is it?"

Felicity had to resist the urge to throw herself into his arms. Here was safety, sanity. Instead, she shook her head and told him as succinctly as she could, her voice almost steady.

"Right." He went first to Kaylyn, who was again staring at the boulders as if they might spring to life. Antony bent over to her, both hands on her shoulders. "Close your eyes, Kaylyn. Breathe."

She obeyed with a deep, shuddering breath.

"Now, say the name of Jesus."

She pulled back fractionally. For a moment, Felicity thought the girl was going to refuse. Then it came out in a whisper, "Jesus."

"Again. Louder," Antony commanded.

Kaylyn took another breath. "Jesus." It was firmer this time.

"Now you." He turned to Evie. She obeyed immediately, almost shouting the name.

Antony nodded and made the sign of the cross on the forehead of each girl. He motioned for Felicity to step closer. "*Kyrie eleison.*"

"*Kyrie eleison,*" Felicity responded.

"*Christe eleison.*"

"*Christe eleison.*"

"*Kyrie eleison.*"

This time Evie joined in on the response, "Lord have mercy."

"We beseech You, Lord, to make powerless, banish and drive out every diabolic power, presence and machination; every evil influence or malefice and all evil actions aimed against Your children…

"The Lord is my shepherd, He makes me to lie down in green pastures, He leads me beside still waters, He restores my soul…"

The calming words of the familiar psalm washed over Felicity, soothing her breathing and lowering her heart rate. "Though I walk through the valley of the shadow of death, I shall fear no evil…" When the prayer ended, Kaylyn was quiet, but her eyes still reflected a trapped, searching look.

They guided the girls to the far end of the mountain, and Antony called the group together. "We're going to say a Station before we go on, but I want to say a special prayer for protection first. Could you all gather in a bit closer together?"

When they were together, Antony extended his arm, his index finger held upward and inscribed a circle around them.

"Protect your servants, Lord, from every threat or harm from the Evil One…"

At the end of their small service, Antony had a quiet word with Nancy. She nodded and began digging in her rucksack. She pulled out two small crucifix necklaces and gave them to Evie and Kaylyn, huddled together as if for comfort a bit apart from the group. Nancy put an arm around each girl and moved them forward. A few minutes later, Nancy's clear, light voice drifted back to Felicity at the rear with Antony: "Walk, walk, in the light." Felicity was almost certain Evie joined in. And could that rich alto be Kaylyn?

She turned to Antony. "Erm—that was a kind of exorcism you just did, wasn't it?"

"Oh, no. Not at all. Just a simple prayer for protection. An exorcism would be much more—er, elaborate. It would need organization. Something to be used only in extreme situations."

That had seemed plenty extreme for Felicity, but she didn't argue. "What was that circle thing all about?"

"Standard practice when praying for protection from evil. The action is a form of prayer itself. It makes the words concrete."

"Like crossing yourself or using holy water?"

"Exactly."

Felicity was still thinking. "But what about exorcisms? You do believe in them, don't you? They aren't just something got up for sensational movies, are they?"

"Oh, yes. I believe."

Felicity would have been less alarmed if his answer had been less fervent. She thought about quizzing him on what he thought about Hwyl's death, but she didn't really want to know.

Chapter 12

Wednesday afternoon

The track plunged so steeply downhill Antony felt like he had to lean backwards and walk on his heels just to stay vertical. His calves were beginning to rebel when they reached the metaled road and the glorious sight of the minibus and the welcome lunch Michael had set out for them.

A few minutes later, his sandwich devoured, Antony gratefully accepted a refill of tea from Lydia and indulged in a third chocolate-covered HobNob. In spite of the gray clouds in the distance he would allow his walkers an extra rest-time. It was much needed—at least by him. The spiritual confrontation at the cairn had been far more draining than anyone would suspect. As was the continued need for prayer and vigilance. He didn't know what was going on or why, but whatever it was, it was obvious it wouldn't do to let his guard down.

He leaned against a grassy mound and observed his charges. What a diverse lot, and yet, for the most part they were pulling together well. Ryan and Colin with their shared interests in the land were natural allies, and Ryan didn't appear to mind Colin's incessant chatter. Lydia, who had seen to everyone's blisters last night with plasters and foam pads, was invaluable and was paying a bit more attention to her little brother after yesterday's scare. At least when she wasn't giving all her attention to Michael. Sometimes it seemed she watched him more closely than the child in her charge.

Nancy, having taken the remains of their lunches back to the minibus, turned to rejoin Kaylyn and Evie, sitting some distance apart. Antony smiled as Nancy broke into an easy run, leaping over the stones and tussocks in her path like a gazelle. Imagine having the energy. The Goth girls were a concern, but he couldn't have been more pleasantly surprised than he had been by Jared—the one he had expected the most trouble from was one of the readiest to please.

Well, they were nearing the halfway point on their walking journey, and then the time at St Non's Retreat was sure to be peaceful. But they had to get there first.

Antony closed his eyes and felt the sun warm on his face.

"If we carry on along the ridgeway walk we'll get to see *Twyn yr Oerfel*—" Ryan's voice jerked Antony out of his light doze.

"It looks really interesting," Colin pointed to the map. "Round burial mounds marked with standing stones—"

"Possibly Neolithic," Ryan added.

"No!" Antony replied more sharply than he meant to. "We've had more than enough of ancient interment sites for one day. Keep to the Rhymney Valley Ridgeway, then down past the old coal tips." He stood to address the group. "All right, troops, a word of advice—there are no roads close enough for Michael to get to us for afternoon tea."

A universal groan met his announcement. "So be sure your water bottles are full, and put an extra piece of fruit or a handful of biscuits—whatever you'll want to snack on to keep your energy up—in your rucksacks."

The way led through a blessedly refreshing forestry plantation. Then on the top of a flat green ridge they stopped to view the broad green Sirhowy Valley to the north and the Rhymney Valley to the south. Antony observed Ryan pointing in the distance to what might well be standing stones, and decided this would be a most appropriate time for a Station.

He motioned for Nancy, carrying the cross, to stand beside him. "Jesus is stripped of his clothing."

Turning their back on the ancient ritual route, the pilgrims' trail once more turned sharply downhill. At the edge of a steep green hill, Ryan stopped and pointed with his trekking pole. "Down there—that's the remains of the Bedwas Colliery. Not much left now, they filled in all the tunnels with rubble when the mine was closed after the miners' strike in the eighties. And here," he pointed almost directly beneath their feet, "is the tip. Covered most of this whole hillside twenty-five years ago."

Now with the vegetation of a quarter of a century doing its best to reclaim the ravages of the industry, it was hard to picture what it must have been like when the whole mountain was buried under millions of cubic meters of excavated mining debris. But still the slag heap loomed over the valley, a harsh black wound. Antony tried to imagine what it must have been like when the smokestacks from the works belched out black coal smoke and the trams dumped carloads of fresh waste on the hillsides daily.

"Don't get too close!" Nancy's warning to Evie broke in on Antony's reverie.

He turned to see Nancy, holding the cross in one hand, reach for Evie with the other to pull her back from the edge of the tip. Whether she reached too far, or Evie jumped back too swiftly and bumped her, or the weight of the cross caused her to overbalance was never certain, but before Antony's horrified eyes, Nancy plunged down the coal tip.

Her sharp cry was drowned by the scrabble of sliding rocks. Nancy was carried downward by the tumbling debris, her scarlet shirt a blood-red blot on the black slag. *Don't let it start a landslide,* Antony prayed. He closed his eyes against visions of the falling rock starting a slip that would move the mountain to the valley floor. With Nancy beneath it.

The rock continued to clatter, sounding ever louder to Antony's desperate ears. But when he managed to tear his eyes open he could see that, although some loose stones were still plummeting downward, Nancy's descent had stopped. Perhaps fifty feet below them she lay on the top of the mound. Unmoving.

"Nancy!" Antony's own voice rang in his ears, but he was aware of others calling as well. He checked his impulse to plunge down the tip to her. The debris was stable for the moment. The worst thing they could do would be to dislodge more on top of her.

Jared knelt and reached over the edge to pick up the cross she had dropped when she pitched forward. He scrambled to his feet as Antony approached. "Maybe we could form a sort of chain down the tip. I could hold the cross out to her—a lifesaver, like. We could pull her back."

Nancy still had not moved or responded to their shouts.

Antony shook his head. "Best to approach from the side, I think. I don't want to loosen any more stones on her." How many had already pummeled her? At least she wasn't buried. He was grateful for that. But she must be badly bruised. Maybe concussed. Perhaps worse.

They scrambled down the grass beside the tip. When Antony judged he was about level with Nancy's feet, he took a tentative step onto the tip. Stones turned and shifted beneath his feet. He waited for them to stabilize, then took another step. This was like trying to walk on marbles. They shifted under him, sending him to his knees. He regretted wearing shorts.

"Father, wait. Let me." Without pausing for a reply, Jared stepped out onto the tip just below Antony. Scuffing each foot to gain a purchase with every step, Jared used the cross like a walking stick on the uphill side, digging it well in with each move forward.

"Be careful. It's looser further out," Antony warned. Looser and steeper as the slag heap mounded.

Two more steps, dislodging more stones each time, and Jared dropped to his hands and knees to accomplish the final twenty feet or so crawling, leaving the cross behind. Antony, likewise crawling, moved over to regain their emblem and held it up, praying.

Rocks crunched against each other and a few more tumbled down the tip as Jared inched forward. Antony held his breath as Jared called, "Nancy? Steady on. Can you hear me?"

Jared turned back to Antony and the others waiting on the verge behind him. "She's breathing."

Thank You, Lord. Now Antony could breathe again.

Nancy gave a soft moan as Jared boosted her to a sitting position. "You're all right. I've got you. Can you just sort of scoot, like, if I help?"

It was a slow process, made slower by the fact that when Nancy put any weight on her right foot she cried out in pain. Eventually they reached Antony, and the two men essentially dragged Nancy the rest of the way to the blessedly firm purchase of the grassy hillside.

"Someone ring Michael," Antony directed. "We need the minibus."

"Already done." Lydia held out her mobile.

"He'll meet us here." Ryan indicated the spot on the map. "It's the closest he can get to us." He traced a mark indicating a narrow track coming off a thin yellow line that ended at the base of the tip.

"That's almost all the way down." Antony's heart sank.

"Here you go, Ryan, we're nearest the same height." Jared grasped his own forearm with his right hand and reached for Ryan's right forearm, indicating that Ryan should likewise grasp his left arm, forming a square seat. "Now, if you'll just, like, put your arms around our necks, we'll have you down in no time." They bent down to where Nancy sat, looking dazed. "You aren't too dizzy, are you?"

Nancy took her hand away from her forehead, leaving a black smudge. All those who had been on the tip looked like chimney sweeps. "I'll be all right. I have a headache."

"Hold on, then." Nancy's rescuers lifted her aloft.

"You're amazing, Jared. Where did you learn that?" Felicity, following behind them with Nancy's rucksack, asked.

"Took a St John Ambulance course. Thought it might come in useful if I was around someone who needed helping."

The line moved slowly with their delicate burden, but even so there was no sign of Michael with the van when they reached the appointed track. "I thought he'd be here by now." Antony assumed he would have been at the church in Bedwas where they were to stay for the night. It was less than a mile away, surely. "Where was he when you rang him?" he asked Lydia.

"He didn't say. It's such a narrow track, though, he couldn't drive very fast."

Still, it was the better part of an hour before Michael arrived, and Antony noted mud on the tires and on Michael's shoes. "What took you so long?"

"Getting supplies," Michael answered. When Antony opened the back of the van to get the first aid kit out, however, he noticed fresh mud on the shovel. Antony frowned.

Lydia put the theory work she had done for her nursing diploma to good use, gently exploring Nancy's ankle. "That's good, nothing broken. You'll need to keep off it for a while, though."

"Thank you. I'm so lucky to have you." Nancy looked around and gave a weak smile. "All of you. Thank you for the rescue."

"What happened?" Adam asked.

Nancy shook her head. "I—" She paused as if considering her answer. "I don't know. My head isn't very clear."

Lydia took a crêpe bandage from the kit and expertly wrapped the ankle. "Wish I had some ice to put on that. We'll buy a bag of frozen peas at the first supermarket we come to. In the meantime, keep it elevated."

"How wonderful to have a trained nurse with us," Felicity said.

"Well, not really trained yet. My practical placement in a clinic starts in September. In Bangor—at the foot of Mount Snowdon. I expect I'll get lots of hillwalking cases to work on there."

Lydia started to close the first aid kit when she spotted the blood running down Jared's leg. "That looks like a nasty gash. Come here, let me clean it." Cleaning the wound took longer than the bandaging, but eventually they were ready to move forward, Lydia sitting beside Michael in the front of the minibus, her two patients behind them. "You want to ride, too, Squib?"

Adam shook his head. "You go on," Felicity waved to the crew in the van. "I'll look after Adam."

He frowned. "I'm fine. I don't *need* looking after."

Antony smiled. "That's all right, then. Want a turn carrying the cross?"

Adam was obviously pleased with the suggestion, because he strode out, even walking ahead of Ryan. Since the track ran along a hedge at the top of the fields and then became hollowed it was easy enough to follow, in spite of the fact that it had started to rain again. Antony, who hadn't bothered to pull up his hood, felt the raindrops making little rivulets in the coal dust on his face. He hoped it wouldn't stain his collar.

Just past a tumbled-down old barn they found a leaning sign that declared the stony track they were following was Old Bedwas Road. It looked unpromising at first, but the path eventually became metaled and led the bedraggled troop to St Barrwg's Church. Antony gave thanks for the welcoming sight of an ancient church with a sturdy, gray stone tower, roof peaks capped with Celtic crosses, set in a green churchyard filled with shapely tombstones overlooking the village of Bedwas.

At the St Thomas's church and community centre everyone smiled when they were served the inevitable shepherd's pie, but familiarity with the menu didn't seem to have dulled anyone's appetite. No one turned down the offer of seconds when their congenial hostesses in flowered aprons offered. Nor did anyone refuse the Spotted Dick for pudding. Father Peter, the rector of St Barrag's, a wide smile on his round, pink face, joined in, urging everyone to eat and enjoy.

After dinner, Ryan and Jared folded the tables and stacked them against the wall to make room for the weary walkers to roll out their sleeping bags, and set battery-powered pumps to work blowing up air mattresses. Michael brought in the first aid kit and Lydia's training was put to use again, placing sticking plasters on blisters. Antony gave thanks that his good boots and doubled walking socks, little used since his days as an undergraduate, were providing effective protection, and took a chair along the wall beside Nancy, who was sitting with her foot propped on another chair, balancing a bag of frozen peas on her ankle.

"How are you doing?"

She managed a smile. "Not too bad. Lydia gave me some paracetamol and my headache is almost gone." She gingerly fingered a lump on her forehead that was starting to turn an angry purple.

"And your ankle? Not too painful?"

"Not unless I put any weight on it. Guess I'm really lucky."

"That must have been awfully frightening. You still don't have any idea what happened?"

Nancy was quiet for a long moment. "Nothing that makes any sense."

"That's all right. Let's hear it." The room was a hive of activity around them with air pumps humming and pilgrims chattering.

"Well, I have the impression of having been pushed."

"You mean Evie bumped you when she jumped back?" Nancy would naturally be reluctant to accuse the girl even of an accident.

"No. I've thought about that, but she was in front of me. She would have knocked me backwards. It felt like a sharp shove from two hands on my shoulder blades." Nancy shook her head, her normally tidy hair falling around her face. "But I must have imagined it, because no one else was anywhere near us."

Antony slipped his hand into his pocket and clutched the crucifix there.

Felicity, assisting Lydia by cutting strips of adhesive as she was directed, noticed Antony talking with Nancy on the other side of the hall. How long had it been since she and Antony had managed a quiet moment for a real conversation? *Antony, talk to me.* She handed a strip of bandage to Lydia.

About us, not just about this blessed pilgrimage. She knew he had a huge responsibility here. And everyone was exhausted. And weird things were happening. *But this was supposed to be a bit of an interlude for us, too. Peace and quiet, you said.*

As if summoned by her thoughts, Antony got up and walked across the hall. "Felicity, we need to talk."

"Yes!" She dropped the scissors back into the kit. Lydia could cut her own tape.

She followed him outside to the quiet churchyard across from the hall. Under an ancient tree at the edge of the yard they leaned against a stone wall. In the dimming evening light they looked across a green field to the mountains beyond. The inevitable sheep in the field were grazing a final bedtime snack or settling down. To their right, long evening shadows stretched down Church Street to the village below. Felicity smiled. How wonderful that he had read her thoughts. She should have known that her Antony wouldn't have forgotten about her feelings. She turned to him with a soft smile on her lips, uncharacteristically letting him speak first.

"Felicity, I'm worried about Kaylyn and Evie."

She put her hands over her face to hide her disappointment and took a deep breath. It was a moment before she could speak. "Yes, you're absolutely right. That was very worrying earlier. Do you want me to talk to them?"

"Just stay close to them, I think. And pray."

She nodded. She would do that. She would learn to put others' needs before her own. "And how's Nancy?"

"That could be even more worrying."

"I thought it was just a sprain."

"I don't mean the injury." He told her of Nancy's impression of being pushed.

Now all thoughts of personal desires drained from Felicity as she felt herself chill. "You mean like Hwyl?"

He sighed. "I don't know. I wish to God I did."

Chapter 13

Thursday
Bedwas to Eglwysilan

Felicity unzipped her sleeping bag to let in some cool air and rolled to her side, facing the wall in an attempt to blot out the dark, distorted images swirling in her mind. Like the apparitions that had confronted Evie and Kaylyn earlier, images of death contorted in her sleep-clogged brain. Half waking, half sleeping, her experiences of the past months intertwined. Hwyl's figure plummeted over the tower and rolled to her feet. But when she looked down it was the battered, bloodied body of her beloved Father Dominic that lay there. The piercing scream that had wakened her was that of Sister Elspeth plunging over the cliff at Whitby, but the ghostly hand that reached out to grab her was that of her murdered classmate, Neville. And through it all, the double-headed snake on the Orbis Astri emblem writhed and slithered. Then Nancy plunged down the coal tip, her hair aflame like Sister Florence, and Felicity tried to scream but it came out as an anguished groan.

"Felicity." Antony was at her side, holding her in his arms as she had longed for him to do earlier. She flung her arms around him, clasping with such force she thought she would never let him go.

At length, though, they drew apart. Antony held out a key. "Father Peter left this with me. I'm going over to the church to pray. Want to come along?"

Felicity nodded and reached for the trousers and sweatshirt lying beside her bag.

Outside, the air was fresh and cool. Felicity drew in long breaths to wash her mind of the lingering dark images. Then the old church closed around them with a warm hospitality, like a comforter. Antony turned on just one light over the altar. They knelt at the rail.

After a time of silence, Antony took a small prayer book from his pocket. "The response is 'We beg you: Free us, O Lord.'" She nodded.

"From anxiety, sadness and obsessions," he began.

"We beg you: Free us, O Lord."

The list was long—hatred, envy, jealousy, rage, death, divisions…

"Free us, O Lord."

"From every sort of spell, malefice, witchcraft and every form of the occult…"

"We beg you: Free us, O Lord." They finished in unison.

Felicity turned and sat on the altar steps, facing Antony. "Witchcraft? Spells? You believe in those things?"

"Not in the way they're popularly portrayed, but evil is real."

"Our enemy the devil goes around like a roaring lion, seeking whom he will devour, you mean?" Felicity knew she didn't have the words exact, but she knew it was from the Bible. "But I don't understand. Kaylyn and Evie with their vampires might be open to the occult. But Nancy—she's in discernment, might even become a priest or a nun."

"Perhaps that's why."

"Her devotion put her in harm's way? But that doesn't make sense. It should protect her. And Sister Florence. And Hwyl."

"It's true enough that the devil flees when Christians pray and when the name of Christ is spoken. But it's also true that the battle is not yet ended. Demons will continue to test the baptized."

Felicity was amazed to be able to return to peaceful sleep and to waken refreshed the next morning. And ravenous. Father Peter had come back, bringing with him a tall, slim, brown-haired woman who set about frying bacon and eggs while he made tea and toast, and the pilgrims rolled their beds up and unfolded the tables.

Nancy hobbled across the room with the aid of two walking sticks. "How are you? How did you sleep?" Felicity asked.

"I slept fine. I'm better already."

Lydia took charge of her patient, insisting that she continue to keep the foot elevated in spite of the fact that the swelling was much reduced.

Antony, however, conversing with Father Peter at the end of the table, had dark circles under his eyes that told Felicity he had not slept well. Even more worrying was the fact that he hardly touched his bacon and eggs.

After breakfast, Felicity started to join the general bustle of clearing tables and loading the van, but Antony touched her arm and led her outside to the far corner of the churchyard. "I told Father Peter some of what's been going on. He had heard of Hwyl's death, but didn't know the details. He didn't seem overly surprised when I told him about some of the other happenings. Concerned, but not surprised. Apparently occult activities aren't uncommon around here." He pulled out his mobile. "He gave me Hwyl's number. Well, the number of his widow, that is."

"Do you know her?"

"No, he wasn't married when he was at college. Dilys, Father Peter said her name is. Means 'perfect' and he thinks she rather lives up to it."

"You're going to ring her?"

"There's too much going on that we need to get to the bottom of." He clicked on the number he had entered earlier. "I'll put it on speaker so you can hear."

A soft female voice answered on the third ring. "Whitchurch Rectory, Dilys speaking."

Antony explained as succinctly as he could who he was and why he was calling, and offered his condolences.

"You were there? The morning Hwyl—"

"I was there almost immediately afterwards. Again, I'm so sorry."

"Yes. Yes, thank you. It's a terrible thing. It's so hard to understand."

"Yes, that's what I wanted to ask you about. If you feel like talking."

"Thank you, Father Antony. Yes, I think it might help. I know it will, if it will shed any light—" Again her voice broke off.

"I wanted to know—was Hwyl worried? Was he sleeping all right? Acting strangely?"

"He had a worrying job. You know…"

"Yes. As I mentioned, he took my seminar, so I helped train him."

"Yes." The lilt was gone from her voice. "Well, I don't know how much I can help you. You'll understand he didn't talk about his work much."

"Yes. I do. But anything you could tell us might help."

"Well, I did think he might be looking for something."

"But you don't have any idea what?"

"Not at all."

"How had Hwyl been feeling? Physically?"

The phone was silent on the other end of the line. Finally Dilys said, "It's strange that you should ask. He'd be absolutely fine." She paused. "And then all of a sudden he'd vomit. All unexpected. His doctor couldn't find anything wrong."

Antony waited without replying.

Even over the phone they could hear Dilys take a deep breath. It seemed obvious she hadn't told anyone else about this.

"And he was having pains in his hands and feet. 'As though a nail was being driven through them,' he said."

"Mrs Pendry, have you found any strange objects in your house?"

"Nooo." She dragged it out as if she were thinking. Perhaps trying to make sense of the question.

"You might take a look. Especially around your bed."

She didn't reply.

"Just one more question, Mrs Pendry. I am sorry to bother you, but do you have any idea why Hwyl went to Kirkthorpe?"

"The police asked me that, too. But like I said, he didn't talk about his work. It was—well, strange. And so much was confidential. He really couldn't. And I think he didn't want to worry me."

"Yes, well—"

"He did say something, though, and I got the feeling... Well, I think maybe he wanted advice." Before Antony could ask, she added hurriedly, "But I don't know what about or from whom."

Antony thanked her and rang off. He looked ashen. "What if he was coming to see me?"

Felicity put a hand on his arm. "You don't know that, Antony. And if he was, it wasn't your fault."

Antony shook his head. "I know. Not really, and yet—it brings the responsibility closer. I was his deliverance lecturer. If I failed to teach him something..."

"Antony," she repeated, "it's not your fault. Besides, why wouldn't he have gone to his bishop?"

Antony didn't have any answers for her.

The group was ready to depart when they returned to the hall. After morning prayers in the church, for which Father Peter joined them, the pilgrims departed with a final thanks to their host.

In sharp contrast to the rural route they had traveled yesterday, today's path skirted around the densely populated outskirts of Caerphilly, taking them through the housing and industrial estates that filled the valley bottom. Felicity found it depressing, and missed Nancy's singing and gentle spirit which never failed to lift her own.

Antony took out the iridescent green vests traffic-control officers might wear. He gave one to Ryan and donned one himself. At every street crossing throughout the built-up area, Ryan crossed first and Antony brought up the rear. Still, with their best efforts to keep the group together, there were always stragglers as someone stopped to look in a shop window or a traffic light changed before they could all cross the street.

Felicity was trying her best to keep a surreptitious eye on Adam. She knew he would be offended if she seemed to be minding him, but someone needed to. Lydia had chosen to go in the van "To watch over my patient" she had said, but Felicity suspected it was an excuse to spend time with Michael, who had shown no signs of rejecting Lydia's attention.

"Have you been here before?" she asked, falling in step beside the lad who was lagging at the back of the group as they walked up Standard Street.

"I've always wanted to. They have a brilliant team."

"Team?"

"Rugby football. Bedwas is the best." His face fell. "Well, they were rather put to the sword last season. But they'll come back. You'll see."

Felicity didn't have much idea what he was talking about, but she admired his spunk. Then she was even more confused a bit further along when he burst out, "Peter's Pies!"

"What?"

Adam pointed to a green and white sign in a shop window. "Their corned beef pasties are the best."

Felicity laughed. "You can't possibly be hungry. We just had an enormous breakfast."

The road became a long, straight route with no cross streets, so Ryan and Antony were no longer required to herd them like sheepdogs. Which also meant that they became even further strung apart. Felicity realized that with Nancy in the van, Evie and Kaylyn had also lost their shepherd. When the girls stopped to look at designs displayed in the window of a tattoo shop, Felicity paused with them.

She listened with half an ear to their chatter, trying to fathom the appeal of having one of these patterns pricked into your skin with a sharp needle, until she caught her breath at a familiar pattern tucked in the far corner of the display. As in her dream last night, the double-headed snake writhed on its triangle. She could almost hear it hissing at her.

Felicity linked an arm through each girl's elbow and commanded, "Come on. Now." Her tug was so sharp she almost pulled Evie off-balance, but both girls obeyed.

They had caught up with the rest of the walkers when Felicity realized Adam was nowhere in sight. She looked frantically up and down both sides of the street. "Where could he have gone? There aren't any other streets." If he had gone into a shop they would be ages finding him. He must have darted off for one of those pies.

"How about that side street back there?" Evie asked.

"Huh?"

"You marched us past it so fast you probably didn't notice— like the devil was on your tail."

Felicity didn't reply, just turned back along the way they had come. Indeed, only a few shops back a small street ran uphill. No wonder Adam had been attracted. A miniature street fair was in progress. Several shops had set tables of their wares on the pavement, a fiddler played a lively tune, attracting several children and dogs, and Adam stood watching them, entranced, munching the final crumbs of a Welsh cake.

Felicity had to laugh. "Where did you get that?"

He shrugged and wiped the crumbs from his mouth. "She gave it to me."

Felicity looked around expecting to see a street vendor, probably in historic Welsh costume. The street was busy, but there was no such vendor in sight—costumed or not. "Who?"

"She's gone."

"I can see that." Felicity's sympathy for Lydia was growing by the minute. "But who was she?"

"The lady from Twmbarlwm."

Felicity chilled. The mysterious lady in the mist. "What does she look like?"

He smiled. "She's pretty."

Felicity sighed. "Yes, you said." It seemed clear she wouldn't get any more out of him.

"I wish I had another one. I'm still hungry."

"Come on, we need to catch up." Felicity struggled to keep the irritation out of her voice.

The way continued on through the busy streets of a built-up industrial area and housing estates. What St David and his monks, moving westward with the gospel, or the later medieval pilgrims following in their footsteps would think if they could see this was unimaginable. Even the more pleasant part when they crossed the bridge over *Nant yr Aber* and the footpath followed the bank of the stream before joining a cycle path bordered by trees was still accompanied by traffic on the busy road beside them, leading past a supermarket and around a wide car park.

At least there was little reason for anyone, even Adam, to dawdle here, although he continued to lag to the rear. Felicity, keeping a surreptitious eye on him, thought he was looking paler than usual, but maybe it was just the late morning sun on his blond hair.

More than an hour later, the buildings began to thin as they followed another cycleway alongside the busy Caerphilly bypass. Finally a footbridge took them over the bypass and Felicity heaved a sigh of relief as they turned up the far quieter St Cenydd Road. A couple of hundred yards on, Angel Lane led them along an old hollow road. This was obviously part of the original route, and now Felicity had no problem imagining earlier pilgrims treading this way.

She turned to say something about that to Adam and stopped still. The boy was ghostly white, bent over almost double, clutching his stomach. She rushed to him, shouting for Antony who was a few paces in front of her, with Colin.

"What is it? What's the matter?" she demanded, although it was obvious Adam was suffering from intense stomach cramps.

He groaned and stumbled off the path to collapse under a tree, still holding his stomach.

Antony pulled out his mobile to ring Michael, but even as he did so the silver minibus bumped up Angel Lane.

Lydia jumped out and ran to her brother. "What is this, Squib? What have you eaten?" She placed her hand on his forehead. "You're freezing." Before she could dig a jacket from his rucksack, Felicity put her own around his thin shoulders.

"He had a Welsh cake at the street market. He said it was the lady from Twmbarlwm." Felicity directed the last statement to Antony, and registered his worried look.

"Nothing else? You've had nothing else to eat or drink since breakfast?" Lydia's voice was sharp.

Adam shook his head. "It feels like a snake in my stomach."

Lydia felt Adam's abdomen carefully with her fingertips. "Right." She reached for the first aid kit Michael had brought from the van. She had her hand on the bottle of Ipecac when Antony held up his hand.

"Wait. Someone doesn't want this pilgrimage to be a success."

Antony turned to the van and returned with a cup of water, which he blessed with the sign of the cross. "Here. Drink." He held it up to Adam's lips.

The boy recoiled.

"Just a sip." Antony looked Adam in the eye; his voice was level, but commanding.

Adam shuddered, but obeyed.

"Now?" Lydia held up the Ipecac.

Antony made the sign of the cross over the small brown bottle and nodded. "Go ahead."

The pilgrims who had gathered around were silent as Adam swallowed the dose.

"Holy Ipecac!" Evie's joke elicited a nervous titter.

But no one laughed when Adam regurgitated a few minutes later. Jared looked at the bit of brightly colored string coiled snakelike on the ground. "That's not in a traditional Welsh cake. My gran makes them all the time."

Wordlessly Antony sprinkled holy water on the vomit, then covered it with dry paper and set it aflame with a lighter from the van. "Let us pray for the protection of the Blood of Christ," Antony directed the small circle. When the prayer was finished and the little pyre had crumbled to ashes, Antony scooped them into a plastic cup. He turned back down the trail. Felicity, following at a distance, watched him sprinkle the ashes into the flowing *nant*, then wash his hands with the remaining holy water.

When they returned, Michael was offering tea to those with stronger stomachs than Felicity. She shook her head when he held a bright orange mug out to her.

"Into the minibus with you, Squib," Lydia ordered. "I don't know what I'm going to do with you. You haven't any more sense than the day you were born."

Felicity wanted to protest that it wasn't really his fault, but the subdued Adam crawled into the van. Through the open driver's window, Felicity noticed that he took the seat in the furthest back corner. It was hard to remember that he was a teen. He looked so young.

"Meet you at Groeswen church," Michael called as he put the van into gear to reverse up the narrow lane.

The small clutch of pilgrims moved forward, Ryan leading with the cross and listening to Colin, Jared making some remark to the Goth girls that elicited a giggle from Evie. When they were a few paces ahead, Felicity turned to Antony. "Now, what was that all about?"

"Norm number 20 of the *Ritual for Deliverance*. If someone has ingested something connected with occult activity it is necessary to vomit." He answered as calmly as if he had been giving a mathematical formula. Then shook his head. "I know the theory. It's the first time I've had to put it into practice. I'm afraid I'm rather shaken."

Felicity didn't know which question to ask first. She settled for, "Even I know holy water is traditional, but blessing the Ipecac?"

"Water, salt and oil are the traditional elements for a ritual against evil. Ipecac is an oil."

"But how did you *know*? Who would have suspected?"

"A rather textbook case, really. The question isn't really what, but rather why?"

"And who?" Felicity added. "So Adam's imaginary lady is real?"

"I'm afraid she's much too much real."

"But why do people do such things? It's just all superstition and fraud— parlor tricks, isn't it? How could anyone be serious about such things?"

"Some are just curious or duped, but most are deadly serious. Power or money—the roots of all evil."

"It still just seems silly. I mean, a bit of string."

Antony spoke slowly, emphasizing the importance of what he was trying to explain. "*Malefice* means—"

"To do evil. From *male factus*. I'm the classicist, remember?"

"Right. For someone who means to do evil—cast a spell would be the popular term—an object like a stone or hair, a length of string, has symbolic value. It's a tangible sign of the will to do harm, offered to Satan to be imprinted with his evil powers. We know Satan often imitates God. In this case such objects become an analogy for the sacraments."

"They are cursed like bread and wine would be blessed?"

Antony nodded. "An inversion of the consecration."

Felicity shuddered. Put like that, it made horrible sense. "But why us—our pilgrims? A priest and an ordinand and a bunch of kids, for goodness' sake. What could possibly be more innocuous? We don't have any power or money."

"I wish I knew."

The walking became easier as they again began following the Rhymney Valley Ridgeway footpath. They stopped for lunch in the churchyard of the small grey Groeswen Independent Welsh Chapel on a green hillside overlooking the valley. A sign said it was the first Methodist place of worship in Wales. Antony called this to their attention: "A good example of the ecumenism this walk is designed to be fostering."

Sandwich and crisps in hand, Colin plopped down on the grass beside Felicity. She hoped he wouldn't want to talk about the morning's events, especially as Adam was sitting not far from them, sipping the black tea prescribed by his sister. But she needn't have worried. Colin, as usual, was engrossed in his surroundings. "Groeswen means 'White Cross.' This was likely a waymarking cross on the medieval route. The village pub is called the White Cross, but that's modern." His dismissive tone showed how little interest that held for him. "But outside the village there's a farm called *Pen-y-groes*. Local tradition says there was an elaborately carved cross there. No record of it has ever been found. I was thinking that would make a brilliant archeology project. Not Roman, of course, but…"

Felicity closed her eyes and let him talk until Antony called the group together for a Station before moving on up the hill. And up was definitely the operative word as, after following hedges around several fields and crossing a stretch of open moorland, the footpath ascended the wide, green side of Mynydd Meio.

Behind them and to their left vast views stretched out across the built-up valley. Ryan stood by the trig point and held his arm out: "Those are the Brecon Beacons to the north. Back there is Mynedd Machen we climbed yesterday." Felicity rubbed her calf as a reflex. "And there," he turned to the south, "is the Bristol Channel. That gleam of white is the Severn Crossing. Beyond you have the hills of Somerset."

Felicity was entranced, but even more fascinating were the paragliders sailing above them like giant prehistoric birds. Orange, red, blue, the wide canopies drifted silently overhead, their small dark shadows following them on the ground. Scattered sheep grazed across the hill, ignoring the aeronautic show above them. A muffled roar rose from the base of the mountain as the silver line of the Eglwysilan Road rushed traffic on its way.

A white canopy with a purple design caught Felicity's eye. She sat down on the smooth, flat mountain top to watch as the giant wing mounted an air current, then seemed to hang suspended against the blue sky before gliding further out over the valley.

"Looks peaceful, doesn't it?"

Felicity looked up to see a suntanned young woman in khaki shorts and a blue shirt standing beside her, watching the same glider her own gaze had been following.

Felicity smiled. "That's just what I was thinking. Like floating on an angel's wing or something." The two women watched silently for a moment. "This hill must be brilliant for gliding," Felicity observed.

"It's fairly friendly as long as they keep away from the power lines, pylons and TV mast—and as long as there aren't too many model aircraft pilots out."

"You sound experienced."

Her companion shrugged. "Not me. Joe." She tipped her head toward the white wing now drifting eastward beyond the hill.

"You're American." Felicity just realized. The woman's voice sounded so normal to her she hadn't registered the difference.

"Yes. Chloe, from Oregon. Where are you from?" Chloe sat beside Felicity.

"I'm from Idaho. That makes us neighbors. What are you doing here?"

"I came over a month ago with my girlfriend. We thought we'd spend the summer walking, sleeping out—had just enough money to buy our food and for an occasional youth hostel. We wanted to meet people and live easy. My main interest is photography." She indicated the camera hanging around her neck.

"Sounds idyllic. How's it working out?"

"It was great for a couple of weeks, then Sue took off with a cute Scotsman."

"And left you all alone?" *Some friend*, Felicity was thinking.

"Oh, no. I tagged along for a few days, but it wasn't really— comfortable. 'Three's a crowd,' you know. Then I met Joe." She nodded toward the distant white speck. "For my sins."

"That didn't work so well either?" Felicity ventured.

Chloe ducked her head. "Well, I got some great shots of his paragliding…"

"But?"

Chloe's cheeks tinged pink. "He, ah, wants more—um, you know—and he's getting awful pushy."

Felicity nodded. How refreshing to find a young woman of her generation who wasn't ready to accept the first fling that came along.

Chloe was silent as if deep in thought. "Where are you going?"

Felicity told her about their youth walk ending with a quiet time at St David's. "That sounds like heaven," Chloe said, with a sigh. "You're walking and staying in church halls and things? I mean, you're er—flexible?"

"I guess so." Felicity wasn't sure what she was getting at. "What do you mean?"

"I hardly slept at all last night. We stayed in a hostel. Joe went out for ages—I don't know where. When he came back, he was... I don't know—high or excited or something. I was frightened."

Chloe hesitated, then took a breath and plunged, her words coming out in a nervous rush. "I need to get away, but I don't know anyone. Can I walk with you? With your group, I mean." She gestured toward the others standing around Antony in his dog collar holding the cross. "I'd be safe with you."

"Well..." Felicity didn't know what to say. The girl needed help, but they didn't really know anything about her.

"I've got all my stuff with me—I told Joe I needed my camera equipment, but really, I was thinking of getting away—" She indicated a rucksack with a bedroll tied on below. "And I could pay. Well, a little bit."

"Let me ask Father Antony; he's in charge." Felicity scrambled to her feet and walked to Antony. Pulling him apart from the others, she explained the situation.

He considered for several moments. "Seems the charitable thing to do. I don't see why we can't give it a try. We'll have to see if it works for everybody."

"Chloe!" Felicity waved her new acquaintance over.

"Everybody, this is Chloe. She's from the States, too, as you'll soon see—well, hear."

"Hi." Chloe greeted the circle with a broad smile and a small wave.

"Chloe's going to be walking with us for a while. I know you'll make her welcome," Antony introduced their small group: Ryan, Colin, Jared, Evie, Kaylyn, and each one responded with a greeting—if Kaylyn's aloof nod could be characterized as such. "And we have four others in the minibus. You'll meet them when we stop for tea."

"That's really great. Thanks so much." Chloe gave a nervous look over her shoulder at the white and purple canopy which seemed to be descending toward the flat, open space alongside the road at the bottom of the hill. "Um, will we be going soon?"

"We can wait a bit if you want to say goodbye," Felicity offered.

"No! Er—that is, it would be simpler... Joe has a temper... I could just leave a note on the window of his Land Rover."

"Don't worry." Antony gave her a comforting smile. "I was thinking of doing a Station here, but no reason we can't move on to the back of the hill first. Right, troops?"

Chloe enveloped Felicity in a hug. "Oh, thank you so much." She turned to Antony. "I won't be any trouble, I promise. I'll meet you on the back of the hill." She ran off to leave her note, and the pilgrims moved into line.

Chloe rejoined them in a few minutes, falling into step beside the Goths. "Hi, I have two kid sisters back home. They're both Illuminated Goth."

Evie held out her bright blue fingernails and touched the magenta spikes of her hair. "Coo, sweet as a nut!"

Felicity blinked. Her only reference of illuminated Gothic was to a medieval manuscript. She suddenly felt old and out of touch. But it was obvious Chloe had made a friend already.

Even Kaylyn seemed to respond a bit as she held out her black fingernails. It looked like their newcomer would be an asset to the group.

Felicity lengthened her stride to hear Ryan informing the others about the long line of dark green bushes topping a bank that descended the hill to their right. "That's the remains of the Senghenydd Dyke. In the thirteenth century it enclosed a vast deer park belonging to the lords of Senghenydd who lived at Caerphilly Castle." He pointed northwestward across the valley. "That next hill is Cefn Eglwysilan. The dyke runs across that, too."

"Yeah, and that's where the Senghenydd Colliery Disaster was—worst mining disaster in UK history." Felicity shivered at the note of relish in Colin's voice. "Four hundred, thirty-nine miners killed in 1921. An electric spark ignited the coal dust on the floor, see, and that raised a cloud and that ignited, too. The shock wave ahead of the explosion raised yet more coal dust, so the whole thing just self-fueled through the tunnels. Those miners not killed immediately—"

"Yes, thank you, Colin." Felicity was thankful that Ryan managed to cut off Colin's flow. "Look, there's tea." Ryan pointed to the sun glinting off the roof of the van below them.

As usual, Michael had everything in readiness, and the walkers, several of whom had eaten more lightly at lunch than usual after the morning's unpleasantness, fell on the array of cakes and biscuits. Felicity took the opportunity to introduce Chloe to the rest of their crew and to enquire after Nancy and Adam, both of whom were looking much better. Felicity was especially gratified when she noticed Adam taking his second slice of flapjack. He gave Chloe a bright, welcome smile and she snapped a photo.

Ryan offered Chloe a cup of tea and sat beside her. "Did you spend much time on Mynedd Meio?"

"No, we only went there because the place Joe wanted to sail was blown out. I'm glad we did, though, or I wouldn't have met you all."

"We're glad to have you." He took a deep drink of tea and finished his slice of flapjack. "I'd have liked to stay up there longer, though. There's a Neolithic burial site I'd have liked to explore."

"Ah, the Shinney," Jared joined them. "Lucky we are to be down from there, I can tell you. My gran warned me."

"What old tale is this?" Ryan smiled around his mouthful of cake.

"The oldest—4,000 years, my gran claims. And not just a tale; they found a bunch of half-burned, painted skulls. The banshee collects them, you see," Jared leaned forward, relishing his tale.

Chloe laughed. "Ohh, tell me more."

"Shinney's the guardian of ways to the Otherworld. She waits on the road at the ford to grab people. She uses the ford to wash their heads before putting them in her collection."

Chloe shivered, encouraging Jared to enhance his tale. "You have to watch out, see, because she's got three guises. She can be really old and haggard like she needs help, or beautiful and sexy, or young and like—lost and alone. Or she can be a combination." He offered the newcomer his wide grin, blue eyes twinkling. "Like you, beautiful but alone, needing help."

Chloe gave a toss of her sun-streaked ash-blonde hair and reached out for Jared, "You see my plan. Now I'll have to take your head for my collection."

Everyone laughed, but later, when Chloe offered to carry the cross after the Station and continued to walk close beside Antony, smiling up at him, Felicity wondered what she might have gotten the group into by taking Chloe under her wing.

Once off the mountain, their way led along the green hillside following Eglwysilan Road, lined with occasional trees and bushes with white sheep and red cows observing them over the hedges. They had been walking perhaps half an hour when Michael came up the road to meet them. "Thought I'd take the chance to stretch my legs. Lovely evening," he observed, looking at the shadows beginning to lengthen across the fields.

Michael went to the back of the group and inserted himself between Antony and Colin. "I settled the others at St Ilan's— unless they've gone across the street to the Rose and Crown already." He grinned. "Typical Welsh village—church and pub. That's the lot." He shrugged. "All you need, really."

Felicity was glad to hear they didn't have far to go, but even a short distance might be too much. She had been feeling distinctly uncomfortable since her second cup of tea on the back of Mynedd Meio. And she had found no conveniently placed bushes. Now the hedgerow offered relief. She stepped off the path and was behind the concealing bushes in a fraction of a second.

She was just pulling up her trousers when she heard a plaintive voice that could only be Colin: "I told you before, I don't know. It was a Roman road. Saint Cynedd followed it in the sixth century, but that's all—"

The angry growl that cut him off was definitely Michael. "That's not good enough. I need something more specific."

"I could try ringing my tutor after supper. Maybe she'll—"

The voices moved on. Felicity adjusted her clothing and rejoined the others as unobtrusively as she could. But what was that all about? Was Michael insisting that Colin help him conduct an archeological dig? Could Michael be trying to steal an ancient artifact? That hardly seemed to make sense, but she couldn't think of anything that did.

The ladies of St Ilan's greeted them with an enormous pot of savory Welsh lamb stew and crusty homemade bread.

They ate in the narthex formed by the enormous, windowless tower that gave more the impression of a medieval fortress than a church. The stew with tiny new peas and fresh herbs was gourmet fare, but Felicity could think of little else but climbing into her sleeping bag—in spite of the fact that they would be sleeping on the stone floor of the church tonight. A twinge of leg cramp, however, reminded her that she had woefully neglected her accustomed stretching exercises the past days. One would think all the exercise she'd endured would have been more than enough but, of course, that was the problem. Too much exercise, and not of the proper sort.

As soon as the meal was over and others had set about folding and stacking the tables, Felicity stepped into the sanctuary and grabbed the back of a pew to serve as a barre and began her *plies.* "Ballet. I did that in infant school." Felicity thought Kaylyn meant the remark as a slur, but to her surprise, the girl grabbed the pew with her black-tipped, be-ringed fingers, displaying the butterfly tattoo on her hand, and began the deep knee bends, her feet properly in second position, her back straight. "I loved it, but Ma couldn't afford to keep up the lessons."

Will wonders never cease? Felicity thought as she moved on to a series of *frappés* with each foot.

The exercises worked a treat to relax Felicity's aching muscles. She wasn't even aware of the stone floor beneath her, or of the activity of the others in the narthex when she crawled into her sleeping bag in the back of the nave, thinking she might not leave it for days.

She had been asleep for less than an hour, however, when Antony wakened her. Her first thought was joy at seeing his dear face bent over her. She reached out to clasp him around the neck and pull him to her for a very thorough kiss.

He responded most gratifyingly, but then pulled back. "We have a problem."

Felicity sat up and peered into the blackness. In the narthex beyond she made out the forms of sleeping pilgrims. And the empty sleeping bags. "Who's missing?"

"Jared, Kaylyn and Evie."

Felicity nodded and reached for her shoes. She had been so tired she hadn't even bothered pulling off her trousers. Just as well.

Michael, sleeping by the door of the tower, roused when the heavy wood grated on the stone. Antony told him what they were doing. "Want me to come, too?"

Antony shook his head. "We'll leave you in charge here."

Michael nodded, and they went out into the fresh night. Beyond the churchyard, the white stucco walls of the Rose and Crown glowed in the dark, pools of light from its diamond-patterned windows falling on the road. "No prizes for guessing where they are," Antony said.

"What time is it?" Felicity squinted at her watch. "Don't they have closing times here?"

"It's not quite eleven, it will still be open."

Evie's giggle was the first thing Felicity heard when she stepped into the warm, low-ceilinged room. One or two other tables were occupied by late drinkers, sitting in relaxed positions on the dark wooden chairs, or leaning against the high-backed booths along the walls. A small, bald man stood behind the bar to their left, wiping the counter with a cloth. He looked up sharply at the newcomers.

"We're closing soon," he began, but Antony waved a hand.

"We're just looking for—ah."

At a table in the corner sat their strayed sheep.

Jared saw them first. "Brilliant. Father, Felicity!" He waved them over with a broad grin. "This is Joe."

Felicity looked into piercing blue eyes in a sharp-featured, tanned face sporting a fashionably stubbly beard framed by white-blond hair. "Hiya. Pull up a chair. What'll ya have? I'm buying."

"You followed us!" Felicity snapped her accusation.

Joe shrugged his slight but well-muscled shoulders. "It was still a free country the last time I checked. They do a good local ale here." He shifted to make room on the bench. "I'm buying." Antony ignored the offer, glaring at his charges' glasses. "They're underage."

"Nah, it's cola, Father." Joe spoke quickly.

"Unusual to serve it in pints." Antony let it drop. "Let's get back." He gestured toward the church. "We've got a stiff walk tomorrow. Ten miles."

No one moved. "Joe wants to talk to Chloe," Evie intervened. "He loves her." Her voice quavered with her determination to bring the star-crossed lovers back together.

Felicity shook her head. "No way. Chloe's with us. For sanctuary." She faced the steely blue eyes. "Chloe doesn't want to see you."

Joe spread out his hands. "It was a misunderstanding. I got my signals wrong."

"You certainly did."

A flash of anger flared in the paraglider's eyes. A tightening of his jaw showed the control required to suppress an outburst.

"We need to be going," Antony repeated with increased firmness.

Jared shrugged and rose. "We were just looking around. We didn't mean any harm, Father."

Evie pushed her chair back with a clatter. "I'm so sorry, Joe. I'll tell Chloe you love her."

Kaylyn sat, glaring defiantly at Antony from her kohl-shadowed eyes. She reached languidly for her pint and raised it to her black lips, taking a long swallow. Antony waited. At last she gave an exaggerated yawn. "Oh well, see you later, Joe."

Now Antony confronted Joe. "Leave Chloe alone."

Felicity could feel the piercing eyes shooting daggers between her shoulder blades as she crossed the room. When she reached the door she couldn't resist glancing back. Joe's smirk was more alarming than any spoken threat could have been.

Chapter 14

Antony woke early, in spite of the fact that merely the palest slivers of morning sunshine penetrated the air vents that were the only openings in the church tower. He had been exceedingly thankful for the fortress, feeling it provided protection against Joe's implied threats last night. Elsewhere, he might not have slept at all. Antony looked into the nave where Chloe had spread her bedroll near Felicity's. What had they taken on? It had seemed impossible to refuse the girl's request for protection, and yet he felt he had more than enough responsibility already.

And if the arcane occurrences that seemed to surround them continued, he wasn't certain that the girl hadn't put herself in greater danger by joining the pilgrimage. He had to get to the bottom of this. But what could he do?

He fumbled in his rucksack for his breviary. His thick socks padded softly over the cold stones up to the altar of St Ilan's. The east window was a triptych of tall, narrow Gothic arches. On each side of the chancel smaller, likewise narrow, pointed windows let in some light. It was enough to read by, familiar as he was with the words. He lit the candles for the comfort of their warmth and redolent, waxy scent rather than for the light.

He knelt at the altar. "Almighty and most merciful Father…"

The collect for peace was a set part of the office. He prayed it every morning of his life. But never more fervently than this morning: "… Defend thy humble servants in all assaults of our enemies; that we, surely trusting in thy defense, may not fear the power of any adversaries…"

His mind filled with the picture of one of his favorite paintings—one he always showed his students when he taught deliverance: *Expulsion of the Devils from Arezzo*, a detail of the life of St Francis from St Francis's church in Assisi—the brown-robed saint standing in front of his church, blessing the city, while behind him a brother kneels in prayer, and over the city walls and rooftops the demons flee in terror.

He knew what to do. He rose and went into the sacristy to prepare. It was the best defense he could offer them. The only sure defense he knew.

By the time Antony was vested and had everything organized the others were awake. "Ask everyone to gather at the front," he directed Felicity.

Antony was pleased with the alacrity with which Chloe took a seat on the front pew. He had no idea of her background. He was equally relieved that Kaylyn offered no resistance. And he was delighted that Nancy barely limped as she came up the aisle. Jared approached almost shyly. "Sorry about last night, Father. Er—my report—like, I wasn't thinking."

Antony placed a hand on his shoulder. "I don't think we need to worry your school authorities about that. But don't wander off again without letting me know." Jared nodded and took a seat.

When all were settled, Antony turned to the pot of water on the credence table. He sprinkled a few grains of salt over the water and marked it with the sign of the cross. Dipping in the apergillum, he turned to his tiny flock. "*Asperges me, Domine, hyssopo et mundabor,*

Lavabis me, et super nivem dealbabor. Miserere mei…" He chanted first in Latin, walking completely around the occupied pews, flinging crystalline drops over all. Then in English, "You will sprinkle me, O Lord, with hyssop and I shall be cleansed. You will wash me, and I shall be washed whiter than snow. Pity me, O God, according to Your great mercy." He completed the circle three times.

Next he took the lighted thurible from its stand, swung it several times to increase the air flow, then again circled the entire group three times, letting the clouds of incense surround them and rise as prayers before the throne of God.

He directed them to turn to the litany in the prayer books he had placed in the pew racks. "… O holy, blessed, and glorious Trinity, one God…"

"Have mercy upon us." All responded.

"… Spare us, good Lord, spare Thy people, whom Thou hast redeemed with Thy most precious blood, and by Thy mercy preserve us for ever."

"Spare us, good Lord."

"From all evil and wickedness; from sin; from the crafts and assaults of the devil…"

"Good Lord, deliver us."

The Great Litany was long and somber, not to be recited lightly, but Antony soldiered on through all the pages, and his flock followed "We beseech Thee to hear us, good Lord."

Until the end, "O Lamb of God, that takest away the sins of the world…"

"Grant us Thy peace."

Then the Eucharist, administering the Body and Blood of Christ, and invoking the protection of Father, Son and Holy Ghost on the body and soul of each partaker.

There was no more he could do. "Go in peace."

And when, after a breakfast of porridge and sausage, they went out into the brightness of the morning to be greeted by birdsong from the churchyard trees and sheep baaing in the field across the way, it seemed that their petition was to be granted. The walking this morning was easy, too, as it followed the road for a mile or so, then cut downhill along a pleasant brook tumbling over stones beneath its green, wildflower-studded banks.

Everyone but Nancy was walking this morning. She had been keen to attempt it, but Lydia advised caution, although Lydia herself had for once chosen to walk rather than accompany Michael. And Adam seemed nearly as frisky as the lambs in the field above them as he almost skipped along beside Jared.

Antony noticed Felicity attempting to engage Lydia in conversation, but their nurse seemed more intent in quizzing Ryan about something on the map. Whatever it was, it had Colin's full attention as well. Since Chloe was again walking with Evie and Kaylyn, Antony was free to enjoy the glories of the June morning. Until they stopped for the first Station of the day, and Ryan and Colin approached him brimming with determination and enthusiasm for their plan. "They aren't far out of the way, Father; we walk right up the Darren Ddu Road, and the trail over to the quarry is well marked." Ryan pointed to the spot on the map.

"The Romans may have worked the quarries. Travertine was their favorite building material. The Coliseum is the world's largest Travertine building…" Colin returned to his favorite subject, but Ryan intervened.

"We wouldn't need to go deep into the caves, Father. The main chamber is just beyond the passage crawl—I've read up on it."

Antony shook his head. "Sorry to stamp on your enthusiasm, lads, but there's no way I'm taking this crew into a cave. Besides, we've got more than eight miles to cover today." Valid enough reasons. No need to mention that there was no way Antony would choose to go into a cave under any circumstances. Just thinking of being in a deep, dark tunnel under the earth made him short of breath. "No chance," he repeated.

Ryan was silent for a moment, studying the map. "Look, Father, Michael is meeting us here at *Penheol Ely* for morning tea, right?"

Antony nodded.

"And then we have lunch here after we cross the Pontypridd Bridge?" He pointed.

"Yes, and I don't want to change the route."

"No, no. Not at all," Ryan hurried on. "Then afternoon tea here by the Clydach River before the path turns west away from the road?"

Antony nodded. The route was clearly set. What was Ryan getting at?

"Then another stop at Mynachdy where the Llantarnam monks had their grange farm." Ryan took a deep breath before launching into his plan. "Now, if Colin and I were to fill our flasks, take some extra cake and make a couple of sandwiches at *Penheol Ely* while everyone is having morning tea, then leg it right on up the road to the quarry without any other stops, that would give us two, maybe three hours to explore the cave."

"We have our torches." Colin emphasized his words by flicking his on in Antony's face. Fortunately the sun was so bright it didn't bother him.

"The limestone quarries were so important to the development of this whole region. I'm certain to be assigned essays on it. You see, Travertine is a sedimentary rock, formed by the precipitation of carbonate minerals from solution in ground surface waters so you get stalactites and—"

"And the Romans—"

Antony held up his hand. "Enough. I'll think it over. We'll see how we're getting on when we get to the Ely Road."

The way started more steeply upward once again as it wound around the gorse, grass and bracken-covered slopes of Cefn Eglwysilan on their right and a patchwork of hedge-bordered fields varying from emerald, jade, pea-green, bottle-green and olive, depending on their crops. Felicity and Chloe joined him, and their chatter about growing up in bordering states, both sharing memories of summer vacations on the Oregon Coast, left him free to enjoy the easy rhythm of the walk.

They reached the meeting point in good time, and Michael and Nancy had their tea awaiting them. Antony noted Colin and Ryan preparing their stores as they had suggested, apparently taking his forthcoming permission for granted. Antony was just finishing the slice of bran loaf stuffed with sultanas the good ladies of St Ilan's had sent with them, when his would-be potholers approached. He held up his hand before they could launch into yet another spiel. "Ask Michael and Felicity to join us."

When they were together again, Ryan explained the plan.

"Are you all right with leading this afternoon, Felicity?"

"Sure. No problem," she agreed readily.

Antony looked at Michael for his thoughts on the matter. "Mynachdy is a bit far afield. I'd rather not get that spread out. Here, where the trail leaves the Ynysybwl Road to head north," he pointed to the map. "That's the best meeting point."

"That's fine," Ryan readily agreed. "And it's nice by the Nant Clydach in case you have to wait."

"No!" Antony was firm. "*You* be waiting for us." He looked Ryan in the eye. "Be early. I don't want to be walking through the St Gwynno Forest after dark."

"Brilliant!"

"Thank you, Father!"

The adventurers set off before Antony could change his mind.

He watched the tall, broad Ryan in his flat cap and the short-legged Colin, swinging his hiking stick double-time in order to keep pace as the trail dropped steeply downward. Antony hoped he'd made the right decision. The morning had been the best walk of the pilgrimage. He didn't want anything to go wrong now.

On the modern White Bridge at Pontypridd, they stopped and looked downstream at the old gray stone bridge arching high over the River Taff. "According to Michael's notes, that's the bridge that gave Pontypridd its name—longest single-span bridge in the world when it was built," Felicity said, after consulting her route information.

Chloe whipped out her camera, adjusted the impressive zoom lens and snapped several shots. "Can we go down there, Father Antony?" She pointed to a path leading down through the bushes on their left to the riverbank. "I could get some great shots from that angle."

The sun was warm, the river murmured beneath them, and traffic noise from the dual carriageway on the other side of the river was muffled. Antony hadn't felt so relaxed since they started this venture. He nodded his assent.

They scrambled down the overgrown path and walked under the modern bridge they had just crossed. Walking along the riverbank on a bed of flat rocks took them under the railway bridge. Chloe was delighted, her shutter clicking a staccato as she photographed bridges, pilgrims and the Taff river rapids from every angle.

Jared challenged Evie and Kaylyn to a rock-throwing contest to see who could lob theirs furthest into the water. Jared was clearly the winner, until a surprise entrant pitched a smooth round stone beyond the second span of the footings with effortless grace. "Wow! How did you do that?" Evie asked the smiling Adam.

Even Kaylyn managed a compliment. "Impressive."

Adam grinned. "Cricket. I bowl."

"That's brilliant," Jared conceded. "Let's see if you can make it two out of three."

The result of the second round was disputed. The third throw would determine the champion. Jared made his best fling. Adam moved closer to the edge.

"Careful, Squib!"

It was uncertain whether it was Lydia's sharp command or a slimy rock that caused Adam to lose his footing, but the ominous splash and Evie's cry brought everyone to the riverbank at once. The cold water ran over Antony's boot tops, soaking his socks as he plunged forward to catch the flailing youth.

The water wasn't above Adam's knees, but he had fallen flat so that he was thoroughly drenched, and likewise soaked his rescuer when Antony pulled him from the water. At least all the stone-throwing contestants had left their rucksacks on the rocks, and Antony had dropped his before swooping to the rescue. They changed their dripping shirts for jackets from their packs, removed their sodden hiking boots, and wrung out their thick walking socks. Now the extra cushioned padding in the trail socks Antony had so carefully selected in an unaccustomed online shopping spree proved to be counterproductive. No matter how hard he wrung them, his socks felt thoroughly sodden when he wriggled his feet back into them. Nothing else for it, though; any other dry clothing was in the van.

Felicity offered her jacket to serve as a towel for his hair as Lydia rubbed at her brother's scalp, chastizing him all the while.

Still, Antony considered, it was a warm day, they would meet Michael for lunch soon, and no one had been hurt—praises be. He refused to let go of his chipper mood over a little wetting.

Although, by the time he had returned to the road, squished his way along a large expanse of grass between several houses and climbed a steep uphill road under a railway overpass to meet the Darren Ddu Road, his optimism was flagging. The day didn't feel quite so warm in walking shorts still dripping little trails of water down the backs of his legs.

His cheerfulness returned quickly, however, when they found Michael at a grassy spot along a stream, and were greeted by the sound and scent of sizzling sausages. Nancy waved at them through the smoke from her position squatting by a charcoal-filled aluminum tray where she was turning the sausages over the grill.

"That's amazing!" Felicity cried. "How did you manage that?"

"Michael bought it at the Tesco at Pontypridd. Brilliant, isn't it?"

"It is. I've never seen a disposable grill. Here, let me help you." Felicity took a fork and began turning the sausages. "How's your ankle?"

"Much better. I might try walking a bit later if the trail isn't too rough."

"*If* your nurse approves, you mean." Lydia joined them.

After a few minutes in the van, Antony and Adam joined them. "You two just wash your hair?" Nancy asked when they approached with dry clothing, but still-wet hair.

Antony explained around bites of hot, spicy sausage in a soft bread roll.

"We didn't pray, Father," Adam reminded him.

"We'll give thanks afterwards. Eat them while they're hot."

Bolstered by dry clothing, a hot lunch and an extended rest time, Antony's euphoria not only held but increased through the afternoon. Walking along the graveled country road with grass growing between the tire tracks, bushes crowding the side, and trees branching overhead gave him a sense of being protected from the encroachment of industrialization, the rush of modern transport and the intrusion of technology. Now they truly could be medieval monks or pilgrims following St David.

The sense of harmony with his surroundings lasted until their road met the metaled secondary road. They approached the minibus parked alongside a field dotted with beech and mountain ash trees. Michael and Nancy sat on the grass. But no Colin and Ryan. "Where are they?" Antony demanded far more harshly than he intended.

Michael shook his head. "I was hoping they were with you. Thought maybe they came down from the quarry and caught you up on the Darren Ddu Road."

Antony looked back the way they had come. "They've had more than enough time. What with the kerfuffle at the river and taking extra time at lunch, I thought we'd find them napping under a bush."

"You don't suppose we're so late they thought they'd missed us and continued on to St Gwynno's?" Felicity joined them.

"I hope they know me better than that." Concern made Antony's voice acerbic. He took a breath and spoke more softly to Felicity. "We aren't that late. And I was very specific about meeting here."

"Could they have gotten on the wrong path? They didn't have a map, did they?"

"Ryan had a map marking the cave entrance. He had done his research. That's one of the reasons I permitted this escapade."

Felicity studied the map she carried. "As to missing the trail, all they would have to do is head downhill. Every path off the mountain ends at the Darren Ddu Road."

Antony took his mobile out of its protective pouch in his rucksack and rang Ryan's number. "Of course, if they're still in a cave there wouldn't be any reception." Wherever they were, there was no answer.

Antony sighed. "Nothing for it but to go look for them."

"No, Father. Let me," Michael offered. "I know the area better." He paused. "And your boots are still wet."

Antony smiled. "Points for tact. You didn't point out that you're in better condition.'

"Well, that, too."

"I'll go with you. In case they need first aid." Lydia started to step forward, but was impeded by Adam clinging to her. "What's the matter, Squib? You're perfectly safe. Just stay out of the river." She shook her arm free. "Anyone would think you're two years old."

Antony saw that Felicity was about to intervene on the part of the boy, but Michael turned to Lydia. "No. You stay here." A long look passed between them as if Lydia and Michael were communicating in an unspoken language.

At last Lydia dropped her eyes. "Right. Off you go, then."

"I've had first aid training. St John Ambulance." Jared stepped forward.

"Get in, then." Michael opened the door of the van. "Enjoy your tea, everybody. Ryan undoubtedly got so busy looking at calcite formations he lost all track of time."

"Or Colin found a Roman site and refuses to leave it. I can imagine him sitting there like Rory guarding the Pandorica." Jared grinned.

Antony looked blank.

"*Dr Who*," Felicity supplied. "Rory becomes a Roman Centurion and—oh, never mind. I'll tell you later."

Bemused, Antony returned to what he did know. "All right, everybody, we'll say a Station, with special prayers for a safe and speedy return for all of them, and then have our tea."

"Prayer and tea, how traditional." Kaylyn's voice was mocking, but she didn't refuse to participate in either.

The tea was long cold in Antony's cup and an ant was crawling over his discarded cake when Felicity sat down beside him. "I know how worried you are." She took his hand resting in the long grass. "Me, too."

"I don't know what to do. I suppose I should ring for help."
He was reaching for his mobile when a jaunty "Heigh-ho, heigh-
ho. It's off to work we go…" rang out from the wooded walk
beyond.

"It's them!" Felicity was first to her feet, but Kaylyn and
Evie were close behind.

Felicity embraced Colin and Ryan, pummeling them with
questions, "Are you all right? Why were you so long? Sorry the
cake's all gone. Are you starved? Where have you been?"

The Goth girls pulled Ryan and Colin toward the others.
Jared followed behind.

"Where's Michael?" Lydia cut through the rejoicing.

Antony looked around. No Michael. No sign of the minibus
coming up the road.

Jared began the explanation: "Our world-famous geographer
here got confused in the cave."

Ryan looked embarrassed. "True. When we came out I
started downhill all right, but it was the north side of the hill. I
would have worked it out, though."

"And the cave was brilliant," Colin broke in. "Past the first
chamber there's this amazing scalloped passage—"

"But where's Michael?" Lydia was more insistent this time.

"I dunno." Jared shook his head. "He went into the cave. I
walked around the hill and found these two."

"So you left Michael?"

"We went back into the cave and called and called. But I
didn't want to go in too far. I thought we should get back. I left
a note on the minibus."

"Did you ring him?" Lydia's voice was becoming increasingly
accusatory.

Jared shrugged. "In a cave?"

Antony had no better luck. "Felicity, you take the others on to St Gwynno's. I'll go back. We'll catch you up. Are you all right to walk, Nancy?"

"I am. I wanted to, anyway."

"I'm going with you." Lydia gave her little brother a fierce look. "No arguments, Squib."

Antony started to refuse, then thought better of it. "Right." He couldn't bear to think of more trouble, but in case Michael did need medical help...

Once his mind started down that road he couldn't stop himself: broken limbs from a fall, bleeding gash from falling against rocks, concussion from hitting his head...

And now Antony was going to have to go into that gaping cavern.

Chapter 15

Felicity had no idea she would feel so alone. Abandoned. Standing on a Welsh hillside with eight pairs of eyes staring at her, awaiting her direction. She ducked her head apparently to consult her map but really to breathe a swift prayer for guidance.

When she looked up, the group had righted itself. Chloe was showing Adam her camera, Jared was adjusting his trekking pole to the length of Nancy's hiking stick to give her a pair for support, the Goth girls had resumed their usual detachment. Felicity considered. She could, of course, hand the map over to Ryan. He would lead as he had for so much of the time. But, in spite of the jaunty air of their return, their geographer was still looking dazed from his recent experience. Even Colin was silent. Odd, really, for Ryan who knew how to read terrain so well, to have gotten so confused.

No, Antony had asked her to lead. She was the adult in charge. This time she turned to the map to study the route. Other choices offered themselves. The one noted as "original" led up the valley through Ynysybwl. What would once have been a pleasant walk along the river was now two miles of metaled road through a built-up area.

The alternative lay just to the west. Felicity traced it: up a lane, through a garden, along the bank of a stream, across a field, over a footbridge, around another garden. Much the pleasanter way, but longer, trickier to follow, and harder walking for Nancy.

"Right, everyone. Let's be off, then. We're going straight up the Ynysybwl Road, so please stay close together. Ryan, are you all right to bring up the rear?" He nodded, looking relieved. "Nancy, just call out if we walk too fast for you." Felicity hoisted the cross aloft in an energetic show of far more bravado than she was feeling.

They had gone only a few yards, however, when Nancy's clear soprano rang out, leading them in the rhythmic South African *Siyahamba*: "We are marching in the light of God." Felicity joined in, not having to fake her warmth.

At the top of the town she paused at the T-junction. They were doing well, but surely Nancy, at least, could do with a rest.

"Oo, cool cemetery." Evie and Kaylyn darted across the street before Felicity could stop them.

Felicity shrugged. "OK. Five minutes' rest before we start up the hill." She raised the cross and smiled as Nancy responded with another song, "Lift High the Cross."

Monuments, sheltered by the branches of enormous beech trees, lay scattered over the Buarth Y Capel churchyard, which was inclosed by a lichen-covered stone wall. Beyond, after a row of modern houses, a green hill rose, topped with the darker green of a conifer plantation.

Felicity caught up with Evie and Kaylyn standing before a gravestone topped with a kneeling angel. "It's like Nightwish," Evie explained. "They have this song about an injured angel and these two guys try to rescue her."

Felicity guessed she was talking about a Goth band. "Mmm." She wished she had asked Antony to leave his Stations booklet with her. They had done two earlier that morning, but she felt a real need for a moment of prayer.

"I've got mine." Nancy held out a small book.

Felicity gasped. "You must have read my mind."

"It just seemed appropriate."

"Will you lead us?" Felicity asked.

Nancy nodded. "Jesus falls for the first time." The meditation was through the eyes of a Roman soldier, forced to goad and kick the Man who only looked at him in love.

At the end of the prayer, Felicity led them out of the cemetery to rejoin the main road. Nancy and the Goths were close behind her. "Sweet. The reading." Kaylyn voiced one of her rare observations.

"Yeah, it's like that song I was talking about, 'Amaranth,' where the villagers burn the angel. She's so beautiful and she's not hurting them," Evie added.

Felicity smiled at the connection, then turned to her map. She was reluctant to take the path that headed out across the field. As long as they followed the road she could hope that every vehicle that passed them would be a silver van with Antony driving. She seemed to miss him more with every step.

Still, she had no choice, so she led across the River Ffrwd where, obeying her notes, she directed the pilgrims to look for the millstone built into the bridge. Jared spotted the large, round stone. "The monks' mill was just below the bridge," Felicity pointed down river. "Where that house is now."

Then, onward. Felicity was beginning to understand about a pilgrimage being like life. A lot of days were like this—just putting one foot in front of the other, no matter how you felt about it. She dug her pole in deeper with every step as the way rose more steeply. Red, beige and brown cattle lowed in the hedge-bordered field to their left. Soon they were trekking through waist-high bushes. The way opened out to a modern farm, and Felicity pointed out the crumbling stone walls of what was once the monks' grange standing beside a green metal implement shed with a red roof.

But she wouldn't let them linger any longer than it took Chloe to snap a few pictures of the ancient stones. The sun was sinking dangerously low in the west, and from here their way was increasingly wooded as they entered the St Gwynno Forest.

Felicity took a long pull on her water bottle, then broke out a box of granola bars from her pack, took one and handed them to Jared to pass around as she studied the map once again. The way followed a road for about an inch— less than half a mile— and then headed into the forest. This was the last stretch for the van to catch them up. She had to resist the desire to walk more slowly to give Antony more time to get there.

A new blister on her little toe made Felicity shift her foot inside her boot. She wanted Lydia with her cushioned plasters, she wanted Michael with his flasks of tea, she wanted Antony's comforting arms to enfold her.

Leaving the vehicle track with reluctance, Felicity plunged into the sheltered silence of the deep wood. Here even the sporadic bird calls sounded muffled. She wasn't certain whether the foliage had likewise muted the intermittent conversations of the walkers behind her, or whether they had fallen silent in a hushed awe.

Felicity was thankful for the long hours of evening light in early June as the westering sun, hanging low in the sky, shot shafts of gold through the deeper shadows of the deciduous and evergreen trees covering the extensive forest. The path was lined by sparse bushes growing in the limited sunlight that reached them beneath tall conifers, their trunks bare halfway to the sky, then sprouting needle-covered boughs.

Huge tree roots reached out to them, requiring care not to trip, and fallen branches tangled the path, demanding valuable time to clear the way before they plunged onward into the deeper shadows.

Felicity was leading more by a sense of where her feet thought the path should be than by any clear sight, when the way before them opened and she stepped out onto a narrow but well-maintained road. And across the way, sitting on its cleared hillside surrounded by leaning gravestones casting their final long, evening shadows, was St Gwynno's Church. So welcome was the sight, Felicity had the strange sense of it looking familiar. Lights from inside the stained-glass windows sent colored lances out to guide them in.

She darted forward. Antony would be here! All the time they had been trekking through the forest, Antony and the others would easily have driven the road that circled the mountain and cut through the forest from the north. Why had she thought them back at the quarry cave all this time just because she hadn't seen them?

She pushed through the iron gate in the wall and rushed around to the door in the south porch. "Ah, ye're here, then! Welcome, luv. Welcome all, ye poor lambs." A tall, broad-shouldered woman swathed in a white apron held her arms out, wielding a wooden spoon. Behind her, two gray-haired ladies, one plump, the other rail-thin, arranged a selection of tarts and puddings on a long table.

"Take yer boots off and sit you down. I'll take an oath yer that starved. We've real Welsh food for you, never fear."

A wave of sickness washed over Felicity when she realized Antony and the others were not there. Their hostess paused long enough to introduce herself as Gladys, and Felicity wordlessly followed her directions, acknowledging the blessed relief of pulling off her boots before heading to the ladies' room. She returned to take a seat at one of the tables set up behind the pews. "Father Antony, he hasn't rung?" she finally brought herself to ask.

"Love you, no. We've heard from no one. We were getting a mite concerned when the sun went down. It gets a deep dark here in the middle of the forest. That's why they chose us for that film, you know."

Felicity didn't know, but she was too occupied worrying about Antony to ask.

Gladys went on with her monologue, "And have they served you shepherd's pie every night of your trek?"

Several of the others admitted the near-truth of the surmise.

"Ah well, it'll be different tonight. Real Welsh food yer getting: Caerphilly cheese, leekie soup and faggots and pease. The Doctor liked my faggots a treat, he did."

Felicity was completely lost.

At least Jared came to her rescue with an explanation of part of her confusion. "That's brilliant! My gran makes faggots. Most people buy them at the butcher's, but Gran wouldn't think of it." He observed Felicity's blank look. "Traditional Welsh meatballs, they are. Gran chops up all the piggy bits and lots of herbs, wraps little balls in caul and bakes them."

"That's right, luv." Gladys gave an approving nod. "Use all of the pig but the squeak. And yer getting them with peas and mash, never fear."

"And extra gravy?" When Jared's plate came out swimming in gravy it was obvious his smile would procure extra of anything he desired.

"There you are. Just like I served the Doctor."

Doctor who? Felicity was about to ask, then realized that was the answer to her question. "Oh! That's why this place seemed familiar. What was that episode called?" Her brothers had been great fans of old black and white videos of the original series and she had grown up watching the tapes with them. She was studying in Oxford when the series relaunched and she had hardly missed an episode in the common room with her friends.

"'The Hungry Earth,'" Jared supplied.

Felicity put her fork down. The first bite of faggot had proved it to be as tasty as promised, but as talk of the excitement of the filming with the great lights set up in the churchyard and that big blue box sitting next to the oldest gravestone swirled around her, Felicity found worry crowding out her appetite.

All too well she remembered the episode they were talking about: holes appearing in the earth and swallowing people up. Too much like the quarries, tunnels, and caves they had encountered in recent days. What had caused Ryan's disorientation? Had Michael been swallowed? And Antony with him?

Thankfully the conversation shifted when Nancy asked about the church. "Twelfth century, this is," Gladys replied. "But the site is much older. There's been Christian worship right here on this spot since at least the sixth century." Felicity felt herself drawing comfort from that fact. Until she realized that wouldn't apply to the Darren Ddu caves. Antony and the others were out there in the engulfing dark. The dark of a cave. The dark of night. The dark of evil.

Felicity shook her head. This would never do. With a sharp reminder to herself that she was in charge, she forced herself to thank Gladys and her helpers for their hospitality, and then gave a hand with the clean-up. When the tables were folded and their hostesses departed, leaving well-filled covered plates for the absent, Felicity gathered her tiny flock at the front of the church and asked Nancy to lead in evening prayers.

"Is it all right to say Compline instead, since it's so late?"

In her nervous state Felicity wanted to snap, *Anything. Just do it.* But instead she merely nodded.

"'He who dwells in the shelter of the Most High abides under the shadow of the Almighty… There shall no evil happen to you, neither shall any plague come near your dwelling. For he shall give his angels charge over you…'"

The reassuring words of the reading continued to enfold them, but Felicity wanted to argue, *Never mind about us. Protect Antony. And the others,* she added hastily.

"Well," she stood at the end of the brief service. "I'm sure the van will be here soon." *Please, Lord,* she added under her breath. "But since our bedrolls aren't here yet," she fought to keep any note of despair out of her voice, "why don't you all, as they say, take a pew." The benches were long, constructed from a mellow wood with scrolled backs. The pilgrims adjusted themselves with good humor, using their rucksacks for pillows and their jackets for covers.

When everyone was settled, Felicity padded stocking-footed up the stone flags of the wide aisle to the Gothic arch framing the altar and stepped up into the most sacred part of the church. The panels of the stained-glass window stared at her, sightless as blind eyes. But the red lights of the sanctuary lamps hanging on either side flickered hope.

Taking a cushion from a server's chair, she sat on the floor. By rights, she supposed she should be kneeling on the bare stones, like a medieval knight keeping a vigil, but she knew her limitations. She tried to form a coherent prayer, but words wouldn't come. Finally, she fell back on the most familiar, *Our Father... Deliver us from evil...* Then she sat in silence.

Every time her mind filled with a worrying image, she blocked it, only to have it replaced by a more worrying one. What if—? What if Antony didn't come back? The void was too terrible to contemplate. She put her head between her knees, a ball of misery.

Time refused to pass. Each breath was an act of will for her.

Dark figures whispering strange words penetrated her consciousness. She shook her head, dizzy with confusion. She must have slept. How else could she have been dreaming?

Slowly her sleep-clouded brain cleared and she realized— Antony! And Michael and Lydia. She was giddy with joy as she jumped to her feet, then had to grab hold of the altar to steady her swirling head.

Antony came to her in a few swift strides and she clung to him. "I was so worried. So worried," she sobbed.

At the back of the church, Lydia and Michael crawled into their sleeping bags. Those pilgrims who had wakened dragged their bedrolls in from the van, then resumed their disturbed sleep. Antony and Felicity stayed in the chancel, leaning against the rough stones of the east wall, hands clasped, fingers entwined. Felicity knew she would never want to let go. At first she didn't even want to talk, just to savor the comfort of his dear presence, the relief of having him returned to her.

But at last her curiosity won out. "Tell me. Where was he? Is he all right? What took you so long? What happened?"

Antony sighed. "I wish I knew. I don't have a clear picture at all. It took us ages to find him, in spite of Ryan's map of the caves. Michael wasn't in the main one Ryan explored, but in a smaller one around the back of the quarry. We almost didn't bother looking in there because the entrance was so low. We had to leave our packs and crawl on our stomachs, pulling ourselves forward with our hands." She felt his convulsive shudder at the memory.

For the first time, Felicity noticed the bandages on his knees. She wrapped her arms around him in an effort to stop his trembling.

"I hope I never have to do anything like that again. Ever. We wouldn't have if I hadn't spotted the mark carved by the entrance."

Felicity chilled. She didn't really have to ask. "Double-headed snake on a triangle?"

Antony nodded and was silent for a moment, remembering. "The passage was maybe ten feet long, then opened out into a wide chamber. Michael was sitting there."

"Just sitting?"

"Sitting and staring. At first he didn't even respond when we spoke to him. It was like we weren't there. Or he wasn't. I thought maybe he was concussed, but he didn't seem to have any head injuries. Finally Lydia brought him around. I don't know what she said to him—I was on the other side of the chamber, praying. Couldn't think of anything else to do." He paused. "It sounded like a rhyme or a sort of chant. Then she clapped her hands and he blinked. It still took him ages to come around to be alert enough to crawl out."

"But what did he say?"

"Something about a pool. A pool being empty."

"Maybe he was thirsty. Caves often have pools, don't they? Maybe he found a pool but couldn't get a drink."

"Maybe. He had left his pack in the minibus and he certainly drank plenty when we eventually got back to it. But I don't know about the pool. Lydia did explore."

"Further in the cave, you mean?"

"She thought it might be important to know what he was talking about. There were two passages branching out of the chamber. I'm afraid I didn't have the stomach for it, so she went. I sat there and tried to talk to Michael. Tried to get through to him. Maybe it helped a little. Hard to tell."

Alarm seized Felicity. Was this like all the other incidents? How could so many things go wrong in such a short time? Was their pilgrimage being sabotaged? But why? And how could they combat anything so amorphous? She came on this walk to get away from the haunting image she thought she had left behind. Now it seemed it had followed her.

"Antony, we've got to find out more about this Orbis Astri thing."

He leaned over and kissed her cheek. "I couldn't agree more. But first we've got to sleep. Don't move. I'll get our bags."

He placed them close enough together that Felicity could reach out and touch him. Hear his deep, even breathing as he fell asleep. She wanted to lay there, looking at him in the flickering red light of the sanctuary candle overhead, but eventually her eyes closed.

Trees surrounding the churchyard morphed into grotesque shapes that chased her toward dark, gaping holes in the earth. Cowled monks processed through the trees chanting the twenty-third psalm. Felicity wakened whispering, "Though I walk through the valley of the shadow of death, I shall fear no evil." The words should have been comforting. Yet she was afraid. Antony had warned her about the real substance of evil. Still, she refused to blame all this on the diabolical. There had to be a rational, human explanation.

Chapter 16

Antony woke the next morning worrying about what he would do if Michael was unable to drive. He would have to do it himself, he supposed, but he felt the need to be with his pilgrims. Felicity had done a fine job bringing them through yesterday, but he didn't want to put that on her today, and with all that had been going on…

When he reached the back of the church where the walkers were busying themselves with filling bowls with muesli and topping it with sliced bananas and cream, however, he found his driver apparently fully coherent, poring over a map. "The road out west off this blessed mountain is too steep for the minibus. I'm going to have to go back the way I came all the way to Pontypridd and take the A4233 around to Penrhys. Were you wanting to meet up in Stanleytown, Father?"

Giving thanks for Michael's clarity, Antony considered. "No, it looks likely we'll get to Penrhys before you do. Let's just meet at the shrine."

Lydia leaned over Michael's shoulder to look at their route, then turned to Nancy. "Right. You're going to ride this morning, my girl."

Nancy looked disappointed. "It really doesn't hurt."

"And we want to keep it that way. It's straight up the hill to that shrine." Lydia turned to her brother. "Squib?"

"I'm walking," Adam declared.

Antony was pleased she had given him a choice.

Still musing on the restorative powers of sleep, Antony shepherded his flock out into the fresh June morning. Maybe a bit too fresh. The breeze felt damp, as if it could blow in a rain, but for the moment the piney scent of the forest offered Edenic refreshment. Ryan showed not the least lingering effects of his former bewilderment as he led the way between the church and the inn across the road, and turned south.

Where the track headed off into the forest they were greeted by a plaque inscribed: *Bendithiaf yr Arglwydd bob amser. Ei foliant fydd yn fy ngenau yn wastad.* Underneath the translation: "'I will bless the Lord at all times; his praise shall continually be in my mouth.' Psalm 34." Antony smiled. A perfect spot for a Station. They were ready for Jesus meets His mother— just the meditation to do before reaching Penrhys.

Felicity, whose attention had been claimed by helping everyone get sorted after their disturbed night, stood next to him close enough for their shoulders to touch, and they exchanged a smile. On his left, however, Chloe stood almost equally close. He shifted slightly under the guise of raising his hands. "The Lord be with you."

"And also with you."

They continued on after the brief meditation. In spite of the steep descent, the walk out of the forest was pleasant. Colin had attached himself to Lydia this morning for his nonstop monologue. Felicity, Jared and the Goths formed a group in the middle and Chloe remained beside Antony. Close beside him. "You'll be going back to the States when your holiday is over?" he asked.

"Yeah, I have a job lined up with a photographer's studio in Portland. This has been an amazing experience, though. And what about you? What do you do when this is over?"

He hoped he didn't sound too pointed. "Felicity and I are getting married after Christmas."

She grinned. "Yeah, I know."

"Oh, Felicity told you?"

"She didn't have to. I could tell."

"How's that?" Antony was surprised; they had spent little enough time together, walking at opposite ends of the line of march as they usually did.

"Your whole face softens when you say her name. If I could capture that I'd make a fortune selling it to a greeting card company."

"With a soppy caption under it?"

Chloe replied, but he missed her words because just then Felicity looked back over her shoulder and caught his eye. She winked at him and he missed a breath. *Next week*, he promised himself. *St Non's Retreat. Peace and quiet at last.*

The way continued to drop steeply and the density of the forest thinned. "Wild strawberries!" Evie's cry caught everyone's attention.

"And daisies," Kaylyn added.

Below them was *Cefn Llechau* farm; from there they would pick up the metaled road down to Stanleytown. A good place to take a break. In spite of the dampness of the grass, the walkers didn't seem reluctant to sit on it. Too bad Michael couldn't have met them here; a cup of tea wouldn't go amiss right now, Antony thought as he took his water bottle from his pack. Felicity strolled over and offered him a granola bar.

As he and Felicity chatted, Antony vaguely noticed Evie and Kaylyn gathering daisies, but it wasn't until the girls approached them did he realize they had made chains. Circlets to be exact. Evie placed hers on Felicity's long golden tresses, worn unbraided today. He smiled and applauded with the others. "Titania!" Evie declared.

Too late he realized what was coming next. "And Oberon!" Kaylyn dropped a circlet on his head. No matter how foolish he felt, there was no graceful refusal. Even when Chloe insisted on snapping numerous poses.

"Now, look at each other," she directed.

"If you sell that I get a cut," was the strongest protest he could make. Felicity, at least, was radiant.

In spite of darkening clouds they carried on in a light-hearted vein down into the valley where Ryan pointed out the eighty terraced houses lining the hillside ahead of them. "They were built in 1895 by the Stanley Building Society at a cost of £166 each." He went on to give more information about the history of the bridge they would cross over the Rhondda Fach river. "*Pontygwaith*, it means ironworks…"

But Antony was too focused on the moment to take it in. Too busy rejoicing. On the other side of the bridge, steps led through the green straight up the hill. With every step Antony repeated to himself, "We made it. We made it. Through it all, we made it. Thank You." Whether he was more grateful or relieved, he wasn't certain.

But when they crowned the top and he saw before them across the wide, flat green space, the gleaming white statue of Mary holding the Christ Child high on her plinth, he had nothing but amazement. He had seen pictures, but he was unprepared for the sheer, majestic height of the figure before him.

Chloe snapped pictures while the others gathered around the base, all craning their necks, studying the face they had come so far to see. Mary stood above them, her crowned head bent toward the Child she held out for all to see. The folds of her robe and cape fell to the carved branches of an oak tree curling at her feet.

Antony's exultation at having achieved their goal faded when he saw the puzzled faces surrounding him. "This is it, then?" Jared asked.

"This is what we walked all this way to see?" Evie's voice held contempt.

Antony considered. How could he make the story of this stone effigy come alive? Eight hundred years of history and devotion, shrouded in mists of obscure legend… He pictured the simple peasants that would have lived here, farming these verdant slopes in the early 1100s. Records said there was a monastery there about that time, but was it there before the statue appeared or built after to shelter pilgrims? Accounts were unclear. Some said it was an order of Franciscans, but St Francis himself wouldn't be born for another 100 years. Surely the Cistercians from Llantarnam were the first.

Taking a deep breath, Antony stood with the statue to his back. How near was this to the place the tree had grown? Legend said it was close. He would do his best. "Why don't you all sit down? With a little imagination I'll try to give you a picture of what it was like here 900 years ago."

Ffodor ap Barris struggled to rise from his straw-stuffed mat in the loft. Dawn rays taunted him through cracks in the eastern wall. In the room below he heard Addfwyn crooning to the bairns as she set fresh oatcakes and ale on the board. Unlike her name, his woman was not meek. Never mind how his muscles ached from the scything yesterday. Today the barley must be gathered. Thank God that the rains held off until the harvest was in. Two more days with the help of his near neighbors, Garnoc and Eurwyn, and all would be safe. Then only the sheep to see to until the rhythms of the year circled round again to seedtime. The endless cycle—seedtime and harvest. And so it would be for him until he was planted in the soil with his fathers.

"Ffodor ap Barris!"

"Aye, woman, Nid ydym am gael rhagor o drafferth.*"*
No more of your trouble he meant, but he knew better

than to be so blunt. He descended the ladder, consumed his oatcake almost whole, emptied his tankard, and lashed on his boots. Addfwyn handed him more cakes and a chunk of pungent sheep's cheese wrapped in a cloth, which he tucked inside his tunic.

"Which garth do you work today?" she asked, filling a stone jug with ale for him.

"Garnoc ap Ynyr." The furthest field, on the top of the hill. It would catch the most wind so they would gather it first.

In spite of his surly mood, however, the late summer air bearing the scent of harvest and the streaks of sun breaking over the hill lifted Ffodor's spirit. He met the others as usual at the ancient well, where they all drank from the communal dipper before starting up the hill.

The sun dazzled Ffodor's sight as he crested the hill almost under the boughs of the spreading oak tree that was its crown. He looked up into the thick green branches, admiring how the light rimmed the leaves. Fall would bring a good crop of acorns to feed the village pigs. His mind was still on crisp bacon and fat hams when he looked higher in the branches.

"What gwirion thing is this?" He stood staring up at the figure that seemed to be growing from the branches.

Garnoc joined him. "Aye, daft, indeed. Who would put a statue of Our Lady in a tree?"

But Eurwyn fell to his knees, crossing himself. "It's a miracle. We must get Father Ilan."

"And will Father Ilan be helping to gather my barley, are you thinking?"demanded Ffodor.

Eurwyn was adamant. The Mother of Our Lord took precedence, even over the harvest. The priest was summoned. And with him all the women and children of the village, including Addfwyn carrying the infant Iddig in her arms.

Ffodor cringed. He was certain to earn a sharp scolding for being the one whose keen eyes had caused all this bother.

His arms spread wide, Father Ilan gave thanks that a miracle had been visited on them. "My soul declareth the glory of God and my heart rejoiceth in God my Savior that the Mother of my Lord should visit us… His mercy is on them that fear Him in every generation, He has shown the strength of His arm…"

When his song was finished, Father Ilan declared, "She must be brought down." And then he turned to Ffodor. "My son, you saw her first, to you belongs the privilege."

Ffodor took a step backward, but Garnoc and Eurwyn grasped him under the arms and boosted him up the trunk of the vast tree. There was nothing for it but to grasp the bottom branch and pull himself up. Below, his neighbors cheered him on and Garnoc called out a rude jest.

Here in the branches the foliage was thick, the bark rough under his hands. He looked up. There she was, the Virgin Mary lodged in a fork in the branches, holding her precious Babe as serenely as if she were in her own home. What daft person had put her here? And why wasn't that troublemaker the one to be charged with getting her down instead of keeping a man from his honest labor in the field?

Ffodor swung up to the next level of branches and reached forward to grasp the smooth carved wooden figure. He hoped it wouldn't be thought a sacrilege if he threw her down to waiting hands below. There really was no way he could climb and carry the bulky statue.

But he needn't have worried. The Virgin was not coming with him. She resisted his first single-handed pluck, so he inched out further on the branch and grasped her more firmly with both hands. The resistance was beyond that of a figure firmly stuck. More resistant even than if he had attempted to dislodge a living limb. The statue was an immovable force.

He couldn't imagine the ridicule he would face when he descended empty-handed, but there was nothing else for it.

Father Ilan, however, didn't seem surprised. "Aye. Go about your labors, then. I'll keep vigil here. This evening we'll hitch a team of oxen and see what they may do."

Ffodor shook his head. "Not if you hitched eight oxen, Father. She'll not budge."

And so it proved, although many others tried.

As soon as the harvest was in, and a bountiful yield it was, too—many said the best they had ever known—all the village set about building a fine wattle and daub shrine chapel with a snugly thatched roof to shelter the holy Mother and Child. Surely when the winter gales blew and snows piled on the bare branches of the oak tree the Mother would deign to bring her holy Babe into shelter then. They prepared a fine alcove niche at one end, and Ffodor himself fashioned a cross to go on the wall. He was no master carver, but long evenings by the fire whittling with his knife had prepared him well enough to carve a loving corpus for the crucifix. All was ready.

In a repeat of the earlier exercise, they gathered at dawn. At Father Ilan's direction Garnoc and Eurwyn again boosted Ffodor to the bottom branches. This time Ffodor swung up full of anticipation. And it almost seemed that it was a matter of the holy Mother moving to him as much as his moving to her. She felt like a living thing in his arms. Prepared as he was this time, he fixed her snugly in the sling he wore around his neck, and they returned lightly to the earth.

Father Ilan bore her aloft; Ffodor followed with his new-carved cross. The village trooped behind them into the chapel—inaugurating what was to become the first pilgrimage to Our Lady of Penrhys.

Nancy, who with Michael had joined them midway through the story, was the first to speak. "What happened next?"

Antony spied the welcoming group from the Uniting Church, who regularly met pilgrims for a special service and tea in their church hall, approaching across the greensward. He also saw the darkening clouds rolling in overhead, and felt the wind whipping up from the south. As a matter of fact, the first spatters of rain had begun to fall from the edge of the cloud bank. He would summarize the rest of the story: "For more than four hundred years, the site continued as one of the holiest sites for Christian pilgrims in Wales. By 1538, King Henry VIII was two years into his process of dissolving all religious houses in England, Wales and Ireland—appropriating their income for his coffers when Hugh Latimer, Bishop of Worcester, wrote to Thomas Cromwell, Henry's chancelor, pleading for the continuation of some of the larger abbeys, but advocating the destruction of such shrines as Our Lady of Walsingham and Our Lady of Penrhys."

The darkness increased overhead, the wind drove harder, slanting the rain at them from the side, rather than on their heads, but the story would not be hurried:

"The shrine's on fire!" Young Gwillan ap Ffodor jumped from his pallet and ran to the door of the cottage his family had lived in for generations. Even here at the foot of the hill he could see the hungry orange flames leap from the roof and lick the night sky. The crackle became louder as he raced up the hill with other villagers roused from their sleep. When they reached the top of the hill, the smoke, whipped by the wind, burned their eyes.

"Our Lady! She'll burn. And her holy Babe!" Gwillan ran toward the door, but strong arms held him back.

"Nae, lad. She's nae there."

"What do you mean? Sure she is. Where else would she be?" He fought to free himself from the restraining grasp.

"Halfway to Lunnon, I've no doubt. Henry's men would nae risk rousing the village until they were well on their way."

"They've stolen Our Lady?"

"Aye, I heard the rattle of the iron wheels of the cart on the path, but I didn't take the meaning of it until I saw the flames. It's the times, lad. The way of the world. There's no use fighting it."

Gwillan shook his head. The words made no sense to him. But he understood one thing. Our Lady was not in the flames. She was gone. But that was not the end. It could not be the end. Our Lady of Penrhys had come to them, bringing her Son, the Lord Christ, to this mountain top. To the surrounding valleys. The white monks had dwelt with her and looked after her, and had ministered to all, far and wide, and taught the way of our Lord. It could not be the end.

"She'll come back. She'll come back and bring her Son." In spite of the sob in his voice Gwillan flung his words defiantly. They must be heard over the roar of the flames. They must.

Antony zipped his anorak, pulling the collar tight around his neck. He longed to turn his back to the driving rain, but that would force his hearers to face into the storm. He could finish the account later, but all were intent. Best to complete it on the spot. "Two months later, on a crisp September day in London, perhaps not unlike the day on which our simple Welsh farmer first discovered her in the branches of the oak tree, Our Lady of Penrhys, Our Lady of Walsingham and two of their Sisters were burned in a great bonfire. Some say the burning was at Tyburn—the traditional place for the execution of criminals in London, and where just a year earlier Henry had executed the leaders who had marched against the closing of the northern monasteries in the Pilgrimage of Grace.

"But wherever it was, the Shrine of Our Lady—even in its empty state—was still visited throughout the following centuries, with records showing devotion up until 1842. In the early twentieth century, a devout lady financed the building of a memorial church in the valley below in Ferndale—complete with a wooden replica of the original statue. In 1936, the Ferndale priest revived the ancient pilgrimage tradition."

A sheet of water hit Antony full from the side. The wind whipped at his words. He raised his voice, determined to finish the story. "This statue—" He raised his face to look up at the modern stone statue towering almost straight above his head, then wished he hadn't as rain sluiced his face. "This statue was erected in 1953, using descriptions from Welsh medieval poetry to reconstruct the original as closely as possible." *Although obviously much larger.*

It was unnecessary to add the caveat, and it would have been futile as the strength of the wind and volume of the rain increased. If Mair, their hostess from the Uniting Church, hadn't turned to lead them down the wet, green slope, they would likely have been washed down.

The tiny stone hut built into the hillside at the bottom of the incline couldn't shelter all their group at once, but those who didn't make it through the small doorway into *Ffynnon Fair*, Mary's Well, huddled against the north wall for protection. Antony was with the last group to duck into the dim interior of the small rectangular building. Stone benches circled around three walls; a cistern occupied the south end. It was a blessed relief to be out of the driving rain, but it was equally chill inside. Until he felt Felicity snuggle close to him. Their exchange of smiles warmed the room. "This is the original building," he told those around him. "Heavily restored, of course. The niche," he pointed to the wall opposite the well, "was said to have held a statue of Mary."

Felicity started to say something, but the sound that emerged was that of chattering teeth. "Right, into the minibus," Antony directed. "We'll have to rearrange the luggage—"

Michael pulled the keys from his pocket and handed them across. "Yeah, here you go."

Thankfully, the violence of the storm let up as they made their way back up the hill to the vehicles. It took some time to shift the bags that had been hastily loaded that morning, largely by the simple expedient of tossing them onto empty seats. Careful packing cleared all but the back row of seats. Antony suggested Felicity and Nancy go ahead with Mair and their other hosts. The rest of them would follow in a minute when Michael caught them up. Antony smiled. Michael had probably wanted to use the shelter of a wall for a comfort stop.

Antony's smile had faded, though, long before he saw Michael's damp, black curls appear over the crest of the hill. "Sorry." Michael jumped into the driver's seat and shook his head, spraying water on those around him. "Didn't mean for you to wait. I could have walked into town."

Antony didn't reply as his attention was arrested by Michael's hands on the steering wheel. A long, jagged scrape on the back of his right hand oozed blood. His nails were darkened by what appeared to be fresh mud. What had Michael been doing at Mary's Well?

He continued to consider as they drove through the wet, gray streets lined with dispirited shops, but could formulate no satisfying theory. The modern yellow brick structure of the Uniting Church offered a bright spot on yet another gray street. And the hearty mugs of hot tea and spicy sausage rolls, accompanied by their hosts' warm greeting, provided a welcome relief to Antony's unformed worry.

"We were built in 1971 by the churches of the Rhondda." Mair's cap of dark hair gleamed, and without her padded coat she appeared much smaller than she had on the hilltop. She continued her explanation to Felicity as she offered Antony a plate of small pork pies. "We're the only church in Wales supported and recognized by eight different denominations. We offer worship and services for all the local community."

"That's wonderful. That's just the sort of cooperation Father Antony's Ecumenical Commission works to support," Felicity said, and Antony smiled around his bite of pork pie.

"It's grand for the whole area," Mair agreed. "We offer after-school homework clubs and music lessons for children, a café, a launderette, a nearly new shop—"

"And hospitality for pilgrims," Felicity added.

Another of their hosts, a plump, bald man in an Arran jumper, brought a refill of tea in a heavy, aluminum teapot. "And where do you go on from here, Father?" he asked, after Antony had sweetened his tea with three sugars and a hearty dollop of milk.

"The Rhondda Heritage Park this afternoon. We stay in Aberdare for Sunday and go on to St David's Monday." Antony's smile showed how much he was looking forward to their time of peaceful retreat.

"Oh, aye, you'll enjoy the Heritage Park. They do a grand job of showing what it was like hereabouts 100 years ago."

Mair shuddered. "Grim it was, Colin. Some things are best forgot."

"I don't agree. We need to remember the struggles of the past to appreciate what we have now."

Mair was adamant. "All those who died in the pits. Or more slowly from the Black Death."

"But there were the good times, too. Family, community, singing—"

"You don't have to go backwards for the music." Mair said to her guests. "If you're in Aberdare tonight and needing to get the coal dust out of your lungs, you'd be more than welcome to come along to the rehearsal of our male voice choir." She smiled at Felicity. "Just six weeks until the Eisteddfod."

Antony turned to find the pastor of the Uniting Church. Their brief midday prayer service was to be a keynote of the ecumenical theme of their youth walk, and Antony felt a great desire to give thanks for their safe arrival after all they had gone through. And to make a fervent request for the bulwark to remain strong.

He knew he would feel better if he could put a face on the dark shadows that seemed to plague them. But they *had* made it. For that they must give thanks.

Chapter 17

T he wind and the rain blew on across mountain and valley, but the glowering dark clouds remained. In spite of the low-hanging canopy, however, they took the scenic route along the fabled Rhondda Valley. Felicity sat glued to her window watching intently as tiny villages tucked in a narrow valley between steep hills rolled by on both sides of the van. Rows of terraced houses sitting on shelves ran up the vertical slopes. She couldn't begin to think how depressing it must be in the winter. Surely it would get dark by two in the afternoon, with what little sun might shine being blocked by the hills.

The clouds hadn't lifted when they arrived at the Rhondda Heritage Park. Their tour of the once-working colliery was led by a burly former miner in a black overall and white hard hat. "For centuries the Rhondda Valleys were a pastoral paradise: clear running streams and waterfalls, lush with trees and plants. The sheep-rearing farmers that populated the scattered farmhouses existed as they had for centuries, as a sleepy rural community." Maddoc, their guide, painted a picture of these hills as they would have been when St David strode over them. "Until the second half of the nineteenth century. Then, coal was discovered. By the end of the century, the Rhondda was one of the most important coal producing areas in the world. At its peak, the coal industry in Wales employed one in every ten persons, and many more relied on the industry for their livelihood. Rhondda alone at one time contained fifty-three working collieries, in an area only sixteen miles long. It was the most intensely mined area in the world, and probably one of the most densely populated."

He continued talking as they walked to the winding house, "In its heyday, Rhondda's coal was as important as the oil produced by the Middle East today. This Welsh Valley helped to power the world."

In the winding house, a multimedia exhibition recreated the everyday life of the miner.

"In the winter, men went to work in the dark, went down into the pit, came up in the dark. They only saw the sun one day a week." The statistics flashed on the screen: "One miner dies every 6 hours. One is seriously injured every 2 minutes…"

The images of disasters leapt at them—fireballs, flooding, explosion. All with actual photos.

Maddoc led on to the lamp room, where they collected their safety lamps and helmets. "Right then, you're ready now, are you?"

Jared and Adam gave enthusiastic answers, but Kaylyn, standing next to Felicity, sounded less sure. "Ready for what?"

Maddoc's eyes glinted as he answered her. "Ready for the cage to the pit bottom, for your underground experience. You'll be descending just like a working miner." He opened the door of what appeared to be a rather tinny elevator. The pilgrims filed in, although Felicity could sense Kaylyn's reluctance.

The door closed. Maddoc turned to operate the control panel, then paused and turned back. "No one here pregnant? Or with a heart problem? Claustrophobia?" Kaylyn tensed and Felicity looked over to see how Antony felt about this. He wasn't fond of inclosed spaces, but his attention seemed to be on something Colin was showing him. Distraction was probably best.

"This winding engine generates 120 psi steam pressure, 2,500 horsepower, it descends to a depth of 434 meters at a speed of 30 a second," the guide continued, and Felicity heard Kaylyn's sharp intake of breath. "All right, then?" Maddoc asked, his hand hesitating over the lever.

Felicity turned to the girl beside her. "You don't have to do this."

She wasn't sure what Kaylyn meant to communicate by her nod, but the tight, white face was enough for Felicity. "No. We'll wait for you in the café." She grabbed the girl's ice-cold hand, and they fled through the door before their guide had it fully opened.

Felicity led her to the café and secured two cups of tea. They sat at a small table next to a window. The lowering clouds seemed to push at the glass like an animal pressing to gain entrance. Kaylyn turned her back to the window, her coal-black hair stark against the gloom. "I'm only mildly claustrophobic. I only panicked the first time."

"First time for what?"

The long jet hair covered Kaylyn's face as she lowered her head. "The first time my ma locked me in a cupboard."

Felicity managed to suppress her gasp. She waited, sensing the girl would go on.

"She didn't want me wandering out, you see. I did once. I didn't understand that her visitors were… business…"

Felicity reached over and took her hand. "Kaylyn, it's all right. There was no need to go down the mineshaft. Although, if it helps any, I think the ride was simulated. But don't worry. No one is going to lock you in anywhere. You're free."

The hand Felicity held started to relax when a growling roar filled the room and the building shook as if from a tremor. "No!" Kaylyn cried, her eyes wide with fright.

"Kaylyn, don't worry. It's part of the exhibition. They're

starting up some of the antique mine equipment." Felicity sounded more confident than she felt. But that must be the explanation. "I'm sure it sounded like this all the time here when the mine was operating." She looked around. The waitress behind the counter calmly put a piece of cake on a plate and handed it to another visitor. "See, no one else is bothered at all."

Kaylyn shook her head insistently. "Can't you feel it? We're being oppressed." *Nonsense*, Felicity wanted to say. That was what she kept repeating to herself, determined that it had to be rubbish. In spite of what Antony had said, she didn't believe in demons. Well, not in that way. Not roaring like lions in a café in a green Welsh valley.

"Through with your tea? Let's walk around a bit. Take a look at what they have in the gift shop." *Anything to get our minds off that earthshaking roar.* Fortunately it had silenced after the third bellow.

They crossed the hall into the brightly lit shop, where a glass case of silver jewelry caught Kaylyn's attention. Felicity was beginning to relax as well. She would buy a box of fudge for Antony—the funny pale gold kind that bore little resemblance to the dense chocolate confection Americans called fudge.

She was paying for it when she noticed a card someone had dropped—or placed—on the counter by the cash register. She picked up the square, white rectangle and turned it over. Then dropped it as sharply as if the two-headed snake engraved there had bitten her.

Felicity took a deep breath. *It's only a piece of paper,* she told herself. But she remained unconvinced. She steadied her hand and picked it up again. The card announced a lecture the Orbis Astri was sponsoring in Cwmdare that night, wherever that was. "*The Golden Dawn* by Israel Regardie, the book that started the modern occult movement. The Third Level. Learn: initiation rituals, equinox ceremonies, consecration liturgy…"

In spite of her reflex to look for a means of burning the invitation, Felicity forced herself to think calmly. The lecture it announced sounded perfectly respectable, she argued. *Nutty, and bad theology, but respectable.*

Yet as she held the card, the snakes writhed. She saw herself picking the paper up not from a glass counter, but from Hwyl's outstretched, lifeless hand. Why was he holding that symbol? What was he trying to tell her?

"Ready to go?"

Felicity jumped at Antony's voice in her ear.

"Sorry. Didn't mean to startle you. Are you all right?"

She shook her head and handed him the card.

"Right." He put it in his pocket. "Later. We need to get on now. Is Kaylyn all right?"

Across the room, the girl was busy showing a red velor dragon to Evie. Felicity nodded.

They drove back up the valley of the Afon Rhondda Fach to the village of Trecynon near Aberdare. The centerpiece of the small community was a vast, green, well-landscaped park, its colorful floral plantings gleaming even in the dim light of the gloomy evening. Michael pulled the van to a stop on a narrow street in front of a tall gray stucco church behind a stone and wrought iron fence. A wide, red-tile walkway led to the porch capped by three likewise red-tiled gables. Above that the second storey rose with three tall, narrow, round-arched windows below the words *Ebenezer Capel ye Annibynwyr.* "Ebenezer Independent Chapel," Michael translated.

A gray-haired lady walked toward them, the wind whipping her red raincoat. "Ah, that's good. You're here, then. I'm Enid. Afraid I'm your only greeter at the moment," she told them in her lilting voice. "The caretaker left for Spain this morning, and the secretary is in Cardiff."

She led them through the iron gates, up the red-tile walk and around to the back. "There are only about a dozen of us now, but we're the mother church of Congregationalism in this region. The Revival spread outwards from here, as you doubtless know. Evan Roberts preached here after the Moriah Chapel."

Felicity was trying to sort that out when their hostess drew a ring of keys from her pocket and opened the door to a vast church hall. "Oh, my goodness," Felicity expressed her amazement at the size of the space.

Enid smiled. "Huge, isn't it? Built in the mid-1800s. The congregation filled it in those days. The sanctuary was built in 1826 and was enlarged many times. Now we do rather rattle round in it, I'm afraid. We have a choir, though." She pointed to a poster on the wall. With another choir they would be performing Fauré's "Requiem" the next week.

"That's wonderful. You Welsh certainly live up to your legendary choral tradition." A rich aroma from the kitchen caught Felicity's attention. "Mmm, that smells good."

"You're getting cawl tonight." Enid looked pleased at her announcement.

Felicity looked blank.

"Have you not had it?" Now Enid looked horrified. "Cawl is the national dish of Wales—a stew of bacon, lamb, cabbage and leeks. Sit you down," she pointed to chairs set at a long table. "I'm sure it's ready."

A few minutes later Felicity savored the tasty concoction filling the bowl in front of her, then considered their surroundings. This all seemed so out of character for her high church Antony. She hadn't realized his ecumenism reached so wide. She finished her bite of potato, then turned to him. "What was she talking about? Revival?"

Antony nodded. "That's why we're here. 1904 it was. An amazing story, but a long one. Dyfrig Griffiths, a local expert on the subject, will tell us all about it tomorrow."

"That will make quite a change from medieval saints."

Antony smiled. "It's all part of the story."

They were just finishing the last of their meal when Chloe joined them. "Enid says the rehearsal hall for the male voice choir is just across the park. We can walk."

"Is everyone going?" Felicity asked.

"I think so. You're coming, aren't you? When will we ever have another opportunity?"

Felicity was torn. She loved Welsh male voice choirs, but she desperately needed to talk to Antony. "It sounds great, but I think I'll give my blisters a rest."

The others spread out their bedrolls in case the rehearsal ran late, then departed, leaving Felicity and Antony in blessed quiet. Felicity attached the battery pump and inflated her air mattress, then made a cozy nest with her pillow and pack as she leaned against the wall.

Antony sat beside her. "All right. Now, tell me what happened with you and Kaylyn this afternoon. You looked like you'd seen a ghost when I found you."

She told him the best she could about the roar, howl, growl, she wasn't sure how to describe it. "Were you the only ones who heard it?"

"I didn't ask. I told Kaylyn no one else was reacting because it was part of the exhibit."

"Did you believe that?"

"I wanted to."

"Did Kaylyn believe it?"

Felicity shook her head. "She said it was oppression. I sort of shrugged it off because I didn't know what to say."

"It sounds like a rather good description of what's been going on. Deliverance ministers often use the term 'negativity.'"

"Which means?"

"Evil influence—headaches, animosities, bad dreams…"

"Strange noises?"

"A rather common occurrence in the case of demonic activity, I'm afraid."

Felicity shuddered. "We talked about being possessed before. Are you talking about that now? Like casting out demons in the Bible?"

"Not that extreme. Oppression involves demonic attack from time to time, causing fear, stress, conflict…" His voice was calm and even. Almost matter-of-fact.

"So what's the cure?"

Again Antony's voice was prosaic, as if they were discussing a routine, rational matter. "Prayer, fasting, the sacraments—especially confession and communion—living a Christian life."

Felicity considered. "That's something I really don't understand. If Hwyl wasn't pushed—if he jumped off that tower because he was under some demonic control—oppression—how could it be? He was a priest. He did everything you just said regularly, surely."

Antony nodded gravely. "I intend to find out when we get to St David's."

Felicity was sleeping lightly when the others returned, chatting about the concert. "Mair was amazing. I didn't realize she was the *director*," Ryan spoke above the others.

Nancy laughed. "Could you believe that little woman could sing over the entire fifty-voice choir—and keep them all in strict order?"

"'Sunrise, Sunset' was really beautiful," Evie added. "Wasn't it, Jared?"

But Jared seemed preoccupied.

Felicity sat up and looked around the room as the others settled into their bedrolls. Then she realized not everyone had returned, "Where are Michael and Lydia?"

No one seemed to have noticed they weren't with them. Finally Adam spoke up. "I don't know. Lyds and Michael went off in the other direction when we crossed the park." His voice indicated he was glad enough to be free of his supervisor.

"Did they enjoy the concert?" Felicity wasn't sure why she asked that, but something didn't seem right.

"Never showed up, did they? Probably got, er—sidetracked." Adam showed a typical disdain of an older sibling's amours.

Felicity resisted the impulse to tuck him in bed. Instead she just said a casual, "Goodnight." And turned away. She had a terrible, niggling suspicion. Too vague even to voice it.

Chloe, the last to return from the ladies' room and snuggle into her sleeping bag, had turned out the overhead light, so Felicity dug in her pack for her torch before taking out the map she had carried all the days of the walking trip. She was quite certain the last page extended from Penrhys to Aberdare.

The pool of yellow light illuminated the red line running up the valley. There, in the center of Aberdare was Trecynon with its open expanse of park. And on the far side was what she feared, but expected. Cwmdare.

She crossed the room to Antony. She was as certain as if she had been told from their own lips. "Michael and Lydia went to the Orbis Astri lecture," she said. "I'm sure of it."

Chapter 18

Pentecost Sunday
Aberdare

ntony felt someone shaking him. It was still dark
and all around him sounded the heavy breathing of
youthful sleep. He struggled to sit up. What now? What
had gone wrong that couldn't wait until morning? He ran his
hand over his eyes. "Jared? What is it? Is it Michael and Lydia?"

"Huh? Oh, no. They came in right after you went to sleep.
Said they had a brilliant evening." Jared whispered close to his
ear. "But I just remembered—I thought I ought to tell you."

Antony was fully awake now. "Go on, then."

Jared continued at a whisper. "Last night, I saw someone. I'm
not sure… But it looked like him, and it made me think."

"Looked like him who?"

"Joe. I didn't want to upset Chloe, so I didn't say anything—
just kept thinking. Then I woke up and I knew." In spite of
having wakened Antony in the middle of the night to tell his
story, Jared now appeared reluctant to continue. He seemed
frightened.

"Go on. You can tell me. You saw Joe at the choir rehearsal?"
It seemed an unlikely place for the paraglider to show up. Unless
he was still following Chloe.

"No, in the park. It was dark, so I'm not sure, but that's what
made me remember."

Antony resisted the urge to pry the story out of him more

quickly. He knew that in cases like this, one had to let the teller do it their own way. "Joe was in the park?"

"Or someone that looked enough like him to jog my memory. It was the setting, you see, behind the bushes in the dark. Anyway, I think I know him. From Cardiff." Jared was quiet. Antony waited. "I'm pretty sure he was a supplier." Quiet again. "I used to be into that. Nothing hard, but cannabis; well, a little ecstasy, too. I don't do that any more, man, you've got to believe me."

Antony just nodded. It was all in the report he had been given.

"You won't put that on my report, will you?"

"I don't see there's anything to report. But Joe was a dealer?"

"Supplier. He supplied the dealers, I think. It's just that I saw them once in the park—"

"This guy that looked like Joe?"

Jared nodded. "Only kind of different. He wasn't so blond then. But he was with the guy that I bought from a few times. I don't think he saw me. You know, if he's recognized me…"

Antony nodded. "I see the problem. I don't think you have anything to worry about, but we'll keep a sharp eye out."

His story off his chest, Jared crawled back to bed and was soon breathing evenly. Antony, however, was awake until dawn. He would contact the local police. He wondered if Chloe knew Joe's full name. Unlikely that even the "Joe" was for real, though.

And perhaps he should ring Nosterfield as well. Could the activities of a drug ring explain what was going on? Many occult groups did use hallucinogenic drugs with their rites. But if Hwyl had found out something like that, why not just contact his local police rather than travel more than 300 miles to see him? If, indeed, that was what Hwyl was doing in Kirkthorpe.

Then Antony wondered about the incident with the Welsh cake. Was that the random attack of an enemy against the pilgrimage, as he had assumed? Or was it aimed more specifically at Jared and the wrong young male pilgrim took up the offer?

Almost two weeks left. He would, indeed, be vigilant as he promised Jared, but could he protect them all when he didn't know who or what he was fighting? And what of Felicity's information last night? Did it matter if Michael and Lydia had gone to the Orbis Astri lecture? They were adults. Still…

Antony finally dozed lightly until Enid and her husband, George, bustled in with their breakfast. And Antony realized it was Pentecost Sunday; one of his favorites in the church year. All through the commotion of the morning routine he was recalling Pentecost services of his past. His favorite was the often-used entrance canticle that began with a solo voice, "*Veni Sanctus Spiritus.*" Then another voice joined in, "*Veni Sanctus Spiritus.*" Then another, "*Veni Sanctus Spiritus.*" Until at last the entire congregation was expressing that heartfelt longing of the disciples waiting in the upper room, "Come, Holy Spirit."

The "Birthday of the Church." Often the Acts 2 account of the Holy Spirit coming upon the church was read in multiple languages, sometimes all at once to give a real sense of what that first Pentecost Sunday must have been like.

And then, a particular, vivid memory from the usually stodgy church Aunt Beryl and Uncle Edward had reared Antony and his sister in. Even at that young age, his sister, so different from himself, had shown little inclination for churchy things, but the day of her confirmation had been an exception. A dozen children, the girls in white dresses, the boys in white shirts, their hands filled with long, flame-colored streamers of red, gold, orange.

He could see Gwendolyn now, standing at the back of the long aisle of the stone church, morning light streaming through the stained glass, matching the ribbons she held aloft. The congregation sang, "Holy Spirit, rushing, burning wind and flame of Pentecost..." The ad hoc liturgical dance group ran, skipped and hopped up, down and around the aisles, clapping their hands and swirling their streamers of Pentecostal flame. And none with more enthusiasm than his sister.

"Holy Spirit, we welcome You, Holy Spirit, we welcome You." Tambourines jangled as robed priests and little gray-haired ladies alike moved to the music. Well, not Aunt Beryl, of course, but others. Then deacons and church wardens from each of the three churches that had come together for this service led the bishop, splendid in red and gold, to the altar.

Gwendolyn was radiant as she knelt and the bishop placed his hands on her head, "Defend, O Lord, this thy child with thy heavenly grace that she may continue thine forever..." The memory made him miss his sister. He must do a better job of keeping in touch.

Antony smiled as he entered the vast sanctuary of the Ebenezer Chapel. He had not imagined it would be so rich and warm. Hanging lights brightened the dull amber walls. Dark wooden pews filled both the main floor and the spacious gallery circling the walls on three sides. In the front, the massive pulpit rose in the center of the platform. And under the pulpit, the hallmark of a Welsh chapel—the "big seat"—a padded bench where the deacons sat in stern splendor facing the flock behind their encircling railing, keeping watch for any misdoing.

After the dismal account Enid had given of the size of their congregation, Antony was surprised as worshipers continued to file in. A few took seats in the balcony. It was explained when the minister welcomed their visitors. "Today, Pentecost Sunday, when we celebrate the coming of the Holy Spirit to the church, we are remembering here in Ebenezer Chapel a special coming of the Holy Spirit to Wales."

The congregation stood to sing a hymn and then the narrative began, not Antony telling this time, but various members of the congregation taking their turn in the lofty pulpit to tell a portion of the dramatic events that shook this valley 100 years ago. A serious-looking man in a dark suit said that because he was a law clerk he had chosen to recount the effects on the courts as his great-grandfather Evan Williams had told him:

Mr Justice Lewellyn, sedate in black robe, bands and white wig entered the empty courtroom and took his seat behind the tall, dark mahogany bench. The room, often so full of scrabbling and swearing that it took several moments to achieve order, today was cold and silent. Might as well be a mortuary. Evan Williams, his clerk, approached the bench and handed him a pair of white gloves, the symbol that there were no cases on the docket for that day. "What! Again?" That made three times this week.

Williams shrugged. "It's the Revival, yer honor."

The judge shook his head. "What's to become of all this I don't know. The theater was closed last weekend. My wife was sorely displeased."

"Aye. And my football club. Disbanded for lack of interest. What's this country without football, I ask you? And only one pub in town left open. That Evan Roberts should be had up, that's what I say."

Wales 1904. It was the same all across the country. Theaters, pubs, football pitches, dance halls, courtrooms—all empty. Chapels bursting at the seams. And yet no one could quite figure out what was happening.

The narrative was taken up by the current pastor of the congregation, reading accounts written by those who were there:

Here at Ebenezer Chapel the sober, sedate congregation that had gathered that morning received a shock. They looked askance when they saw their minister's place occupied by a young man, accompanied by maidens. The service should have begun with an orderly announcement of the opening hymn. Instead, one of the young women burst forth in a song. The whole congregation gasped.

She sang of her new experience, tears streaming down her cheeks. In spite of the raised eyebrows and pursed lips of the congregation another young woman stood and sang with her. Whatever next?

But the young minister in the pulpit remained absolutely silent, his body shaking as tears coursed down his pale cheeks. Then a strange stillness fell upon the people, like the quiet presaging an electric storm. It soon broke when one of the proudest members of the assembly fell on her knees in agonizing prayer and confessed her sins. Others followed rapidly and spontaneously. All over the chapel, men and women, young and old knelt in the pews and aisles, claiming "the blessing."

When the confessions ceased, extempore hymns began. The service lasted all day. Evan Roberts did not preach at all, only uttered such injunctions as, "Obey! Obey! Obey the Holy Spirit!" And his most frequent prayer, "Bend us, O Lord, Bend us."

One man who was given a seat on the deacons' bench recorded the scene: "With my back to the pulpit, I witnessed a sight that made me feel faint. Confronting and surrounding me was a mass of people, their faces aglow with divine radiance…" One section of the congregation was singing. In another part of the building scores were engaged simultaneously in prayer, some wringing their hands as if in mortal agony, others joyous in their newfound experience. Welsh and English were extravagantly intermingled.

All over the room people were testifying: A well-known singer, a radiant young woman, an elderly deacon, a Presbyterian minister, a young man with a stammer… A

man with a powerful voice spoke above them all, "Lo, the
winter is past, the rain is over and gone; the flowers appear
on the earth; the time of the singing of birds is come, and the
voice of the turtle is heard in our land."

When the glorious spiritual tumult was at its height,
there was a sudden calm. Evan Roberts stood in the pulpit. He
read St Paul's great love chapter, I Corinthians 13: "... and
though I have all faith, so that I could remove mountains,
and have not love, I am nothing—nothing—nothing." He
repeated the final word three times, then was silent.

A member of the congregation attempted an interruption,
but he was drowned out by ecstatic singing. Trying to force his
way to the pulpit, the would-be disruptant was overcome by
conviction. In a few moments the shout went up, "He has
been saved!"

"Haleliwia!"

"Praise the Lord!"

"Diolch Iddo!"

"A'r Ei ben bo'r goron!"

And then, one of the most remarkable elements of all
that remarkable day—the entire congregation began singing
in English, "Throw out the lifeline, throw out the lifeline..."
Never before would an English chorus have been sung in
such an orthodox assembly. To make the attempt would have
been rated almost a "sin against the Holy Ghost."... But this
Revival burned all linguistic barriers.

Through it all, the young Evan Roberts stood in the
pulpit, quiet and serene. Calmly, Roberts would direct
workers. "There is a woman outside to the left of the church
in spiritual distress. Will you go help her?" Some went. She
was there. They helped. "There is a young man at the far end
of the gallery, anxious for salvation. Will someone please help
him?" Someone did.

Other accounts followed of the events that covered all of Wales in a two-year period. The service closed with a final hymn and all were invited to the hall for a Jacob's join, which Felicity called a potluck. "What did you think of that?" Felicity asked around bites of pork pie after they were seated at a long table.

Antony had been asking himself the same thing. "I'll readily confess the emotionalism makes me uncomfortable. But I'm not certain the biblical account of Pentecost isn't just as strange—and many of the stories of the saints as well."

"It's sad, isn't it, that's it's all so—well, lifeless now."

Antony nodded. "I've read about this. I'm not an expert, but some have speculated that there might have been more lasting results if it had all been followed up with more solid teaching, especially for the new converts. And perhaps making room for women and young people to have a more active role in the church."

"But still it was remarkable."

"Absolutely. Perhaps one thing it demonstrates is that Wales has always been a thin place." Antony shivered at his own statement. A thinning of the veil between heaven and earth was a good thing. But there was more than one kind of spirit.

Felicity bit on a crisp, then chewed thoughtfully. "Julius's and Aaron's martyrdom, David's preaching, the Revival—are you saying they're part of a continuum of spiritual power?" She thought again. "So something must have promoted that power?"

"Of course, any priest will tell you. But it isn't something, it's Someone—the Holy Spirit specifically."

Felicity grinned. "Hey, I'm a theology student, remember. I know. But I mean something concrete. Like you're always on about what I've learned to call a means of grace. Like the Bible or the Eucharist or baptismal water—those things are concrete."

"Something that promoted faith, you mean? Something that gave believers courage to speak and act?" Now it was Antony's turn to ponder.

"Right, and that then could be perverted for evil? Something a power-hungry person or group would want to get their hands on?"

"That's an interesting speculation." Antony wasn't ready to commit himself, but he could see a certain fragile logic to what Felicity suggested.

"It needs to be more than speculation. Something is going on," Felicity insisted. "Hwyl's death wasn't an isolated event. Whatever it was is following us." She started to look over her shoulder.

Her gaze was met by a tall man with deep-set, dark eyes and waves of steel-gray hair approaching them with a wide smile. He introduced himself as Dyfrig Griffiths. "I understand you're wanting to know more about the Revival, if this morning's presentation hasn't answered all your questions. Grand service, wasn't it?" Dyfrig's lilting voice made the most ordinary statement sound like poetry.

"It was remarkable." Antony stood and shook his hand. "I'd say it's raised far more questions than it answered."

"You're Father Stephen, are you?"

Antony introduced himself and explained about the substitution.

"How many are you?"

"Eleven in addition to myself."

"Ah, that's grand. Just grand. Now, if you have transport, I'll take you to the Moriah Chapel in Loughor where it all started. It's not far—just outside Swansea. Good dual carriageway all the way."

Antony rode with Dyfrig in his small blue car, the others following in the minibus. Dyfrig talked all the way in his sonorous voice of the remarkable renewed interest in the Revival in recent years. "A wellspring has sprung up seemingly from all over the world. Several times a week I'm called on to give tours. People just like your good self and your group, Father. From India, South Africa, New Zealand, Korea, America, the Congo, Canada... They've all been here recently. God is bringing us together. He's not restricted to denominations. We have a prayer meeting every week, just as they did here in 1904."

The narrative in Dyfrig's restful, undulating voice brought them to a stone church, golden in the afternoon sun. Three persimmon-colored doors stood behind the entrance arches and a row of curved windows above. Dyfrig held open the gate in the iron fence and waited on the flagstones for his hearers to gather round.

When they were assembled, he took his place in front of a tall, black marble memorial to Evan Roberts and the Revival. Antony scanned segments of the inscription: "God hath visited and redeemed His people. Gloria Deo." "God's man and God's Word." "Hope for a spotless generation, The opening of the heart of a nation." On the other side was a raised sculpture of Roberts's head with the words: "'Remember Jesus Christ.' E. Roberts."

"Roberts was raised right here in Loughor in a solid, religious family. Friends described him as sincere, serious, solemn, persistent in Bible study. Although he worked as a blacksmith and a coal miner, he had a passionate desire to preach. Evan Roberts prayed for thirteen years for a visitation of the Holy Spirit on Wales.

"But Roberts was no one's idea of a typical revivalist. Half-educated, he began working in the mines as a young child when his father broke his hip. He was soft-spoken, undemonstrative and not a fluent speaker. He entered grammar school at age twenty-six to prepare for the ministry, and left a few months later to begin preaching.

"Shortly after that he felt that he should return to his home church at Loughor. His mother met him at the door in some alarm. 'Where have you been? Why are you not at school? Are you ill?'

"'No.'

"'Then why have you come back home?'

"'Oh Mother, the Spirit has sent me back here to work among our own young people at the chapel at Moriah. We are going to have the greatest revival that Wales has ever seen.'

"He went to his pastor and asked permission to hold services for young people. That night, after the Monday evening prayer meeting, he invited the young people to stay behind as he wanted to speak to them."

Dyfrig pointed to a long, low building beside the chapel. "They met there, in the school house. Sixteen adults and one little girl. 'God send the Holy Spirit for Jesus Christ's sake,' Evan Roberts prayed, then turned to his bemused congregation. 'Now we can go home. He has come.'

"And that is how it started," Dyfrig ended his lecture.

"Now we'll go around back." He led the crocodile of pilgrims along the path between church and school, and stopped at a large square structure some two feet high. The rim of the cement footing was capped with black marble bearing inscriptions in Welsh. The center was filled with gravel.

Antony was startled to see Michael, who had apparently slipped away from the group unnoticed, sitting on the rim with his hand in the gravel like a child playing in a sandbox. "The Roberts family tomb," Dyfrig explained.

Evening shadows fell over the churchyard filled with more traditional graves. "And so it ends quietly," the bardic rhetoric resumed. "Perhaps the effects of the Revival were most notable in the coal mines and in the homes. A man could go mad down the pits. Tales are told that a man might curse at a tram that had left the rails until he was almost too weak to stand, then kick it until he fell to the ground, cursing God. And like the trams, the mules and pit ponies were flogged, kicked and cursed—it was the only life they knew, man and beast—the only language the animals ever heard.

"When revival changed the hearts of the miners, the horses were bewildered to hear hymn-singing from the beginning to the end of the shift. Instead of the steel prod, booted kick and harsh curse, the animals were patted and encouraged to work: 'Come on now, laddie. Try harder this time.' It's little wonder they didn't know what to do.

"And lunch hours were even stranger. The men started Bible studies and prayer meetings in the mines. At one mine men even went down into the pits an hour early so as not to trespass on employers' time when they took extended lunch hours for Bible reading and prayer.

"Colliery managers claimed that the Revival made the men better colliers; wives claimed that the Revival made them better husbands and fathers. The miracle of Jesus turning water into wine is well known. In Wales he changed beer into furniture. Miners who had been accustomed to spending most of their time and wages in the pub, now spent their time at home and in prayer meetings, giving their wages to their wives for food and family necessities."

Antony continued to mull over Dyfrig's remarkable story. And Felicity's question. So much power. If there was an esoteric secret attached, it was little wonder someone would want to get to the source of it.

There was no question that if Evan Roberts had been asked for something concrete he would have pointed to the Bible. It was said that young man could stand in a pulpit and by merely measuring with his thumb down the side of the holy book, open it instantly to the passage he sought.

Julius and Aaron would have had scrolls, letters, tablets of tile and wax, as they had seen at the Roman museum. David would have had beautifully hand-illuminated volumes. Was the answer that obvious?

Certainly, it was all too possible for the unscrupulous to pervert those teachings to their own advantage. Could it be that simple?

And yet that explained nothing: Hwyl's mysterious death, Michael's strange behavior, the objects in Adam's Welsh cake, the noises bombarding Felicity and Kaylyn... Antony would be glad to get to St David's.

Chapter 19

Monday
Aberdare to St David's

Felicity looked out the window of the van as they drove down the Vale of Neath, leaving the abandoned coal tips of the Rhondda behind them. The golden sunshine and blue sky were a relief after the gloom and lowering skies of recent days. Something of a party atmosphere pervaded the cocoon of their vehicle as they rejoiced in surviving the rigors of the walking pilgrimage, and looked forward to the promised days of relaxed retreat.

And no one was in higher spirits, Felicity noticed, than Lydia. She seemed elated, almost giddy, quite a change from the controled, rather domineering person Felicity had thought her. It must be the relief of no longer being responsible for her little brother. She chatted animatedly at some length at how happy Adam had been to be back at school, how his friends had been watching out for him and had come to greet him. The group had delayed their departure from Aberdare until Michael and Lydia could return from delivering Adam to Abergavenny College. "College?" Felicity had been confused when she heard of the plan. "But he's only thirteen years old."

"No," Antony explained. "Not what you'd call a college. It's a prep school. A very good, very expensive one. And they begin term today." Adam was the only one with a schedule that wouldn't allow for the second half of the pilgrimage, since the other young people were home-schooled, on their gap year, or on work experience. Whatever the reason for delay, Felicity had been happy enough for it since Enid had thoughtfully invited the pilgrims to her home for breakfast and offered them the use of her bathroom and washer and dryer. Felicity didn't even want to think how long it had been since she had washed her hair, but now, with it hanging loose and dry across her shoulders, she was sure her head was measurably lighter. Or maybe that was just the effect of the sunshine.

In the back, Jared entertained Evie and Kaylyn with some nonsense which they seemed delighted to respond to. Evie's giggle was a familiar enough sound, but Kaylyn's light laughter was a new and delightful experience to hear. Chloe sat beside Felicity, silently watching the landscape. Behind them, Ryan informed Colin and Antony about the geology of the area. "Waterfall Country, they call this. There's a large number of spectacular falls all through here—on tributaries of the River Neath through valleys deeply incized by glaciers during the succession of ice ages. You see, what happened was that these tributaries cut down into their own beds as they adjusted to a base level lower than in pre-glacial times. The underlying geology…"

"Roman camp!" Colin cut into the narrative when he spotted a roadside marker. "That said 'Roman Camp.' Father—"

Antony held up his hand. "We need to get on, Colin. They're expecting us at St Non's."

"Oh, but—"

"It's right along St Illtyd's Walk," Ryan added.

Lydia, sitting beside the driver, gave Michael a nudge which Felicity only caught on the edge of her vision. "And St David was educated by St Illtyd," Michael chimed in from the front. "We could just take a tea break there, Father."

Antony threw up his hands and laughed. "Only if there's chocolate cake for tea."

There was. And the falls were, indeed, spectacular. They picnicked in a sun-filtered wood beside a white water river that made Felicity think of the rapid rivers in her native Idaho.

The water burbled beside them, insects buzzed nearby and birds sang overhead. "This is glorious." Felicity sighed and leaned back against the rough bark of a tree trunk. "Can you believe that rain in Penrhys was only two days ago?"

"That was an absolute pig of a day, wasn't it?" Jared agreed around bites of chocolate cake.

Felicity hoped her laughter didn't scare the birds.

Antony, who had been beset by Colin, Ryan and Michael, agreed—not too reluctantly—that they could extend the stop long enough for those who wished to explore the Roman camp. "But only briefly," he insisted.

Felicity chose to walk the shorter, but extremely bendy, way up St Illtyd's path with Jared and the Goths to a cairn circle. "This trail was laid out by a German," Jared informed them as a twist in the path made an almost 180 degree turn.

"Really?" Kaylyn asked.

"Yep." Jared grinned. "Herr Pin."

Felicity laughed with the others, then let them go on up the trail as she stood listening to the gentle sough of the breeze in the scattered conifers, and the occasional birdcall. How wonderful to be away from the sense of oppression that had dogged them for days. Here in the clear air she could almost tell herself she had imagined the whole thing. She had always had a very active— some would say overactive—imagination.

She turned toward the cairn circle. Then froze at the moaning sound. No. She shook her head and strode forward. It was merely the wind in the trees.

And it must, indeed, have been no more than that because in less than an hour the group reassembled just as Antony had directed, with no one lost or victim of an accident.

At the end of the valley Michael slipped the silver vehicle into the whizzing stream of traffic on the M4. "Right. We're on our way to Rome," Antony announced to the pilgrims.

His declaration was met with a chorus of surprised questions.

"Well, all right. Halfway to Rome, that is." He smiled, then explained. "In medieval times, two pilgrimages to St David's counted as a pilgrimage to Rome. It's a sign of how holy St David's was considered. And how difficult the journey was."

Their time on the motorway was short-lived and they were soon driving through green, undulating farmland. The pleasant way trundled along a winding road through countryside that became increasingly flatter with many pullings-over and backings-up to allow passage for tractors and trailers stacked high with hay bales.

"All right, boys and girls," Antony called for their attention. "Just a quick history lesson here."

The chorus of groans was overdone enough to make it obvious they were teasing. "A very brief one. Promise. Just more of a footnote, really. But you'll encounter Giraldus Cambrensis, Gerald of Wales, at St David's and I want you to know this is the same route he took when he made his famous seven-week journey through Wales in 1188. Gerald accompanied Baldwin, Archbishop of Canterbury, to raise Welsh troops for the Third Crusade. Gerald was a scholar, a churchman, a gossip, an indefatigable traveler, and a prolific writer with an obsessive desire to record his observations for posterity.

"Seventeen of his books survive, but his two on his beloved Wales are his most important: *Itinerarium Cambriae* and *Descriptio Cambriae*. Gerald recorded Welsh history and geography and his reflections on the always rocky relations between the Welsh and their English neighbors.

"In the past, that is of course," the English Antony was quick to add.

It was Kaylyn, one of their English pilgrims, who spoke up, sounding very disappointed. "But, Father A, aren't you going to act it out for us?"

Felicity smiled. She'd been thinking the same thing, but most remarkable was the fact that Kaylyn, who had seemed so detached, if not actively hostile, was now willing to admit she had actually enjoyed Antony's lessons. Felicity remembered only a few months ago undergoing a similar metamorphosis in her own attitudes.

Antony's warm grin showed he was appreciative of the transformation, too. "Thank you, Kaylyn. I'll try not to disappoint you next time. But I did warn that this was just more of a footnote. You see, Gerald was a canon of St David's and responsible for much of the rebuilding of the cathedral. He was a powerful man with many titles, but he most frequently styled himself Bishop-elect of St David's. Becoming Bishop of St David's was his most fervent desire, but it was denied him. Although his name was twice put forward for the position, King Henry II refused to appoint him. The last thing Henry wanted was an intelligent, powerful, well-organized, well-connected bishop who insisted on the independence of his see from Canterbury."

Felicity was wondering if she should add Giraldus Cambrensis to her list alongside Julius and Aaron, St David and possibly Evan Roberts of supernaturally aided leaders, when Antony added, "Gerald retired, a disappointed man. Eight centuries later his vision was fulfilled. In 1920 the Church in Wales became independent."

The way became increasingly rural as they turned northwestward beyond Haverfordwest across the steep, rocky, wind-swept peninsula. "In spite of Gerald's fondness for St David's, he didn't care much for what he observed as he and Baldwin rode this way," Antony continued. "'Remote, rocky and riverless; its soil too barren to sustain trees and pastures; exposed to winds and inclement weather; caught between warring Flemings and hostile Welsh.' That's how he described it."

Felicity was about to agree with Gerald's evaluation when the road curved and a stunning blue sweep of bay spread before them. Steep cliffs ran down to a strip of black rocks, and beyond that perfect white sand stretched out to molten silver water. A fringe of white surf lapped the sand and seagulls swooped above. "The Atlantic!" Felicity cried. Beyond that was home. Except that this side of the Atlantic was home now, she reminded herself.

"St George's Channel, I'm afraid," Ryan corrected. "St Brides Bay, to be precise."

"So New York isn't the next stop?"

"Ireland, I'm afraid. Unless you dodge around a bit to the south."

Felicity was still wishing for a good atlas when the road cut steeply downward, and around another turn she was presented with one of the most picturesque villages she had ever seen. The tiny hamlet stood at the head of a narrow bay, sheltered in a deep ravine. Color-washed shops and cottages lined the street in storybook fashion: pink, blue, pink, yellow, red, pink, blue... "What is this?" she asked, turning in her seat for another look to be sure she hadn't imagined the fairy tale scene.

"Solva," Ryan replied. "Solva Harbour is a good example of a glaciated meltwater channel. The coast all along here is pockmarked with caves, and the rocks contain fossils from the Cambrian age."

But it was Nancy who provided the most delightful bit of information: "Solva had the first butterfly farm in Wales. It's closed now, but we did a school trip here once. These cliffs are a great place to see butterflies and dragonflies."

A few minutes later they swept into the smallest cathedral city in Britain. Felicity was enchanted by the narrow, curving street lined with shops. At the corner, Michael pulled into a parking spot, but didn't turn off the engine. "Here you are. Just a pause for a peak at the cathedral."

Beyond the low stone wall in front of them, a smooth green churchyard dotted with crumbling gravestones swooped downhill to the cathedral below. How odd to meet a cathedral almost eye-level with its crenelated roofline. Beyond the massive square tower rising to the evening sky, smooth green hills stretched toward the bay.

"How extraordinary—to build a cathedral in a hollow," Felicity said.

"Apparently to protect it from sea raiders," Antony replied. "At least that's the theory. If that's the case, it didn't work very well, though. Exposed as it is to the sea here, the cathedral was host to frequent Viking raids during the tenth and eleventh centuries."

"Oh, that's what you meant when you said Gerald rebuilt the cathedral. So is this Giraldus Cambrensis's cathedral?"

"Somewhat. Although there was a great deal of rebuilding and restoring through the centuries. The greatest builder of St David's, though, was Bishop Gower in the middle of the fourteenth century." Antony pointed to an enormous picturesque ruin behind the cathedral. "Henry Gower's Bishop's Palace."

"Good grief, it was bigger than the cathedral!"

"Gower was a passionate builder, to say the least." Antony said no more as Michael put the van into gear and turned down the street, but she suspected there would be more to the story.

They were quickly out of the city, driving along a narrow track out onto the peninsula. Bracken and gorse covered the fields on both sides, and the lowering sun gave a special golden quality to the light. Cattle grazed in fields that stretched to the cliff edge with the shimmering ocean rolling on to the horizon. At the end of the lane a sturdy stone building sat stark against the sky. A few white clouds softened the sweep of blue, and out toward the cliff edge, seagulls swooped and called.

"Welcome to St Non's—Seek beauty and you will find it," the sign greeted them. And then they were taken in charge by Alma and Nora, the two Irish Sisters, in their modern dress. "Our crosses are our habits," Alma, the shorter, more effusive one, explained in her melodic lilt. "I'll just take those, my dear." She had picked up Felicity's bedroll and pack and headed up the wide stairway before Felicity could protest.

Along the hall, the sister opened the door onto a glorious sight. Felicity gasped and rushed to her window. "What an amazing view!"

"'Tis, tisn't it? The hotel at the beginning of our track was voted one of the grandest views in the world. We think ours is better."

Below Felicity, intense green grass covered a terraced lawn running down to a path skirting the cliff edge. Beyond that, the blue waters of St Non's Bay sparkled. On each side the rugged cliffs curved into water that foamed and splashed over the black rocks. Felicity stood mesmerized for several moments, then remembered herself. "Oh, it's wonderful! Thank you."

Reluctant to turn away, Felicity opened the side window. The curtain billowed as the roar of the waves and a cry of gulls blew in with the ocean breeze. Felicity leaned out and looked across the field to her right. "What's that?" She indicated a crumbled stone wall inside a rail fence.

"To be sure, that's St Non's Chapel. Where the blessed David was born. The holy well is just along the path on your way." Sister Alma pointed, although Felicity couldn't make out the well.

"And that," at Alma's direction Felicity looked almost straight down on the roof of a small stone building sitting on the lawn of the retreat house, the pointed top of the tower marking the arched entrance, nearly on a level with Felicity's window.

"That's our modern St Non's chapel. We no longer use it for regular worship, though, because in a gale the wind will drive the rain right through the stone walls."

Felicity found that hard to imagine, until she recalled the force of the wind-driven rain she experienced at Penrhys. "You'll not have to worry, though," the sister assured her. "It's sure to be fair while you're here."

"Dinner in an hour, so you've plenty of time to settle in." The ebullient nun was at the door when she turned back with a twinkle in her eye. "Do you like fish?"

"Yes, I love it."

"Well, you're not getting it." Alma smiled. "It's lasagna tonight." She left Felicity with a merry chuckle.

The pilgrims would join the nuns for Compline in their chapel on the lower level of the retreat house later, but after dinner they were free to ramble. Felicity had no doubt as to the top of her agenda—time alone with Antony in this incredibly beautiful place. At last they were free of the responsibility of herding pilgrims over precipitous Welsh mountains. They were here to relax and commune with nature and with God. And Felicity wanted to commune with Antony.

Apparently his agenda matched hers. "Want to go for a stroll? Over to the old chapel or something?"

"Yes! That sounds great, Father. Let's go to the well, too."

Felicity managed to suppress her groan. Antony had spoken specifically to her, but Colin had answered. She wanted to tell him she was quite certain it wasn't a Roman site, but instead she mustered a faint smile.

In the end it amounted to another pilgrimage as everyone but Chloe and Lydia chose to trail after them. The beauty of the evening and the freshness of the air soon revived Felicity's spirit, however, as she followed Colin along the flagged path below the retreat house. A green hedge grew almost as high as Felicity's head on the right, and to the left the tussocky grass was dotted with mounds of bright pink balls, waving on their slender stems. "Thrift," Nancy informed her. "Or sea pink. It grows in the rocks all along here."

Felicity bent forward to check the cushion of pink for scent, then pulled back as three bees flew up at her. Nancy took her arm to steady her. "I should have warned you. Bees love it. It's heavy with pollen."

A few more yards on and the path dropped down to a small pool of clear water under the dome of a white stone arch. Felicity knelt and dipped her hand in, letting the crystal drops fall from her fingers. "Put some on your eyes," Nancy said. "It's supposed to be very healing, especially for eyes." Felicity obediently did so. It was certainly refreshing.

"This has been considered a holy well for 1,400 years," Antony informed them. "It was a favorite with medieval pilgrims." Apparently it was still popular, Felicity thought, because the bottom of the well was shiny with coins tossed there by votives.

She stepped across the path to let others have a turn at the waters, and paused at the grotto. An arched stone dome mimicking that of the well covering held a statue of Mary, her hands spread wide in welcome. The image made Felicity think of her own mother, to whom she had been so recently reconciled. She stooped to pick a small handful of the pink flowers and placed them at Mary's feet. Her brief prayer, however, was interrupted by a series of sneezes. Nancy was right about that pollen.

When Antony joined her, they ambled on across the field toward the broken walls of St Non's Chapel. "So this is where Non is supposed to have given birth to David?"

Antony smiled. "Close enough, I imagine. It was along this coast somewhere, above Whitesands Bay, and this building marks an ancient spot. So this could well be where Nonnita took refuge with the holy Sisters to give birth to her remarkable son during a violent storm."

Felicity recalled Alama's words about the force of the driving rain on this cliff. She hoped Non's walls had been waterproof.

Felicity was running her hand over the smooth, cool surface of the white, lopsided oval stone incized with a slim Celtic cross that Antony had identified as St Non's Cross when Jared, Kaylyn and Evie joined them, and Antony turned to tell them of the birth of St David:

... Hour after hour, as black as night in the middle of the day, the sound of the howling wind and crashing sea pounded in Non's ears with increasing ferocity as the intensity of her pains grew. The noise of the storm, the shaking of the conical thatched roof over her head, and the relentlessness of her gripping pains were so all-consuming that she was not aware of the ministrations of the nursing Sisters, but hung all the more tightly to the large, smooth stone beside her pallet, giving her something to push against in her labor.

The peak of the storm and the peak of her labor climaxed together...

At first Felicity thought the cry she heard was her imagination, identifying with Non in her birthing pangs. Then she realized it had come from the well.

"Father Antony!" Michael's shout was clear enough.

They all turned to scramble for the path. Felicity's long legs were the first over the rails and carried her across the field and up the path in seconds. Even before she was there, though, she could hear the harsh, strangled gasps of someone struggling desperately to breathe. She rounded the corner and saw Colin kneeling on the ground, his body bent double. In front of him a particularly large hummock of sea pinks bobbed in the breeze.

"It's the pollen!" She shouted and darted forward. "Where's Lydia? Jared," she turned to the youth behind her and pointed to the retreat house. "Get Lydia, quick!"

It would be several minutes before Lydia arrived, and already Colin's pale skin had a blue cast to it. Michael and Ryan knelt beside the struggling youth, looking helpless. "We need to get him away from this pollen. Can you two carry him?" Felicity didn't really know anything about it, but it seemed logical.

The chunky Colin was much heavier than the petite Nancy Ryan and his team had carried a few days before, and Colin's whole body was shaking, making the task much harder. But with Colin's arms slung around their shoulders, Michael and Ryan managed to as much drag as carry him away from the polluted air.

They were halfway to the retreat house when Lydia came running down the path. "Does anyone know if he's been remembering to take his meds?" No one answered. She dug in his pocket, pulled out his inhaler and administered it. "He needs epinephrine." She shook her head. "Well, get him inside—out of this air." She ran up the path ahead of them. "Bring him to the bath. We need to get all the pollen off him. And his clothes will need to be washed." She pulled out her mobile as she ran, and pushed 999.

The emergency services still hadn't arrived by the time they had Colin in the tub of warm water. And Felicity, standing outside the bathroom door could hear his breath still coming only in strangled gasps. Antony arrived with pajamas and the bottle of allergy pills from Colin's pack. More splashing and grunts sounded from the bathroom as Ryan and Michael got the patient out of the tub and dressed him.

Lydia took the pill bottle and shook it. "Still pretty full. He probably hasn't taken one for days. I should have been administering them." It sounded like she was accusing Antony.

"His mother didn't want him to feel embarrassed," Felicity said.

"Well, we need to get some inside him now, but he could never swallow one in his condition. Spoons. I need two spoons."

By the time the paramedics arrived, Colin was in bed and Lydia was spooning drops of pills crushed in water into his mouth. The emergency team administered an EpiPen in his thigh, and in a few minutes Colin was able to get a full breath. "He should be all right now. Keep him quiet. He probably needs to sleep. And be sure he takes his tablets regularly."

Lydia seemed to interpret the medic's instructions as an affront. The color rose in her cheeks and she took a step toward him. "Thank you so much," Felicity intervened. "We'll keep a careful eye on him. Lydia is an excellent nurse."

"Be sure you bring him to the doctors tomorrow if there's any doubt." The medics zipped their bags and left, escorted down the stairs by Sister Nora.

Felicity turned in time to see Lydia approaching Colin with a look in her eye that said she was going to give him a telling-off for neglecting his meds. "You were great, Lydia. No one else would have had a clue what to do. You probably saved his life."

"Hmph." Lydia turned back to the bed, but only straightened Colin's covers. "Try to sleep now, you."

Antony closed the door on the patient's room. "I need to ring his mother. Will you come with me, Lydia, in case she wants to ask you anything?" Antony and Lydia went to the lounge where they could make their call without bothering anyone else.

Felicity turned to her room with dragging feet. Her golden evening had turned to ashes. This retreat was to be their peaceful, safe haven. A place she and Antony could have some time alone. Away from whatever had dogged their steps so threateningly across the width of Wales.

But now she knew. They had not escaped. Whatever it was had followed them. Or had been here ahead of them. Waiting for them.

She pulled the curtain across the wall of obsidian glass that earlier had been such a glorious picture window. She knew no thin veil of fabric could keep this blackness out, but it made her feel less exposed.

She pulled off her jeans and put on her pajamas. At least she had a real bed to sleep in. If she could sleep. Felicity closed her eyes against the dark. But she couldn't keep it out of her mind.

It was the weight that wakened her. Like something sitting on her chest. She felt as if an unseen hand was trying to squash her—an unknown force trying to suck the life out of her. She was in a strange darkness. She was breathing, but no air was entering her lungs.

For a moment she pictured herself giving in to the weight. Just sinking to the bottom of the pool and letting the waters close over her. No more struggle. Just let go. Relax. Give in.

"No!" She flung her covers from her and sat up in bed, wet with sweat. She stumbled across the room and jerked her window open. Cool, fresh sea breeze flooded the room. She filled her lungs. Deeply. Again and again she breathed in the pure air.

Then she stuck her head out the window and yelled to the elements, "No!" A single, defiant word. But it was enough.

She had flung down the gauntlet. This was intolerable. In this beautiful spot, hallowed by centuries of worship, this oppression was not to be allowed. Whoever it was. Whatever it was. She would get to the bottom of it and she would stop them.

Chapter 20

A ntony toyed with his porridge, gazing out across the bay through the wide windows of the dining room. It was a clear day, the water an intense, morning blue, the sky a cloudless sweep to the horizon. Around him the pilgrims chatted, Lydia giving everyone a good report on her patient: still some allergy symptoms—stuffy nose, a little cough, a bit weak— but otherwise normal. She smiled. "He's talking about evidence of Roman occupation in Pembrokeshire—coins at Pembroke Castle and the floor of a high status Roman villa uncovered somewhere near here." She shook her head. "I think he's on the mend, but I'll keep him quiet today just to make certain."

Antony just wished his mind felt as clear as the atmosphere. He had spent a restless night, his sleep interrupted by disturbing dreams. Once he had been certain he had heard Felicity shouting, but then had drifted back to an uneasy slumber. He looked around the room. Where was Felicity? He could hope she was having a restful lie-in, but it was unlike her to miss a meal.

He pushed his porridge aside, excellent Irish oatmeal though it was. Toast, crisp. And coffee, black. That was all his stomach could handle this morning.

He was returning with his toast to his seat at the long table, arranged to offer maximum views of the bay to as many guests as possible, when he saw Felicity walking on the terraced verandah beyond the window. In spite of the neatness of her shining golden braid, and the brilliance of her red sweater against the blue backdrop he could see by the droop of her head and the jerkiness of her walk that she was troubled. He abandoned his uneaten toast.

Felicity turned to him at the sound of the retreat house door closing behind him. Her smile made his heart wrench. He could see what the effort had cost her. The circles under her eyes were darker than those that greeted him in his mirror that morning. Her cheeks paler.

He put an arm around her and led her to the shelter of the little stone chapel where they could talk unobserved by the breakfasting retreatants. The rough stone walls held the cool damp of the night, but the air was scented by a few candles flickering in a stand before the altar. The narrow stained-glass window of St Non, swathed in blue, at the front, and David, robed in red, at the side, warmed the faint light, giving a sense of shelter, rather than gloom.

Antony pulled Felicity to sit on one of the chairs along the wall. His arms around her, he gave her several light kisses on her cheeks, her eyes, her mouth, then pulled back. "You look terrible, my love."

Indignation flared in her eyes, then she sighed and her shoulders sagged. "I am terrible. I'm a mess. Last night I was so frightened. Then I was determined to fight. I wasn't going to let this—this thing—win. I shouted at it."

"Ah, that *was* you. I thought I'd dreamed it."

"It was me, all right. That was the good news. Then I went back to bed and argued with myself the rest of the night."

"Who won?"

"Do I look like I won?" She pushed to her feet and began pacing the stone floor with steps far heavier than her normal dancer's tread. "Every time I determined to fight, I asked myself how? Who? What? And I couldn't answer. But I refused to give in, so then it all went around again." She stopped her pacing and stood, wringing her hands.

Antony got up and took her in his arms. He held her close for a minute, then pushed back and held her at arms' length. "All this worry—it's not like you. Caution—certainly. Realistic assessment of danger—that's great. But not endless, useless worry. Don't let this rob you of your shining courage." He wanted to say more, but his mind was so filled with the image of the Felicity he knew so well—dauntless and gallant—that he couldn't find words.

At last she smiled. "Don't lose my courage, just my rashness?"

He returned her smile. "Can't you find a balance, woman?"

"Right. So no worry. But action." She nodded. "What do you suggest, then?"

"I had thought I'd take the group to see the cathedral today, maybe do the Bishop's Palace, too, but perhaps we can leave our retreatants to their own endeavors. Whatever is going on, it revolves around Hwyl. I can't get away from the idea that he was at Kirkthorpe to see me. And if I hadn't been working in the sacristy—if I'd been at the tower that morning, as he would have expected..." He clamped his lips shut. That was a useless line of thought. "I think we should call on Dilys Pendry. Maybe she's found something or remembered something."

After another cuddle and a rather thorough kiss they walked hand-in-hand back into the retreat house. Antony was pleased at the renewed lightness to Felicity's step and sparkle in her eyes. He wasn't sure whether it was due to their plan of action or the more concrete comfort he had given, but he was glad for it.

Hwyl's widow agreed readily to Antony's suggestion that he and Felicity visit her. "Yes, please. I don't know whether or not I have anything useful for you, but I would be happy to have some company."

When Antony returned to the dining room the others were still there, lingering over second—or third—cups of coffee or tea. Antony was pleased that Felicity had helped herself to cereal from the sideboard and was eating a good breakfast. A sure sign she was feeling better. He made himself a fresh piece of toast and joined her. "I'm going to leave you on your own today. We'll postpone our tour of the cathedral until tomorrow," he told the group.

"That's fine, Father." Ryan was the first to speak. "I was hoping to explore the caves around Caerbwdy Bay. I'd be happy to take anybody with me who wants to go along."

Ryan's suggestion received an enthusiastic response from everyone but Kaylyn, who was undoubtedly remembering her attack of claustrophobia, and Lydia, who said she would stay with her patient. Antony asked about transportation, since he and Felicity would take the minibus. "You can drop us in the center of town. I noticed a bike rental shop right across the street from the cathedral yesterday." Ryan pulled a map out of his pocket. "It isn't far—just the second bay over from St Non's. Caves all along there." He pointed. "We'll go down this inlet to get below the caves." Several heads bent over the map.

Antony caught Michael's eye, recalling his driver's bad experience in the cave at the Darren Ddu quarries, but Michael nodded reassuringly. "It's fine. These caves aren't deep. I'll go with them, no problem."

Antony and Felicity left the group in front of the bike rental shop and drove out of town, back along the way they had come the day before. Felicity picked up the map and studied it for a few moments. "Do you find Whitchurch?" He asked. "We take the B road up here a bit."

"Oh, I see. It's just above Solva."

"That's right, they're in the same parish."

When they drove into the village that was no more than a cluster of scattered houses, however, it was clear that Whitchurch was anything but the tourist attraction the nearby Solva was. St David's Church stood on a slight rise of ground with leaning, lichen-covered gravestones dotting the verdant grass of the wide churchyard. A small, modern vicarage stood nearby. And all around, a bleak, desolate sweep of flat fields ran as far as one could see. Felicity shivered. "Oh, this is depressing. Poor Dilys. I wouldn't want to live here alone. No wonder she sounded happy to have visitors."

The young woman who answered the door on their first ring was small with a neat cap of curly black hair framing a round face. She wore jeans and an oversized plaid shirt with the sleeves rolled up. "You'll have to excuse me—and the house— I'm packing." She shook her head. "You wouldn't think we could have amassed so much stuff in just five years, would you? Of course, there are all of Hwyl's books…" Her speech faltered as if she'd run out of breath. She stepped back, holding the door for them to come in.

Half-filled packing boxes littered the floor. Their hostess turned to move a stack of folded blankets from the sofa. "Do sit down. I've put the kettle on."

"I'm so sorry to bother you." Antony made his way across the jumbled room to take the offered seat and Felicity followed.

"No, no. Not at all. As I said on the phone, I'm happy for company."

"Don't you have anyone to help you?" Felicity asked.

"People have been very kind. I've had so many offers. People from the parish bring in far more food than I can eat. Rhys Morgan and others Hwyl worked with have offered to help clean out his study. But I…" She sighed. "I'm just not ready. My sister is coming up from Penzance on Friday. But I wanted to make a start." Dilys looked around as if she was uncertain where she was. "I needed to work through it myself. There's so much—" She swallowed. "So much I don't understand. I'm hoping you can help me."

"That's what we're hoping, too," Antony replied.

Felicity made a more literal application of her words. "Let me help you with the tea."

When the women returned, Dilys took a long sip of her sweetened tea, then leaned back. "I've given a lot of thought to the things you asked me, but I don't know that I have any answers. Have you learned anything new?"

"I'm afraid we mostly have more questions," Antony replied. "You haven't found anything?" Surely, if there was anything to be found it would come to light with the job Dilys was doing turning everything out. "What can you tell us about how Hwyl seemed to be in recent weeks—within himself?"

Dilys shook her head. "Nothing more than I told you on the phone, really. He was preoccupied. He spent a lot of time in his study with the door closed—but then, priests do that." Antony nodded his understanding.

"And the pains you said he had?"

"That was odd. I kept telling him to go to the doctor—but he was so busy. He'd say, yes, yes, he'd do it. And then he would be fine for a day or two and forget all about it."

"In his hands and feet, you said."

Dilys pointed to the palms of her hands and the arch of a foot. "Sharp. Piercing. Like a nail, he said. Sometimes he would cry out."

Like stigmata. Antony couldn't suppress the thought. "And stomach?"

"That was more general. He had an uneasy digestion at the best of times anyway, and then when the pressures of his job weighed on him..." She was quiet for a moment.

"But it seemed worse just of late?"

Dilys nodded. "He was hardly eating anything. I worry about that. I keep thinking, if he'd eaten more he would have been stronger, been able to resist..."

Antony took a deep breath. "Mrs Pendry…"

"Call me Dilys, please."

"Dilys, I'm sorry to have to ask you this, but do you know of any reason Hwyl might have…"

"Committed suicide?" She completed his sentence. "The police asked me that, too, but you should know better, Father Antony. He was a priest. A faithful priest. Suicide is a sin."

"Yes, but…"

"If the 'balance of his mind had been disturbed?' The police asked that, too. My husband was worried. Overworked. He was not insane."

Dilys herself seemed so very rational. Antony had confidence in her words. "What about people he was working closely with recently? Especially people who might have come to the house?"

Dilys set her empty beaker down on the floor. "I made a list for the police. I should have kept a copy."

"I'm sorry."

"No, I don't mind. Truly. I appreciate what you're trying to do. I told the police everything I could, but there was so much they didn't really grasp about his work. I know you will understand." She paused. "Well, people from the parish, of course. It's a combined parish; he had charge of three churches. Then everyone at the diocesan office. And this committee to restore the Bishop's Palace. He thought that was a bit mad, really, but the chairman asked him especially, and sometimes they met here just to save him the drive into St David's. Very thoughtful, really."

"But did he have anyone special he was counseling at the moment?"

Dilys made an attempt at a grin. "Was he working with anyone possessed, or doing any exorcisms just recently? We can speak plainly, you know."

"Sorry. Yes, that is what I meant."

"None that I knew of. But I wouldn't necessarily. He never talked about his work. Besides the seal of the confessional, I mean. He just didn't like to bring those things home with him." She was quiet a moment. "He did, though, of course. Sometimes I thought that if he would have talked to me about it more he wouldn't have had to carry so much inside. I longed to help, more than making him bacon sandwiches at all hours of the day and night and running the flower rota at church. And now it's too late." She dropped her head into her hands. Felicity went to her and put an arm around her.

Dilys didn't sob or shake but when she raised her head her eyes were red. Felicity picked up the teapot and took it to the kitchen for a refill.

"Do you know why he went to Kirkthorpe?" Antony asked.

"There was a monk or someone there he wanted to talk to. He received a note in the mail. Right after that he said he had to show it to the man who taught him deliverance."

Antony dropped his head. He had been that man. And it explained why Hwyl was holding a paper with the Orbis Astri symbol on it. "But why didn't he take it to his bishop?"

"Hwyl felt Bishop Harry was a truly good man, but rather, ah—naïve in some ways."

Antony took a pen and notepad from his pocket and made a rough, quick sketch of a triangle and double-headed snake. He held it out to Dilys. "Have you seen this emblem before?"

Dilys grimaced. "The police asked me about that, too, but I haven't. Evil-looking, isn't it?"

When Felicity returned with the tea, Antony accepted a top-up and drank slowly, trying to evaluate what he knew; what he needed to know. It seemed all too likely that Hwyl was under occult attack. By far the most common form of such attack was a malefice where some object was used to transfer evil. Certainly if the contaminated Welsh cake Adam had eaten had come from this same satanic group—if all the strange events of late were related, and they must be—then that would likely be their favored mode of operation.

But Dilys said Hwyl ate little and she had prepared his food. So it was likely to be something external. The intermittent sharp pains sounded like a voodoo doll. But it was also possible something had been introduced into Hwyl's environment. "Dilys, may I see your bedroom?"

She looked surprised, but she didn't object, just stood and led the way down a short hall and opened the door on a tumbled room. "Sorry. I haven't had the heart to start packing in here. Or to clean. I've slept in the guest room since…"

"No worries. It's better this way. Everything is pretty much like…"

"Like it was when Hwyl was here?" She nodded. "Except a lot messier. I never left the bed unmade."

The bed was exactly what Antony wanted most to examine. His knowledge of the occult was all from study, not personal experience. He had lectured ordinands, and assisted other priests and deliverance ministers in cases needing extra prayer support. But now more than head knowledge was called for. He turned to Dilys. "Can you get me a bowl of water, please? And some salt."

While she was gone, he took the opportunity to search under the bed, between the sheet and mattress and between the duvet and cover. He felt the pillows carefully. Nothing came to light. But he hadn't really expected it to. He opened all the drawers in the bureau and pulled the bed out from the wall just enough to allow room to walk around it.

Dilys returned with a small glass bowl of tepid water. "Is this all right? There's holy water in the church."

"No, this is fine." He shook some salt into the water and made the sign of the cross over it. "In the name of the Father and of the Son and of the Holy Ghost. Amen."

Antony dipped his fingertips in the water and, walking clockwise around the bed, sprinkled it with holy water. He made three complete circles, observing the duvet, mattress and pillows carefully. Nothing came to light.

He set the bowl aside and took his rosary from his pocket. "Which side of the bed did Hwyl sleep on?" Dilys pointed to the left. Antony placed the crucifix on the pillow, mattress and duvet. Nothing.

Could he have been completely wrong? Antony wondered.

He pushed the bed back into place and turned to Dilys. "Thank you for your patience. I'm afraid I haven't been much help."

She gave a slight shrug. "I appreciate your trying." They were back in the front room when she added. "I don't suppose this would mean anything to you?" She held out several sheets of paper. "I've been trying to sort out Hwyl's desk."

Antony examined the printout of a lengthy email from a Professor Leo Meyerson, lecturer in biblical archeology, Cardiff University. It appeared that Hwyl had contacted him for information about letters from the first century. Apparently Hwyl had printed it for more careful study. Little wonder, as the answers appeared to be long and detailed. "May I keep this?"

"Of course."

Antony thanked Dilys again and promised to contact her if they learned anything more. She promised to ring him as well, if her packing turned up anything else of interest. He put his hand on her arm briefly. "God be with you." She nodded solemnly.

Back in the van, he handed the sheaf of papers to Felicity. "Why don't you read this aloud? I don't know whether or not it's of any importance."

Felicity snapped her seatbelt and took the papers. "Sure. But first, what was all that hocus-pocus with the holy water and crucifix back there?"

Antony started the engine and backed out of the driveway. "Not hocus-pocus. Established practice in such cases. Most of the time if anything external—"

"By external you mean a cursed object?"

He nodded. "That's right. If anything like that was being used against Hwyl, the most likely place to put it would be in his bed. Often such items don't come to light—even if the objects are cut open—until they're asperged and a crucifix is placed on them."

Felicity frowned. "And then they would just *appear*. Magically?"

Antony sighed. "Felicity, I have to admit it. I'm in way over my head here. I've read books written by priests who have had years and years of experience with such things. I've even lectured from them. But I've never done this before. All I know is that Satan does give power to his devotees. It's a second-rate power, but it can be very enticing to people who want power for themselves. Even if we don't really understand it, it doesn't do to scorn it."

"Yeah, I know. I just can't get my head around it. But I do trust your judgment." She turned her attention to the printouts in her hand and read silently for a few moments. "Well, it would help if we had the questions this is answering. Pity the professor didn't just hit reply so we'd have Hwyl's query on the bottom."

"Or maybe he did and Hwyl didn't print it all. I suppose it would still be on his computer if we need it."

"True. But I think we can figure it out. It looks like Hwyl asked what a letter from Rome—or maybe from Jerusalem— to somewhere distant in the empire would have been like, because Meyerson discusses language and writing materials and appearance. It's rather free-flowing and what-if. The professor must have dashed this off from the top of his head. But he apparently knows his stuff."

"Just read, we'll analyze it afterwards."

"OK, sure. 'Personal correspondence would have most likely been on wax tablets or on wooden leaves like the Vindolanda correspondence. I doubt they would have used papyrus unless there was an Egyptian connection (because papyrus was cheap there). If the writer was Jewish as you seem to indicate, parchment made from animal skins is more likely. And only from a kosher animal, such as a lamb. No pig skin! And no fish because the skins smell...'Yuck! Imagine writing a letter on fish skin."

"Read."

"Yeah, right. 'All Torah scrolls are still written on parchment with special inks and quills with no metal implements. Only black ink is acceptable. In ancient times, the ink used for writing a Torah scroll was obtained by boiling oils, tar and wax, and collecting the vapors. Afterwards, that mixture would be combined with tree sap and honey, and then dried out and stored. Before its use, it would be mixed with gall-nut juice. Such ink might have been used for non-sacred writing because it was handy.'" Felicity lowered the paper. "If Hwyl wanted to know that, I'd guess he had found something and wanted to know whether or not it was authentic. But it would have taken a chemist..." She looked up at Antony. "Oh, I know—*read*.'Keep in mind these rules are only for sacred texts (Torah Scrolls, the scrolls inside a mezuzah, etc.). Other legal documents—ketubot (wedding contracts), divorce papers, forms filled out by a mohel after a circumcision, etc.— don't have any restrictions.'

"'In the first century, I would expect a letter to be written with a quill (probably from a turkey; doubtful a non-kosher bird like a griffon vulture would be used, although they are native to the area).'" Felicity sighed. "This is fascinating, but could any of it possibly have a bearing on Hwyl's death?"

Antony shook his head. "I don't see how, but let's finish it."

"OK. This bit is about the Sanhedrin and languages: 'The Sanhedrin was largely a religious body. They used Aramaic, the *Lingua Franca* of the area, for secular dealings, and Hebrew for study and prayer. They would likely have had enough scholarship to write in either Greek or Latin, as well; whichever was the recipient's usual language.

"'Of course, it's essential to consider not only what language the writer worked in, but also what would be intelligible to his recipient. If the family member lived in the eastern part of the empire, then Aramaic is likely. If in the west, then Greek is likely.

"'In Britain, Latin is more likely. It prevailed there, since most people who made it that far west were in the Roman army, and Roman soldiers would have spoken Latin among themselves.'

"Oh, now, on this last bit the professor did copy some of Hwyl's questions and interlineated his answers. Pity he didn't do the whole letter that way: '[Now, may I ask more? What form would it likely be in? A sealed scroll?]

"'Probably. Or if it's just a small letter, then maybe a single sheet.

"'[How big?]

"'Hmm, not all that big. Depends how much they had to write.

"'[Perhaps in a leather pouch? In a clay jar like the Dead Sea Scrolls?]

"'Could be either. I don't think there were any rules on how one could send something like that. It's more a matter of how it was preserved. Do let me know how you get on. I'd be happy to take a look if you locate it.'

"And then he signs it with all his credentials. Good grief, they run off the page." Felicity folded the sheets and sat in silence. The reading had taken them back to St David's.

"Sounds to me as if Hwyl strongly suspected the existence of a letter from the Holy Land and wanted a description of what he was looking for," Antony mused as he drove slowly through the city.

"I agree." Felicity was quiet for a moment, then added, "I hope the others have had a good outing."

"And I hope Colin is fully recovered," Antony added, his mind still trying to figure out what to make of this new information. If anything. "Colin would appreciate Meyerson's reference to the Romans, at least."

"Yes, he was very interested in the clay table letters in the Roman museum in Caerleon," Felicity agreed. Then she caught her breath. "Wait! That's not all. That night in Caerleon, I went out for some air and Colin and Michael were talking. Well, arguing, really. I almost had the feeling Michael was threatening Colin and he referred to some letter, but Colin declared he didn't know anything about it."

"If Colin is feeling up to it we can have a talk with him. If some such artifact was involved in some way, we need to know about it."

When they arrived back at St Non's, though, the retreat house was silent. "Colin must be sleeping. Obviously the others haven't returned yet from Caerbwdy." Antony opened the door on Colin's room quietly so as not to disturb him. But the room was empty. The bed stripped.

"His mother came to collect him." Antony started at Sister Nora's voice. He hadn't heard her approach. "She came shortly after you left. She was in a great hurry. Not even time for tea."

"How was he?"

"He didn't want to leave, the poor laddie. He kept insisting he wouldn't forget to take his tablets again. He said he needed to do something."

Antony thanked her. As soon as the sister disappeared down the hall, he turned to Felicity. "I need to think." Felicity made a move toward him, but he stepped back. "I'll be in St Non's chapel."

He spun around abruptly. But not so abruptly he didn't register Felicity's bewildered look. He had to work through this, though. Alone.

The tiny chapel was warm this afternoon. Antony chose a seat along the west wall where the stones had been heated by the afternoon sun. He knew he had been brusque with Felicity, but prayer, silent prayer, was what he needed.

The silence, however, would not come. Hwyl's limp form, Adam's pale, retching figure, Colin gasping for air... The images filled his mind that should be emptied of all but the holy.

At last he gave it up and turned to active thinking. Who should he talk to? The police were unlikely to be open to any notions of the paranormal. Hwyl's bishop seemed a natural choice, but apparently Hwyl hadn't confided in him.

What about an ancient document, perhaps a letter, being involved somehow? Was it possible such a letter could reveal some lost arcane rite that would be of interest to satanists? Or might it be something truly holy that they wanted to pervert for their use? It was generally accepted that corruption of anything sacred to Christianity or any other major religion would strengthen a ritual or curse.

All those times Michael seemed to disappear. Could he have been looking for something for such a purpose? It seemed unlikely. Michael worked closely with Father Stephen and had mentioned that he wanted to become a Religious Education teacher. Or Colin? Was that his unfinished business? But he was still a child. Surely...

At last Antony's mind would form no more questions. Neither did it offer any answers, but at least the questions quit plaguing him. The peace of the chapel, the scent of the candles, the distant rhythm of the waves seeped into his soul and he could pray.

Chapter 21

*F*elicity woke from a fitful sleep. Sometimes being in love wasn't much fun. She hated it when Antony shut her out. She was well aware that he could appear cold and a touch pedantic to those who didn't know him. But she who knew him so well usually had only to look to see the tenderness underneath. So many times on this pilgrimage, though, there had seemed to be a barrier she couldn't broach. And yesterday's parting had been the sharpest. She knew he was worried. She was worried, too, for goodness' sake. And she hated feeling isolated.

Right. She flung her duvet aside. Lying here worrying wasn't helping anything. She crossed to her window and pulled back the curtain. Pink-tinged clouds hung low over the bay. A herd of red cows grazing near the ruined chapel lowed softly. And at the foot of the garden Antony stood observing the same scene from ground level. "Antony!" She stuck her head out of the window and called, hoping she wouldn't disturb Nancy in the room next to hers.

He turned and waved. Not a vigorous wave, just an acknowledgment, but it was enough. She was beside him in a few minutes. Without speaking she put her head on his shoulder. Barely moving, he put an arm around her and spoke as if she had shared the contents of her thoughts with him. "We will get through this. But we have to know what's going on."

"Yes." When she was with him she could believe it. "But don't shut me out, Antony. Whatever it is, we have to face it together."

"Yes. You're right. I'm sorry."

"And I'll try to be less cynical. I'm not really, you know. I think it's a defense mechanism—my way of dealing with fear."

He kissed her forehead. "Just try to keep an open mind. Today should be easier. We'll take the crew to the cathedral. That shouldn't be threatening."

Nothing could have been less threatening a few hours later when Felicity walked under the archway of the gatehouse beside its massive octagonal tower and stood at the top of the steep green slope of the cathedral grounds. The sun shimmered on the dewy grass dotted with lichen-encrusted stones spreading before her. Then she lifted her gaze to watch the crows cawing and circling around the tower, and beyond that to the spread of woods and sheep-grazed fields—all bathed in clear, golden sunshine. It seemed startlingly rural. And safe.

"When St David brought his band of monks here from Caerleon to found his monastery in the middle of the sixth century…"

"By the same route we traveled," Jared interrupted, looking very proud of himself.

Antony smiled. "Yes, indeed, by the very same route—he knew what he was getting into, having been born so near. But even so, the choice was a challenging one. *Glyn Rhosyn* it was called, 'The valley of the little marsh.' The entire valley was a bog, dense with bushes, but David found a relatively dry platform at the bend of the river to build his church on." He paused and glanced up at the gatehouse tower. "You'll note I said 'relatively dry.' When the cathedral bells destroyed by Cromwell's forces were replaced, they chose to hang them up here to prevent adding weight to the water-logged foundations.

"But this wasn't at all an eccentric choice for David. It was normal for Celtic saints to seek out deserted, waste places for their communities. And this was especially right for David, who is known for his rigorous asceticism as much as for his vigorous preaching. It was David's rule that all his monks engage in heavy manual labour.

"It was said that David turned his monks into oxen. Of course, that meant that he made them work as hard as oxen. In order to maintain a penitential spirit in his community, he forbade the use of any cattle in tilling the soil. His monks were allowed to speak only upon absolute necessity and they never ceased to pray, at least mentally, during their labor. After a day of such toil they returned to the monastery to read, write and pray. Their food was only bread and vegetables, seasoned with a little salt. They drank only milk and water.

"The evening meal was followed by three hours spent in prayer and adoration. Then, after a little rest, they rose at cockcrow to pray until it was light enough to return to work in the fields."

Kaylyn and Evie looked aghast at the idea of such a life.

"Not many takers for the job, I'll bet," Jared said with a grin.

Antony returned his smile. "Amazingly, it seems that there were. Not only those who applied, but those who persevered as well. It wasn't just a matter of showing up. When any one petitioned to be admitted to David's monastery, he was required to wait for ten days outside, suffering harsh words, repeated refusals, and difficult labors. So that he might 'learn to die to self,' it is said."

"It would have been easier just to die," Jared joked.

But Nancy seemed affected by the story. "So much love." Her remark was directed to Chloe, standing beside her.

"Love?" Chloe gaped. "It sounds abusive."

"It does, to the modern mind." Nancy nodded. "But it also

shows determination and total devotion to sanctify the land David loved so much."

Still thinking about Nancy's appraisal of David's energetic asceticism, Felicity followed Antony down the wide stairway. "Locals call these steps the '39 Articles'—for the similarly numbered articles of religion of the Anglican Church. They were—" The rest of Antony's sentence was drowned out by an exuberant cascade of bell-ringing from the gatehouse tower behind them. Felicity walked on with the changes tumbling down the hill around her like a waterfall. Such a joyous sound. She flung out her arms as if she would catch the silver sounds.

Inside, however, the cathedral was quiet. The stone walls completely blocked the sound of the bells. Felicity, who loved change-ringing, considered going back outside to hear the rest of the ring, but stopped still in her tracks at the sight of the graceful beauty of the sanctuary before her. She gazed at the flow of the stone arches supported by pillars running the length of each side of the nave below clerestory windows with clean morning light streaming in. Then she lifted her eyes higher to the wooden ceiling with its carved filigree arches and pendants. The sight that took her breath away, though, was the scalloped lines of the golden oak case enclosing the ranks of gleaming organ pipes, which made her think of angels' wings.

A tall, blue-robed verger approached, smiling. "A medieval attempt to create a vision of heaven. I can't help feeling they did rather well in the attempt." Felicity smiled her agreement.

The guide followed the upward line of her gaze. "This is the 'new' ceiling, installed in 1530 as an architectural expedient. The walls were leaning outward due to inadequate foundations on the marshy ground. But necessity became virtue, and the Irish oak ceiling—it's said they insisted on Irish oak to avoid using English oak—is one of the glories of the cathedral." Her guide pointed out a medieval Green Man and Renaissance dragon-shaped dolphins and delicate fretwork carving, then offered to show her more.

"Thank you, that was very interesting, but I need to catch up with my group."

"Right on up the aisle, then," he pointed. "Literally up. The nave slopes upward 14 feet."

Felicity stopped, trying to discern a rise to the stone floor. "Why?"

The guide smiled. "Some say the slope is due to the fact that the cathedral was built on marshy, ill-drained land; others that it is simply because it was built on a hillside. The more poetic say it's to get the worshiper nearer to heaven."

Smiling, Felicity hurried forward through the rood screen with the statue of St David to her right, up the stairs across the mosaic-tiled floor of the choir, rich with warm wooden stalls, to the high altar. Behind the presbytery she found her friends in the Holy Trinity Chapel. Felicity looked for a moment at the statue of Giraldus Cambrensis with the bishop's miter he so desired but failed to achieve lying at his feet. Antony, however, was pointing his little group of pilgrims to a niche tucked away in the back of the wall. An oak casket was almost hidden inside the niche behind a sturdy iron railing. "The chest contains bones—long believed to be those of St David. When David died in 589, the monastery is said to have been 'filled with angels as Christ received his soul.' His final words to his followers were: 'Be joyful. Keep the faith. Do the little things that you have heard and seen me do.'

"David's asceticism had a great influence on the Irish church and brought many pilgrims to St David's, until it was ravaged, first by warring Welsh kings, then by the Vikings. In the eleventh century, a visitor found David's shrine hidden in the undergrowth and the site abandoned. Our friend Giraldus Cambrensis was one of the rebuilders in the next century."

Antony pointed to the statue of Gerald Felicity had observed earlier, then turned to lead the group around to the front of the altar, and stood before three simple Gothic arches set into the north wall. "In medieval times, pilgrims queued to see David's shrine. It was destroyed at the Reformation, but his relics, being in a portable casket, were secreted away. There is currently an appeal for funds to restore the shrine and return the relics of St David to their rightful place."

"Oh, aye, there is. And it was coming along right fine until this absurd notion got going that it was the Bishop's Palace that was needing restoring." Everyone turned at the words of the verger who had guided Felicity earlier. "I ask you—a few thousand pounds to restore a place that was hallowed for 1,500 years," he pointed to the barren arches of what was once a glorious memorial, "or millions of pounds to restore Bishop Gower's tribute to his megalomania? I don't know what people are thinking." He shook his head and stomped off down the north aisle.

"What was that all about?" Felicity gaped at his departing, stiffly erect back.

"Sounds like competing appeals for funds," Ryan remarked.

"Wonder which side he's on?" Nancy laughed.

"Actually, that's not a bad segue," Antony said as he led back through the choir and under the rood screen, which he referred to as a pulpitum, to the statue of St David. Beside the statue a compartment was built into the massive stone screen, surrounded by an ornately decorated Gothic arch. A sarcophagus topped by a stone effigy lay behind an iron railing. "Bishop Gower's tomb," Antony said.

"Sweet," Kaylyn observed, peering through the grille.

Felicity surveyed the grandeur of the tomb. "Was the guide right? Was he a megalomaniac?"

Antony shook his head. "By all accounts, Gower was an able and energetic bishop who served both church and state."

"And also his own memory," Ryan added.

Antony nodded. "That, too. But we have him to thank for much of the beauty we see around us in the cathedral today. Of course it's been restored and remodeled continually through the ages, but Gower's work in the fourteenth century transformed the cathedral and its precincts."

"When's lunch?" Jared's abrupt question was seconded by the Goths.

"I noticed a fish and chips shop back up the street," Evie said.

That settled the matter. The shop had an open courtyard with tables set in the sun. Felicity closed her eyes and leaned back while Antony ordered their fish. When he returned with the baskets of crisp, golden cod, she savored the first bite. "Mmm." After the second succulent mouthful she looked around at their pilgrims. "Where are Lydia and Michael?"

"I think Lydia was going to look up an old friend here," said Antony, "and Michael went for a walk."

Felicity finished her last chip and, observing a large tabby cat curled up sleeping in a sunny corner of the patio, was thinking how good it would feel to take a nap, when Antony rose to lead them back to the cathedral close.

This time they went on beyond the entrance and the west front of the cathedral, across a curved bridge over a crystal, flowing stream, and through the gatehouse of the intriguing-looking ruined building. A wide courtyard carpeted with lush grass filled the interior of the structure that sprawled before them on three sides of the lawn.

"Safe." "Sweet." Kaylyn and Evie spoke together.

"This must have been amazing in its day." Ryan stopped mid-stride.

"Oh, this is a photographer's paradise!" Chloe removed her camera from the case she always wore around her neck, and began adjusting the telephoto lens to focus on interesting angles.

Antony pointed to the two-storey range topped with a distinctive arched parapet walk on their left. "The east wing has the private episcopal apartments, then the bishop's hall, solar, and his private chapel." Now he pointed straight ahead of them across the courtyard toward a wide stairway leading up to an arched entranceway beneath the parapet which crowned the length of the building. "That's the grand processional entrance into the south range which housed the Great Hall, parlour and Great Chapel for the entertainment of distinguished pilgrims."

"He could have entertained royalty," Felicity said.

"He undoubtedly did. Bishops were considered equals with princes," Antony replied.

The pilgrims had waited politely while Antony pointed out the general plan of the building, but now they wandered off to explore the enticing ruined chambers, hidden stairways and shadowy undercrofts.

Felicity turned to the barer, more broken walls to her right. "What was on that side?"

"The west range was probably used to house lower status visitors, and the north, behind us, would have completed the square with stables." Antony pointed to their left. "Shall we start in the bishop's private chambers?"

Felicity led up the small staircase to the bishop's solar. Chloe stood along the far wall, her camera aimed upward at a small, perky face peering at them from where the ceiling beams would have abutted the wall. "Aren't these corbels wonderful?" Chloe snapped a picture. "Each face is different. They have such personality—like the sculptor knew each one personally. I've spotted human heads, animals, and mythical creatures. There must have been dozens—hundreds—of them." She took another shot as Felicity and Antony moved on into the bishop's private chapel.

"Can I ask you to stand in that window opening? It'll make a perfect frame." Felicity obediently posed in the aperture of the enormous Gothic window that filled the end of the chapel. "Great. Thanks. Now will you take one of me?" Chloe showed Antony which buttons to press. "From the outside, if you don't mind." Chloe climbed into the window opening while Antony went back outside for the photoshoot.

Felicity wandered out of the chapel and on across the length of the bishop's hall toward the kitchen, when a scrabbling noise in the arcaded parapet made her look up. A large black crow took flight, leaving two of his brothers perched on the rim. Felicity smiled and started to turn away when she saw a shadow that wasn't a bird. She shivered, recalling recent days when their steps had been dogged through London and across Norfolk by a shadowy figure. But this was a sunny June day in Wales. It was undoubtedly another tourist drawn to the enticing walk circling the top of the bishop's structure.

A passage led from the kitchen to the grand south range. Antony joined her in the Great Hall where she stood gazing up at the rose window. "It's still beautiful even without its glass. Dinners here must have been magnificent." At the far end, a small stairway in the corner led up to an alcove that opened onto the parapet walk. "I wonder what this was for," she mused. Did it hold someone reading or singing? Or maybe listening to the company below?

Felicity walked out onto the parapet and leaned over the arcade, observing the unique checkerboard decoration formed by different colored stones: purple and cream sandstone, and white quartz. With Antony behind her, Felicity continued on around the rim of the Great Chamber to look down on the Great Chapel. "The altar stood there," he pointed, "below what was a three-light east window. And there, to the right note the piscina. It's considered one of Gower's most graceful touches."

He turned to say something else when a tall, stocky man with thick black hair curling over his forehead entered the chapel below them, lecturing a small group, "Now, the Great Hall would have been limewashed white to set off the deep red, ochre, and purple of the Caerlwdy stone. The whole place would have been a blaze of color. But this is where I believe we should begin." He directed the group to the niche for washing liturgical vessels. "This piscina is the jewel of the room; it has great architectural value, and it should be restored to its full glory." His booming voice carried upward. "This now-bare stonework would have been entirely covered with paint. There may have been an illustration of a saint..."

Felicity saw Jared, Evie and Kaylyn walking across the broad lawn below them and waved. She and Antony made their way back down to the Great Hall, then out the magnificent ceremonial entranceway to join their friends on the grass. "There's supposed to be an exhibit in the undercroft," Evie said.

"Sounds interesting. Let's take a look." Felicity walked beside Evie.

The first archway they entered under the hall led to a cold, dark cavern. Evie shivered deliciously. "Oh, this is spooky. I like it."

Felicity smiled. "It might be atmospheric, but I don't think we found the right place for the exhibit." A series of undercrofts that had once served as various storage and service rooms ran beneath the entire palace. They tried two more entrances before they found the one that offered models of reconstructed rooms, paintings showing how the rooms had been used, and posters appealing for funds to "Restore the jewel of St David's to its former glory."

Kaylyn and Evie studied a painting of horned, forked-tailed demons tormenting medieval humans. "Medieval people believed themselves poised on a knife-edge between heaven and hell and always threatened by tempting demons," Kaylyn read out. This spurred the girls and Jared to a lively discussion on the existence of demons.

Felicity moved on to an exhibit about the bishopric in Gower's day: In 1326, the bishop had 2,000 tenants' lands worth £333 a year—twenty times the income of a knight, she read, then turned to Antony. "I was just wondering how Gower managed to finance all this. This explains at least some of it."

Antony considered. "I'm not sure. That makes it sound rather a lot, but I read that Gower's annual income was less than that available to most other bishops of England and Wales. And only about one-eighth of the size of rich dioceses such as Durham or Winchester."

"Maybe he had private wealth."

Antony shook his head. "A lot of bishops did, but not Gower. And along with all this grandeur he built a large hospital for the poor and sick in Swansea."

"Hmm," Felicity considered. "I wonder how he managed it." Should she add Gower and his achievements to her list of power points in Wales along with Julius and Aaron, St David and Evan Roberts? Such a diversity, spread over so many centuries. And yet in the very path they had trod.

Felicity realized Antony was continuing his lecture. "… reformed the lives of the clergy and was a brilliant ruler of his flock. The greatest medieval bishop of Wales, and a scholar and chancelor of Oxford university as well."

Felicity moved on to read from the next board: "Gower came to St David's in 1328 and found 'a lodging for servants and animals where there ought to be a palace.' Twenty years later he had created the finest bishop's palace in Britain." Again her mind turned to the question of financing.

But not for long. The booming Welsh voice they had last heard floating up to them from the floor of the Great Chapel interrupted further thought. "Now, we can see from this reconstruction exactly what it should look like." The speaker caught sight of Antony's clerical collar and left his group to stride across the room to him. "Welcome, Father. Interested in our reconstruction, are you?"

Antony shook the hand thrust out toward him and replied that the display was very interesting.

"Rhys Morgan," the exuberant guide introduced himself. "Chairman of the Reconstruction Committee. We're holding a tea in the cathedral hall to present an update on our work to the public. I'm just showing some of the early comers around a bit. You'll come, won't you? Starts in just a few minutes. Should be there right now myself, but my wife will have it all in hand."

"Thank you, but I don't think—"

"Thank you, Mr Morgan, that's very kind of you." Felicity stepped forward. "We'd love to hear more about your work. And, frankly, a cup of tea sounds wonderful."

"Ah, grand. That's just grand. We'll see you in a few minutes, then. North side of the cathedral, beside the cloisters."

Antony looked at her quizzically, but she waited until Rhys had left before she explained. "Dilys said the committee met at their home. She mentioned the chairman had been in and out several times. That must be our effusive friend."

Antony smiled. "Right you are. Do you think we can bring the troops?"

Felicity surveyed their always-hungry friends and shrugged. "He said public." She interrupted their examination of a display showing the rats and other items from a medieval sewer. "Jared, Ryan, everybody, we've been invited to tea."

They left the palace precinct and walked back toward the cathedral, crossing the tiny River Alun at the stone bridge with its Narnia lamp post. Rhys saw them approaching and strode toward them. "Ah, right. So glad you all came. Just what we need—to get the word out." He waved his arm at the structure to the north side of the cathedral. "St Mary's College, this was, in the fourteenth century, to house the clergy that conducted the continual round of offices in the cathedral. Reformation put an end to all that, of course. But it was restored in the last century. Serves as the cathedral hall, a refectory open to the public, an art gallery." Even with Felicity's long legs she was having trouble keeping up with Rhys Morgan. "It's a good start, I say. An excellent example of what we can accomplish on a much grander scale with the Bishop's Palace."

He led across a small cloister garden into a light, airy room with ivory floors and pale gold walls. "Now, see what I mean." He addressed their whole group. "Original stone walls, windows glazed, good solid roof, all the mod cons. There's no reason the palace couldn't be put back into running order. Talk about prime real estate. It's wicked to let it go to waste."

Felicity considered. "Yes, I see what you mean. But the Bishop's Palace is vast. What will you use it for?"

"Oh, there'll be no end of uses: meetings, conventions, tourist accommodation… All things we can charge for, as well, so the restoration will be an investment. In time it will turn a profit."

A tall, slim woman with her pale blonde hair worn in a sleek roll detached herself from a group sipping tea and nibbling biscuits to cross the floor toward them. "Ah, here's my wife. Anne, my love, meet our pilgrim group. They've come all the way from Caerleon in the steps of St David."

"How wonderful! You walked all the way?" She directed her question to Antony.

"No, no. We drove from Penrhys."

"Ah, very sensible of you. I'm sure my husband has filled you in on his little project."

Felicity laughed. "I don't think I'd call it 'little.'"

Anne waved a hand tipped with bright red nails. "Oh, to a visionary like Rhys, it's all in a day's work."

"Thank you, my dear, but I must say that credit for this really goes to my charming wife. It wasn't my idea."

Anne looked her husband straight in the eye. "Yes, it was, darling. You've forgotten." Her voice was so soft the words were barely audible over the clink of teacups and chatter in the room.

Rhys smiled. "Oh, yes, love. Of course, you're right."

"Rhys is a natural for this work. He's a genius at real estate." She patted her husband's arm. "I don't know a plot from a plat, but I do have a small shop in the high street." She turned to Felicity. "You must drop in while you're here."

"Oh, a dress shop?"

Anne smiled. "I like to think of it as a place of healing. Chakra Health, I call it. Scented candles, poetry books, herbs. Marissa, my assistant, does massage and aromatherapy. Let her give you a massage if you have time. It's so relaxing, and you must have sore muscles after your pilgrim walk."

"Still some blisters," Felicity admitted.

"Do help yourself to tea and nibbles," Anne invited. Jared headed the beeline to the refreshment table, but Anne stopped Antony with a hand on his arm. "Here, you must have one of our information brochures. I know Rhys would love to involve you on the committee. We do need more clergy input. You must come around to our house on Monday evening. We're having a little group over. You'll want to visit more with Father Antony, won't you, Rhys?"

"Oh, sorry, love, I forgot to tell you that Monday evening won't work. Something came up at the office."

Anne looked at her husband. "That was taken care of, darling. You want to talk to Father Antony."

Rhys threw his head back and laughed loudly enough to draw attention from across the room. "What a lady. I ask you! She knows my mind better than I do." He handed Antony his card. "Address is there. Monday at seven."

Felicity turned toward the refreshment table, then stopped in surprise when she saw the amber-haired young woman pouring out cups of tea. "Lydia, I didn't expect to see you here."

Lydia held out a cup of tea with milk and no sugar, the way Felicity liked it. "I did rather get roped in. But I don't mind. Anne Morgan is an old family friend."

Felicity smiled and watched their hostess approach a group of newcomers, offering them brochures. "Forceful lady. In a velvet glove sort of way."

Felicity turned to the exquisite selection of luxury biscuits, but before she could decide between white chocolate or Jaffa, a movement in the garden beyond the window caught her eye. She watched for a minute, then burst out laughing. "Oh, look at that!" Four of their pilgrims were doing "Y. M. C. A." in the cloister. Early in the pilgrimage she would never have imagined their former juvenile delinquent would be leading two Goths and a prospective nun in cheerleader choreography. "Oh, where's Chloe? I want a picture of that."

But the amateur photographer was nowhere to be seen. "Here," Lydia dug in her pocket and pulled out her mobile. "The camera on this takes pretty good photos." She clicked the buttons to get it to camera mode. "Just push here. It's aim and fire."

"Thank you." Felicity abandoned her tea and ran out into the cloister to capture the moment.

She had taken several snaps when Ryan joined her. "They're great, aren't they? Here," he held his hand out for the phone/camera. "That'll take video, too."

By the time they finished filming, the dancers were ready for another cup of tea. Felicity started to follow them back into the hall when the phone in her hand rang. She considered rushing to get the phone to Lydia, but the vision of bumping guests and sloshing tea was daunting. She pushed the green button. "Hello. This is Lydia Bowen's phone."

She had intended to offer to get Lydia, but the caller apparently mistook her for the answerphone. "This is George Watson, headteacher at Abergavenny College. Please contact me immediately. We are very concerned that we have not heard from Adam Bowen since term began. If he is ill, please let us know if we will need to arrange for tutoring to keep him up with his class."

Long moments after the message had clicked off, Felicity stood staring at the tiny blank screen in her hand. Adam had disappeared? Had never arrived at his school? How was that possible? Lydia had taken him there herself, Lydia and Michael, Monday morning while the others waited in Aberdare. She was certain she remembered correctly. Lydia had gone into detail about how happy he had been to be back.

What could have gone wrong? Had Adam been faking his happiness and then run away? Or had it been something even more sinister?

Chapter 22

Thursday
St David's

*B*ack at St Non's, Antony sat alone in the darkened chapel in the retreat house going over the events of the past hours in his mind. Lydia, as baffled as everyone else, had rung the headmaster immediately, but she could offer no explanation or advice beyond Antony's insistence that she tell them to call the police.

There was little point in ringing Adam's parents. Their father was a top executive for an oil company based in Dubai, but they could be anywhere in the world. "But surely your mother—" Felicity had insisted.

"Adam's mother, you mean," Lydia had replied with a hint of bitterness in her voice. "My mother has been dead for years. Of course, Father would probably hire a helicopter and fly to Abergavenny. He dotes on the little twerp. But what could he accomplish other than ordering everybody around and getting in the way?"

"What's he like?" Felicity had asked.

"Father?" The acrimony had been more than a hint, then. "Rich, powerful, a snob. Demanding. With everyone except Adam. He spoils him. Mostly, he bosses women around. He completely trampled my mother. I was only five when she died, but I could see it even then. I stood up to him. He hated that."

And then she had repeated it all for Detective Superintendent

Thomas Pool, the senior investigations officer from the Dyfed-Powys police in Haverfordwest who interviewed her at the request of the Gwent Police. Pool had also questioned Michael, who recounted watching Lydia accompany her little brother to the door of his House, and then going to the gas station to check oil and water levels on the minibus as well as the air pressure in the tires before filling up with gas while Lydia helped Adam settle in.

After the policeman departed, Antony had gathered the pilgrims in the chapel for a special prayer time, then sent them to bed. Felicity had gone up with Lydia, offering to stay with her for as long as she might want company.

And now he sat, his mind as dark as the lightless room around him. Nothing made any sense. This had to be yet another of the diabolical events that had plagued them this entire time. But how? No matter how often he reminded Felicity of the reality of the power of Satan, he did not believe that force extended to making a human being simply disappear. This sounded far more like human action.

But that didn't mean it was any less evil. Antony was certain that if he could discover what Hwyl had been doing, he would have the key. Tomorrow he would ring Dilys again. And then he would have to approach Hwyl's bishop.

Questions continued to gnaw at him as he climbed the stairs to his room through the echoing retreat house. A tinge of pink and gold dawn was showing around the edges of Antony's curtain before he finally fell into a restless sleep. He awoke a few hours later with a splitting headache.

He was in the guest lounge making a cup of tea when Felicity came in. "You don't look like you slept any better than I did," he said.

"Hmm, you do know how to make a girl's heart go pitter-pat." She gave him a peck of a kiss, then sighed. "But, no, you're right. It's all so worrying. Do you think whoever killed Hwyl has abducted Adam? Could there possibly be a connection?"

Antony added an extra scoop of sugar to his tea. "I think it's all connected. If I could just see how…"

"We had thought Adam's poisoning was random, or maybe a mistake, but now I wonder. Did anyone think to tell the police about that? Or about the 'lady' from Twmbarlwm?"

Antony's reply was to take out his mobile and ring the number Detective Superintendent Pool had given him, while Felicity made herself a cup of tea and joined him on the sofa. The superintendent wasn't in, so Antony left a message with Pool's assistant, who identified herself as Constable Gwen Owen.

Ringing Dilys was next on his list. She was delighted to hear from him; she sounded perkier than she had the day they visited, and was happy to answer his questions. But Antony felt they were just going over old ground.

"Interests? Hobbies? Not much time for that. We loved walking. We'd done almost the entire Pembrokeshire Coastal Walk. In bits and pieces, of course. I loved the flowers, Hwyl concentrated on the birds. Puffins. They were his favorite. Looked like a child's stuffed toy, he said. He even collected puffins—for when we…" She stopped.

"Dilys, I'm so sorry." Felicity spoke softly into the speakerphone.

Dilys caught her breath with a little hiccup. "Yes. Thank you. We'd hoped for so long."

"Any other hobbies?" Antony thought it best to move on.

"Archeology. Roman artifacts. Like that email I showed you was apparently about."

"Yes."

"Did that help?"

"I'm not sure. You haven't found anything else, have you?"

"I'm afraid I didn't get much accomplished yesterday. My sister will be here tomorrow, then we'll get stuck in."

"Good. Thank you for your help. We'll check back in a few days."

After he rang off, he and Felicity looked at each other. She was the first to shake her head. "Not much help, huh?"

"And nothing new about Adam?" Antony rubbed his throbbing temple. The sugar and caffeine were beginning to do their work.

"I spoke with Lydia just before I came down here. She had rung all of Adam's friends she knew, although she said she didn't know many. Apparently the police had already spoken to them. If anyone knows anything, they're not talking."

"Surely his friends couldn't be responsible?"

Felicity shrugged. "Well, one hates to think of it, but you do read about terrible things kids get up to."

"Or maybe whoever removed Adam has frightened the others into keeping quiet."

"If that's the case, the police will get it out of them soon enough, I'm sure." Felicity took a sip of her tea. "What's our agenda for today?"

Antony smiled. "The point of a retreat is not having an agenda. At least, that's the theory. Actually, I think I need to talk to Hwyl's bishop if he can make time to see me. What about you?"

"I thought that after lunch I'd take Anne Morgan up on her invitation to visit her shop." Felicity flexed her shoulders. "I can't even imagine how good a massage would feel."

Antony rang the diocesan office. The bishop's personal assistant said Bishop Harry could see Antony mid-afternoon. "You're fortunate; he's at the cathedral office today and tomorrow. That'll save you a journey to Carmarthen." Antony was pleased. That would give him plenty of time to see that the young people, under Michael's direction, were organized for the walk Ryan was leading. After lunch, he and Felicity stood on the verandah, waving the more energetic of their group away as they set off up the Pembrokeshire coast armed with a rucksack full of flasks and biscuits, and a bird book and binoculars supplied by Sister Nora. Nancy had elected to spend a quiet afternoon reading, and Lydia wanted to ring an aunt and some distant cousins on the off-chance they might have heard something from Adam.

As it was such a beautiful day, Antony and Felicity chose to walk into town. "So the diocesan office isn't in St David's?" Felicity asked.

"Carmarthen is probably forty miles east. Much more accessible for an administrative office. It's on the train line, even."

Felicity smiled. "I suppose that makes sense, but that's one of the things I like best about St David's—the sense of being set apart from the hurly-burly." The rolling landscape covered with bracken and gorse stretched as far as they could see—to the cliff edge above the sea on their left and to meet the blue, cloud-puffed sky on their right. A slight rustle of the breeze in the foliage at their feet and the distant cry of a seabird were the only sounds besides their own footsteps.

"What do you know about the bishop? Have you ever met him?"

"I met his predecessor at Hwyl's ordination. Harry Wynn has only been bishop for a couple of years, but he sounds like a good man. I looked him up on Sister Nora's computer. Son of a vicar from Cardiff, he's served his whole career in Wales. Was archdeacon of the diocese before being elected bishop. He's an historian, too."

"Oh, you'll get along just fine, then." Felicity grinned.

She went on up the street to her massage appointment and Antony turned down the steps to the cathedral. Bishop Harry welcomed him into the cathedral library, located over the chapel beside the high altar. "I thought this would be more pleasant than meeting in my rather stuffy office in St Mary's Hall." He indicated that Antony should take a chair by the brick fireplace along the far wall, and seated himself on the other side of the empty grate. "My assistant, Jane, tells me you knew Father Hwyl." The bishop shook his bald head. "Tragic loss. I can't imagine how I'll replace him. He was excellent at his job. Both as a parish priest and with the more esoteric duties he undertook for me. Frankly, I don't have much time for all that myself."

"Yes, that's what I wanted to talk to you about. As you may have heard, it's rather likely Hwyl's deliverance work may have contributed to his death."

Bishop Harry looked skeptical as he raised his eyebrows behind wire-rimmed glasses. "The strain, of course, can be severe. But I always thought Hwyl could handle it. He had a marvelous ability to be quite laid-back when he wasn't working. That's an ability more of us need to cultivate, I always feel."

Antony ran his hand backward through his hair, then stopped himself. Yes, he knew about being too intense about one's work. "Bishop, I realize much of Hwyl's work would be confidential, but were you aware of anything he was working on that would have caused him special concern?"

"I wasn't aware of anything out of the ordinary. I would have known if he was planning a full exorcism, but that is very rare. I wouldn't necessarily be aware of his day-to-day calls. Father Hwyl does—er, did—a great many house blessings. We get a lot of creaky stairs and cold spots in old farmhouses hereabouts. I don't mean to minimize that. St David's is a very ancient holy place. That can be a magnet for the wrong sort of spirits as well."

"Yes. Do you know anything about a group that calls itself the Orbis Astri?"

"Yes, Hwyl mentioned it. He brought me some information—a leaflet about a lecture series on spiritual empowerment, as I recall. The thing that does stick in my mind is the image of that rather sinister-looking double-headed snake. I don't think he had any more information than one could find on the Internet. Groups like that can be very worrying, of course, if a highly charismatic person gets hold of them. It can be a real power trip for some individuals."

"Enough to kill for, would you say?"

The bishop raised his eyebrows again. "Power can be a very, well—powerful motivator."

"To manipulate people for personal prestige, you mean?"

"Prestige, money, any personal goal. 'I will give you all the kingdoms of this world,' Satan promised our Lord." Bishop Harry leaned forward in his chair. "I don't have to tell you, Father, it's mostly smoke and mirrors, but there can be a real danger."

Antony nodded and was silent until the chill of the bishop's words generated receded. "What do you think about the drive to restore the Bishop's Palace?"

"I can see that the idea of developing a retreat and convention center might hold appeal to some of the more energetic members of our community. I personally wouldn't like to see the lovely peace of St David's disturbed. That is, after all, why David came here. I think we could lose something very precious. Besides the issues of the staggering amount of money involved and the difficulties of getting planning permission to rebuild anything of such enormous historic value, I'd have to say that the campaign to restore St David's Shrine is far more practical, and I would hate to divert attention away from that." Bishop Harry removed his glasses and rubbed his eyes. "Of course, I don't suppose I should be seen as showing favoritism, since it was a predecessor of this office who is responsible for destroying both."

Antony blinked. "A bishop? Of St David's? Surely, Henry VIII…"

"No, I fear the culprit was closer to home. William Barlow, bishop here in the mid-sixteenth century. He was determined to break the hold of 'superstition' here, so he stripped the shrine of David of its jewels and confiscated the relics. It was his plan to remove the cathedral from St David's to Carmarthen, but he only got as far as moving the bishop's residence." The bishop smiled. "It is more convenient, I suppose. But convenience isn't everything. Barlow was blamed for stripping the lead from the roof of the Bishop's Palace in order to provide dowries for his six daughters, but that may be no more than gossip."

Antony thanked the bishop for his time and made his way back through the cathedral, wondering if he had learned anything useful. Interesting, certainly. But was there anything there that could get him closer to the cause of Hwyl's death? If there was, he didn't see it.

Up the street from the cathedral close, Felicity was waiting for him at the lace-curtained Corbels Tea Shop. He surveyed the copies of various corbels copied from the Bishop's Palace ringing the ceiling. Little human heads, animals and mythical beasts peered down at him. He turned to Felicity and smiled. "You look relaxed. Did you get a massage from the magic-fingered Marissa?"

"Don't mock. There wasn't time for a real massage, but she did something she calls energy work on my neck and shoulders—I couldn't believe how many knots I had in my neck. Feels great now." Felicity rotated her neck like a rag doll to demonstrate her flexibility.

"Was Anne there?"

"No, she was out, but the shop really is quite lovely in a New Agey sort of way; stained glass and crystals catching the light in the window, bells and wind chimes tinkling through sitar music, a little waterfall splashing. And the smells! All kinds of scented candles and aromatherapy oils." She leaned forward so he could smell her neck. "She used lemon oil and lavender on me. To relieve stress, she said."

Antony looked at his companion's serene smile. But he was still uncomfortable about all this. "Felicity—" He wasn't sure how to express his discomfort. "Crystals, chakras—all this new age stuff just isn't compatible with Christianity. Be careful."

"Yes, I know. It all seemed great until I was leaving and spotted these." She pulled a flyer from her pocket and handed it to him. He knew what it would be. The act of unfolding the paper made the double-headed snake printed there appear to slither.

"Another empowerment lecture," Felicity began, but then her placid look vanished.

It or they were all around them. And yet Antony could see nothing. He had a sense of the corbels circling the room laughing and jeering at him. *You'll never get us. We're stronger than you are. Smarter, quicker and more powerful,* they mocked.

Chapter 23

After breakfast the next morning, Felicity followed Lydia out onto the terrace where Nancy, Evie and Kaylyn were already sitting on a bench overlooking the bay. Lydia stood apart and Felicity joined her. "How are you holding up, Lydia? Has there been any word about Adam? This must be so worrying for you."

Lydia shook her head. "I'm worried about Adam, but not in the way you think. I'm sure he's fine. They'll find him holed up with a friend no one knew anything about, or having a grand adventure in a deserted shack in some woods. He's done things like this before. I worry because I can't imagine what we'll do if the school kicks him out."

"So you don't think he's been abducted? The police…"

"Oh, I know. They have to do all the 'missing child' search things. Doing their job. That's good. But he'll turn up. I told them."

Jared, Ryan and Michael joined them. "Pembroke Castle today," Ryan declared. "Who's up for it?"

"Pembroke Castle?" Felicity asked.

"An enormous oval castle with a huge circular keep," Michael replied. "Pembroke Castle may have been a base when the Roman fleet patroled the Bristol Channel."

"What a pity Colin isn't here to go with us," Evie said.

Felicity smiled at the Goth's immediate enthusiasm. Pilgrimage was often life-changing, but the change wasn't usually so dramatic. Nancy, however, chose to remain at St Non's. "I think I'll have a quiet day."

Michael turned to Lydia. She shook her head. "I'm sure you can take care of it without me. I'm going to see if I can get hold of some more of Adam's school chums. His bunks don't usually last this long."

Michael placed a hand on her shoulder. "God help you, Lydia. I can't imagine how worried you must be. Do you want me to stay with you?"

"No, of course not. You've got your job."

Michael turned to Felicity, "You up for an outing?"

"It sounds like a great—" Felicity started to join in the plans when Antony came around the corner. The morning sun seemed to highlight the worry lines at the corners of his eyes. She didn't finish her sentence, but went to him.

"Two things," he said, walking on toward the corner of the lawn where they wouldn't be overheard by the others. "Chloe has some photos she wants to show you, and Dilys rang. She's found some things in Hwyl's desk. I think we ought to go back to see her again." He nodded toward the group on the terrace. "That is, unless you…"

"No, no. But I think Michael is planning to use the van—they want to visit Pembroke Castle. I'd rather go with you, though." *Always and anywhere*, she finished silently.

"Good." He gave her a brief smile. "That sounds a good plan for them. I do appreciate Michael seeing to the youth when I've got all this on my mind. I'll ask Sister Nora if we can borrow their car."

Felicity returned his smile. "Right. You arrange that and I'll see what Chloe wants. Where is she?"

"Sister Nora's office. Chloe borrowed her computer."

Felicity found her American friend busily cropping and enhancing her photos from the Bishop's Palace. "Looks like you got some great shots."

"I thought you'd like to see the ones I took of you. They turned out so well. It's great of Nora to let me use her computer. I get so far behind on my editing. And I love to keep up my photo journal blog when I can. Everyone at home is following me."

Felicity pulled a folding chair up to sit beside Chloe. "Oh, you did a great job of framing me in that window."

"So glad you were wearing red. Nothing photographs better. Especially against the brown stone. And with your golden hair."

Chloe turned through several photos, some of Felicity and Antony together. "Oh, not fair. We didn't know you were taking a picture." The photo was of Antony kissing her.

"You're darling together. You don't mind, do you?"

"Of course not." Actually she liked it. "How did the ones we took of you come out?"

Chloe clicked on through her album. "And these of the corbels are fun. I used my telephoto so I could get interesting angles and show their features." She turned through a variety of pictures of little medieval heads. "This is a fun one. I caught Michael looking around the parament, just like one of the corbels. I'm sure he had no idea I was there."

No, Felicity agreed. She was certain he didn't know. Why had he pretended he wasn't there that day? And wasn't that part of the parapet walk closed off? What was he doing there?

She was still puzzling over it when Antony came to tell her he had their transportation sorted out. "How nice of Sister Nora to loan us her car," she said as they started down the lane.

"She was more than happy to when I told her we wanted to call on Dilys Pendry. Father Hwyl was much loved here. He had led healing retreats for the Sisters several times."

"What has Dilys found?'

"She didn't go into detail. She said it would be best to show us. But she sounded worried."

And Dilys looked worried when she answered the door of the vicarage. "Thank you for coming." She stood back to hold the door for them to step in. "I was cleaning out Hwyl's desk." She began immediately, without preamble or further greeting. "I thought since my sister is here I didn't have any more excuses to put it off." She led the way down the hall to the office, crossed the room to the desk and picked up a file. "You asked me if I'd seen that emblem before." She shoved the papers at Antony as if they stung her fingers. "I wanted to burn them, but I know they're probably important."

Antony sat at the desk chair, and Felicity stood behind him, leaning over his shoulder. The first thing in the file was one of the ubiquitous fliers for the Orbis Astri empowerment lecture. Below that were notes in Hwyl's handwriting, apparently on research he had done on satanic ceremonies. Antony nodded. "Yes. We covered some of this briefly in my seminar."

"Are these notes from your class?"

"I wouldn't think so. But perhaps remembering something we discussed there led Hwyl to dig deeper into these practices."

"Seven high holy days a year: Christmas, Easter, Guy Fawkes, beginning of the four seasons. Blood sacrifice required, usually an animal..." Felicity shivered. She didn't want to consider what the blood sacrifice would be if it *weren't* an animal. "A mix of Christian and national and pagan celebrations," she mused. "The beginning of the seasons... June 21, summer solstice..."

"The Eve of Corpus Christi. The Solemnity of the Most Holy Body and Blood of Christ." Antony finished her thought. "Next Wednesday. The day Christians around the world prepare to celebrate the Body of Christ, consecrated in Holy Communion."

"And occult practice requires a blood sacrifice." Felicity's voice was barely above a whisper, yet it seemed to echo in the room. She counted on her fingers: today was Friday, Sunday would be Trinity, celebrating the three persons of God—Father, Son and Holy Spirit—then three days to the Eve of Corpus Christi which this year fell on the summer solstice. If the Orbis Astri was planning something more sinister than one of their lectures, they had just over five days to figure out what was going on. So many questions. So little time.

Dilys moved to ascend a small stepping ladder by the book case. She lifted down a rectangular wooden box perched on the top shelf. "I found this, too. It looks very old. Maybe valuable." She took a rolled sheet of paper from the case and handed it to Antony.

He very gently unrolled a few inches of the sheet. "Mmm, very old, yes. And brittle. I don't want to destroy it."

Felicity looked at the edge of the exposed drawing. The arcaded parapet was distinctive. And the checkerboard decoration. "The Bishop's Palace. Do you suppose that's an original plan? Think how valuable that would be."

Antony smiled. "Wouldn't Rhys Morgan's committee love to have this, if it is?"

Dilys looked worried. "I don't think—"

"No, I don't think I'd recommend you give it to them. If that's what it is, I suppose it's rightly the property of the current bishop."

"Would you like to take it to him?" Dilys asked. "He would know who could safely unroll it, at least."

Antony nodded. "I'll be happy to take care of it for you. I think his assistant said he would be in St David's today."

As they spoke, Felicity gazed around Hwyl's study. An office could tell you a great deal about its occupant. Hwyl's numerous books were carefully shelved. His desk was less tidy, but that could be the result of his wife's cleaning-out. Some files were stacked on the floor, but they gave the impression of someone who was busy, focusing hard on their work, not of haphazardness.

Crucifixes hung over the door frame and above the window. A statue of St Anthony stood on a table by a lamp. A fine print of Botticelli's *Head of Christ* hung over the desk. And Hwyl's fondness for seabirds was evident in two nicely matted and framed photographs, one of a puffin and one of a sooty tern. "Did Hwyl take these?" Felicity asked.

"Yes, shortly after we moved here. I had them framed for him for Christmas that year." Dilys bit her lip.

Felicity nodded. "You said he loved puffins." Perched around the room, on the edge of a book shelf, in the windowsill, on the lamp table stood the stuffed puffins Dilys had mentioned he collected. The ones he would now never be able to pass on to a child. Felicity picked up a particularly appealing one tucked in the corner of an easy chair.

But she dropped it immediately. It didn't feel cuddly. "Ooo, that was cold."

Antony was immediately attentive. He regarded the appealing-looking toy in the large overstuffed chair. "Did Hwyl use that chair a lot?"

Dilys nodded. "It was his favorite chair. He often sat there to read. That's why he placed it under the window." Her face softened. "Sometimes I would come in and find him dozing. He didn't always sleep well at night—especially the last few months—so I was always glad when he could…" She turned away abruptly.

Antony nodded solemnly. He took a vial of holy water from his pocket and pulled out the heavy crucifix he wore under his shirt that day. He made the sign of the cross over the stuffed seabird and placed his crucifix on it.

Felicity was never certain whether the metal of the cross sliced the fabric as Antony placed it on the plush toy or whether it came apart miraculously, but she knew she cried out when the three iron nails fell from the bird's belly.

Dilys gasped. "What is that? What does it mean?"

Antony emptied his small bottle of holy water over the nails before he answered. "It's what I suspected when we were here before, but I looked in the wrong place."

"Imitative magic…" Dilys's voice was so soft Felicity feared she might be going to faint. She led the small woman to sit in the desk chair. "Like the nails…"

"That pierced Christ's hands and feet," Antony concluded.

"But how could they have been effective… "Felicity began, then stopped. This wasn't possible. It was something out of a Halloween story. Scary. Done to produce nothing more than chills. But this wasn't childs' play.

"I don't expect the hex was effective on its own. Not against a person of deep prayer. But whoever put these here believed they would work."

"But he had the pains," Dilys protested.

"Did Hwyl have arthritis or anything like that?"

Dilys shook her head. "Not that I was aware of."

"Well, whoever was doing this could have worked on him with psychological suggestions as well."

Felicity could tell Antony was making excuses, trying not to add more to Dilys's worries, but she felt certain Antony was wondering if his former student might have let his spiritual defenses down.

Antony, however, turned to the business at hand. "Is there a shovel in the garden shed?" When Dilys said there was and gave him the key, he scooped the nails and torn toy into a box sitting on the floor. "This won't take long."

Felicity started to go with him, but he suggested she help

Dilys put the kettle on. "The river is near. I'll burn the puffin and bury the nails in the riverbed. When I come back I'll cleanse the room. See if Dilys can remember anything that might be helpful."

Dilys's sister, Tressa, already had the tea brewing in a big brown pot. The three women sat around the kitchen table. "What a beautiful name," Felicity said. "Is it Welsh?"

"Cornish," Tressa replied. "Our father is Welsh, mother Cornish."

They talked about the beauties of the Cornish coast, and Felicity was trying to find a way to get the subject back to Hwyl when Dilys, who had been very quiet for some time, said, "I had been so worried. I urged him to go to his bishop. He was so distracted. I don't know, it just seemed like he spent more time on other things lately."

"What things?"

"If only I knew. I had the feeling he was looking for something."

"Do you think he found it?" Felicity asked. "Do you think that's why…" She paused as Dilys just looked at her wordlessly.

"Do you have any idea who gave him the puffin?" Felicity resumed softly.

Dilys shook her head. "We don't have a church hall, so it's pretty much open house at the vicarage most of the time—was, that is. Anyone could have left it. It just appeared one day. Hwyl said it must have flown in." She attempted a smile.

Before they set out for St David's, Antony had phoned Bishop Harry's assistant and was told the bishop could see him for a short time at the end of the day. "Perfect," he'd commented. "Time to have a late lunch, and to take you back to St Non's."

Felicity agreed, although when they stopped for lunch in St David's the thought of the malice that would put cursed spikes in a child's toy took her appetite away. Antony, however tucked into a plate of Welsh rarebit quite happily. They had had a silent journey; Felicity not wanting to ask Antony for details regarding the puffin toy, and Antony apparently lost in thought.

"Did you learn anything more from Dilys?" Antony asked at last.

"She didn't really say that Hwyl had let his devotional life slip, but she hinted at it. And she said she had the impression he was searching for something. I wonder if that document she found had anything to do with it."

Antony frowned. "So much speculation. Perhaps the bishop will be able to help us on that score."

The day was warm and Felicity had been unable to shake the stifling feeling she'd got from Hwyl's office. She pushed her sandwich aside. "Don't bother taking me back to St Non's. I'll walk."

"You're sure?"

"Absolutely. I'm desperate for some fresh air." She looked around as if the walls of the little café would close in on her. No matter how she reasoned with herself she couldn't get her breath. "I'll see you later." She almost ran from the coffee shop.

It was a good thing there was only one main street leading out to the countryside and St Non's Lane or she would surely have lost her way. She walked with her head down and more than once almost cannoned into a passerby on the narrow sidewalk. She wanted to get out on the coastal walk. Away from buildings. Out where the sea breeze blew unhampered. That would blow away the darkness.

It was perhaps an hour's walk back to the retreat house on the cliff above the bay. Felicity wouldn't have stopped at St Non's at all, but she was choking for a drink. She would just get a glass of water and use the loo. Then she would walk and walk and walk until she was free of whatever was hovering over her. She clutched at her stomach. Something wanted to get in, like those nails had been in the bird.

The bracken along the sides of the lane offered protection without smothering her, and she began to relax. Until a gull swooped over her head and she ducked as if being attacked.

"Oh, Felicity, hi!"

She startled and almost cried out. Once she reached the dirt lane she had felt as if there was no one for miles around. "Chloe." She forced her mind to clear. What nonsense had she been thinking, anyway? "Hi. What are you doing?"

"I'm off for a photoshoot. Will you come with me? I'd really like some company. Everyone else had gone."

"Oh? I thought Nancy and Lydia were still here."

"Lydia left right after you did. I haven't seen Nancy all day."

"I'm sorry. We didn't mean to desert you."

Chloe smiled. "That's OK. I didn't really mind, but the day did get a little long."

Felicity ran in to the retreat house to use the facilities and to leave a note for Antony. She grabbed a sweater, too, as it could get cool along the coast when the sun went down.

"Where are we going?" she asked as she rejoined Chloe.

"Back to Caerbwdy. As soon as I saw the natural arch out on the point I knew I had to return at sunset."

"I thought it was a long way. You rented bikes."

"It was a fun ride out from town, but it's only about a mile and a half walk." Chloe continued to chat about her photo journal and comments she had received on her blog, and Felicity found it easy to push the earlier shades from her mind. There would be a rational explanation. When this was over, she would be embarrassed that she had given in to such alarms.

They walked on over the flat, barren land with the sun hanging low in the sky to the west when they approached the blue waters of a bay. To their left, the warm evening sun bathed a greengold headland extending far out into the water with a tiny teardrop of a rocky island just beyond it. "Ryan said the promontory is the site of an Iron Age fort dating from about 3000 BC." Chloe snapped several photos. "He said the purple sandstone used to build St David's cathedral was quarried here, too."

"Is this what you came to photograph?"

"Not really. This is Caerfai Bay. We want the one on the other side of the promontory." She put the cap back on her lens. "Let's hurry. The sun is sinking fast. I want to frame it in the natural arch." Chloe set out across the jutting point at a trot. Even with her long legs, Felicity had trouble keeping up.

When they arrived, though, Felicity saw instantly that their trek had been worth the effort. On the shady side of the headland, the rocks were no longer warm and golden, but cold and black. The women stood at the top of a sheer cliff, the surf splashing white on the rocks far below them. "How do we get down?" Felicity asked.

"Around here. Ryan knew the way or we'd never have made it before." Chloe led her along the path to a draw that was invisible until they were almost on top of it. The land sloped steeply up on either side of a narrow track. Rough rocky outcrops thrust through coarse grass. Clumps of pink, white and yellow wildflowers grew in the shallow soil, clinging to the cliff side.

The path delivered them to a half moon beach covered with shingle and pebbles. Chloe crunched ahead. "We're in luck. We wouldn't be able to get there at high tide. I was hoping I'd timed it right."

Beyond the beach they made their way around the base of the promontory, scrambling over boulders and clinging to any handhold they could find. Occasionally spray from a large wave showered them. "Aren't you worried about your camera?" Felicity called to Chloe above the crash of the waves.

"Waterproof case!" Chloe shouted back.

Well, my clothes aren't waterproof, Felicity thought. She was beginning to be seriously concerned about the wisdom of this venture when they rounded the tip, and the rose and peach evening sky that had been blocked by the cliff came into view. The fiery ball of the lowering sun sat on the horizon. "Perfect!" Chloe shouted.

Chloe knelt on a boulder and leaned forward so that the natural arch extending into the water made a perfect frame. Felicity watched in amazement at the glory of the scene before her. Nothing could have been a sharper contrast to the horrors she had been dealing with only a few hours before.

The sun continued to sink as Chloe shot photo after photo from various angles. At the last, breathtaking moment, the glowing ball seemed to flare brighter, and then it was gone. "Did you see that?" Felicity cried. "It turned green. At the last second it turned green before it disappeared. I haven't seen that since I was a child watching the sunset at Seaside with my brothers." For just a moment she clutched the cold, wet rock so hard it bit into her hand. The other side of the world. The other side of her life. Encompassing a security she had left behind her.

"Let's get back to the beach before it gets dark." Chloe interrupted Felicity's long ago and faraway thoughts.

"Summer solstice next week," Felicity said. "We'll have a long twilight."

Back on the crunchy shingle, Chloe began examining the rock formation of the cliff wall. "Mm, great shadows." She adjusted the settings on her camera and sought a firm perch to steady herself. "I'm going to try some timed exposures. This could make a cool line of Halloween cards."

Felicity wandered up the tiny, secluded beach, looking out for the tide pools she had so loved as a child visiting the Oregon coast. Closer to the water where the rocks were larger, she found what she was looking for. Hollows in flat rocks, exposed by the receding tide, held seaweed and tiny snail shells. Then, as she went further out, the pools formed between the larger boulders contained beautiful grey, green and purple anemones growing on the rocks; tiny fish and spider crabs swam in the water.

Chloe joined her and they continued to move along the edge of beach, fascinated with their findings until the lingering glow in the sky was inadequate to spot marine life in the pools. Felicity was ready to suggest that they should be getting back, especially since her stomach told her they had missed dinner, when Chloe pulled a torch out of her pack. "Here, shine this on the pool. That will be a great effect if I can capture it." She adjusted her camera. "No, don't shine it straight down. Angle it right at the waterline." This called for the intricacies of more timed exposure photography. "Can you hold it still?" Chloe asked, as the light shook in Felicity's hand.

"Sorry." Felicity concentrated to control the shivers caused by her wet clothes.

"You more of them nutters?" The harsh male voice coming out of nowhere made both women jump and cry out.

Felicity looked at the stooped old man with long white hair and missing teeth. The deep lines in his weathered face spoke of years of exposure to wind and weather. She hoped Chloe wouldn't ask him to pose for her. "Nutters?" she laughed. "I don't think so. What do you mean?"

He jerked his head toward the gaping dark hole in the cliff on up the bay that suggested a cave. "That lot what do their hocus-pocus in there."

As he spoke, Felicity glimpsed a shadowy form approaching the mouth of the cave. "Hocus-pocus? What do they do?"

The old man coughed and spat. "Nowt much. Burn candles. Mumble 'n' chant. All foolishness, but each to 'is own, I says."

Sure enough, Chloe asked if she could take a picture of the stranger. The idea seemed to amuse him. He told them his name was Emrys, and he and Chloe walked closer to the cliff where she could pose him against the jagged rocks for her flash photographs. Felicity, watching for more dark shapes to enter the cave, moved as quietly as she could across the gravel toward the entrance. 'Hocus-pocus. Candles and chants,' he said. Had they stumbled on a meeting of the Orbis Astri that was less public than their lectures? Did their hocus-pocus include hexing iron nails to embed in soft toys?

She was almost to the cave mouth when a flickering orange light on the far wall told her their informant had been right about the candles. She held her breath and edged forward, hoping the loose shingle under her feet wouldn't give her away. Indeed, the rhythmic, sing-song chorus coming to her on the breeze could be described as a chant, although she couldn't make out any words or identify a language. A few phrases sounded vaguely Greek, or maybe Latin, but certainly nothing she could have translated for a Classics paper.

She jumped when a hand touched her shoulder. "Shhh," Chloe whispered in her ear. "It's me. Sorry, I didn't mean to startle you. Sounds like Emrys was right about the nutters."

"I want to see what they're up to." Felicity put a finger to her lips, and moved forward stealthily.

The view of the cave entrance was blocked by a pile of boulders, which also served as a screen to prevent the participants from seeing the women on the beach. Felicity looked around carefully in the dim light, thinking they might have posted guards, but didn't see any lurking figures. The light inside the cave projected long, swaying shadows on the walls. There appeared to be perhaps a dozen or more participants in the ritual. The shadows indicated they were wearing hooded robes.

Pebbles turned under Felicity's feet with a crunch that made her heart leap. She froze, but there was no break in the rhythm of the dancing shadows to indicate that they had heard anything. "Go on," Chloe nudged her.

At last they gained the shelter of the rock screen. Squatting down, Felicity flattened herself against it, then slowly raised up to peer over the top. The cavern was lit by a circle of thirteen tall, fat candles. In the center of the floor, five additional candles lit what Felicity guessed to be the points of a pentagram—or the angles behind the menacing snake emblem. The swaying figures wove an undulating pattern between the candles. The robed dancers blurred almost as if one body, but two caught Felicity's attention—one so fat the motions were more a rolling than a bending, and one so tall and thin Felicity could think only of a dancing stick.

In the center, a statuesque figure stood as a still point amid all the circling motion, arms extended high, hands clasping a dark object. Against the back wall, three additional robed figures sat on a rock ledge, observing. At least, the two larger appeared to be observing. The small one in the middle looked to be asleep or dazed.

Chloe nudged Felicity to the side, and balanced her camera on the top of the largest boulder. Felicity held her breath, praying no one would hear the telltale shutter click. But there was no sound as Chloe adjusted her settings and continued to take exposures.

The speed of the dance increased, as did the intensity of the chant. With the repetition certain words began to form a pattern in Felicity's mind: *cum, cum, cum, congregatio…* The chant repeated over and over, then changed: *dies sanctificatus* only once, but very clearly. Then new words floated out from the mouth of the cave as if the cavern itself were speaking: *potentiae, obiectum, potentiae, potentiae, obiectum…*

At last the dance ended, and the votaries stood against the wall. The central figure, obviously some sort of leader or priest, moved for the first time, to sprinkle powder on the candles. When the powder hit the flame, a cloud of smoke rose and the smell of sulfur reached the hidden observers. Felicity pinched her nose to keep from sneezing.

The priest nodded and the three figures sitting against the wall rose and moved to the center, the smaller one supported—almost dragged—by the two larger. They knelt before the tall figure and those along the walls began a high-pitched wail that sounded an odd mix between anguish and ecstasy.

The priest extended long arms as if blessing the suppliants. The ululation rose in pitch, echoing and reverberating against the walls of the cave with its importuning tone: come, come, come…

And then it stopped. The silence rebounded as loudly as the chanting had.

And then Felicity sneezed. The priest pivoted toward the mouth of the cave. This time the long arm pointed directly at the spot where Felicity and Chloe crouched. Felicity froze.

A rough hand grabbed her from behind and jerked her toward the cliff wall beyond the cave. Away from the lightspill from the cavern mouth, she was blinded. Her abductor pulled her toward the cliff until she felt her body slam against the rock wall. Then a hand pushed her head forcefully down into the ground. She barely had time to turn her face to avoid getting grit into her eyes and nose. She realized Chloe was lying beside her. Apparently Felicity's captor had snatched Chloe with his other hand.

"Stay still! They'll give up soon enow." She recognized Emrys's voice in her ear.

For all his warning, she looked up. Robed figures, carrying tall black candles were combing the beach and searching both directions along the path. Felicity quickly ducked her head down again.

Eventually the priest blew a long, deep note on an instrument that must have been related to the auroch's horn used by Druids, and the searchers dispersed up the path Felicity and Chloe had descended hours before.

Emrys raised his head and sniffed the air. "Right. The stench is gone. Off wi' ye. And have better sense next time. This lot don't take kindly to bein' spied on."

Felicity hugged Emrys and thanked him, wondering what Antony would say about her evening's adventure, then gratefully accepted the torch Chloe held out to her and turned to ascend the steep path. She had no idea what time it was, but it must be getting on for midnight. And they still had the walk back to the retreat house ahead of them, through desolate country. What if one of the cultists was lying in wait for them along the path?

It wasn't a robed occultist waiting for them at the top of the cliff, however, but a uniformed police officer with the blue light blinking on the patrol car behind her. "Felicity Howard? I'm Constable Gwen Owen."

Felicity took a step backwards and almost knocked Chloe over. "What have I done?"

"You've driven me to distraction, woman!" Even filled with irritation as it was, Antony's voice was the most welcome sound Felicity could have imagined. He emerged from the patrol car and strode toward her.

"Oh, thank God! How did you know where to find us?" She threw herself into his arms, not the least bit worried about how angry he might be with her.

"At least you had the sense to leave a note. I didn't worry until it started to get dark. Then I was so foolish as to think you might be in trouble, so I called the police. Ryan knew Chloe wanted to photograph the arch and gave us directions." He returned her hug. "Oh, Felicity. I had visions of you being trapped by the tide and washed out to sea. What have you been doing all this time?"

A shiver shook Felicity's body. "I'm cold. Could we talk in the car?"

A few minutes later, they were heading across the peninsula back to the retreat house and Felicity and Chloe were talking, in turns and in tandem, about the night's adventure. "It was the Orbis Astri. I'm sure of it. And now you know where they meet." Felicity spoke to Constable Owen, "you can watch for them and arrest them."

Gwen Owen laughed. "Unfortunately, you can't arrest people for being nutters. Well, maybe fortunately. The jails wouldn't hold them. There's no law against dancing around in robes on public beaches."

"Yes, but they're evil. They do awful things. I'm sure they're behind Hwyl's death. And who knows what all else?" But Felicity knew her protest was futile. It sounded insubstantial to her own ears.

She snuggled into the warmth of Antony's arm, but when she closed her eyes she saw the grotesque shadows of the dancers writhing on the walls of the cave. The image was so strong she smelled the sulfur again and exploded in a sneeze. Antony pulled a handkerchief from his pocket and handed it to her.

The gesture was so comforting she had to squeeze her eyes and clench her teeth to keep from crying.

Chapter 24

Saturday
St David's

At first Antony thought the pounding was the surf dashing rocks against the cliff below St Non's; then he realized it was someone knocking on his door. "Just a minute."

He staggered out of bed and pulled on the clothes he had left on a chair the night before.

"Antony, come quick. You've got to see this. In Sister Nora's office. Chloe uploaded her pictures from last night." Felicity raced ahead of him down the stairs, her long golden hair flying. Antony wondered how she could be so energetic after last night's experience.

But when they got to the little room he saw that she was anything but the picture of health she had appeared. "Felicity, are you sick?"

She sneezed and blew her nose. "It's just a cold. I'll be fine. Sister Alma gave me some Lemsip. It's very energizing."

He could tell she was trying to make light of it, but she looked dreadful. "Did you sleep last night?"

"Not much, but it's not important. Look at this."

Chloe sat before the monitor manipulating the picture on the screen. "I'm afraid that's the best I can do. It's pretty fuzzy. My telephoto lens is a prime, but it loses some quality with the time exposure… Still, I think Felicity is right."

Felicity bent toward the screen. "Oh, that's better. You brought the contrast up, didn't you? Yes, what do you think Antony? It's him, isn't it?"

Antony examined the image on the screen. A small figure in a white robe with a hood covering half the face. Could be a boy or a girl. "Who?"

"Adam, of course! The Orbis Astri have kidnapped Adam. And not only that, I was doing some Internet research on the Orbis Astri. There's a blog called 'Witch-finder' and they say the Serene Imperator of the Orbis Astri is known to have said prepubescent boys make the best sacrifice. Now maybe the police will listen to me."

Antony peered closer. "Yes, we should show these to the police, but I'm not convinced that's Adam. Have you asked Lydia?"

"Oh, Lydia, of course!" Felicity stopped to blow her nose before rushing off to find Adam's sister. "We should have called Lydia first."

"Someone looking for me?" Lydia appeared in the open doorway. "I was coming to find you, Father. We found the prodigal."

"Adam? You found him? Where?"

"I was certain he would be hiding out with a friend, so yesterday I rang everyone I could think of from his old school. Then in the end, they rang me. Sure enough, he was holed up with a friend from Builth Wells. The parents just returned from holiday—thought their son was in school, too. They'll deliver Squib back to the arms of his loving housemaster today. Pity they've outlawed caning—it's what he deserves."

"Still, you must be so relieved," Felicity said.

"Yes, of course. If he'll just buckle down now. It all comes of his being so spoiled." Lydia tossed her auburn hair. "What did you want to see me about?"

"Well, it's not important now. Chloe took some pictures—" Felicity gestured toward the computer.

"Good grief!" Lydia bent closer to the screen. "Where did you get these?"

"I took them last night. We were walking along Caerbwdy Bay," Chloe said.

Lydia frowned. "Wrong time of the year for a Halloween party."

"We thought…" Felicity began and pointed to the small figure. "Rather, *I* thought it looked a lot like Adam."

Lydia considered. "Yeah, it does a little. That kid's smaller, though." She shook her head. "He doesn't look too happy. Or maybe she—it's hard to tell. Not that Adam deserves to be happy, either, of course."

"I'm glad Adam's all right." Antony realized as he spoke how very relieved he was. He hadn't quite realized how responsible he had felt for the youth that had been under his care for ten days.

"Well, he'll be all right until I get my hands on him. It took me most of the day yesterday to talk the school into taking him back. I even had to walk into town just to get my mobile topped up at the newsagents."

"We'll give thanks at morning prayer. Everyone has been worried."

"Yes, of course. Thanks." Lydia turned toward the door. "I need my morning coffee now, though."

"I still think we should call the police," Felicity insisted. "That's obviously a minor in the photos and he was so still, so zombie-like. I think he must have been drugged."

Yes," Antony agreed. "I'll ring Detective Superintendent Pool."

"And there was that awful stuff the priest threw on the flames," Felicity added. I wouldn't be surprised if that was something illegal."

Antony shook his head. "Probably just incense. That's normally used abundantly in occult practices. Fragrance offered to Satan as a counterpart to the liturgical incense we offer to God."

Chloe turned on through her pictures, showing Antony the figures caught in frozen distorted positions in their ritual dance. Felicity clapped her hands over her ears as if she were hearing the wailing again and turned away from the monitor. "'Come, come, come…' It made me think of our singing *Veni, Sanctus Spiritus* on Pentecost."Then she stopped. "But wait. They weren't chanting in English. It wouldn't have been *come*. At first I thought it was Greek. Then it started sounding more like Latin…"

"If it was a known language at all," Antony reminded her.

"Yes, but whatever it was, it was very intentional. Not gibberish. So if it was Latin it would have been *cum*."

Antony nodded. "As in union."

"Yes. Or together. A coming together."

"Did you get any other words?" Antony asked.

Felicity thought. "I couldn't hear very clearly—what with the cave echoing and the waves splashing behind us. But I thought I might have caught *potentiae obiectum*."

"Article of power," Antony translated.

"*Potentiae obiectum*," Felicity repeated almost under her breath. "Something Hwyl found, maybe?"

"Or was looking for," Antony suggested. "Perhaps that's what he was enquiring of Professor Meyerson about."

"What about that drawing of the Bishop's Palace Dilys showed you? That couldn't have been it, could it? What did Bishop Harry say?"

"He was very interested, very appreciative that I'd brought it to him. He thought it should be looked after by the cathedral librarian, and asked him to come in. They're calling in an archivist to humidify it so it can be unrolled without damage. We can check back today."

"Great! I can't wait—" A sneeze interrupted Felicity's sentence. "To see it," she finished.

After breakfast and morning prayers, Antony did his best to convince Felicity that she should spend the day in bed. But, of course, she wouldn't hear of it. "And miss out on all the fun?" Antony smiled. He wasn't sure what he adored most about her, but her energy and sheer grit had to be near the top of the list.

The librarian greeted Antony at the cathedral library. "Ah, Father Antony, come to see your treasure, have you?"

"It is a treasure, then? I was hoping it would turn out to be."

"It's early days. Tests must be run, but we are anticipating exciting results."

Antony introduced Felicity to George Phipps, the librarian, and he led the way to a work room where a small woman in a neat navy blue dress was bending over a long table. "Ah, may I present Mary Ware, our archivist. Well, not really our archivist. We called her in from Cardiff University." He introduced their visitors. "How is your work progressing?"

"Splendid. It should be dry now. We had to re-humidify it, you see. It had some pretty severe cracks. I'd say it had been forced open by someone." She looked at Antony accusingly.

"No. I brought it straight here," he assured her.

"Good. Any more such violence and it might have been too late to save it. Vellum is particularly tricky to work with." She turned back to her table. " But I find the laminate stack usually works very well." She indicated several items on the end of the table. "I placed the document on a sheet of Gore-Tex over a damp blotter, then put on a polyester cover to hold the moisture in. Gore-Tex, you see, is a very dense material that will only let water pass through it as a vapor, so it provides gentle humidification."

"How long did it take?" Felicity asked.

"Oh, not long. I watched it carefully. You can tell when

it's done because the document relaxes. This took about fifteen minutes, I suppose." She moved to another stack, this one still assembled. "Drying takes longer. This has been here more than twelve hours, so it should be all right." She lifted the Plexiglas cover to reveal the document lying flat between two blotters. She touched one corner of the sheet gently. "Yes, you may examine it. But very carefully."

Felicity started to reach out. "Ah, aha," Mary stopped her and produced a pair of white cotton gloves for each of them.

"Can you tell how old it is?" asked Felicity.

"We'll run some tests on the vellum, but I'd say fourteenth century, judging by the style of the work." She pointed to the words across the bottom of the page. "You'll note how the Gothic lettering has a broad, open look. That's very characteristic of the mid-fourteenth century. Also, the spreading branch of the ornamental brackets. Earlier you would have had a single bud, rather than a vine. By the next century the bud would have flowered."

"So this could be an original plan of the Bishop's Palace?" Antony asked.

"Not a working architect's plan, if that's what you're thinking. It's too ornamented for that. But it could have been done at that time. Perhaps for Bishop Gower himself, rather like one might take a photograph of their home today. But, of course, that's speculation."

"I wish we knew where Hwyl found it," Felicity mused, leaning over the drawing, but not touching it.

Antony agreed. He longed to know the secret he felt sure this document must hold. He too, was reluctant to touch. Besides, they could see perfectly well with it laid out flat before them. What clues did this hold to the secret Hwyl must have died for?

Mary moved around the room, tidying her tools and supplies. "Any ideas?" Antony asked Felicity.

"What are we looking for?"

Antony grinned. "It would be helpful to know, wouldn't it?"

"Do you think this could be the *potentiae obiectum*?"

"It's possible, but I think it's more likely a clue to its location."

"A treasure map?" Felicity's eyes widened.

"If you like."

Felicity pulled a chair up to the table and picked up a pencil and notepad lying there. "I'll work on translating the writing. You look for X marks the spot."

For several minutes the only sound in the room was the scratching of Felicity's pencil. At last she set it down with a conclusive air. "Got it. Listen, this is interesting: 'Bishop Henry built his *clausum honestum*'—that translates 'cathedral close,' doesn't it?" Antony nodded and she continued, "'To safeguard canons, vicars and ministers of the cathedral from the depredations of the bishop's temporal officers.'"

"That is interesting," Antony agreed. "I wish we knew what temporal officers: civil servants, lay workers or something further afield?"

"I wonder if the Orbis Astri existed then?" Felicity answered her own question: "I wouldn't think so. But I wonder what depredations: Physical safety? Wars? Thievery? Personal attack? Spiritual safety? Protection from heresy?" She removed her gloves, pulled a tissue from her pocket and blew her nose. "Oh. This is frustrating—too many questions; too few answers."

"Learn anything?" Mary returned to the table.

"We certainly learned a great deal about unrolling brittle vellum." Antony smiled and pulled off his gloves. "Thank you so much for your time. I'm glad your work was so successful."

"Thank you for bringing this to us, Father. It will be a wonderful addition to the cathedral archives. If you learn anything about its provenance do let us know."

Antony promised and led the way through the cathedral and back out the south door. Warm sunshine greeted them when they emerged into the close, as did the joyful voices of the youth choir scheduled to perform a concert there that evening, assembling with exuberance for a photograph on the 39 Steps. But Antony turned around back toward Bishop Gower's palace.

"Antony!" Felicity caught at his arm. "Where are we going? Did you spot something on that plan?"

"Well, maybe. It's worth a look, anyway."

"What? Where?"

"Whoa, just wait. I'll show you. If it's still there."

They paid their admission fee at the gatehouse and entered the broad green courtyard. Tourists milled about them on every level of every range of the building. That could make any snooping difficult; or perhaps provide useful cover on the off-chance anyone was watching them. Antony hoped their investigations had managed to elude observation by anyone who might be seeking the same goal they were—but for vastly different purposes.

He led up the outside steps that ran from the courtyard directly into the bishop's private chapel, then slowly along the south wall dividing the chapel from the bishop's solar. Craning his head back, he examined each corbel carefully.

"If you'd tell me what we're looking for I could help you," Felicity pleaded, following so closely she nearly stepped on his foot.

"I wanted to be sure…" He stopped in the corner. Looking up at the features on the face he felt his spine tingle. Yes, even in its ruinous state he was certain. Making sure they were alone in the chapel, he pointed. "There. That corbel. Tell me what you see."

Felicity considered. "It's in a somewhat protected corner, so it's in better condition than some." She tipped her head to the side, looked at the others protruding at their intervals along the wall, then looked back. "Yes, I thought so. It's larger."

"Right. Very good. Anything else?"

"Well, it's hard to say, but the features… Definitely a man. Not a beast, demon, or angel. And yet… Is it a depiction of Christ?"

"Bingo! That one was drawn as a pop-out on the plan. It could have been out of respect. Or…"

"It could have been our X marks the spot!"

The anticipation was mounting inside him so that Antony could only nod. The stairway to the parapet walk in the corner of the bishop's solar was roped off. Broken steps in the ascending spiral gaped like missing teeth. Still, it didn't appear to be impassable. "I need to get a closer look." He turned to Felicity. "Stay in the chapel. If anyone comes in, distract them. Get them to look out the window or something."

Felicity didn't seem happy with the idea of being left on the ground when there was climbing about to be done, but she didn't argue.

Antony clung to the rough stone walls with both hands. Even the remaining triangular steps were uneven and broken. Falling down the ruined stairwell could result in nasty injuries. The first missing step still had a stone protruding from the wall, large enough to support his right foot. He gripped the step above it and pulled himself up.

He breathed slightly easier now. At least he was high enough to be hidden from the view of anyone passing the open doorway. The second gap was harder to negotiate as two steps in a row were missing. He strained to reach a step high over his head, then, bracing his feet against the stones of the wall, heaved himself up. His purchase was almost secure when the stone under his left foot broke free and clattered to the floor below.

Antony held his breath. Would anyone notice? Maybe come to investigate? "I'm so sorry." Felicity's voice traveled up the shaft. "We've had a report of falling stone. The inspector will be finished soon, but this part of the palace is closed off for safety at the moment. Perhaps you'd care to check back in half an hour?"

Antony couldn't hear the reply, but no one came chasing up to haul him down.

When he reached the rampart, he had to lie flat on his stomach to avoid being observed from visitors walking along the arcade on the south range. He could hardly expect Felicity to close down the entire palace. He inched his way forward, painfully aware of the violence the jagged stones were doing to his clothes. His scraped skin would heal, but this would cost him a new shirt and pair of trousers.

When he judged he was over the Christ corbel, he raised his head and looked around. The chapel was empty. But the corbel was further from the walkway than he had judged from below.

He tried to reach it by sliding as far as he could along the rampart, then extending one arm while holding on for dear life with the other, but it was no good. His only hope was to extend one leg over the side and stick his foot into the hole left by one of the wooden ceiling trusses. With one more look to be certain the coast was clear, and a quickly breathed prayer, he went for it.

The fingers of his left hand tingled as he grasped the stone head. He was here. Now what? If his guess had been right that Bishop Gower had designed a type of medieval safe to secure his treasure, how did he now access it?

He grasped the head more firmly to pull himself forward. For a moment his tug was secure, then the corbel twisted in his hand.

It was only his frantic grasp at the edge of the parapet with his free hand that kept him from pitching headlong to the floor below. He clung there for a moment, gasping, while the rush of blood receded from his head. It was only a few seconds, but it seemed like hours before he could relax and open his eyes to examine the bishop's hidey-hole.

A cavity, perhaps eight inches in diameter, extended into the stonework behind the angled corbel. Feeling carefully, Antony slid his hand into the hollow. His disappointment at feeling only rough stone was severe.

And then his fingertip grazed something that felt like wood. Once again he strained forward, clasping at any available handhold with his right hand and stretching his left. He had to get a firm grasp. If he merely pushed the object deeper into the cavity he would be unable to retrieve it.

At last he could feel the dimensions and realized it was a wooden box of some sort. Carved, from the feel of it. Sweat poured from his forehead and ran into his eyes. His heart was pounding so loudly in his ears he wouldn't have been able to hear if someone had shouted at him from below. One more inch and he had it.

He removed the small casket with one smooth gesture. Placing it on the rampart he arched over one final time to replace the corbel, then rolled onto his back on the walkway, grasping the precious object and gasping for air.

It wasn't until he was safely back in the bishop's solar with the little wooden box chafing the skin under his shirt, that he thought to breathe a prayer of thanksgiving.

Felicity threw her arms around him, squealing, "Oh, well done! I watched from the doorway. I almost shrieked when I thought you were going to fall! Oh—" She squeezed him even tighter, pressing the box into both their chests. "What is it? What is it? What did you find?"

"I don't know, but we can't open it here."

"Where? I can't wait!" Felicity was pulling him toward the exit.

"The cathedral, I think," Antony replied. "It is their property, after all."

The library was deserted, the staff probably at lunch. Antony unbuttoned his shirt and drew out a wooden rectangle less than a foot long and six inches wide. The dark oak, weathered with time and damp, was held together with tarnished, but ornate brass fittings, the top inlaid with ivory and semiprecious stones in the shape of a cross. Gold leaf highlighted the carved vines in a similar pattern to the brackets on the palace plan drawing.

"Open it!" Felicity urged.

Antony took a breath and lifted the lid.

Felicity pulled back at the sight of a bone with shreds of rotting flesh clinging to it. "Eww. Disgusting."

"Yes. And worrying." He set it on the floor as if afraid it would cut his fingers.

"What—" Felicity began.

"I'm guessing it's a curse of some sort. A very recent one."

"But the box looks ancient."

"Yes, and whatever ancient relic or artifact it held has been removed and replaced with an instrument of evil."

Felicity moved back. "A curse on the person who finds it?"

In spite of himself Antony shivered. "Possibly." He took out a clean handkerchief, wrapped the case in it and picked it up again. "Come on. I'll deal with this."

Antony led the way out of the cathedral grounds and around the back where a small stream flowed freely under a thicket of trees. He set the case on the ground, unwrapped it and opened the lid, then knelt down and scooped water into his cupped left hand, making the sign of the cross over it with his right hand. He sprinkled all with the blessed water. He tipped the malefice into the stream and held the case in his hand. "Lord, I beseech You, cleanse this vessel. Drive out every evil power, presence and influence and all evil actions aimed against Your servant. Where there is malice, give us an abundance of goodness, endurance and victory. Amen."

"Amen," Felicity responded and crossed herself as Antony did.

He rinsed the box in the flowing water and wiped it dry.

Now Felicity felt she could look at it properly. She sat down on the grassy bank. "It's beautiful. What is it?"

Antony sat beside her. "I would guess it's a *scrynne*— a forerunner of a shrine. Used to contain precious writings or sacred relics."

"Do you think this is what Hwyl was trying to protect?"

"More likely what he was trying to find."

"But he had the plan." Felicity wrinkled her brow.

"He might not have had the plan for very long. If he had unrolled it, it would have been cracked."

"But it's just a case, isn't it? I mean, it's beautiful and very, very old and probably valuable, but the point of a *scrynne* was what was inside it, right?"

Antony nodded and Felicity continued, "So either Hwyl found the relic or artifact or whatever was in here and put it someplace safe…"

"No. Hwyl wouldn't have left a hex. Someone else has it and has taken it out to use it," Antony concluded. He thought for a moment. "At that coven or whatever last night, did you see anything used in their ritual that that would fit in here?"

Felicity closed her eyes, thinking. "I think the priest—Serene Imperator—had something in his hands. It might show in one of Chloe's pictures." She thought more. "It might have been a pouch. Leather or a heavy fabric, maybe. About that long." She held her hands about ten inches apart, then looked from them to the casket. "Yes, it would fit in there." Her eyes grew wide as she continued, "*Potentiae obiectum*, I'm certain that's what they were chanting. Well, I think so, anyway. So you're thinking this had the article of power in it?"

Antony was silent for a long time. Felicity leaned over and gave his temple a peck of a kiss. "What was that for?"

"I love it when I can see your wheels turning. That's to grease them."

"Good. They're squeaky right now, but here's what I'm thinking. There seems to be a thread through all the history we've seen in the past weeks, starting with Aaron and Julius—devout Christian Romans; Aaron, probably Jewish. If they brought a valuable Christian artifact or document with them, or something was sent to them…"

"Why?"

Antony shrugged. "As valued personal property? A family treasure? For safekeeping?"

Felicity nodded. "That is possible. Britain was the safest part of the empire for Christians." She was quiet for a moment. "Some document or something that bolstered their faith enough to stand strong as martyrs."

"Yes, and then, David found it."

"That's not too far-fetched, is it? He was at Caerleon, after all." Felicity leaned forward and grasped his arm. "And Aaron and Julius would have kept their treasure hidden from the Romans, after all. Maybe in one of those tunnels under the monastery."

"Oops—" Antony held up a hand. "You're letting your imagination run ahead of you there. The monastery wasn't built yet."

"Yes, but wasn't it built on ground where the fort was? So maybe they found it when building the monastery. Anyway, just say David found it—whatever 'it' is—somewhere at Caerleon, and that gave him the assurance to stand so strong against the heretics that the ground rose up when he preached."

Antony nodded. "Well, if there was such an artifact, it's certain David would have taken it with him when he moved his bishopric to Menevia."

Felicity was quiet, as if watching David and his entourage moving westward across ancient Wales. Eventually, she spoke. "So David carried his relic across Wales, just where we walked? All the ancient sites—Roman, some much older—all along there show it was a trodden way. And he could have stopped at Aberdare."

Antony laughed. "Well, that's probably stretching it. It's unlikely there was even so much as a clutch of mud huts there then. Certainly no coal mines. But the rest is just possible. Although the Cistercian Way linking the ring of monasteries around the border of Wales only goes back to the twelfth century."

"But those monasteries were built on the work of St David, weren't they?"

"Yes, he and his monks founded twelve monasteries, but we're getting a bit far afield."

"Oh, yes. Sorry. Well, never mind about Aberdare. Although I do think—"

Antony cleared his throat.

"Right, I'll try to stay on track. But it's hard to know what the track is. So say David brought our artifact thing here."

"Why would he hide it?"

"Maybe he didn't. Not at first, at least. But later, when Welsh kings attacked, it was hidden somewhere here at *Tyddewi*."

"'David's House'—well done." Antony nodded to encourage her reasoning. She said she loved it when his wheels turned. He loved the quickness of her mind.

This time, though, she was quiet for a longer period. "You'll say I'm really reaching here, but Giraldus Cambrensis—he was an author and scholar. So he might have learned something about this. Then when he traveled around Wales with the Archbishop of Canterbury and helped the Bishop of St David's rebuild the cathedral, he would have been looking for it, too."

"Are you suggesting that his failure to be elected bishop was somehow due to his failure to find the sacred object?"

"Possibly. But whether or not he found it, maybe he heard rumors and wrote about it. You said he was something of a gossip, so if he heard anything he would have recorded it."

Antony saw where she was going. "So you're thinking that Gower, who was a scholar, would have read whatever Gerald might have written."

"And could have found it when rebuilding the cathedral. Then when Gower was desperate to build his palace—you said it was a bit of a mystery how he managed to finance it— he used it somehow."

Antony considered. In spite of all the guess work, there was a logic to what Felicity said. "How would he have used it, I wonder?"

Felicity shrugged. "Do I have to do all the work? You tell me."

"Well, it depends on what the object was. Whether it offered a threat or a promise. He could have promised special prayers for donors. Even charged to let wealthy patrons touch it, perhaps. Rich pilgrims brought lavish gifts to shrines in those days."

"He wouldn't have sold it, would he?"

"Then why build a cache for the *scrynne* in his palace? Complete with a floor plan marking its whereabouts." Antony considered. "The question seems to be whether he hid it to use for personal power or to protect it."

The flash of a camera made them both jump. "Sorry," Chloe said. "I hope you don't mind, but your expressions were a priceless study of deep concentration."

"How did you find us?" Antony asked, wondering how long she had been there, how much she had heard.

"I was just wandering around, looking for good subjects. I was photographing the Great Chapel in the palace, but then all these people came in—those people that invited us to that tea the other day."

Antony nodded. "The committee for the restoration of the Bishop's Palace."

"Yeah, them. I think they were planning a meeting or a service or something there. They were talking about where to place an altar, candles, censer, that sort of thing. Anyway, I couldn't really work with them all over the place, so I wandered out back and climbed over that broken place in the wall."

"I'm glad you did." Felicity indicated the small, ornate casket. "What do you think—whatever the Serene Imperator was holding up in the center of the pentagram last night. Could it have fit in here?"

Chloe considered. "I would think so, but it's hard to say for sure. I didn't get a very clear look. That's really beautiful, though. What is it?"

Felicity explained what a *scrynne* was, but not where they found it.

"Is it all right if I photograph it?"

"Yes, please do. Then we'll give it to the librarian. It's cathedral property."

A short time later, Antony was back in the librarian's office, feeling a great relief at being able to turn his find over to a cathedral employee.

"It's magnificent. Where did you acquire it?" George Phipps beamed at the object Antony placed on his desk.

"It's complicated. I'd rather explain to the bishop, but I want to be certain it's in safekeeping."

Phipps drew a ring of keys from his pocket. "The dean and chapter will decide, but for the moment, I'd feel best if this were locked in the Treasury. You can be assured we'll take good care of it. It seems that once again, St David's Cathedral is in your debt, Father Antony."

Antony was about to reply that he was grateful to the cathedral staff for taking such excellent care of these objects, but a loud sneeze followed by a nose-blowing from Felicity reminded him that he had another, more important, responsibility. "I'm worried about that cold, Felicity. Let's get you to bed."

It was even more worrying that she didn't resist.

Chapter 25

Trinity Sunday
St David's

In spite of red, watery eyes and a streaming nose, Felicity was on time for breakfast the next morning. Two things were at the forefront of her thought: a cup of hot, strong tea with honey in it to soothe her throat, and talking to Antony about what had been on her mind through a long, restless night.

The tea was easily obtained, but Antony didn't appear in the dining room. With a little wave to the other pilgrims gathered around the tables facing the panoramic view of morning sunshine as it turned the cliffs and bay golden, Felicity refilled her mug, adding a more generous dollop of honey this time, and hurried upstairs to find Antony.

If she was right they might not have any time to lose. She stopped on the third step to let a chill pass over her body. A chill that had nothing to do with her plaguing cold. What if they were already too late? What if she had the day right, but the ceremony was for sunrise? What if—

"Felicity? Are you all right?"

Antony's voice brought her back to the present with such a jolt she almost spilled her tea. "Antony, I was looking for you."

"And I for you. I was hoping you'd still be asleep, but when I found your room empty—"

"We've got to talk."

"Yes, I think you should stay in today. I'd have brought your tea to you."

Felicity shook her head impatiently. "No. I'll be all right. I've remembered something. Today. This is the day. They only said it once. That's why I didn't think of it sooner. Finding the *scrynne* and recalling the ceremony with Chloe must have jogged my memory."

Antony took her arm and led her up the stairs. "Woman, you're babbling." Two chairs were set in a little alcove along the hall. He guided her to one of them. "Now, take a deep breath, blow your nose, and tell me what you're on about."

Felicity obeyed. Just being with Antony calmed the thoughts that had been jumbling in her head through so many dark hours. "*Dies sanctificatus.* It wasn't repeated over and over like everything else seemed to be. It was a sort of culmination. And their pronunciation was eccentric. Of course we don't know how the original was pronounced, but—"

"Felicity."

"Oh, sorry. Babbling again."

Antony smiled and nodded. "Don't worry. I love your babbling. But we need to get this clear. At that coven ceremony they chanted something about a convergence or assembly or something—"

"*Cum*—with or when, and *congregatio*—assembly. Only like I said, their pronunciation—"

Antony smiled again. "Yes, I got that. And then they ended with a reference to a holy day?"

"Yes, yes! That's what I'm trying to tell you. And this is Trinity Sunday."

Antony was quiet for a moment. "Yes, I see what you're getting at: the only day in the Christian calendar that celebrates the Holy Trinity. A week after we celebrate the coming of the Holy Spirit at Pentecost." He nodded thoughtfully. "The unity of the Godhead is important. Someone wanting to disturb that unity might want to disrupt this day."

Felicity was on her feet. "We need to get over to the cathedral. Warn the dean. We need to keep watch—" An explosive sneeze ended her speech.

"Felicity, you need to be in bed."

"I'll ask Sister Alma for another sachet of Lemsip. I'll be all right."

Antony looked thunderous.

"I'd just fret if I stayed here."

He surrendered. "I'll see if anyone else wants to go with us now in the minibus. The others can walk."

Michael had pushed his bowl of porridge aside and was on his feet even before Antony finished explaining about wanting to get to the cathedral early in case someone wanted to cause a disturbance. "I'll go with you."

Lydia, Ryan and Chloe were also ready. Nancy said she would come later with the Sisters. Jared and his Goth friends were out on the terrace, so had to be consulted separately. Kaylyn and Evie said they wanted to visit St Non's Well first, so they would all walk into town later.

"One advantage of coming early is there's plenty of parking," Michael said as he pulled the van into an empty space.

"I've been thinking," Felicity said. "Since we don't know what anyone might try or where, maybe we should spread out in order to watch for trouble anywhere in the cathedral."

"What exactly are we looking for?" Lydia asked.

"That's the problem. We don't know. We've come across some information, though, that makes it look like an occult group calling itself the Orbis Astri might want to co-opt the Trinity Sunday Holy Communion for their own purposes."

Lydia looked horrified. "Surely not. That's impossible."

"I hope so," Antony agreed. "But just in case, I intend to

warn the dean, and I want us to keep our eyes open."

"I agree it sounds far-fetched," Michael said. "But I'll be happy to stake out the north transept."

"I'll take the Lady Chapel," Lydia said. "It's my favorite bit of the cathedral."

Antony looked at his watch. "Good, you should be in time for the Welsh language service."

Ryan shrugged. "South transept for me, then."

"Isn't the Holy Trinity Chapel the most likely?" Felicity said.

"I'd thought of that." Antony turned to her. "I was going to suggest I take that, and you and Chloe take the nave, if that's all right with you."

Once again the glorious tintinnabulation of the cathedral bells rang out from the gatehouse tower, and crows circled over their heads as they descended the 39 Steps. Sun shone on the green scene before them, and Felicity wondered how anything evil could possibly be at work in such a place. And yet the very history of the stones before her was a chronicle of destruction and rebirth.

Worshipers leaving the early Holy Communion service spilled out onto the lawn, and people entering for the Welsh service hurried forward, each group greeting the other, putting to rest Felicity's fears that they might already have arrived too late. And yet, could some of these faces around her, faces lifted to the morning sun or smiling at their neighbors, have been the same ones she had glimpsed shadowed under loose white hoods? The very thought seemed incredible. Still, those very same people would probably look entirely normal if met in a sunny, green churchyard on a Sunday morning.

Inside, the cathedral was dressed for the feast day of the One, Holy and Undivided Trinity. White and gold paraments adorned all the altars, baskets of white flowers stood on either side of the rood screen, and all was bathed in the clear morning light streaming through the clerestory windows. Felicity chose to take a seat at the back where she could have a panoramic view of the length of the nave. Chloe moved to the front, in the hope of being able to see into the choir through the pulpitum.

A gentle murmur of the service in the chapel was punctuated by the footsteps of blue-robed servers walking back and forth across the stone floor, getting all in readiness for the main morning service. Felicity knew she was supposed to be keeping watch, but her eyelids were so heavy...

"Hello. How lovely to see you this morning. Are you alone?"

Felicity jumped at the lilting Welsh voice in her ear. "Oh, good morning. Anne Morgan, isn't it?" She started to offer to shake hands, then thought better of spreading her cold germs.

"Yes. Do you mind if I sit with you? Rhys is a sidesman, so I'm on my own."

It took Felicity a moment to translate. Oh, yes, usher. She noted the tall, broad, dark-haired Welshman conferring with a server. "Please, join me." She patted the space on the pew beside her.

Anne looked like one of the Trinity altar cloths herself, in a perfectly fitting white suit, her golden hair in a gleaming chignon at the nape of her long, white neck. It made Felicity wish she had taken time to redo her braid that morning.

"Are you enjoying your visit to St David's?" Anne whispered so as not to disturb the early worshipers kneeling or meditating in their seats.

"Oh, yes, it's absolutely beautiful."

"How much longer are you here?"

"Just three days. We leave the morning of Corpus Christi." Felicity thought back to Ascension morn when this had all begun. It seemed a lifetime ago. And yet it had gone so quickly. So much had happened; and yet so little had happened to get them closer to solving the puzzle of Hwyl's death. For a moment she was back on that dew-sparkled hillside where a broken body had crashed through the exuberance of the morning. She looked at her hand, and for a moment it wasn't a worship folder she held there, but a piece of paper with a two-headed snake. She shuddered and dropped her folder.

Anne retrieved it and handed it to her. "Are you all right?"

Felicity resisted the impulse to sniff. "Thank you. I'm fine."

Then the stifled sniff burst out in a sneeze.

"You're not all right. You have a cold." Anne dug in her soft, ivory leather handbag and drew out a small card which she handed to Felicity.

The picture was of hands, held upward as if in prayer, filled with light radiating outward over the amethyst background. Felicity turned the card over. *Healing Hands. One Free, Lymphatic Drainage massage*, it said, and gave the address of Anne's shop. "Marissa is absolutely magic. Come by tomorrow. You'll feel worlds better," Anne assured her.

"Yes, I know she's good. And thank you. I will." Felicity slipped the card in her pocket, then blew her nose again.

The nave filled rapidly with worshipers, and soon the organ atop the pulpitum was pealing out the chords of "Holy, Holy, Holy," the threefold ascription to each person of the Holy Trinity. Felicity stood with the singing congregation as the white and gold-robed clergy and red-robed choristers processed up the aisle behind the crucifer. In spite of her months of training, Felicity, busy wiping her watery eyes, might have failed to acknowledge the passing cross had her seatmate not bowed so low.

In spite of their earlier alarms for the service, it proceeded without a hitch through scripture readings and prayers. "Almighty and everlasting God, who has given us thy servants grace by the confession of a true faith to acknowledge the glory of the eternal Trinity, and in the power of the Divine Majesty to worship the Unity: keep us steadfast in this faith, and evermore defend us in all adversities; who livest and reignest, one God, world without end."

"Amen." Felicity was thankful for Anne Morgan beside her, who kept her on track with the responses as she found her mind wandering.

Felicity made no attempt to focus on the sermon, but the calm, confident air of the dean as he delivered it reassured her. If Antony had succeeded in warning Dean Williams of possible peril, it had not flustered him. She also found it reassuring that Rhys Morgan and other sidesmen, as well as robed vergers, stood along the walls of the side aisles as if posted there for vigilance. So perhaps Antony's warning had been taken seriously.

At the conclusion of the sermon, Felicity stood with the others to recite the familiar words of the Nicene Creed, then realized that this was Trinity, the one Sunday in the year when the Athanasian Creed with its powerful Trinitarian affirmations was recited. "We worship one God in Trinity, and Trinity in Unity, Neither confounding the Persons, nor dividing the Substance…"

Felicity fumbled to find her place in her worship folder. "… The Godhead of the Father, of the Son, and of the Holy Ghost, is all one, the Glory equal, the Majesty co-eternal…" Anne's firm voice beside her helped her pick up the unfamiliar rhythm. "… The Father eternal, the Son eternal, and the Holy Ghost eternal.

"So likewise the Father is Lord, the Son Lord, and the Holy Ghost Lord. And yet not three Lords, but one Lord…" And then the clergy, which had been sitting in front of the pulpitum for the service of the Word, processed through the choir to the high altar for Holy Eucharist. Felicity smiled, knowing how this would please Antony, who didn't hold with the popular practice of celebrating Eucharist at a nave altar in replacement of the high altar.

After the consecration, which Felicity could hear but not see, the communicants moved forward, up the sloping aisle, up the steps to the pulpitum, through the choir with the choristers singing on either side of them, "I bind unto myself today/ The strong Name of the Trinity,/By invocation of the same/ The Three in One and One in Three…" And on through "St Patrick's Breastplate" as Felicity, following Anne, continued her ascending journey to kneel at the altar rail and receive the Body and Blood of Christ.

"Immortal, Invisible, God Only Wise," the clergy and choir recessed at the end of the service, leaving Felicity relieved that nothing untoward had happened, and yet a bit deflated. They had been wrong. *She* had been wrong. It made such perfect sense. But had she imagined the whole thing? Had she completely misunderstood or mistranslated what she thought she heard that night outside the cave? She had to admit a certain amount of it had been guesswork. But still…

"Are you sure you're all right?" Anne Morgan touched her arm.

Felicity jumped. "Oh, yes. Thank you. No, really, I'm fine." She stifled a sneeze and wiped her nose with a hanky. "I was just thinking."

"You'll be much better after that massage tomorrow," Anne assured her. "Are you coming to coffee now? In St Mary's Hall?"

"Oh, um, I'm not sure. I need to find Father Antony."

"Of course. Well, I'll see you in there if you do."

"Yes. Thank you. It was lovely to worship with you. Thank you for sitting with me." Felicity meant it. She felt that, distracted as she was, she might not have made it through the service without Anne's assured prompts.

Antony slid into the pew beside her. "I'm so sorry," she began. "I feel such a fool. But I was so certain. I hope I didn't make you look foolish in front of the dean."

"Not at all. No worries. He appreciated the caution. You noticed the guards he posted?"

Felicity nodded.

"And he thanked me for the *scrynne*, although he hasn't heard the story yet of exactly how I found it." Antony grimaced, undoubtedly dreading having to confess his snooping.

It was the mention of their adventure in the Bishop's Palace and Chloe's joining them at that moment that made her recall what Chloe had heard there yesterday. People planning a service in the ruined chapel. Had they been watching the wrong place? Had another group taken advantage of the fact that everyone else would be in the cathedral to hold a black mass or something— with the instrument of power? With a blood sacrifice?

Felicity jumped up and remembered where she was, just in time to temper her voice. "We've been looking in the wrong place; I'm sure of it. Come on, maybe we aren't too late."

She all but ran around the cathedral to the gatehouse of the Bishop's Palace. But it was boarded tight. "Open 1:00," the sign said. "Yes, of course, they wouldn't hold a black mass during visitors' hours." She thought for a moment, then called, "Come on, this way." Chloe had mentioned scaling the unrestored garden wall behind the palace; Felicity could get over it easily.

Glancing over her shoulder, she saw that Michael, Ryan and Lydia had caught up with Antony and Chloe, who had followed her out of the cathedral. Good. She had back-up.

It was a lengthy sprint through the trees around to the crumbled bit of the wall, but Felicity felt fueled by the assurance that she was on the right track at last, and had very little time to make up for her mistake. What if they were too late and the desecration had already occurred?

"What do you think you're doing?" Lydia demanded when she caught up, panting for breath.

"We were in the wrong place. It wasn't the cathedral. Chloe heard them talking. I misunderstood." Felicity grasped the stones on either side of the breech in the wall and pulled herself upward.

It was a maneuver she would normally have had no trouble accomplishing, but her cold and sleepless night had weakened her. Her fingers slipped and she felt herself sliding back, until Antony caught her and she was through the wall with a single boost.

She heard Antony instructing the others: Michael to come with him, Ryan, Lydia and Chloe to watch the exits. Go for help if need be. Antony and Michael were by her side in a moment. Her impulse was to rush across the courtyard and up the outside stairs leading to the Great Chapel, but that was far too exposed. Anyone glancing out one of the broken window arches would see them approaching. Instead she ducked into the darkness of the undercroft and made her way as if through a tunnel. At the end, she and the others emerged next to the stairs.

Crouching to avoid observation, Felicity started for the steps, then turned back. "I'll go up this way. You two cover the other doors in case they run."

"Um, Felicity," Michael said. "In case who runs?"

She looked around. She didn't see anyone else. She listened, straining over the pounding of her own heart. She heard nothing but the birds in the woods beyond the walls. Well, she would check for herself. Straightening her spine she ascended the stairs to the Great Chapel where Bishop Gower had held Holy Communion services for his honored guests. The room was deserted.

She heard Michael stifle a guffaw as he went back down the stairs, but Antony came to her. She examined the floor under the east window, looking for—what? Scratches of a pentagram? Feathers from a black rooster? Blood from…? There was nothing. She walked to the piscina and ran her hand over the smooth purple sandstone, even examining the drain hole. All was dry. No vessels, holy or otherwise, had been washed here.

She dropped her head into her hands. Antony put his arms around her. "Am I going crazy?" She whispered. Maybe the strain of the past weeks had been too much.

She leaned into Antony, feeling so safe, so secure. They stood there for some time. The sun was warm on her head. The gentlest of breezes murmured through the open windows. She felt her body relax.

And then they both jumped. It was a voice. And yet it was unvoiced. Standing apart from Antony, Felicity craned her neck, examining the shadows in all the crannies of the arcaded parapet, expecting a ghostly face to appear in any of the arched openings. It was unnaturally quiet. Not even the twitter of birds reached them. And then she heard it again. Not a voice. Not a roar like they had heard at the coal mine exhibit. It was more of a vibration. The vibration of high tension wires that could sound like singing. But there were no wires anywhere around. The sound swirled around them—a high tension shriek with the whisper of voices over it. Felicity wanted to clap her hands to her ears, but she knew that wouldn't keep it out.

By common consent they walked the length of the chapel to the northwest corner where the belfry rose, capped by its spirelet. Antony put his head through the opening and looked up. He withdrew, shaking his head. "Nothing."

And then, just when Felicity thought she would scream to blot out the sound, it quit. Felicity's knees buckled and she sank to the floor with relief, as one might do if a strong wind they had been leaning into suddenly ceased.

"We were right," she said. "They were here, but we couldn't see them. They were laughing. Mocking us."

Then she realized how hysterical that sounded. She had no idea who "they" were. She forced herself to take a deep breath. "No. There has to be a rational explanation. It must have been some kind of an echo."

"It sounded electronic to me," Antony said. "You sit here. I'll check around, just in case."

Felicity was more than happy to wait. But when Antony

returned from a careful search of the parapet, adjoining chambers and even the undercroft, he had found no evidence to support any assertion of the rational.

Chapter 26

Candles flickered on the altar of the tiny, womb-like St Non's chapel as Antony sat with his prayer book open on his knees, his mind awhirl. Only three days remained of their pilgrimage/retreat. He couldn't remember a time when he had ever spent so much effort on an endeavor and accomplished so little. Actually the account was all to the negative: there had been little spiritual refreshment, much encounter with apparent evil; the renewal he had promised Felicity had turned to exhaustion, her cold worse this morning; he had no answers for Dilys, so the appalling verdict of suicide would stand.

But to accept that would be to let evil win. His whole life was built on the premise that the power of good was stronger than the power of evil. That the good would ultimately win. He could not, would not abandon that foundation. But faith was all he had. Blind faith. No plan of action.

He closed his prayer book and knelt on the cold stones before the altar. A votive candle flickered before the gleaming brass cross. An aureole of white light radiated from the arched window. He was engulfed by the numinous. All he could see was light. He was surrounded by light. Hidden in light.

He breathed the light into his soul. Opened himself to the light.

Feeling stunned, all but blinded like St Paul on the road to Damascus, he stumbled from the chapel.

"Father Antony."

Antony put up his hand to shade his eyes, straining to identify the female Welsh voice carrying a note of authority.

"Constable Gwen Owen," the speaker supplied. "We're hoping you can help us. Dyfed-Powys police are clamoring for action. They're getting leaned on by Abergavenny. That missing lad's father has turned up and is raising the roof. Apparently your lot are the last ones to have seen him."

Antony registered that at least she didn't say *last to see him alive.* "But I don't understand. He isn't missing any more. He turned up. Lydia got a call from the school. No, the parents of a friend of Adam's…" Antony felt chilled as the realization washed over him. Whoever had kidnapped the boy must have rung Lydia claiming to be friends. She hadn't actually spoken to Adam, had she? "Well, I don't remember exactly what she said. Lydia can tell you." Antony turned toward the retreat house.

"We'd like that very much, only Miss Bowen isn't in her room."

"Someone will know where she is." Antony led the way to the dining room, where several of their group were lingering over breakfast.

No one, however, had seen Lydia that morning, and they were aghast to hear that Adam was not, after all, back at his school.

Felicity, red-eyed and red-nosed, spoke up from the end of the table. "I knew it! That was Adam we saw in the cave. The Orbis Astri have him. I knew it all along. Do you think they have Lydia, too? Chloe, show them your pictures."

Sister Nora efficiently turned her computer over to Chloe and the police officer. Antony and Felicity peered over their shoulders. Antony felt Felicity shiver beside him as the familiar images of the strange ritual filled the screen.

Constable Owen nodded. "Yes, we found wax on the rocks. Powdered lime on the hard earth of the floor—could have been used to make a design like that triangle diagram you described. Who knows?"

"But nothing more?" Felicity asked. "No fingerprints? No DNA?"

"You can't get prints from rocks. And everyone was shrouded head to toe; they even wore gloves. As good as SOCO protective gear."

Chloe pulled up the best picture of the small figure that Felicity believed was Adam. "I don't care what his sister says. I think that boy is the right size. It's Adam, I'm sure of it. And he's drugged. Chloe, show Constable Owen some of the pictures you took of Adam on the walk."

"Sure. I got some good shots of him that first day we met." She opened a folder labeled Mynydd Meio and began turning through them. "Adam wasn't on the mountain. I met him at the tea break—"

"Wait! Turn back," Constable Owen ordered.

Chloe started back at the beginning of that folder with pictures none of the group had seen before. "Who's that?" Owen asked.

"That's Joe. Joe Clempson. I took those shots just before I met these great people."

Gwen Owen shook her head. "I don't think so. Of course, he looks different here," she pointed to the screen, "Tanned, bleached blond, stubble… But it's him, all right. Brian Wright-Stilson. Wanted for drug dealing."

Antony groaned and smacked his forehead. "Oh, Jared said he thought he recognized him from Cardiff. I'm sorry. I didn't think."

"Where did you see him last?" The constable pulled out her mobile.

"Aberdare. A week ago. Jared thought he saw him in the park after the choir rehearsal."

"Right. That might be worth following up. And I'll need a detailed description of your missing woman." Constable Owen turned to her phone.

Antony turned to Felicity. "Let me walk you back to your room. You should be in bed."

"Nope, I'm going to get a massage. Free, even. The gift of Anne Morgan." Felicity drew the card from her pocket and showed him. "Lymphatic drainage—whatever that is. Supposed to do wonders."

Antony considered. He didn't like Felicity going there, but he had no concrete reason to dissuade her. "Then I'll drive you into town. I need to see the dean anyway."

A short time later, he pulled up in front of the lavender storefront with the row of crystals gleaming in the window. "Are you sure you're all right on your own?"

She gave him a saucy look. "What, you want to observe my massage, Father?"

"Get on with you, baggage." His answer was light-hearted, but he couldn't help worrying. Something was going on and it was impossible to know who was involved or what their motive was. "Be careful," he added as the door closed.

The dean welcomed him into his office and was effusive in his thanks for the recovered *scrynne*. "We'll have it tested carefully, of course, but at an initial observation our archivist thinks it likely it could date from Bishop Gower's time."

"Any idea what it held?"

"Mary Ware, the expert from Cardiff who is still here working on the floor plan you produced—what a treasure trove you are, Father—says it's most likely too large to have held a relic; she expects it to have been a document, although further tests may reveal more. Now, if you could just find that document,

Father, we would have to name a hall in your honor."

Antony all but blushed. "I think I'd better confess how I found this." Haltingly, he told his tale.

When he looked up, the dean's face was split in an enormous grin. "Well, well. Our own Indiana Jones, I must say. But I'm curious as to why you didn't go through more—ah, *normal* channels."

"We thought there might be some urgency." And Antony laid out the entire tangled tale to Dean Williams.

Now the dean wasn't smiling. "This does sound serious. You've informed Bishop Harry, I assume."

Antony assured him he had, and promised to keep the dean informed if anything else should come to light.

There was still some time before he needed to meet Felicity, so Antony strolled across the cathedral close and back up to the narrow, winding streets of the quaint city, noting the names as he went: The Pebbles was an obvious reference to the surfacing material of the road; Goat Street spoke of a wandering lost goat or of chevre milk and cheese for sale; Nun Street evoked images of habited women of long ago walking in a tidy procession.

Antony turned to follow a small, shadowed lane leading off Nun Street. He had only gone a few strides, however, when he pulled back at the sound of angry voices ahead of him. He started to turn around when he caught a voice he was certain he recognized. "No, wait, I didn't." That was Michael's voice. What was his driver involved in?

Antony pushed himself against an angled wall as the voices got louder and he heard footsteps coming from behind the building ahead of him. "I owe you nothing. Now get lost. And don't try this on again." Antony peeked around the corner to make certain. Yes, the speaker was Rhys Morgan, with Michael alongside him.

And he caught a glimpse of the muscled, tanned young man with the peroxide blond hair. Constable Owen would be interested to know that Joe Clempson, or rather, Brian Wright-Stilson was apparently demanding money in a hidden lane right here in St David's.

But first he must collect Felicity. Then find a phone. He had left his mobile at the retreat house. Felicity saw him coming and dashed out of Chakra Health, leaving the bells on the door tinkling behind her. She grabbed his arm and propelled him toward the minibus. "You'll never guess who was in there."

Antony held the van door open for her. "Joe?"

Her mouth fell open. "How did you know?"

Antony closed her door and went around to the driver's seat. "He was in the alley threatening Michael and Rhys Morgan."

"Curiouser and curiouser." Felicity leaned over and kissed him. "By the way, I feel great. That massage was amazing."

"Wonderful," he said. "But now, tell me."

"I was in the massage room, all cozy under heated sheets, dim lights, nice smells, New Age music—" She held up a hand. "Don't say it. I know—not compatible. But you didn't expect them to be playing hymns, did you? Anyway, the point is, while I was waiting for Marissa I heard this voice in the hall. I was almost certain it was Joe. He wanted to know where Anne was. Sounded really angry," she paused. "No, not angry. Desperate, when Marissa said she didn't know. Then Marissa came in and I asked her who that was. She called him Evan. Apparently Rhys wants Anne to give him a job in the shop. Marissa said they don't really have any work for him, but Anne doesn't want to turn him away because he's Rhys's nephew."

"And you're sure it was Joe?"

"Fairly sure. I only heard his voice that one night in the pub."

"Right." Antony drove back to the retreat house, anxious to

ring Constable Owen to tell her of this new development, and to enquire if there was news of Lydia.

He had just turned into the lane leading to St Non's, however, when he recognized the narrow-shouldered, broad-hipped figure striding ahead of him. He pulled up alongside and rolled down his window. "Want a ride?"

Lydia slipped into the passenger seat. "Thanks."

Antony put the minibus into gear. "I must say, I'm glad to see you. We were worried when you disappeared."

"Disappeared? What an ominous word. I went shopping."

Antony frowned at the explanation, since she carried no packages, but that was a minor detail compared to Adam's continued absence. "Lydia, I'm afraid I have some bad news. The police were here while you were gone. It seems that phone call you received about Adam was a fake. Your father—"

"My father!" She swallowed. "What do you mean a fake? Where's Squib?"

Antony stopped outside the retreat house, and before he could answer, Lydia was out of the vehicle, punching the keys on her mobile, apparently anxious to get hold of her father.

Later, Antony still felt no clearer about what was going on as he and Felicity walked into town to attend the Restoration Committee meeting at the Morganses home. Late afternoon was the loveliest time on the headland, with the westering sun turning all the landscape to gold, the lengthening shadows lending a sense of quiet peace. But Antony felt no peace. The golden shrubs seemed sharp-edged, and the shadows felt ominous.

He had been looking forward to the walk as a time to talk through events with Felicity, but even though they walked hand in hand, she seemed distant, distracted. And it got no better when they entered the cream and white Georgian house on New Street.

"Ah, Father, welcome. I'm so glad you've come." Anne Morgan put a crystal sherry glass in his hand, and pulled him into the room filled with people chatting in small groups. It had far more the feeling of a cocktail party than a committee meeting. Anne steered him around the room, introducing him to various committee members: a tall, thin woman named Clarissa, who was wearing a very short skirt; a man in a red shirt and maroon trousers with a name starting with T; a fat woman he had difficulty stepping around… He quickly lost track of the names. The sherry was sickly sweet and the room overheated. For the life of him, Antony couldn't remember why he had agreed to come. Something to do with Hwyl, but the connection seemed tenuous now. He caught a glimpse of Felicity across the room, talking to Rhys Morgan. Perhaps she would learn something useful.

At last Rhys called the meeting to order. Antony started to sink into a small sofa at the back of the room, thinking there would be room for Felicity to sit beside him, but Anne grabbed his arm and guided him across the thick Persian carpet to a chair next to her by the fireplace. Antony caught Felicity's eye. She raised her glass of cranberry juice in salute with what looked like an amused smile at his having been ambushed.

Rhys presented the group with impressive charts showing an architect's concept of the restored Bishop's Palace and projections of the income that would be brought into St David's by pilgrimage groups and conventions, then asked for reports from various committee chairs on the progress of fundraising and planning permission. The numbers jumbled in Antony's head. A tiny trickle of sweat ran down the back of his neck. Antony had never been uncomfortable in a clerical collar, but tonight it felt like a thrall's neck ring.

At the conclusion of the meeting Anne turned to him, radiant with rays of the sinking sun through the window lighting her smoothly coiled hair. "Inspiring, isn't it? Rhys is so far-sighted." She placed a hand briefly on Antony's arm. "I do hope you've caught the vision, Father Antony, because we—well, Rhys, really, of course, but he doesn't mind my speaking for him—we are so hoping you'll agree to fill Hwyl's place on the committee."

Antony frowned. Could he have heard her right? "Me? But I don't live here."

Anne was unfazed. "Oh, that's part of the point. Our members are really quite far-flung. I'm sure you realize that if our efforts are to succeed, they need a broad base. International, even."

"Yes. Well, it's an honor to be asked. I'll need to think about it." He hoped he didn't show the desperation he was feeling as he turned toward the door. "We really must be getting back to St Non's… Responsible for our pilgrims…" Were his words slurring?

"Oh, now, Father, you don't think you're going to escape us that easily, do you? You must stay for supper. Just a few select members of the committee. They're all anxious to meet you."

Antony's head was ringing. He couldn't form an answer.

"That's so kind of you, Mrs Morgan. I know Father Antony would love to get better acquainted with your group. You really are so well organized." Felicity's voice was clear and firm as she gripped his arm with both hands, steadying him.

"Wonderful. And you're invited, too, of course, my dear."

"Thank you so much. We would be delighted another time. Unfortunately, I just received a text. One of our pilgrims went missing a few days ago, and the police are waiting at the retreat center to talk to us."

"Oh, how terrible. But surely—"

Antony moved slowly in obedience to Felicity's tug on his arm, his feet feeling ensnared in the pile of the carpet. Felicity shoved him out the door. The fresh, early evening breeze revived him a bit. Antony took a deep, wavering breath, expelled it and repeated the process. He still felt confused, but at least he could breathe. "What happened in there? There must have been something in my drink." He took one more deep breath. "What do you mean text from the police? You don't even carry a mobile."

Felicity grinned. "Quick thinking, huh? I didn't think Sister Alma's name would carry the same weight, and I needed to talk to you."

"Hmm?" Antony followed Felicity's guiding down the street. He felt he was walking through treacle.

"Are you all right? What did Anne want of you? What did you think of Rhys's presentation? Can you walk any faster?"

"I don't know." That answered it all. "What did you think?"

She waited to answer until they were through town and back on the lane to the retreat house. "That's what I wanted to tell you. Two of those committee members—the fat blonde woman and the tall, skinny one with the freaked-out hair—of course it was covered by a hood before—but I'm really sure… Well, pretty sure—" Felicity talked so fast he was only getting one word in every two or three.

"What?"

"Aren't you listening? I know you don't feel good. I suppose you're coming down with that cold I had. I'll call Marissa and book you in for a massage tomorrow, but try to concentrate. This is really important. I'm convinced some of those women were part of that witch's coven thing we saw in the cave—especially the tall one. Not just her height—the way she swayed when she moved. And, listen, now that I saw him again—standing in front, leading the group—I'm sure Rhys Morgan was their leader. He had the same commanding presence. Like he expected people to kneel down to him."

Rhys Morgan? Leading a coven of witches and warlocks? Even in his enervated state, that seemed laughable to Antony. "He's one of the most respected men in the city."

"Right. Powerful, a real leader. Just what a group like that would need. Or maybe just what he needs. You're the one who's always saying there's real power in that stuff."

Antony just nodded and concentrated on continuing to breathe deeply. The closer they got to the bay the fresher and saltier the air became. It was exactly what he needed. When the path branched up to the house, he steered Felicity to the lower walk along the cliff. "Let's not go in yet."

"I should call Constable Owen. Tell her about those women."

"Ten minutes won't matter. The sea air is helping. I'm feeling much clearer." As he said it he realized how much better. The walking-in-treacle feeling was gone. His steps felt light. He began to stride along the path as if he had wings on his heels.

"Isn't this amazing! I'm so glad you're feeling better. I love this walk." Felicity skipped on ahead of him as the path was too narrow to walk side by side.

Yes, he was feeling amazingly refreshed. It must have just been that overheated room filled with chattering people. The sun was almost setting now, gilding the tops of the cliffs a gleaming gold, and leaving the stones of the sheer rock face below them a menacing black as they disappeared into the surf at their feet.

The mat of green vegetation ran like a thick, verdant carpet from the path and smoothed the way over the precipice. Pink, white and yellow wildflowers grew in cascading tendrils down the cliff face like a colorful waterfall. He stepped off the path, drawn by the beauty of the scene, the amazing contrasts of the softness of the flowering vegetation and the harshness of the jagged rocks; the golden brilliance of the light, the Stygian darkness of the shadows, the stillness of the air, the crashing surf.

And then it was the sound, rather than the sight that overwhelmed him. The mesmerizing rhythm of the waves beating, beating, beating on the rocks; the call of the seabirds soaring over the water harmonizing with the buzz of insects drinking nectar of the flowers; the vibration of the breeze, rustling the grasses at his feet, calling him onward. *Come, come. Float with the birds. Soar. Come…*

An inch closer. Antony looked down. Straight down. The water swirled, making delightful patterns, washing the rocks, splashing, foaming like lace. Laughing, singing. *Come, come, come.* He took another step forward. It was all so clear, so right. To be one with the breeze. One with the birds and the salt spray. One with the universe…

"Antony!" Felicity's arms closed around him, pulling him back from the brink.

Chapter 27

The midmorning sun glittered on the bay spread before them as Antony and Felicity sat on the bench along the wall of St Non's. As breathtaking as the scene spread before them was, Antony had no desire to get any closer to it. He squeezed his eyes closed and then opened them wide just for the sheer relief of being able to do so. To be able to look, to breathe, to think. Had he really come as close to dying as Felicity's account made it sound? His own memory was a vague muddle of walking with weights on his feet, then wanting to fly. All followed by a splitting headache which he had only partially slept off.

He shifted on the bench to push his back more firmly against the solid boards. "Did I say thank you for saving my life?"

Felicity squeezed his hand. "My pleasure. Any time. But what happened?"

Antony shook his head. "I'm not sure. I keep going over it in my mind, but it's pretty much a fog. I felt good, I remember that. Great, actually. Like a king. Or a god. Invincible."

"And drawn to the edge?" Felicity added.

"Oh, yes, definitely that." He shuddered.

"Like Hwyl?"

Antony turned to look at her. Her eyes were wide. "What are you saying?"

"I'm not sure, but if you had gone over the edge no one could have proved it wasn't suicide or an accident, could they?"

He shook his head. "I suppose not. Unless they had done some sort of drug testing. *If* drugs were involved. I don't know what happened. Or almost happened. But I'm awfully thankful it didn't."

"No more thankful than I am." Felicity scooted even closer to him on the bench and gave his arm a squeeze with both hands. "But whatever it was—do you think that's what happened to Hwyl?"

"It would explain a lot. If it was, it means he went off that tower thinking life was beautiful and that he could be one with the birds."

"So he wasn't pushed?"

"Pulled, is more like it."

"Do you think it was drugs—or something more... er— inexplicable?"

"You're still not comfortable naming evil, are you?" He looked at her fondly. "But absolutely, whether it was drugs or a spell or some other type of mind control, it was definitely evil. Hwyl knew something someone didn't want him to tell me or anyone else."

"Well, if drugs were involved, Joe could be the link. And what a cover it would be for Joe to work in a herbalist shop if he's dealing drugs." Felicity was quiet for a moment, thinking. "Yes. I'd like to get a closer look at the storeroom behind Chakra Health. You really should get a massage for that cold you're coming down with."

"I'm not..." Antony started.

"Look, I'm sure Rhys is behind all this somehow. What a perfect set-up—get drugs from his nephew, and hide them in his wife's herbalist shop."

"Well, I suppose so." It all seemed pretty circumstantial to Antony.

"And something else. I really hate to say this, but Michael—"

"What about Michael?"

"Well, if he was in the alley with Rhys and Joe, like you said, he must be involved somehow. I mean, he helped take Adam back to school—or wherever it was he disappeared from."

"Felicity, you can't be saying you think Michael kidnapped Adam."

"I don't know what I'm saying. I just think the drugs angle needs to be investigated. And Michael questioned more closely."

"I agree. I'll call Constable Owen."

Felicity hesitated. "But don't the police need some kind of evidence to get a search warrant? If we can get some evidence for her, then Constable Owen can take over from there."

Antony opened his mouth, but his argument was interrupted by a sneeze.

"Right." Felicity jumped to her feet. "A lymphatic drainage massage for you. Essential oils all over your body, feather-like strokes from Marissa's tensile fingers. You'll love it."

"Felicity. I really don't—" But she was off.

Half an hour later, Antony was quietly reading when a whole delegation entered the library. "Your first herbal massage! That is so totally cool. You'll love it, Father A." Kaylyn shook her shaggy, kohl-black hair and curved her black-lined lips into a smile.

"And a whole shopful of crystals! I'm, like, totally into crystals," Evie added. "Let's buy one and hang it in St Non's Well, huh, Jared?" The chubby Goth looked up at her lanky, red-haired companion, the slightest pink tinge staining her chalk-white cheeks.

"Sure, if you like. Whatever, really."

"Felicity, what *is* this?" Antony came to his feet.

"Nothing," Felicity protested with an innocence he knew she never possessed. "I told them we were going into town and they wanted to come along. I couldn't see why not. They can just browse around the shop a bit."

Antony looked at her through narrowed eyes. "You mean Kaylyn and Evie can distract anyone in the shop while Jared, who knows something about drugs, slips into the storeroom."

"Antony! What a brilliant plan. Why didn't I think of that?"

"No way." He grasped her arm harder than he intended to. He forced his fingers to loosen a bit as he turned to the others with a steely look. "Out. Everybody. Felicity and I need to talk."

As soon as they were alone he turned Felicity to him with both hands. He wanted to be gentle, but he had to get his point across to her. "This has gone far enough. I'm not having any more of your dabbling in this... this—whatever's going on."

She started to protest, but he cut her off. "And I'm certainly not going into that shop and lay down like some kind of sacrificial lamb. And I will not endanger our teens by taking them there. We'll ring Constable Owens and tell her everything we know and what we suspect. The authorities can make of it what they will. They'll have to get their own proof."

Felicity stood there in stony silence, her body rigid. He waited for her outburst. He had never spoken to her so harshly before. Would she cry? Shout at him? Storm out of the room?

Instead she turned to him coldly. "Right. You've made your position quite clear. I'll be in the front parlor if Constable Owens wants to talk to me."

Alone in the room he sank into a chair and put his head in his hands. He had never felt at more of a loss in his life. They had both been through so much and he had accomplished nothing. He had so wanted to help Dilys. He could only hope that his experience last night would be of some small comfort to her. It was certainly evidence that her husband had not committed suicide in cold blood. It was the best he could offer her. He felt responsible to the former student who had been coming to him for help, but he could do no more.

Tomorrow they would celebrate the Eve of the Feast of Corpus Christi; the pilgrims would dispense the next day and that, thankfully, would be the end of his obligation to this whole ill-conceived endeavor. Had any venture ever started out with such high goals and gone so badly wrong? He was certain he had never failed more spectacularly in his life. He could only pray that the police could recover Adam.

But he was through. And that was the end of it.

A short time later he led Constable Owens into the parlor with some trepidation. He had no idea how Felicity would react to his presence but he could see nothing to do except carry on. To his surprise Felicity nodded at them both and began telling the constable about the evening before in precise detail.

The story became more disjointed, however, when Felicity started in on the theory that Morgan's nephew was a drug dealer hiding his wares in the Chakra Health storeroom. The constable looked up from her notepad filled with hasty scribbles. "So let me get this straight. Are you accusing *Rhys Morgan* of dealing in illegal drugs?"

Felicity gulped. "Well, no, not *accusing* as such. But I do think it's a line of enquiry you should look into. I mean, Antony did feel very strange, and he was inches from going over the precipice and I'm sure—well, almost sure—well, I really do think Rhys's nephew is a drug-dealer—and…"

"Constable," Antony spoke up for the first time. "What about the possibility of doing a drug test on me, and on Father Hwyl Pendry's corpse?" They needed to get back on firmer ground if they hoped to be taken seriously.

"We can certainly try. As to the possibility of detecting a drug administered yesterday, it depends entirely upon the type of drug used. If it was a date rape-type drug, it could be gone in a few hours after ingestion, but a heavier drug could still be in the system for up to maybe three weeks or so."

"And a corpse?" Felicity asked in a hushed voice.

"Actually a corpse would be better. Since the body is no longer absorbing or burning off the elements, everything is stagnant. So if a person died with a drug in their system it would still be in the fatty tissue, especially in the organs, years after the death. I can enquire, but I expect the Yorkshire police have already seen to that. I believe they have a very good forensics department there."

Antony opened his mouth to say that he thought the widow should be given any such information, but a pounding of footsteps on the stone verandah just outside accompanied by shrieks and sobs stopped his words. The door flew open and Kaylyn and Evie burst in with Jared just behind them.

"Joe! I know it's him."

"At the well! We went to hang a crystal…" Evie held up the brilliant prism and burst into sobs.

Jared stepped over the threshold. "It's Joe all right. Face down in the well. I think he's dead."

Chapter 28

F elicity paced the verandah in front of the retreat house. The last day of their retreat. Some retreat. Antony had promised her rest and peace. It had been anything but that: struggling up steep trails with blistered feet, injuries, illnesses, alarms, terrifying encounters with manifestations of evil…

And there still had been no opportunity to sort things out with Antony. After she calmed down she had realized that Antony had been perfectly within his rights to refuse a massage. And perhaps her idea was a bit hare-brained. Not that she intended to admit that to him, of course. But they did need to talk.

All of yesterday afternoon and late into the evening had been consumed by the discovery of Joe's drowned body in St Non's Well. Constable Owen hadn't been able to prevent the pilgrims following her to the well after the hysterical announcement that roused everyone in the house. Felicity had glimpsed the kneeling figure slumped on the stones beside the well, his face in the water as if he were drinking from the small pool.

The constable didn't comment, but it seemed to Felicity that there were no apparent signs of struggle; the delicate fronds of the fern near his head bent in graceful, unbroken arches, the moss between the flags around the well was undisturbed, and a small clump of yellow wildflowers grew by his head as if someone had placed a posy beside the body. Had he truly knelt down for a drink and had a heart attack or something, as it appeared? Or had he been in a drug-induced state so that he had allowed someone to hold his face in the water? Or was the explanation even darker than that?

Felicity had been about to comment when Sister Nora arrived, acting the feisty sheepdog to herd everyone back to the retreat house.

Chloe had identified the body, with drops of water still clinging to his white-blond hair, as the man she knew as Joe Clempson. Felicity and Antony had stayed with her as the police questioned her about her former relationship, and Antony related what he had heard in the alley. Joe's death certainly gave new significance to the fact that he had been pressuring Rhys for money, or a job, or something.

Michael couldn't be questioned about this until later. He and Ryan had taken Lydia on a cliff walk in the hopes of calming her agitation. She had been able to give Constable Owen very little new information about Adam, and had not yet made contact with her father. Now the nurse who had attended to everyone else needed care herself. It was probably just as well Lydia wasn't there; it would only have added to her distress.

Felicity had put personal relationships aside for the moment and tried to get Antony to speculate. "But what do you think? Was Joe blackmailing Rhys? Did the Orbis Astri cast some kind of spell? It's all just the power of suggestion, isn't it? The mind worked on by fear?"

Antony nodded. "That's certainly an element. But don't dismiss fear. Manipulating a person's emotions for harm is no less evil than casting a satanic spell."

That had been late last night and she still shuddered to think of it. It was all such a muddle and she longed to know the truth of all that had been going on, but Antony continued to remind her, somewhat pompously, she thought, that everything was in the hands of the authorities now, and their responsibility was to their pilgrims.

And now when she needed to talk to him he seemed to be avoiding her, spending ages with Sister Alma in the tiny St Non's chapel preparing everything for the first Evening Prayer of the Feast of Corpus Christi. Antony said he wanted it to be a special service, a solemn choral Evensong with incense because it would be the last service of the pilgrimage. "So fitting to celebrate together the day set aside in the church calendar to give thanks for the gift of the Holy Eucharist. Christ's Body and Blood given to strengthen his followers," he had said when he announced the service at lunch.

Okay, she got that. But surely he could have made time for her if he'd tried. She looked at the sun hanging low in the west. It still felt like afternoon, but it must be far later than she thought. Judging the time by the position of the sun was deceptive on this, the longest day of the year. She would just have a cup of tea and a slice of the dark, rich fruitcake Sister Nora kept on the sideboard in the guest lounge and then she would find Antony and insist they talk.

She thought she would be alone in the lounge, but Evie and Kaylyn were there. Felicity blinked. She had never before seen Kaylyn dressed in anything but solid Goth black. Evie occasionally varied her wardrobe, but only to include a dark wine red or deep forest green. Both girls now wore pristine white. And even more surprising, had flowers in their hair. The effect was startling as it made their hair look even darker, their skin more alabaster.

"Wow! You look—different. Er—lovely. Really pretty, both of you."

Kaylyn gave a shy smile. "Summer solstice."

"Nature in full bloom, the land flowing with abundance," Evie poured out in a breathless voice, then stopped and giggled.

"Um, sure. And also Corpus Christi. You are coming to Evensong, aren't you?"

"Of course."

"See you there." They set their cups down and fled.

While her tea brewed, Felicity picked up the leaflet Kaylyn had dropped. "The History of Litha," she read. "Among the great festivals of the pagan Celtic year are the two solstices and the two equinoxes. In folklore, these are referred to as the four 'quarter-days' of the year, and modern witches call them the four 'Lesser Sabbats,' or the four 'Low Holidays.' The summer solstice, or Litha, is one of them."

Felicity cut a slice of cake and read on, "Although Litha is a lesser sabbat in the ancient parlance, it is celebrated with more revel and merriment than any other day on the wheel of the year. The joyous rituals of Litha celebrate the verdant earth in high summer, abundance, fertility, and all the riches of nature in full bloom. This is a madcap time of strong magic and empowerment…"

Felicity crumpled the paper before dropping it in the bin. It was nonsense; and yet, she couldn't help feeling uneasy. The Feast of Corpus Christi, the Wiccan festival of Litha on the same night. Surely it didn't mean anything. A lot of Christian feasts were predated by pagan rituals. Some said that disproved the validity of the Christian observances. Antony would say it simply evidenced the universality of Truth—Common Grace.

Getting sidetracked with Lithia, however, meant Felicity had let it go too late. Now there would be no time to confront Antony. Why did she think of it as a confrontation? They just needed to talk. That should be easy enough. Talking was the thing they were both good at. They had always been able to talk through their differences. Always before, that is.

A sudden chill shook Felicity. She was glad of the warm evening air as she stepped outside to make her way to St Non's chapel. The small room usually offered chairs around the walls for private meditation, but tonight Antony had arranged seats in traditional rows facing the altar, just enough for their group and the Sisters. When Felicity arrived she was pleased to see Jared and the Goth girls in their astonishing white attire already there, sitting in the front row. Michael sat in the middle of the next row and Felicity took the seat to his left, leaving the one on his right for Lydia, as she assumed they would want to sit together. Michael, however, made no protest when Chloe slipped into the chair. Nancy and Ryan chose the next row, leaving the seat behind Felicity vacant for Lydia when the Sisters took the back two chairs.

Felicity, who loved organ music, was surprised to find that the silence of the stones, the distant crash of waves and the evening call of birds filled the air with an even more vibrant music. The western windows magnified the rays of the sun as it sank into the sea, filling the tiny space with a rose-gold warmth and enhancing the lighted candles around the room.

In her clear, sweet soprano, Nancy began the entrance canticle:

Pange lingua gloriosi
Corporis mysterium,
Sanguinisque pretiosi…

In her own mind, Felicity translated:

Sing, my tongue, the Savior's glory,
of his flesh the myst'ry sing:
Of the blood all price exceeding,
shed by our immortal King,
On the night of that Last Supper
seated with his chosen band,

He, the paschal victim eating,
First fulfills the law's command;
Then as food to his apostles
gives himself with his own hand.

Word made flesh, the bread of nature
by a word to flesh he turns;
Wine into his blood he changes...

And then the soft clink of the thurible chain and the swish of heavy fabric as Antony entered in a white cope borrowed from the cathedral, and the chapel was filled with the musky scent of myrrh, the most ancient of embalming spices, reminding them of the gift brought to the holy infant by the wise men, presaging His entombment.

Standing before the altar Antony spread his arms, holding his hands out to the tiny group. *Like a father at the head of the table on Thanksgiving,* Felicity thought. "In the Feast of Corpus Christi we celebrate the greatest gift our Lord has left us: His Body and Blood in the Eucharist—the source and summit of the Christian life, the fullness of the life of God, contained in this Sacrament..."

The service continued through its familiar rhythm of prayers and scripture readings. More than once Felicity glanced over her shoulder. The chair behind her remained empty. Where was Lydia? As the nurse to their group there wasn't a person here she hadn't ministered to by bandaging a blister, supplying aspirin or salving a cut. The woman must be distraught over her still-missing brother, and Felicity had hoped this service would be a comfort to her. Now Felicity realized she hadn't seen Lydia all day. The image of Joe face-down in St Non's Well flashed into Felicity's mind. *Dear God, let her be all right.*

They had reached the final collect, "Gracious and merciful

God, in a wonderful sacrament you have given us a memorial of the passion of your Son Jesus Christ; grant—" when Felicity noticed Michael taking his mobile out of his pocket.

She told herself she wasn't really snooping; the screen was in her line of sight. Well, if she looked just a little sideways, and given that she didn't have her eyes closed during prayer, of course. Still, the message jumped out at her with the impatience of the writer: WHR R U? PLCE NOW! LYD

Michael scraped his chair against the stones as he lunged to his feet and barged out of the room, his footsteps pounding on the stone floor.

Antony waited until the echo had died away, then motioned for them to stand. "Let us join our voices together in saying: *The Grace…*"

Felicity contained herself just long enough for the *Amen* to be pronounced, and then she dashed forward. No time for an orderly, prayerful recessional. Something was going on. Something Michael and Lydia were excited or disturbed about. Whatever it was, it had to have something to do with the strange things that had been happening and she meant to find out what.

Antony frowned at her garbled report. "A demand from Lydia that he meet her now? At the PLCE—what place? I was disappointed that she missed our last service together, and we all know Lydia is capable of being more than demanding, but I'm sure Michael can take care of himself."

"No, I don't feel right about it," Felicity insisted. "It's something important. I know it." Felicity took a deep breath. She had given in to Antony last time. This time she would stand firm.

"But we have no idea where this place is. What can we do?"

Their discussion was interrupted by an argument from the back corner of the chapel. "Nah, I don't really want to, and I don't think you two should go alone."

"Oh, come on, Jared, it'll be fun." Kaylyn and Evie were pulling Jared toward the door.

Nancy looked from one group to another. "What's going on? Is something wrong?"

"I think—" Felicity began.

"It's just a bonfire," Evie pleaded. "To increase the sun's energy."

"Bonfire?" Felicity asked. "Where?"

"Well, we don't really know. We went back to Chakra Health today to get another crystal, and we heard some people talking. When we asked they were really vague. But everyone knows solstice fires are always on hilltops, so it should be easy to spot."

"The hillside beyond the cathedral seems obvious," Kaylyn added to Evie's lengthy explanation.

"Hill?" Felicity asked.

"Well, hummock," Kaylyn amended. "The ground's definitely higher there."

"It's a wild goose chase. You don't even know for sure it's a bonfire. And if they wouldn't tell you where it is, it must be a secret," Jared said.

"What else would it be on Midsummer's Eve?" Kaylyn asked.

"And everyone will see it," said Evie. "A fire on a hilltop will show up, so it can't really be a secret."

"That must be the place Lydia meant in her text," said Felicity.

"What text? What did she say?" Ryan asked.

Felicity shrugged. "I don't know; just PLCE—you know how text messages are."

"Yes, I do," Ryan said. "Could be place, but just as easily it could be palace."

"The Bishop's Palace!" several said together.

"Did Michael take the van?" Felicity asked.

"No, I have the keys." Antony said.

"Then we could easily catch him," she replied.

"Wait. I don't think…" Antony began.

Felicity turned and glared at him. "You don't have to go. But I'm going." She held out her hand. "May I have the keys?" She started to add *please* but realized it would sound sarcastic rather than firm.

"I agree there's something going on—the same thing that's plagued this whole pilgrimage—and we can't just turn our backs on it now." Ryan looked at Antony. "Father?"

"All right, we'll see if we can find Michael."

"You're going to stop them, aren't you? The people causing all this trouble." Nancy moved closer to Ryan. "I want to come with you."

Antony answered her. "No, you stay here and pray. Get the Sisters to pray with you."

"But—" she started to protest.

Antony put a hand briefly on her shoulder. "I'm hoping this will be a simple bonfire, but if we are to encounter active evil, nothing is needed more than faith and prayer. It's the first thing I teach my deliverance ministry students—to have a group of people praying concurrently with, but separately from, the work of the priest." His voice carried a ring of authority that he seldom summoned.

"Right." Nancy turned and darted up the sloping lawn to the retreat house.

"We…" Evie got no further before Antony stopped her.

"Don't even think about it. Jared, you take these two to the house. Lock them in their room if you have to."

Jared grinned and took each protesting girl by an arm. Antony turned to Chloe, who was clutching her camera like a weapon.

But this time he was preempted. "Don't worry. I'll stay way

back. Freedom of the press and all that. Besides, you might need documentation."

Antony shook his head. "I don't have time to argue." He tossed his hastily shed vestments on a chair and ran out toward the minibus.

They were almost to the end of the lane when they saw a figure jogging in the dusky light. But when they came alongside, Felicity saw that it wasn't Michael. Michael was nowhere to be seen on the road leading into St David's. "Could he walk that fast? We couldn't have missed him, could we?"

"Not unless he ran all the way, or someone came to pick him up in a vehicle," Antony said. "I suppose he could have gone an entirely different direction."

"Let's carry on to the Bishop's Palace, in case our guess is right," Ryan urged.

"It's definitely not on a hilltop, and it'll be closed at this hour," Antony argued, but he continued driving.

Rather than approaching from Nun Street, which would take them to the cathedral, Antony turned down a country lane that ran behind the east range of the palace and parked beneath a clump of trees lining the way. Beyond the low stone wall, the field stretched flat and green—and completely devoid of any activity.

"Well, there would be plenty of space to build a bonfire here," Ryan began.

"But no one did." Felicity let her discouragement show in her voice. They sat observing the deserted, bucolic scene spread before them. In the growing dark, the arches of Bishop Gower's distinctive arcaded parapet topping the broken wall, and the wheel window of the Great Hall with the belltower of the Great Chapel behind it took on a ghostly distinction that brought to life the powerful impact this building must have made on medieval visitors. Indeed, Felicity felt its magnetic force even now.

Then she caught her breath. "Antony!" She grabbed his arm and pointed. "There! At the end of the arcade. Did you see that?"

"What? I didn't see anything."

Felicity blinked to be sure her eyes weren't playing tricks. "I'm sure I saw a movement." She paused. "There! Again. There's someone up there."

"Could just be a bird," Antony began, but Felicity was already out of the minibus, darting across the road. She was barely aware of the scratchy bushes and the crumbled wall that had once surrounded the property.

Vaguely aware of Antony and Ryan behind her, she set out at a lope toward the more modern wall, erected to make sure visitors didn't enter without paying the entrance fee. But even this hardly slowed her down as she grasped the rough top and jammed her toes into whatever foothold the uneven stones provided, completely heedless of the scuffing it gave her shoes. Now she was inside the enclosure, looking up at the magnificent wall before her. A solid wall. If she had, indeed—and she was sure she had—seen someone moving about on the parapet running straight above her head, how was she to get up there? The tall arched window opening two floors above stared back at her like a dead eye.

Antony and Ryan caught up with her. "What do you mean by darting off like that?" Antony began, but she put her finger to her lips.

She heard something. It could have been the breeze playing in the stone arches, but equally it could have been a murmur of voices. A chant, even. She looked to her left. Was that a faint glow of light through the wheel window? Were the girls right? Was someone building a bonfire— inside the Bishop's Palace? Keeping to the shadows, she moved along the solid stone barrier.

Felicity pointed emphatically to her right, indicating that Ryan should investigate the east range, then to her left for Antony to take the west.

"We'll be right back," he whispered. "Wait here."

She had little enough choice, since she was faced with a stone wall. Then she saw the opening. A small arched passage that hardly showed in the dark. Of course. The undercroft ran all the length of the range, and the supply rooms under the Great Hall would have been some of the most important. It was undoubtedly where the wine had been stored to provide for the guests at Bishop Gower's magnificent banquets. A delivery cart would have unloaded here; there would be a stairway directly up to the hall. If only it wasn't broken beyond ascending.

Felicity groped her way through the total blackness of the undercroft, her hand trailing along the stones to guide her to the inside wall, and then the stairwell. Now she felt with both feet and hands, instinctively stooping to protect her head. Her feet found the wedge-shaped stones, worn slick-smooth by centuries of use, ascending in a tight spiral. Her fingers slid over moss growing on the wall; then, thankfully, she grasped the thin pipe railing installed for the safety of modern visitors, although such a nighttime invasion would hardly have been envisioned.

She held her breath as she approached eye level of the hall floor. It was unlikely anyone in the Great Chamber would notice her mole-like entrance, but she wanted to be prepared for whatever she was to face.

The Great Hall was dark and hollowly empty. She scanned the arcaded parapet. If she had seen someone up there—and she was still convinced she had—they were gone now. She shivered. She had rushed off without a jacket and now, as night drew on, a chill rose. Should she go back? Find the others and bring them up?

Then she heard it again, the sussurrant sound that was more a disturbing of the air than an actual noise. This time followed by the tinkle of a small bell. The breeze stirred. Was that a waft of incense? Whatever it was, it was coming from the chapel beyond the far end of the hall. And surely there was a flickering aureole of light in the empty space where there would once have been a ceiling.

Hugging the outer wall to keep in the blackest of the shadows, she slipped toward the stairway she remembered from that day, which seemed so long ago now, when she and Antony had explored the building in the sunlight and presence of other innocent tourists: the stairway that led to a tiny chamber looking down on the dais where the bishop would have entertained his most honored guests.

She paused at the top, looking down now into the vast emptiness, remembering seeing Rhys Morgan escorting a group of visitors through here, and then into the chapel. Now she wondered, had that been a simple tour promoting his restoration project, or had he been planning something more sinister?

Here the wall above the room was intact with the parapet walk open on the outside of the building. That meant Felicity could walk with little fear of detection. But at the end of the Great Chamber the arcaded parapet ceased. The way now was not a grand walk, but instead a narrow outer ledge leading to the Great Chapel. Felicity hugged the rough wall and inched forward, feeling every step carefully with her foot. And now, as she drew closer, there was no doubt. The sounds, lights and scents were issuing from the Great Chapel.

The arcaded parapet began again above the chapel, giving Felicity a firmer foothold and vantage point. She dropped to her hands and knees and crept forward until she could stick her head through the first of the arches. A soft sigh broke from her lips. It was beautiful. She didn't know what she had expected, but certainly nothing so lovely. So—orthodox.

What a wonderful idea! Surely this was Rhys Morgan's doing. It wasn't sinister after all. Nothing could be a more powerful argument in favor of his restoration project. A reenactment of a high mass just as Bishop Henry Gower must have celebrated it here for select guests almost four hundred years ago. The altar stood, as it would have in Gower's day, below a three-light window which her imagination could easily fill with radiant stained glass in the soft glow of dancing candlelight. Golden statues filled the niches flanking the windows, and candles burned on the altar and flickered from the darkest corners of the room, shedding just enough light to make the enormous, newly installed altar glow; it was covered with a rich white and gold frontal. The altar cloth was one of the most beautiful Felicity had ever seen. Antony would love this. She should go back and find him.

Before she could move, though, a white-robed acolyte entered carrying a large circular pan of glowing charcoal, and placed it on a stand to the right of the altar. When it was in place the server sprinkled a few grains of incense on the coals, bowed slightly and withdrew. The glowing charcoal from the incense burner lit the altar cloth from a new angle, and Felicity looked again.

She drew back so sharply she hit her head painfully on the stone arch. The scene was not at all what she had at first taken it to be. The intricate design on the frontal, worked in such rich golden thread, was not the traditional symbol she had assumed it was at first glance, but rather the double triangle with writhing snakes that symbolized the Orbis Astri.

Now she scrutinized the scene more carefully. Her gaze fell on the piscina in the wall just beyond the incense burner. She recalled Rhys Morgan pointing out this ornate liturgical fitting which the celebrant would have used to wash the communion vessels at mass as the "jewel of the room." And what was that it now held? Felicity squinted at the small, elegant alcove lit with a single votive candle. A packet of something partially encased in what appeared to be a crumbling leather pouch, perhaps ten inches long and five inches wide, leaned against the purple sandstone blocks backing the piscina.

She knew without doubt that this was what she had seen in the hands of the Imperator at the ceremony in the cave. And she was certain it would fit perfectly in the *scrynne*. The object Bishop Gower thought valuable enough to build a special cache for in his palace. What part was it meant to play in this night's proceedings?

"I've read of this, but never seen such a thing." Antony's voice, close to her ear, surprised Felicity so she almost cried out.

"Antony!" She groped in the dark for his hand, found it, and held on so tight she thought she might never let go again. "Oh, I'm so glad you found me. This," she gestured to the scene below them. "This is—chilling. Whatever it is."

"It's called a service of sacralization or destitution—turning something important to Christianity, or to any other religion, into a sacred symbol consecrated to Satan. I think it's a rather common practice in occult circles."

"But why? What do they hope to gain by it?"

"Power. What we would call a means of grace."

Felicity shuddered. "So it's turning everything on its head."

"Exactly."

"Should we ring the police?" Felicity's hand went to her pocket; then she remembered that, as usual, she didn't have her mobile with her.

She more felt than saw Antony shake his head. "I'm not certain what they're doing is actually illegal. Except maybe breaking and entering—and it's possible they got permission. Under false pretenses, of course."

"Can you ring the bishop?" Felicity startled at Ryan's voice coming from behind Antony. She hadn't realized he was there.

Antony handed Ryan his mobile with Bishop Harry's number in it, and Ryan faded further back into the shadows. Felicity and Antony leaned forward for a better view as the sound of chanting and chime of handbells grew louder. The procession, which had apparently been forming on the lawn outside the chapel wound its way up the outside stairs at the back and moved toward the altar at a stately pace. Leading them, the white-robed, hooded, "crucifer" carried a long pole topped by the Orbis Astri insignia. Next, two acolytes bearing processional torches. The figure following them broke from the line as they neared the altar, drew the pouch from the piscina and continued the procession, holding the artifact aloft as a server in the cathedral would have carried the Gospel book.

Felicity turned back to Antony. "I think that's what was in the *Scrynne*."

Antony nodded. "Seems likely. I'd like to get my hands on it."

The votaries now entered in pairs, hands folded, hoods covering their bowed heads. It was impossible to tell anything about them—age or gender. Certainly not identity.

Felicity was getting a leg cramp, crouched there on the cold stones. She shifted, trying to find a more comfortable position, then froze at the sight of the final entrants.

At the very back walked the Serene Imperator, a golden headdress with the familiar triangles and double-headed snake over his hood. But the thing that riveted Felicity's attention was the two robed figures walking in front of him. Instead of the gifts of bread and wine they might be carrying in a Eucharistic procession, they bore the limp form of a boy on a stretcher between them.

"Adam!" It took all the control Felicity could muster not to shout his name. Instead she gripped Antony's arm hard with both hands. "He isn't dead is he?"

"About to be, I'd say. The sacrificial lamb. It's the convergence—summer solstice with the Feast of Corpus Christi. They believe a black mass with a special sacrifice will bring the Orbis Astri great power."

"We have to stop them!" Felicity prepared to spring to her feet.

Antony grabbed her arm. "Indeed we do. But there are too many of them." He turned back to Ryan. "Is the bishop on his way?"

"He's in a service in the cathedral. I told his chaplain to come as soon as they could—with help." As he spoke, the cathedral bells rang, indicating the service had begun. Apparently the black mass had been timed to synchronize with the cathedral's mass of Corpus Christi. "But I'm afraid he may be too late."

"Ring 999. We've got a crime now."

"We need a diversion." Felicity said, looking around for loose stones or something they could throw. As she did, she saw dark figures running across the field toward the palace. Were the police here already? "Look!" She pointed. "We'd better go tell them what's happening."

By the time the three of them had descended the stairs as quickly as they could, not bothering too much about quiet as the chanting in the chapel was steadily rising in pitch, the dark figures materialized into recognizable forms.

Jared reached them first, Evie and Kaylyn right behind him. "Jared, I told you to—" Antony stopped at sight of Nancy. "You're supposed to be praying."

"Don't worry," she said. "I am. But I left the Sisters to it at St Non's."

"We thought you might need some help," Jared said.

"Well, as a matter of fact…" Felicity began.

Antony filled the newcomers in succinctly as they ascended the stairs from the undercroft, and made their way toward the chapel, this time simply walking straight across the hall as the intensity of the ritual in the next room covered any sound they might make.

Leaving the others, Felicity slipped along the small passage leading into the chapel and, keeping to the shadows, observed the circle of figures rapt in their mesmerizing dance around the Serene Imperator. Adam, who now lay on the altar, was the only one in the room not caught up in the dance. Felicity sighed with relief when she saw him move his head. At least he was still alive. For the moment.

Back in the hall, Felicity was the first to speak. "It would take quite a diversion to distract them. They're spellbound by what they're doing." As she said it she realized that was the answer.

"Kaylyn, your white dress. Change clothes with me."

"What?" Antony's cry was more of a protest than a question.

"Don't you see? I'll look like one of them in white. Evie, let me use your sweater for a hood. It's only a few feet around to the altar. I can match their dance step— no problem. I can be to Adam in ten steps."

"No way." Antony reached out to grab her, but she stepped aside.

Kaylyn handed her the flowing white dress. "Don't put the belt on— it'll look more like a robe."

"Felicity, don't!" The anguish in Antony's voice was almost enough to make her stop. But not quite.

By the time she reached the door the words of the chant became distinct:

> … *Circle round, compass, wheel and wreath, we become*
> *as one…*

She peeked into the chapel, vibrant with the warmth of dancing, singing bodies. It seemed even the candles flared brighter. She could have wished for deeper shadows.

She took one swift glance back at Antony and was glad to see he was praying. With a final gulp of air, she stepped into the room, the motion of her body matching that of the circling dancers. Unfortunately, the worshipers were circling clockwise and the altar lay to their right. Felicity hoped that if she swayed and shuffled sufficiently it wouldn't be obvious that they were moving in a different direction. It was only a few steps but, fully exposed as she was and moving at a snail's pace, it seemed like miles.

> *… at magick's hour we call the winds and timeless*
> *powers…*

Felicity was so lightheaded by the time she reached the altar she likely would have fallen even if she hadn't planned to sink down. Leaning against the altar she breathed a sigh of relief and realized she had been holding her breath.

She shot a quick prayer upward and turned to her task. Fortunately, they had relied on the drugs to keep Adam still and hadn't bothered tying him. "Adam, can you hear me? Can you move?"

A soft moan and a movement in the form above them served as reply.

"Try to roll off. I'll catch you." She held her hands at the edge of the altar. "That's good. Just a few more inches. I've got you." She put her hand on Adam's leg to guide him.

Felicity was shocked at the weight when he rolled into her waiting arms. Still screened by the altar, she lowered the lad to the floor and helped him sit up.

> *… we catch the fire from out the Goddess's eye…*

Thank goodness they were still looking inward at the circle, wrapt in their ritual. Felicity prayed the chant would have another verse. She feared the litany would end at any moment and that they would turn toward the altar.

"Can you walk? We need to get you out of here." She grasped Adam's shoulders and shook him gently.

Adam nodded. It was clear that he was still dazed, but he was aware enough to manage a half nod. "Yeah. Let's go."

Felicity held her breath again as they rose to their feet. Adam was sufficiently unsteady; it wasn't necessary to tell him to sway like a dancer. Felicity grasped his hand for support. They were halfway to the door when a dancer stepped out of the circle and approached the censer. As she did so, her hood slipped back. Felicity gasped. Lydia! She must have realized the Orbis Astri had her brother after all, and come for him.

Just then Felicity's worst fears were realized. The chant ended and the Imperator turned to the altar. "Run!" Felicity shoved Adam toward his sister.

With horror she realized the boy must be more addled than she knew because Adam turned and ran the opposite direction— toward the Orbis Astri. A tall figure stepped out and swept him off his feet. "No!" Felicity shouted.

And then the stars fell from the sky. Or were they setting off fireworks?

Chapter 29

Later

Circling pinwheels and shooting skyrockets again pierced the thick blackness. Felicity groaned at the pain in her head, then realized someone was binding her hands behind her back. She struggled to hit at them.

"Hold still. I almost have you untied. There's no time to lose."

"Ryan?"

"Yeah."

"What happened?"

He continued to work at her bindings as he spoke. "The Serene High Mucky-muck wasn't very serene. Hit you hard."

Felicity nodded. That explained her throbbing head.

"They dumped you here for the moment, but they're sure to be back soon to finish their work." The cords cutting her wrists fell loose.

She realized Nancy was untying her ankles. Chloe stood at the entrance, keeping guard.

"We were watching from above," Ryan went on. "Chloe went up to get pictures. It seemed best to stay. Wasn't much else we could do to help."

"Smart." Felicity rubbed her unbound hands to restore circulation. She gingerly fingered the pulsing lump on the back of her head. "Where are we?"

"Um, best I can tell it's the latrine block."

"Oh, great." She looked around. "Where's Antony?"

Nancy squeezed her shoulder. "They have him. He rushed forward when that priest hit you."

Felicity jumped to her feet so fast she almost blacked out again. "Where? We have to get him." She started forward, then paused. "We lost Adam. They're going to…" She turned and, ignoring the dizziness threatening to engulf her, hurried down what seemed to be a wide corridor toward a dim light at the end. She didn't know where she was going— what she was doing— but it appeared to be the only way to go.

At the end of the corridor she realized she was back in the Great Hall, where the others were. She pulled Evie's tattered dress off and tossed it to her. And now she could hear the service proceeding in the room beyond. "And so, you see, my sister votaries, the graciousness of the goddess. She has sent us a far more powerful sacrifice than an innocent youth." The seductive female voice rose in a triumphant pitch. "Tonight we sacrifice a priest! My sisters, the kingdom and the power and the glory are ours."

Shutting her ears to chorus of exultant praises, Felicity crossed the hall in a few strides. Only Ryan's restraining hand on her arm kept her from charging straight into the chapel. "We need a plan."

"You have one?" she asked.

"Well, we have surprise on our side. If we go in through different entrances they might think they're surrounded. With luck we can grab the candlesticks and statues to use as weapons. Chloe, Evie and Kaylyn can run across the lawn to the outside stairs. Jared, Nancy and I'll go in here."

Felicity saw the sense at once. She looked around. "The east window." The altar was directly below it. That would get her to Antony most quickly.

Ryan shook his head. "This isn't the ground floor. It must be 20 feet off the ground."

"More." Felicity nodded, then wished she hadn't because it stirred the throb in her head. "I'll go across from this window." She strode across the floor toward the last of the tall, arched windows looking out over the courtyard. It was only a step up to the sill. Grasping each side of the opening firmly, she looked across the space to the chapel wall jutting out at a right angle from the end of the hall. She judged she could reach it all right. But could she grasp the stones framing the window and swing herself over? Or would it be better simply to leap from one window to another? Her legs were long enough, her ballet dancer's muscles well-conditioned for such an action. But was her aim good enough? She hesitated.

"Tonight, on this night of powerful convergence, we have two sacrifices," the priestess's voice floated clearly across the space. And now Felicity recognized the voice. Anne Morgan. The Serene Imperator—Imperatress—wasn't Rhys Morgan. It was his wife.

Felicity's mind filled with the image of Anne Morgan standing at the altar, triumphant over a bound Antony in the place Adam had been. In the danger Adam had been. Or still was. That must be what she meant by two sacrifices.

Below her across the corner of the courtyard she could see Chloe and the girls ascending the outside stairs to the chapel. In a moment everyone would be in place. Inside the chapel the chant rose:

> *Spirits of fire come to us; We kindle the fire,*
> *Spirits of fire come to us; We kindle the fire,*
> *We kindle the fire; We dance the sacred circle round…*

A wafting scent told Felicity a fresh scoop of incense had been placed on the glowing coals.

Fire, Fire, Fire; Kindle higher,
In thy flame naught else remains:
But Fire, Fire, Fire…

Now the Imperatress extended her hands full above her head, high enough that Felicity could see through the crumbling window arch that she held something in both hands. A knife, to plunge into the sacrificial victim? A knife that in the next moment would be dripping Antony's blood?

Felicity lunged. She caught the near rim of the opening with both hands, and her right foot found purchase on the sill. Her left foot scrabbled the wall for the smallest projection or hole. Anything to restore her balance. It was no more than an uneven stone in the weathered wall. But it was enough.

Her arms aching with the strain, Felicity pulled herself closer to the opening and peered around. Thankfully the priestess no longer stood behind the altar, but had moved aside to stand before the incense burner, its red coals billowing smoke. And beside her stood her deaconess.

Felicity blinked; even through the clouds of incense, there was no doubt. Lydia Bowen stood second in rank to the Imperatress.

"On this night of double power, we offer two sacrifices." Now Felicity could see that she held not a knife, but the artifact from the piscina. The Imperatress raised her arms again and drew the object from the pouch, brandishing it in triumph. A folded parchment. They were going to burn a document that had been preserved for 2,000 years. And then a human sacrifice. The horror was inconceivable.

"This account has helped the enemy for far too long. Hidden for centuries, it resurfaced too often when spirits lagged. It will surface no more!" She returned it to the pouch and handed it to

Lydia who held it likewise aloft, awaiting the moment to put it on the coals.

Fire blaze, Fire burn: Make the wheel of magic turn
Work the wish for which we pray: Eo-deo-ah-hey-yeh

The high priestess turned to the altar. And this time she, indeed, held the long-bladed knife Felicity had imagined before. Reflections of flames flashed from the razor edge as she raised it high in both hands.

Blood of Ancients pulse in our veins,
Forms may pass, but circling life remains…

As the chant rose, exceeding fever pitch, Anne Morgan raised the knife over Antony's inert body.

With a shriek that carried above the cantillation, Felicity flung herself from the window at Anne Morgan, knocking them both to the floor.

Barely aware of the chaos engulfing the room, Felicity focused on her one task—to wrest the knife from the woman's hands. Whatever it took, she had to keep Anne Morgan from plunging it into Antony.

Grappling on the floor, the roaring cacophony and frenzied melee blended with the pain in Felicity's head, all but blinding her. Anne Morgan was the larger, stronger woman. For a moment Felicity grasped the knife, then felt it wrenched from her hand.

Felicity flung her arm out. And her hand brushed the stone the priestess had hit her over the head with earlier. Her fingers closed on it and she swung upward with all her might.

With a groan Anne Morgan slumped to the side, releasing her grip on the knife. Before it could clatter to the floor, Felicity grabbed it. She pulled herself unsteadily up by the altar. The room was spinning, but she sawed at the bonds on Antony's wrists.

And then she felt herself slipping. The blackness was winning.

Chapter 30

Later

Felicity had no idea how much later she came to. For a moment she didn't know where she was or what she was doing. But she knew all she needed to know. She was in Antony's arms.

She looked around and realized they were sitting on the floor of the Great Chapel of the Bishop's Palace, leaning against the back of an altar. The air was scented with incense. A few candles flickered but not enough to compete with the stars in the sky above the roofless room. She could hear voices and people moving somewhere off, and yet it was as if she and Antony were inside a wonderful bubble of peace. "What are we doing here?"

Antony laughed and squeezed her. "My lovely heroine. You mean you don't remember taking on the entire Orbis Astri practically single-handed?"

Felicity blinked as images flittered across her mind. Robed figures, swaying, chanting... glowing coals, something about to be burned... a small figure on an altar... No, not small. The whole world—her world. Antony. Still and bound. With a knife gleaming above him.

She sobbed and turned her face into his chest. "Antony, they were going to..."

"Yes." He paused. "I had it wrong. Not a heroine; an angel."

"Huh?"

"The story in the Old Testament. Abraham was about to sacrifice Isaac. God sent an angel to stay his hand."

Felicity shook her head and took a deep breath of the night air. It was coming back to her now. "And then you rushed in to rescue me and they got you. Fine pair we are." She sat for a moment, reveling in being held by Antony. Then she thought. "Adam?"

"Michael has him."

"Michael? Oh, no!" She struggled to sit up.

"Hush, it's all right. He'll explain. I don't really have the story yet, either."

Felicity glanced sideways and saw the censer laying on its side, a trail of coals spread across the floor. "The artifact! It was from the *scrynne*, wasn't it? Lydia burned it." Her heart sank with the sense of loss. "Now we'll never know what it was."

"She would have, Ryan tipped the censer over and rescued it. A few scorchmarks on the pouch, but after 2,000 years, what's a couple more marks?"

"You mean we won? But there were only six of us."

"No, my lovely. You're good, but you aren't quite that good. Constable Owen arrived with the troops. Then the bishop swept in like an avenging angel just about the time the police were rounding everyone up."

Just then, Ryan and Nancy, holding hands, appeared around the corner of the altar. "Are you ready to go?" Ryan asked. "The police will want to talk to you more tomorrow, but I think I've satisfied them for the moment."

Nancy grinned. "They have their hands more than full with that lot." She jerked her head toward the courtyard where angry sounds of protest sounded.

"Bishop Harry said to tell you that the Requiem Mass for Father Hwyl will be at ten o'clock tomorrow morning, in the cathedral. He'll do a cleansing of the palace after that."

"Great." Antony grinned. "I think Bishop Harry's a convert to the importance of deliverance ministry." He got to his feet, then held his hands out to Felicity to help her rise. Her head swam and her knees almost buckled, but Antony's arm was firm around her. She made no protest at being all but carried back across the field to the van.

At St Non's, sunk deep in the cushions of the softest sofa, Felicity held Sister Nora's steaming mug of hot chocolate in both hands. Antony sat close beside her like a protective shield against all the horrors that had passed. It seemed more as if she had been the one so nearly slaughtered on the altar of a pagan god. She let go of her mug with her left hand, and sought Antony's.

She looked around the room. The band of pilgrims. Unbelievable how much they had been through together. Everyone looked exhausted—shattered. And yet, on every face there was a glow. Confidence. Satisfaction. The sense of a job well done.

In the furthest corner Michael sat in an oversized chair, a sleeping Adam sprawled against him. "Michael," she began. "I must apologize to you. I thought…"

Michael nodded. "Don't apologize. I know how it looked. And I did go along with it all at first. I was trying to find the artifact for Lydia."

"But why?"

Michael stared at the floor. "I had applied for a job with her father's company. A brilliant job that would more than finance going back to uni. She said she would help me if I would help her. It's no excuse. I knew it was wrong. But she was very persuasive." He paused so long Felicity was afraid he wasn't going to say more.

Then he shook his head as if to clear the memory. "If Lydia looked deep into my eyes and said I was going to do something— well, I did it. I can't explain it. I just did. I had no idea what it was for, though. I swear. You must believe me."

Antony nodded. "Yes. It's quite a simple method of mind control, actually. A common occult practice. I'm sure Anne Morgan used it on Rhys as well."

"And one other thing," Michael spoke with more assurance now. "I also stayed close to her for Adam's sake. I could see there were problems there and I really wanted to help him. He's so much like my little brother." He looked at the tousled head on his shoulder.

Felicity frowned. "But you were there when she abducted him—at his school."

"No." He shook his head. "She must have handed him over to someone from the coven when I took the minibus to the garage. Perhaps 'the nice lady' who danced with him on Twmbarlwym— if she was real at all." His voice took on a bitter note. "I had no idea she abducted her own brother—until I got to that vile ritual tonight. I was looking for a way to rescue him when you two showed up. All I had to do was grab him and run." He smoothed the pale hair on the sleeping head. "I hope he'll be all right now."

"I think he'll give evidence against Lydia on a kidnapping charge. With her and her jealousy out of the way, maybe he can have a more normal relationship with his parents," Antony replied.

"So that's why you were doing all that digging?" Felicity said slowly, still working through it all. " But the Orbis Astri already had the document. The *Scrynne* was empty." Then she gasped, recalling Chloe's picture of Michael's head peering over the corner corbel. "You found it."

Michael nodded, looking ashamed. "I'm so sorry. Lydia came on the walk specifically to search for it. She had a map with exact locations marked where she was to search. Places they thought it likely to be hidden. The Bishop's Palace was the last marking."

"Rhys must have seen the floor plan at Hwyl's. Or Hwyl took it from him. I'm not very clear on that," Antony said.

Felicity shivered, then drank deeply of her hot chocolate. "So were the Orbis Astri people following us all the way?" It was obvious, really.

"But why?" Antony asked.

Michael grinned briefly. "Because of you, Father. They couldn't be sure Hwyl didn't make contact with you before he fell. They couldn't be sure you didn't know too much."

"What do you think he wanted to tell you, Father?" Ryan, sitting at the far end of the room with Nancy, asked.

Antony sighed. "I can only guess. But I think he must have learned somehow about their plans for the mass and was coming to me for advice." Antony shook his head. "Nothing in that seminar I taught could really have prepared anyone to handle this in more than just a general way."

Jared spoke up for the first time, "This whole black mass thing—I don't get it. Why were they doing it?"

"The convergence..." Antony began

"No, I got that. I mean, what did they want the power for?" He shrugged. "I suppose everybody wants power in some general way, but I mean, this was really OTT."

Antony smiled. "Over the top is certainly an understatement. I've been thinking about that, too, and from some of the talk I heard at the Restoration Committee meeting, I think it was the rebuilding project. I think they planned to use the chapel as a satanic cathedral—more powerful because it was on the site of ancient Christian worship."

"And Hwyl found out about this from serving on the committee?" Felicity asked.

"He must have learned enough to make him guess. They probably let things slip that only someone especially attuned to spiritual nuances—of all sorts—would pick up on."

"I still can't get my head around the fact that it was Anne, not Rhys, behind all that," Felicity said. "He must have been absolutely besotted by her to let her talk him into such a scheme."

"I guess you could say he was 'bewitched,'" Evie giggled.

Antony smiled. "I think the correct term is Black Widow—a woman who preys on men for her own ends—sex, power, money, whatever."

"Yes, Anne Morgan was using her husband, just as Lydia was using Michael."

"She was using everyone; Marissa at Chakra Health, all the followers in her coven, everyone on her committee…"

Sister Nora came in with a fresh pitcher of hot chocolate and walked around the circle of seated pilgrims, refilling their mugs. Felicity had the sense that she was giving each one of them a special benediction as she did so. When the Sister had gone out again, Felicity's gaze fell on the scorched leather pouch lying on the table next to Ryan. "Oh, there it is."

Ryan looked a little embarrassed. "Yeah, I put it inside my jacket when I grabbed it, and in all the excitement I forgot. Actually, Lydia was coming for me and I—well, I'm not sure what I did. I remember pushing her. Then she sort of flew at me and then…" He shook his head. "I don't remember."

"I remember," Nancy grinned. "I grabbed her by the hair and pulled her off you. Then I hit her with that pole with their disgusting symbol on it. Whacked her a good one. That was about the time the police arrived."

Ryan put his arm around her. "Thanks."

"Don't mention it."

"But what is it?" Felicity hadn't thought she would ever want to leave her cozy nest beside Antony, but she set her hot chocolate down, shoved herself to her feet and crossed the room. The ancient leather felt hard as a board when she picked it up.

"It's amazing this has survived. It should be in a controlled climate. Like the Dead Sea Scrolls."

Antony joined her. "I'm sure it soon will be. We'll take it to the bishop in the morning. Reunite it with the *scrynne* and let the cathedral archivist take it from there."

Working with great care so as not to crack the brittle parchment, Felicity drew two sheets out of the packet. She pulled the top open just far enough to be able to see a few lines of writing, then shook her head and handed it to Antony with a sigh. "I can't read this. I don't even know what language it is."

Antony looked carefully. "Aramaic, I'd say. I'm guessing first century. That was the common language of the time. Scholars will undoubtedly be poring over this for some time to come."

"But this," Felicity held up the second sheet with a flourish. "This is Latin. Just my cup of—hot chocolate." She sat on a small wooden chair and held the document under the lamp on the table beside it, studying the page carefully. At last she looked up, trying to suppress the excitement she was feeling. She could be wrong, of course. But… "Well, this is only a guess. This needs lots of study, too. And the Latin is very bad. Probably because it's late. The translation may have been made as late as the fourteenth century."

"Fourteenth century? That was—" Antony began.

"Bishop Henry Gower. Exactly." Felicity nodded. She took a breath. "It could be a translation Gower made of the parchment before he sealed it away." She took another breath. "Of course, I could be completely wrong and it could be much earlier."

"You mean…" Antony began.

"Yeah. It *could* be as early as the sixth century." She paused, shaken by her own audacity. "Well, David *was* quite a scholar. He definitely would have known Latin."

"Oh, never mind that!" Evie burst out. "What is it? What does it *say*?"

Felicity bent over the small sheet. "It seems to be a letter. From a Roman soldier. Cornelius, centurion, Cohors II Italica Civium Romanorum…"

"Cornelius?" Antony's exclamation was so sharp Felicity jumped.

"Yes. That's what it says." She looked again. "Yes, I'm sure. Does that mean something to you?"

Antony bit his lip. "It might. What does he say?"

"Well, I don't have it exact, but he seems to have had some kind of vision, and he sent an officer to get someone named Peter and—"

"That's it! This is a letter from Cornelius—the centurion who sent for Peter…"

"That's what I just said. It is, if I'm reading the translation right."

"Don't you see? This is a firsthand account of the first Gentile conversion. It's in the book of Acts. Cornelius's coming to faith showed that the gospel was for all people, all nations."

"Oh," now Felicity understood. "It's your ecumenical thing."

"Wait. Let me get this straight," Michael spoke up. "This Roman centurion wrote a letter to someone in Britannia. Someone like Aaron or Julius, maybe?" He stopped. "No, that can't be right. They were 300 years later."

Antony nodded. "They were. But Aaron or Julius is a very good guess. We know of their devotion and their strength. This could have been in one of their families, and brought with them when they went to the furthest edge of the empire; or sent to them for safekeeping when persecutions became severe in their homeland."

"A powerful reminder to give them assurance when they had to stand strong," Felicity added. "Then David discovered it at Caerleon. But how would it make his preaching against heresy to the synod more powerful?"

"We don't know that it did," Antony began.

"The Orbis Astri must have believed it. Anne Morgan said it had resurfaced to add power. That's why they wanted to burn it."

"We'll probably have a better idea after the scholars analyze it. Perhaps David quoted from it. Or perhaps having it gave him confidence so he spoke with greater authority."

"So why would he hide it? Wasn't that what you were digging for in Caerleon, Michael?" Felicity asked.

Michael nodded. "I don't expect he meant to hide it. I expect he was guarding it for safekeeping."

Kaylyn leaned forward. "But then David took it from Caerleon to St David's along the same route we walked? Sweet!"

Antony nodded. "I think that's more or less what happened."

"And Gower found it when he was restoring the cathedral. Then he needed money to build his palace, so he sold it to wealthy monks—the Cistercians near Penrhys, maybe? And Evan Roberts—" Felicity ground to a halt.

Antony laughed. "Whoa, too much conjecture. Let's leave that to mystery."

Felicity made a face. *Mystery.* She would rather know. But some things they couldn't know. She sighed. "I suppose I'll have to accept that. But Hwyl—did he jump under some kind of spell, or was he pushed?"

"We'll probably know when the police get the toxicology report. But it was murder, either way, and we have the people responsible. Even if the police can't prove Hwyl was murdered, I'm sure they'll find plenty of evidence to convict those responsible for Joe's death."

"Why do you think they killed Joe?" Chloe asked with a catch in her voice.

Antony shook his head. "I hope that wasn't our fault. We told the police who he was. When they started asking questions Anne must have been afraid he would give too much away."

"Or maybe Rhys told Anne that Joe was pressuring him for money," Michael suggested.

Felicity sighed and closed her eyes. Well, it wasn't all tied up, but it was enough for now. She leaned her head against Antony's shoulder and gazed around the room, observing those there and thinking of those not there: Lydia, "helping the police with their enquiries;" Adam, asleep with his head in Michael's lap, awaiting his father's arrival; Jared, sitting between Kaylyn and Evie, looking pleased with himself as Evie whispered in his ear and Kaylyn smiled; Ryan, holding his mobile out to Nancy, sitting very close beside him, who read out a text from the fully recovered and still chatty Colin: his tutor predicted an A for him in his archeology exam; he hoped to make an original find. Would any of them do a dig with him? He asked.

"What a shame Colin had to miss this. He would be so excited." Felicity missed him.

"My fault again, I'm afraid," Michael said. "I was worried I'd involved him too much. I called his mum."

"Well, when this winds up in a glass case back in the Roman museum in Caerleon, the plaque must have Colin's name on it as a member of the discovering party," Antony said.

Chloe was the first to move. She thanked the group, especially Antony, over and over. "If you hadn't come along, taken me in as part of you, I don't know what might have happened." She choked. "I'll send you all pictures. Gotta go pack." And she swiftly left the room.

Felicity smiled. Pilgrimage was designed to change, broaden, perhaps even purify the pilgrim, but could any of them possibly have foreseen such outcomes as they had experienced?

"We'll all be heading home tomorrow, so we should get some sleep." Antony made a motion to get to his feet. But Felicity still didn't want to move. They had all shared so much, been through such amazing experiences together, and they would likely never see each other again—not in a group. Not like this.

Nancy spoke up. "Father, before we go, let's say *The Grace* together."

"Excellent." Antony held out his hands to Felicity and Nancy on each side of him, and the circle closed.

"The grace of our Lord Jesus Christ," everyone entered in; there was even a very drowsy voice from Adam, "and the love of God and the fellowship of the Holy Spirit be with us all, evermore." Felicity felt her own fervency rise as she joined in a wholehearted, "Amen."

She turned to Antony. Exhausted, but infinitely grateful, she gave a weary smile. "Let's go home."

Felicity and Antony's adventures continue:

Look for *A Muffled Tolling*, Book 4 in THE MONASTERY MURDERS

Permissions and References

Gabriele Amorth, *An Exorcist Tells His Story*, San Francisco, CA: Ignatius Press, 1994.

Michael Boag et. al., ed. *A Week of Simple Offices (prayer)*, Mirfield: Community of the Resurrection, 2000. Used by permission, Fr Nicholas Stebbing.

Rebecca Brown, MD, *He Came to Set the Captives Free*, New Kensington, PA: Whitaker House, 1992.

Eifion Evans, *The Welsh Revival of 1904*, Brigend: Bryntirion Press, 2000.

Dion Fortune, *Psychic Self-Defense,* San Francisco, CA: Weiser Books, 2001.

Brynmore P. Jones, *Voices from the Welsh Revival 1904–1905,* Brigend: The Evangelical Press of Wales, 1995.

David Matthews, *I Saw the Welsh Revival,* Chicago, IL: Moody Press, 1951,

Johanna Michaelsen, *The Beautiful Side of Evil*, Eugene, Oregon: Harvest House Publishers, 1960 (1982 ed.).

James A. Stewart, *Invasion of Wales by the Spirit Through Evan Roberts*, Asheville, NC: Revival Literature, 1963.

Jack Dover Wellman, *A Priest's Psychic Diary*, London: SPCK Publishing, 1977.

Author's note: All of the occult occurrences in my story were fictionalized accounts of events recorded in the above nonfiction books or based on reports from people to whom they happened.

About the Author

Donna Fletcher Crow is the author of 40 books, mostly novels dealing with British history. The award-winning *Glastonbury, A Novel of the Holy Grail*, an Arthurian grail search epic covering 15 centuries of English history, is her best-known work. Besides The Monastery Murders series she is also the author of The Lord Danvers series of Victorian true-crime novels and the romantic suspense series The Elizabeth & Richard Mysteries. Donna and her husband live in Boise, Idaho. They have 4 adult children and 11 grandchildren. She is an enthusiastic gardener.

To read more about all of Donna's books and see pictures from her garden and research trips go to
http://www.donnafletchercrow.com/

You can follow her on Facebook at:
http://ning.it/OHi0MY